A Brothe

Jill Bray

A BROTHERLY DEVOTION

Copyright © Jill Bray 2025.

The right of Jill Bray to be identified as the author of this work has been asserted by her in accordance with the Copyright, Designs and Patents Act, 1988.

First published in 2025 by Holand Press.

JILL BRAY

To my mum and dad – I miss you both every day.

And to Anna Mazzola - without your continued encouragement & help, this novel would never have happened.

A BROTHERLY DEVOTION

CHAPTER 1

YORK - JULY 1224

Brother Clement could feel the soothing warmth of the evening sun on his back as he walked along the bank of the River Ouse back to the Abbey of St Mary. The air was heavy with the scent of cut grasses and the flowers that bloomed along the edge of the river. It had been another hot day and, in the city, the air clung to buildings like a suffocating blanket. The streets had been thick with the unpleasant stench of rotting food and foul water, and the breeze that occasionally wafted through them only served to increase the repulsiveness. Brother Clement found it a blessing to be outside of the city walls for once, and to enjoy the sweeter smells of the countryside. The summer heat had lasted for several weeks now, and without any rain, the river was lower than he had ever known; the mud banks cracked and hard under his feet. Even during the nights, the temperature did not drop much, and the stone walls of the Abbey buildings including the dormitory, held the heat all night so that there was no respite from it.

It was unusual for Brother Clement to be out of the Abbey precinct, but Abbot Robert had been quite insistent that he should be the one to tend to Lady Maud de Mowbray as she grew more frail. He had been making regular visits to deliver poppy juice to ease her pain and make her more comfortable. He had also been charged with hearing her confessions and delivering Gods' grace to the ailing widow who was a notable benefactor of the Abbey.

It was late and he had already missed vespers, but he was not far away now and could see the buildings of the Abbey silhouetted along the skyline as dusk fell. He had to admit that it was a beautiful evening, and one which made him marvel to see the hand of God at work in the landscape around him. Brother Clement was a private man; accustomed to spending time alone in the building he used for concocting his herbal remedies which he supplied to his brethren and the hospital. Lost in his thoughts and contemplations he didn't hear the approaching horses and their riders.

He was taken by surprise and before Brother Clement knew it the men had dismounted and surrounded him. Suddenly, he felt very afraid. He wasn't sure what the men wanted with him. He gave them a blessing and wished them good evening, but his instincts were telling him that they were not there for him to dispense the Grace of God. He felt a fear rising inside him that he hadn't known for many years, and although he wanted to trust God to deliver him safely back to the Abbey, he sensed it was not going to be. The men were quick, and before he had time to think, they had grasped hold of him. A hand came down hard across his mouth to prevent him calling out and he found he was helpless to resist. It was all over so quickly and as he lay prostrate on the riverbank, the life seeping out of him, he prayed to God to save his soul and deliver him to heaven.

Abbot Robert de Campo Longo was in his office when Brother Michael approached the door. It was early morning, and the Abbot was using the time after Prime to complete some essential correspondence; he was not expecting visitors. The Abbot thought highly of Brother Michael; he was an intelligent, calm man, who was seldom flustered by events. However, this morning, he appeared harassed, and Abbot Robert instantly noticed his agitation as he stood in front of him; it told him straight away that something was very wrong indeed.

"What is it Brother Michael?"

"Abbot something most terrible has happened. Please come at once!" The note of urgency and distress in the monks' voice alarmed him.

He rose quickly from his desk and followed Brother Michael outside and towards the western gate and the Porters Lodge. The large wooden gates were open, and through them a man was leading a horse and cart into the abbey precinct. On the back of the cart lay a body dressed in the black habit of a Benedictine monk. The Abbot drew breath sharply and realised instantly that it must be Brother Clement, as he was the only one of the brethren who had been outside the grounds of the Abbey the previous day. He had also noticed last night that Brother Clement had not returned for vespers or compline and had assumed that he was still tending to the Lady Maud. It had never occurred to him that there could have been another explanation for his absence. He wondered what had happened, an accident? A fall perhaps?

Other monks were quickly gathering around, and Abbot Robert gestured to Brother Michael to keep them back, until he had ascertained exactly what had happened. He approached the man leading the horse and greeted him, to which the carter gave a nod of respect.

"What has happened here?" The Abbot asked, walking with the carter to view his cargo.

"I found him at first light." The carter said, roughly. "Down by the river, father. Nasty business," he continued. "I was driving the cattle down to the river to drink and there he was lying there in the grass he was. At first, I thought he must be asleep, and tried to wake him, but then when I turned him over, I saw the blood."

Abbot Robert reached over the cart and pulled the cowl back so that he could see the face. It was Brother Clement as he suspected. However, what was not expected, was the bloodied gash around the front of his throat. Abbot Robert drew breath to steady himself as bile rose in his mouth, and he closed his eyes momentarily. He had never seen something so violent happen to a person he knew so well. He had been Abbot at St Marys for over twenty-five years, and he had seen many things in this time, as both Abbot and monk before then, but never anything quite as horrific as this; and inflicted on one of his fellow brothers too.

"Thank you for bringing him back to us. We owe you a great deal." Abbot Robert tried to remain calm. "We will take him from here and reunite him with his brethren." He turned and signalled to three of the other monks to come forward and to take the body from the cart. "Take our dear Brother Clement and lay him out in the sacristy please," he instructed them.

"But father." One of the monks protested. "He should be laid in the main church before the altar, where we can all pray for him, and God can receive his soul."

Abbot Robert paused briefly trying to keep his composure. "You are right, of course Brother, but the sacristy has no windows and is far more appropriate in this hot weather than keeping him within the abbey." He tried to reassure the monk, whilst keeping his demeanour as calm as possible, though he felt anything but. "And please ensure that his body is not touched or washed until I say so." He turned his attention back to the carter. "Good man, will you care to show me exactly where you found our dear brother?"

The carter shrugged, then shook his head, looking a little uncomfortable. "But I need to get back to the farm, Father, there is much to do you see. It's almost harvest." He shook his head again. "Not that there will be much to bring in this year."

Abbot Robert realised that a little persuasion was needed. "I assure you it won't take long and there will be a jug of good ale and some bread waiting for you here, once we are through."

The carter thought for a moment, then nodded and walked back to the horse pulling the cart. Then, taking the reins, he urged it on, so that it started to walk around and turn back towards the gate.

"Brother Michael, accompany me – if you will." Abbot Robert summoned his trusted aide.

The huge wooden gates were opened for them, and the

Abbot and Brother Michael followed on behind the cart through the west gate of the Abbey precinct. Once outside they turned left and followed the path down to the bank of the River Ouse.

The Abbot was a tall man, now in his late fifties, he had taken holy vows as a young man. With an English mother and French father, he was fluent in both languages and when they had travelled to England for his father to work on reconstructing the Abbey of St Mary in York, he knew he had found the place where he wanted to be. He had a quiet and thoughtful demeanour and that had made him a natural leader for the Abbey when the previous Abbot, Robert de Harpham, had been deposed. At the time he was still a relatively young man, and the appointment had been somewhat of a surprise. Although he knew he was well liked by his fellow monks he had not once thought that he would ever be selected to be their spiritual leader. Initially, when he had entered the abbey as a novice, his mastery of the English language had not been perfect, and he always used a thoughtful pause before he replied to consider the words he would use. Even though he now spoke the language incredibly well, he still found himself taking his time to consider what he said.

The walk took them about half a mile along the riverbank towards the north-west. When the carter stopped and pointed to the area of flattened, dry grass alongside the riverbank, the Abbot made him stop short of the area.

"Can you point out exactly where you found Brother Clement?" The Abbot inquired.

"Just over there, Father;" the carter replied pointing to an area of flattened grass that were heavily stained with dried blood. "By the river; just there."

The Abbot nodded. "Please, both of you stay here," he instructed them, before carefully walking across to the area. He was reluctant to go too close but looked thoughtfully at the place the carter had indicated. Then he fell to his knees and started to pray. Brother Michael observed the Abbot and did likewise. For a short while both of them were focused on their Latin verses. When they were finished the Abbot got to his feet and Brother Michael followed.

"Thank you, my good man for showing us where our dear brother met his untimely end. If we return now, then I will ensure that you are well compensated for your troubles."

Simon de Hale sat in his room within the newly built keep of the castle at York going through papers that had been delivered to him that morning. At forty-two he was still a handsome man, with blond hair that was tinged with grey at the temples. His angular face was set alight by piercing blue eyes that could change from ice blue to grey, depending on his mood. He was surprisingly tall and had managed to avoid the onset of middle-aged spread that had beset so many of his contemporaries. He sat back in his chair and picked up a document to work on, he was hoping that focusing on the papers would take his mind off the problem of his youngest daughter who he found out, had once again, left the castle enclosure yesterday without his permission. They had only been in York for just over a year as part of his position as Sheriff of the county, and he was beginning to think it would have been better if he had left her back at their home in Northamptonshire. The King had appointed him to the position the previous year and he had moved to the city of York with his youngest daughter, Katherine. It had seemed a good idea at the time, though he was now beginning to have doubts. His eldest daughter, Angharad, was already married, and he knew he could have left Katherine with her, but she had wanted to go with him, and he found it difficult to deny her anything. He had been meaning to confront Katherine about her escapades since they had been in York; it wasn't the first time that she had done this, but it was growing more regular, and he had to ensure that it stopped. It was unbecoming, nor safe, for the daughter of the Sheriff to be seen riding outside the city walls unaccompanied. Especially now since he had recently been approached regarding her betrothal. He knew that his daughters strong-willed behaviour wasn't something that would be allowed by her new husband and he needed to speak to her about it as soon as he could.

Lord William Fitzwarren, a local knight and landowner, had approached Simon a week ago, regarding a union between himself and Katherine. At first Simon had been surprised by the request, but listening to Lord William speak, he realised that the man would be a good match for his head-strong daughter. Simon knew it was high time that Katherine was married; his eldest daughter amongst others, had told him as much, and Angharad was usually right about these things. He shook his head; if truth be told, his daughter Katherine, reminded him so much of her mother, his late wife, and there was a part of him which loathed the thought of losing her. Simon knew he had indulged his youngest daughter far more than he should have done, especially after his dearest Ellen had passed away shortly after Katherine had been born. Simon had cherished his daughter as a reminder of everything he had loved in his wife. Now his daughter was seventeen and proving to be quite a handful. She was a beautiful, intelligent girl with a strong character, all of which he greatly admired, but he knew it was not appropriate for a girl of her age not to be married or at least betrothed. Katherine sneaking out of the castle enclosure without her maid, hadn't gone unnoticed by the servants either, and when it had been brought to his attention, he knew he really had to address the problem. He had set himself the task of confronting her later in the day, but for now he had work to occupy him.

The Royal Justice was due to hold the assize court shortly and, as sheriff, Simon needed to ensure that all the court papers were in order before his arrival. If he was truthful though, he also needed them to be a distraction to his worries over his daughter. Simon was a lawyer by training and enjoyed the detail of documents and was just getting engrossed in the specifics of the first one, when his steward appeared at the door.

"Sire, Abbot Robert requests an urgent meeting with you."

Simon looked up from his desk. The request surprised him; it was not usual for the Abbot to pay him a visit. It must be something serious for him to leave the Abbey complex and venture to the castle, and at this early hour as well.

Simon nodded to his steward. "Send him in."

Simon rose from his chair and walked forward to greet the Abbot as he entered the room.

"Abbot Robert, it's good to see you again. Please come and sit with me."

"Simon; may God's blessing be upon you. I wish my visit was a social one, but unfortunately, I come with dreadful news and in need of your help." Abbot Robert took a chair opposite Simon.

Simon gestured to the steward to bring them both some wine and sat back down in his chair. He could tell by the expression on Abbot Roberts' face, that something quite serious had occurred. Simon watched the Abbot sigh heavily as he accepted the goblet of wine. He observed how drawn and pale the Abbot looked, certainly not his usual serene self.

"Please enlighten me, Father." Simon prompted.

"Yesterday, I sent Brother Clement out to see Lady Maud at the Manor House. She is very ill, and I sent him with herbal potions to ease her pain as well as to administer the communion and to pray with her. I knew he would be away most of the day but expected him back before nightfall. When he did not return, I thought she must have grown worse, and he had decided to remain with her. Then, this morning, a carter came to the Abbey." The Abbot paused to gather his thoughts and sipped at his wine. "The carter had been down by the river bank this morning taking the cattle to water when he came across the body of our dear Brother Clement. The carter was a man of good countenance who saw it in his way to bring our dear Brother back to us at the Abbey. But I'm afraid there was nothing to be done for him."

"An accident?" Simon inquired.

The Abbot shook his head. "I wish it were. But no, not an accident. It seems our dear Brother Clement was murdered; his throat had been cut."

Simon was shocked by the news. Murder was not an entirely unusual occurrence amongst the community – from drunken brawls outside taverns, to jousting knights in tournaments; but the murder of a monk was something quite dreadful; and so very, very wrong. It was an abomination against both the city and the church.

"I'm very sorry Abbot Robert."

"Thank you. And now you know the reason for my visit so early in the morning. I realise that as Sheriff you are a busy man, and that a murder would generally be handled by one of your deputies, but I would like to ask if you could see your way to giving this matter your personal attention."

Simon could see just how shaken the Abbot was by the event and he nodded.

"Of course, I will take personal responsibility for this," he assured the Abbot. As Sheriff of the county, it was not a given that he would personally deal in such matters. However, when it was a monk who had been murdered it did warrant his personal attention.

"Thank you, Simon. I had the body of our dear brother laid to rest in the sacristy. In this hot weather, I thought it the coolest place for him to remain until we hear from his family as where they would like him to be buried." He paused. "I also had the carter show me exactly where he had found Brother Clement. I thought..." He turned the goblet slowly in his hands. "I thought that you might want to view the site to see if there is any information that can be gleaned from it."

Simon nodded, somewhat surprised at just how practical and astute the Abbot was.

"That was very insightful of you. And yes, I would like to view where Brother Clement was found." He put his goblet down on the desk. "Shall we depart now, before the sun gets too high in the sky?"

The Abbot nodded. "I was hoping you would say that."

The two men were very similar in many ways, both intellectual, thoughtful and reserved. But their looks were quite different. Whilst Simon was tall, fair and blond, the Abbot was shorter with a darker complexion from his Mediterranean parentage.

Simon summoned his steward and requested that his horse was made ready for him to ride out; and also, to arrange for his deputy, Adam and another of his men at arms to be saddled and prepared to ride with them. Whilst they waited, the two men exchanged pleasantries and news that was lighter in tone than the events which had brought the Abbot to see him.

The two men walked out of the castle keep, and into the bailey where Simons' horse had been made ready and his deputy, along with two men at arms, were waiting for them. Mounting easily, Simon waited whilst Abbot Robert was helped onto his mule. Together they rode west out of the castle along the main road through the city to Bootham Bar in the western wall. Even though it was still early morning and the bells for terce had only just sounded, the city was alive with merchants and tradesmen all vying for customers along the street front. Simon watched the people going about their everyday duties and wondered if the news of the murdered monk had filtered through to them yet. Gossip always seemed to move quickly in the city and if they weren't aware of it now, then it would not be too long before the news was out there. He observed that hardly anyone was paying attention to him or to the Abbot, and he concluded that this indicated the gossip still had not percolated through the city. The carter must have been more reticent about telling his story to everyone than Simon expected.

Outside of the city, the Abbot led the party down to the

river and then along the bank towards the north-west. It wasn't long before the Abbot halted them and went to dismount.

"I came here earlier with the carter who found Brother Clement," he told Simon. "But I made sure not to walk over the area where I was told he found him, in case there was anything of importance still there. I thought it was best for you to take a closer look at the place."

Simon nodded. He was grateful for the Abbots shrewdness, though he doubted there would be anything much to find. He dismounted and signalled for Adam and his men at arms to join him in the search.

"Look carefully men. Anything that you see could be of importance."

Simon stepped carefully over the ground towards the riverbank. The ground was hard from the lack of rain over the last weeks and there were no footprints of any note. He saw trails along the riverbank of where something had been dragged but considered that this was likely to be where the carter had dragged the body. In a patch of dried grass, he saw the darkened redness of aged blood. Looking around, he thought he could detect the downtrodden undergrowth where a scuffle had taken place. This was undoubtedly where the monk had been murdered. The blood had dried on the grass and was already attracting the attention of a number of flies. He swatted them away and as he moved, something glinted in the sunlight, half hidden in the grass. Carefully he reached forward and separated the grass so that he could take a closer look at it. As he peered more closely, he could see that it was a small, polished red stone set in a metal fitting. It had probably come from the end of a hilt of the dagger that had been used to slit the throat of the monk. He picked it up carefully and looked at it. It was spotted with blood that had now turned dark and more brown than red. Simon supposed that at the time, the red stone would have been well hidden amongst the red blood. It was only now that the blood had dried, and the sun was shining on it, that he had noticed it.

"What is it?" The Abbot asked him, standing apart from the men searching the area.

"A red stone," Simon replied, holding it up so the Abbot could see. "Maybe a garnet or something like that. It looks as if it has come from the hilt of a dagger. Possibly the dagger that killed Brother Clement. It has specks of blood on it, so it hasn't found its' way there since he was killed."

The Abbot peered at it carefully. "But it could have been there before?"

"Possibly, but I would think highly unlikely. A stone from the hilt of a dagger, lying in the residue of blood, in the exact location where a man had his throat slit?" His voice rose slightly at the end of the statement illustrating it as a statement not a question.

Simon placed the stone into the pouch suspended from his belt and stood up, looking around himself slowly in case there was anything else that might be hidden. He very much doubted there would be, but then he hadn't expected to find the stone.

"Sire!" Adam, his deputy called out to him.

Simon went over to where Adam was standing next to a bush and his deputy pointed to some horsehair that had caught on a projecting sharp twig.

"It looks as if there were horsemen around here." Adam said. "And one of them rode a grey."

"It may not relate to the murder." Simon mused. "It could have happened days or even weeks before this incident." However, he leant forward and unpicked the strands of horsehair, placing them with the stone in his belt bag.

"Is it important?" The Abbot asked him.

"I don't know." Simon replied. "But if the man that did this was on horseback and has a dagger that is decorated with precious stones, then we aren't looking for a drunken serf as your murderer. Whoever did this is likely to be a knight, or a nobleman."

Simon returned to his horse and gestured for his men

to do the same.

"I don't think there is anything further that we can find here," he added going to mount his horse. Then turning to the Abbot. "Did you say that you had the body of Brother Clement at the Abbey?"

"Yes, as I said earlier, I instructed him to be laid in the sacristy where it is a little cooler."

"Then that is where I would like to go next. If you would permit that?"

The Abbot nodded. "Of course."

Simon and his men on their sturdy chargers rode in silence behind the Abbot astride his small mule. Simon mused that they must look a comical sight as they rode back along the bank of the River Ouse towards the Abbey precinct and the city, but outside the walls of the city, there was no-one to see them. The huge timber gates of the abbey, opened for them as they approached and a number of monks were gathered in the courtyard beyond the gates, waiting for the Abbot. One monk approached and took charge of the mule as the Abbot dismounted. Other monks took the horses from Simon and his men.

"Will your men wait here?" Abbot Robert asked Simon. He nodded and the Abbot turned to a monk who was at his side. "Brother Peter, see to it that our guests have some ale and bread please."

The monk nodded wordlessly. Without having to be asked Simon unfastened the belt that held his sword and handed it along with his dagger to Brother Peter for safe keeping.

The Abbot smiled at his gesture. "I appreciate that you understand our request that no-one should bear arms within the house of God."

"Of course." Simon replied as he followed the Abbot across the courtyard and up the steps into the Abbey building. As they entered through the main west door at the end of the nave, Simon had to stop momentarily to allow his eyes to adjust to the dim light within the building.

The Abbot graciously stopped as well, in order to wait for the sheriff. Then together, they walked together down the nave and up to the crossing point where the tower soared above their heads. Simon looked up at the soaring columns and exquisitely carved stone arches, raising far into the sky. He had only seldom been in the abbey before and had never actually stopped to look at the splendour of the building. The sound of their footsteps on the tiled floor, even though not loud, sounded intrusive in the perfect silence of the space. After the crossing point the Abbot went to his right towards a wooden door in the south wall of the abbey. Turning the handle, he opened the door onto a side room which was the sacristy. The room was completely dark, and the Abbot took a candle from beside the entrance to light his way into the room. He quickly lit the candles on the wall sconces, before stopping in front of the small altar in one corner of the room and genuflected before it. Simon repeated the sign of servility and respect before following the Abbot, and noticed that it was slightly cooler in the sacristy than the main body of the Abbey. Simon assumed this was due to the thick stone walls that surrounded the room and the lack of windows. He considered that it was unfortunate the Abbey did not have a crypt below ground which would have been the obvious place to store a body in this incredibly hot weather. As if sensing his thoughts, Abbot Robert turned to face him.

"I thought it best to place Brother Clement in here, separate to the main church. I'm not sure how long it will be until I hear back from his family as to where they would like him buried, and the smell of the body by then would prove to be quite awful should he be in the main abbey. At least in here we can contain the smell of death."

Simon reflected that it was a wise decision given the impossible heat that gripped the city. The room had large coffers lined up against the walls and a sturdy wooden chest adjacent to the small altar. He assumed that the Abbey's religious silverware for communions, altar linens and Abbots' vestments must be stored here, well away from the temptation they might pose to others. The body of the monk was laid on a large wooden table in the centre of the room.

"Have you sent word to his family yet?"

The Abbot nodded. "Yes, I sent one of the monks to go to their manor this morning with a letter informing them."

Simon nodded. "Good. Will you let me know when they intend to visit?"

"Of course."

Simon looked around at the room and then said. "You could use some river water in buckets in the room to keep the air cooler."

Abbot Robert nodded. "If that would help, I will make sure it happens."

Simon turned to look at the table in front of him where the body had been laid. The black habit of the Benedictine order adorned the body and he knew that this must be Brother Clement. The Abbot stood in front of the body and crossed himself as he spoke a prayer in Latin.

"Requiem aeternam dona eis Domine, et lux perpetua luceat eis."

Simon lowered his head as the Abbot spoke in respect. He remained silent and still for a moment until the Abbot finally moved to one side.

Simon approached the body slowly and carefully looked at the external appearance of the dead monk and in particular the habit that he was wearing. He was looking for anything that was out of place; perhaps something caught in the fabric; or a tear that should not be there. There was nothing.

"Do you mind if I examine him?" Simon asked politely.

He saw Abbot Robert draw a silent breath. "It is not usual for us to allow this, but then these are not usual circumstances, so I will agree."

Simon reached out and carefully moved the black cowl away from the head of Brother Clement. There were no other marks on his head except for the gash across his throat. He had wondered if there might be the sign of bruising on his temple, or across his face if he had been hit or stunned before his throat was cut. Simon leant in to look more closely at the cut across his throat. As he did so, Abbot Robert moved nearer to him with the candle so that the cut was lit and not in shadow.

"See this," Simon pointed to the cut, "it's deeper on the left-hand side than it is on the right. If the man who did this was standing behind him then we are looking for a right-handed man. But, if he was standing in front of him, then we are looking for a left-handed man."

Simon noted that the cut was very clean and not at all jagged. It had been a sharp blade that had perpetrated this wound, and not a worn or barbed blade. It was definitely a dagger that had caused such a precise wound, Simon mused. An ordinary, everyday knife carried by most people would never be as sharp as that, nor would it give the precision of cut that could only have been made by a blade sharpened on both sides and not just one.

"Do you mind?" Simon asked, indicating that he would like to move the sleeves of the habit in order that he could look at the arms of Brother Clement.

The Abbot nodded in agreement, standing to one side he lowered his head and started uttering prayers for departed monk in front of him.

As Simon pushed the left sleeve of the habit upwards above the elbow, he saw that there was faint bruising on the upper arm. Moving around the body to the opposite side, he did the same thing and confirmed his thoughts when he saw that there was slight bruising also on the right arm.

"You see this," he indicated the bruising to Abbot Robert. "The bruising on both arms shows that he was held whilst his throat was being cut. From the shape of the bruises, I would say that someone held him from behind, whilst his throat was cut from the front. That means that we are looking for more than one man; and the man that cut his throat was also left-handed. Look," he added pointing to the hands of Brother Clement, "there are no cuts on either hand, meaning that he had no chance to defend himself. However dreadful this may be, mercifully it appears that it was a swift death."

The Abbot nodded and looked away, finding himself quite affected by the sight of the body and considered what Simon had said. He knew that minutiae were often the most important things and often overlooked. He had noticed how Simon was an observant man, with an eye for the smallest of details. The man certainly saw things that would go entirely unnoticed by another.

Simon looked at the feet of Brother Clement and saw no marks on them to suggest that he had been dragged anywhere, so it was likely that he had died where he had been found. After further careful examination failed to reveal anything more, Simon nodded to Abbot Robert that he had finished. He straightened himself and let Abbot Robert say a final prayer over the body, before covering it with a shroud. Then they both left the sacristy, and the Abbot locked the door behind them.

"If there is nothing more you need of our dear departed Brother then, with your permission, I will have his body washed and prepared for burial." He said as they walked together back into the Abbey nave.

Simon nodded. "Yes of course. That will be fine."

"If you will excuse me then I need to return to my office," the Abbot said, as they approached the west door. "It will soon be time for our devotions at Sexte and I must be there to lead the prayers for our dear departed Brother."

"There was just one other thing." Simon noted. "You mentioned that the reason Brother Clement was outside the Abbey precinct was that he had been administering to an infirm lady."

"Ah yes, Lady Maud de Mowbray. She and the Earl live out at the manor house at Overton. Lady Maud has been ill for some months, but she has become quite frail of late. Brother Clement was ministering to her and hearing her confession."

"I see; thank you, Abbot." He gave a small bow of respect to the Abbot. "I will leave you to prepare for your devotions."

Simon knew there was not much else he could do at the abbey. He would get his men to carry out some inquiries around the city, and he also needed to return to his own work.

"Thank you, Simon. I value your assistance in this, and I hope you are able to find the perpetrator quickly."

"I will do my best." Simon nodded, then added. "As soon as I get back to the castle, I will organise my men to start their investigations; the local alehouses are normally a hive of gossip when something like this has happened. And, whilst the majority of it is really quite useless, sometimes, just sometimes, there can be a point made or a sentence remarked on, which is of interest." He paused. "And, whilst my men are doing that, I will ensure a full record of what has transpired today is made; including what we found in the area where the murder occurred; and also, what I have observed about the body. When we find the villain who has done this, I want to have all the evidence ready to be able to convict him."

The Abbot nodded. "Then I will leave things with you, my friend. Please do keep me informed if anything of interest comes to your attention."

"I will do." And with that, Simon bowed his head again in respect for the Abbot and made his leave.

CHAPTER 2

Katherine was late to rise that morning. When her maid Jennet came into her chamber, she groaned inwardly as she pulled the cover over her head. Katherine wanted to stay in bed and daydream again about what happened yesterday when Alexander had proposed to her. She wanted to remember every single word they had said to each other and play the hours she had spent with him over and over in her head. Sir Alexander de Ros, third son of Lord Robert de Ros, Baron of Helmsley castle to the north of York was in love with her. He had told her as much when they parted last night, and she was glowing with the remembrance of everything that had happened.

Grenulf, Katherines wolf-hound stirred on the floor as Jennet busied herself.

"It's another beautiful day outside, my lady." Jennet said, as she laid out the dress for Katherine. "I put out your lilac dress to wear today."

Katherine reluctantly hauled herself out of bed; she supposed that she would have to put Alexander to the back of her mind, at least for a little time. She quickly washed in the basin of water that Jennet had brought in, then dressed herself in the lilac dress over the top of her shift that Jennet had left out for her.

Jennet was still talking to her as she sat down in the chair whilst Jennet stood behind her to brush and then plait her long auburn hair, so that it had a resemblance of elegance.

At seventeen Katherine was a tall, beautiful girl, with haunting eyes and a wildness of spirit that no-one, not even her father seemed to be able to subdue. When her mother had died shortly after Katherine had been born, her father had initially shunned the baby in favour of her elder sister. The pain of remembering how his beloved

Ellen died had been too difficult for him. But then, as Katherine had grown older, her courage and intelligence had won him over. She had started to remind him more and more of his beloved wife, whom he had loved with all his heart.

The young girl's spirited character had earned her a reputation by a succession of tutors, of being impossible to teach. Katherine had no interest in learning courtly ways, dancing or fine needlework. Instead, she loved nothing more than spending time with her father reading books and learning from him as he worked as a lawyer. She was always inquiring and asking questions; wanting to know why and how things were so. Her father had been constantly warned by his staff that it was quite inappropriate for a lady of his daughters standing to be behaving in such a way. When her father had told her that they were moving to York due to his appointment as Sheriff by the King, Katherine had railed against him. She hadn't wanted to leave her home or her friends and had been angry with him for insisting that she came with him. She believed herself old enough now to remain at their home, in Earls Barton in Northamptonshire, where she would oversee and run the household whilst he was away. After all, she had told him, she was old enough to be married and run her own household, so she couldn't understand why her father wouldn't consider it. He'd tried to explain that it wasn't appropriate for his unmarried daughter to remain alone at the manor; but Katherine hadn't understood. Eventually, he had given her the ultimatum that either she accompany him to live in York or, she could go and stay with her elder sister Angharad and her husband. The thought of staying with her sister and her husband was even worse than the alternative of going to York.

Her sister, Angharad, was two years older than Katherine and the two girls could not be more different. Whilst Angharad had grown up wanting nothing more than to be married and in charge of her own household,

Katherine had been reluctant to settle down. Angharad accepted the match her father had made for her and had married a man twenty years her senior. She was a serious and devout woman who had, it seemed to everyone, prematurely aged to fit in with her new husband's life and friends. The two sisters were as different in character as they were in looks. Katherine could think of nothing worse than being stifled by her elder sister into behaving like a proper lady, or being reproached every time she said something that wasn't approved of.

At first Katherine had hated York, she didn't know anyone there and her father was constantly busy with his new appointment. There was only Jennet, her maid, who was her constant from her life before. Then, at one of her father's dinners in the great hall, she had met Alexander de Ros. She recalled seeing him for the first time across the hall and had been instantly intrigued by him. He was there with his father who was part of the local nobility, dining as guests of her father at the castle. Part way through the dinner she had caught him watching her; she smiled at him, and he raised his glass in acknowledgement. Suddenly, butterflies started to dance in her stomach.

It had been another two weeks before she had seen him again and, that time, Katherine was sure he had engineered the meeting. She had been going out to the stables and planning to ride out of the city, when she had seen him leading a horse towards her.

"Lady Katherine," he had greeted her and smiled.

"Lord Ros." She replied, feeling as though her insides were in turmoil at the sight of him.

"Are you going out riding?" He asked. "I hope you aren't planning to go out alone?"

Katherine smiled; she had the distinct feeling that he was teasing her.

"Yes, I am going riding, but not alone; my maid Jennet will be coming with me." She looked directly at him with a challenging stare but found his gaze quite unnerving.

He turned and patted the neck of the sturdy horse next

to him and Katherine found it hard to breathe for a moment. He really was quite handsome, with a quick smile and kind eyes under the cropped black hair. He was taller than her and well built, but more than that, it seemed that whenever their eyes met, her heart did the most enormous somersaults.

"Would you mind if I accompanied you instead? My father has business to carry out here that doesn't require my presence, and I expect that he will be some time."

Katherine put her head on one side and considered what he'd said. "So, if his business doesn't need you, why did you come with him?"

If she hadn't been watching him quite so closely then she would have missed the slight colour that spread across his face.

Alexander smiled. "I was actually hoping that I might see you. Is that wrong?"

Now it was her turn to feel the colour rising in her cheeks.

"No, not at all." She stammered, her mouth feeling quite dry. "But my maid Jennet will still need to ride out with us. It would not be appropriate for me to ride out alone with you, my Lord." She teased.

He nodded and gave her a warm smile. "So be it."

Alexander waited patiently as the stable hand readied the two horses for both Katherine and Jennet. Then together they rode out of the castle gates to the south and took the road leading down to the river. It was early May and the leaves on the trees were only just beginning to change from the new light green to a darker green colour that would deepen more over the coming weeks. The air was warm during the day and away from the city walls the hub-hub of activity disappeared to be replaced with the calm of the countryside. Katherine would have loved to be walking along the banks of the River Ouse on her own, but her father had strictly prohibited it. She was the daughter of the Sheriff of the county and there people out there who would not think twice about harming her. There were times when she wished she had been able to remain at the manor in Earls Barton. At least there, she was a 'nobody' and could come and go as she pleased. But today was one time when she was glad of the company – at least of Alexanders' company. They had ridden together along the riverbank with Jennet following on behind them at a suitable distance to allow the two of them to talk freely.

Katherine recalled that first meeting so clearly. Her heart had known straight away that Alexander was special; and she knew that the feeling had been mutual. They were both captivated with each other and had managed to arrange many meetings over the last couple of months. Their latest had been yesterday afternoon and for once she had managed to sneak out of the castle without Jennet and to meet Alexander on her own. She had ridden along the riverbank to the place where they always met; the place where the trees thinned out a little, but it was still private enough for them to remain hidden. The sun had been glistening on the water of the river as she dismounted her horse and tethered him loosely to a tree branch. Walking up to the river she closed her eyes and allowed the sun to warm her face, before sitting down in the grass. Her maid Jennet hadn't been pleased that Katherine was still seeing Alexander and hadn't told her father about him yet. Jennet had told her quite firmly that if Katherine didn't tell him, then she would do so. The veiled threat had made Katherine angry; she didn't like being backed into a corner by her maid, even if she did love the woman like a mother. Her father had already made it clear that it was time for Katherine to marry and that he was speaking with the King's advisors about a suitable Earl or Baron for her. She had been told it would be a good match, commensurate with her fathers' standing; and one which the King would personally approve. There was never any mention of love and that was the one thing Katherine wanted more than anything. She wanted to be loved; the same way she was told her father had loved her mother.

Her thoughts were suddenly disturbed by a movement behind her, and she started, suddenly afraid of who might be there. She looked around and saw the figure standing at the edge of the trees; it was Alexander, and as he approached her, he removed his cloak, letting it fall to the ground next to her. He gazed down at Katherine, and as their eyes met, she felt her breath quicken. Then he lowered himself on to the ground beside her. Alexander was a little older than Katharine and quite a few inches taller. He was a powerful, muscular man, who was a fine knight and would one day be a great Lord of one of his father's estates.

Katharine smiled at him, then looked away, returning her gaze to the river. Her heart beat so quickly every time she looked at him that she was sure he must be able to hear it.

"You came here on your own?" Alexander observed, raising a hand to move a lock of hair that had come loose and fallen down the side of her face.

His touch was like electricity.

"Yes, I managed to get away without Jennet noticing. But I don't think I will be able to do it again. I'm afraid that Jennet is going to tell my father if we keep seeing each other." She said the words quickly, as though it would make it disappear if she spoke quickly.

He smiled gently and took her hand in his. "We've been lucky so far." He watched her carefully. "I suppose it could never last forever; our secret meetings."

He paused and Katherine was suddenly afraid of what he was going to say next. For some unknown reason she was suddenly worried that he was going to end it with her and her eyes searched his face looking for reassurance. She could not imagine her life without him now. He had become such an integral part of her existence, that thinking of a future without him was unbearable.

"Perhaps it's time that you told your father, and I told mine." Alexander said.

Katherine momentarily gasped with relief and then stared at him trying to compose herself.

"Are you sure?" She asked. "What do you think your father will say? Aren't you supposed to be betrothed already?" The words tumbled out of her mouth.

They had been seeing each other for a few months now and although she was sure of how she felt about Alexander, he had never before spoken about his feelings for her. She had only been able to assume that he felt the same from his gestures, but he had never said anything directly. Katherine felt her head whirling as she tried to take everything in. It was all that she had ever wanted; to fall in love with a man and marry for love and not because it was a political match. She wanted what her parents had had, and Alexander was offering her that dream.

"I am supposedly betrothed, but it has never really been formalised. And it's not as though I'm the heir to my father's title and estate. I'm the third son. I'm not important; I'm just another nobleman's son who is a knight. Whereas you......" He paused and looked at her.

Katherine nodded, understanding what he was trying to say. "I am the youngest daughter of the Sheriff of Yorkshire. A man who was appointed by the King and has his favour." She laughed. "Yes, it's probably going to be more difficult for me to persuade my father to allow us to be together, than it will be for you. I know my father is a reasonable man, but I am just a daughter, and I fear that I won't get much say in the matter of who I marry. But, if you were to ask him for my hand..." She gave him a pleading look.

Alexander looked at her tenderly. "Then, let me talk to him, my darling. Once I've told my father, I will arrange to see your father and ask him personally if I can marry you."

Katherine let out a small squeal of delight. She had scarcely dared to dream that Alexander would want her, as much as she wanted him. It was so much more than she could ever have hoped for. It was a perfect moment in time.

The sun was glowing in the evening sky and the warmth and scent of a summer evening on the banks of the river, made if feel magical. Especially when the man she loved had just told her he wanted to marry her. Then, to make it even more perfect, Alexander leaned in, and their lips met in a kiss. It was the briefest brush of his lips on hers. She could feel the warmth of his breath on her face. Then, closing her eyes, she moved towards him until their lips met once again, this time more passionately. Alexander put his hand around the back of her neck and gently pulled her towards him until their bodies were touching. The warmth of his body against hers was intoxicating and she found it hard to maintain her composure. She wanted him so badly that it was hard to resist him, but she knew she had to. She felt a gentle pressure from Alexander to entice her to lay down with him on the ground, but she gently pulled away.

"We can't. I'm sorry, but we can't," she breathed, pushing him away. It wasn't that she didn't want him; every part of her was aching for him, but she realised that she needed to be sensible. She wasn't one of the serving girls, who was good for a laugh and a quick fumble in the stables. She had seen what could happen to girls like that, and that was the last thing she wanted. "If our fathers agree, then we can marry quickly and I will be all yours; until then, we mustn't."

For a moment he seemed to freeze as if angry with her, then a smile slowly spread across his face, and he kissed her gently.

"You're right, I know. But don't think that I don't want you, Katherine."

"I know and I'm grateful for your restraint. But I don't want to give my father any reason to stop us marrying, and if he found out that we had lain together then I would probably be sent away to my sister back in Northamptonshire and we wouldn't get to see each other again."

"That is the last thing I want." He got to his feet and

held out a hand to her. "I will speak with my father in the morning. And then, once I have his agreement, I will ride here to see your father and ask him for permission to marry you."

When Katherine thought of their conversation, it still brought shivers of delight to her. Now all she had to do was to speak to her father before Alexander arrived at the castle and tell him that she was in love and wished to marry Sir Alexander de Ros. Her father could hardly refuse him on grounds of his family not being part of the nobility. His father was Robert de Ros, Baron of Helmsley and, according to her father, a man well respected by the King. There was nothing disagreeable about him.

"Is my father around this morning?" Katherine asked Jennet, anticipating the conversation she was going to have with him about her intended betrothal to Alexander.

"No, my lady. He went out early this morning with the Abbot." Jennet replied as she finished braiding Katherines' hair.

"The Abbot?" Katherine spun around to face Jennet with surprise.

"Talk is that a monk was murdered out by the river, my lady." Jennet replied eager to impart the gossip, and then adding a little more sharply. "That's why I didn't want you to go out, it's not safe out there. I know you went out last night on your own, and I think your father knows as well. He's not going to be happy with you. He won't be happy with me either, allowing you to go out all those times. At least then I was accompanying you, but yesterday – you going out alone, it's not right my lady; it's really not appropriate."

"I was only with Alexander and it's not as if you don't know that I've being seeing him."

"What I'm saying is, that you shouldn't be seeing him on your own my lady. It may be acceptable for a servant, but it's not right for a lady of your standing. Your father would dismiss me if he were to find out that you had gone out without a chaperone."

"Then I won't tell him" She turned to face Jennet, whose face was stern. "And I hope you won't either?"

Jennet sighed heavily. She disliked keeping things from her master, he was a good man, and he had always treated her fairly. She knew how lucky she was to have him as her employer. She had first come into service for him when he had married the Lady Ellen. Back then, Lady Ellen had been no more than a young girl herself, only a year older than Jennet and they had travelled together after the wedding to the manor in Earls Barton. Lady Ellen had only met Simon de Hale twice before the wedding, and both she and Jennet had found themselves in a strange manor, with no-one they really knew. Their shared experience of being homesick and missing their families had bonded them and made them friends and confidents. However, Jennet had always been conscious of the difference between Ellen, as lady of the manor, and herself as a member of her staff, and managed to keep a dutiful distance.

Jennet was unusually tall for a woman, with a slim figure and a warm face; her long blonde hair was kept hidden from view by her wimple. Katherine had been merely days old when her mother had died. Jennet hadn't left the side of Lady Ellen trying everything she had learnt from her mother to try and break the fever that had taken hold of Ellen following the birth, but nothing seemed to work. Then suddenly, one evening, the Lady Ellen appeared to rally, and it looked as though Jennets' remedies had finally worked. The master had been overjoyed to see his beloved wife looking better. But then, in the middle of the night, the fever returned suddenly and viciously and there was nothing that Jennet or anyone could do. As the sun rose, and the first light bathed the room with gentle golden rays, Lady Ellen had died peacefully. The Master had been distraught and refused to move from the bedside until finally one of his squires had persuaded him to leave. There was nothing more that anyone could do for her now.

Jennet had been equally distraught at the death of Lady Ellen; she had been not just her mistress, but her friend as well. All she could do now was to ensure that her daughters were taken care of. Angharad was almost three years old and was already being cared for by one of the maids, but it was the new-born child that Jennet focused her attention on. She could do nothing more for Lady Ellen now; all she could do was promise her mistress, that she would do everything in her power to look after her youngest daughter. Jennet had found a wet nurse to suckle the tiny waif and then had busied herself organising everything in the household. The master had been too distraught to do anything, and Jennet had ensured that at least the household was taken care of; the tradesmen were paid, and the pantry was kept full.

Jennet had become a surrogate mother to the tiny baby, trying to love her as though she were her own flesh. Initially, the master had wanted nothing to do with the baby girl, the memories of his beloved wife, all too fresh and painful for him. But as the years passed, and the girl had flourished, he had begun to take more of an interest in her. Jennet had taught her to read from the gospels and instructed her on needlework, which Katherine had loathed. Instructions on running a household had been only marginally better received, but when her father had sat her next to him and explained details of the law, or of a land dispute he was hearing on behalf of the King, she became alive with questions and engaged him in numerous discussions. Jennet had watched as the bond between the master and his youngest daughter had finally grown and flourished. And now, her master seemed unwilling to let her go. The small girl had grown into a beautiful young woman, and one that should have already been wed by now, like her older sister, Angharad. But the master seemed reluctant to make the decision. Jennet sensed that he thought of Katherine as his last link to his dear Ellen and that once she had left his house, then Ellen too would be gone from him. It wasn't right though, and Jennet had urged him to find a good husband for Katherine. He had not wavered in making a good match for his elder daughter Angharad, but he kept saying that there was time enough for Katherine. Finally, when Lord William Fitzwarren had approached Simon to make a treaty between the two families, Katherine's father had relented and agreed to the marriage. But it seemed the only thing he hadn't done, was to tell his daughter of this. Jennet knew it was not her place to tell Katherine, and only her master could do that.

Lord Fitzwarren was a good man; a man of wealth and standing in the Shire. His first wife had passed away, but he was still relatively young and not bad looking. It helped that he was on good terms with both the young King, and his advisors and it seemed the this had finally helped the master to agree to the marriage. Lord Fitzwarren had a reputation as a good soldier and knight, brave and fearless, even if he was quick to anger, but Jennet doubted that would matter much as he would rarely be at home. Jennet knew she was trying to convince herself that he was the right man for Katherine, whereas in her heart, she knew he wasn't. Nor was he the man that the girl loved. Jennet shook her head; it was not her place to say anything; this was a matter for her master to deal with.

"I haven't said a word to your father about Alexander." Jennet told Katherine. "But I suspect that he may already be aware of the situation. Even without me telling him, there are those who would do so; the stable hand for instance; and your father is very observant, my lady. There is very little that he doesn't notice."

"Yes, of course, you're right." Katherine sighed. "Then I will need to speak to him as soon as he returns and tell him everything." She stood up and walked across to the window embrasure. "Alexander wants to marry me, Jennet. Isn't it just wonderful news? He's going to tell his father first and then come here to speak with mine."

Katherine turned to face Jennet, her face alive with

happiness and love. Jennet looked at the pretty face of the girl who was quickly becoming a beautiful, if slightly wild young woman. She felt her heart lurch at the news that Alexander wanted to marry her. She had watched the relationship blossom and knew she should have put a stop to it earlier. She loved the girl as though she was her own daughter, but it wasn't her place to tell her about the already arranged betrothal to Lord Fitzwarren; that was down to her father. Whatever he had planned for her, it would be with his daughters' best interests at heart. Jennet repeated the statement to herself, as she needed to believe it. The master was a good man, and he cared so much for his beautiful daughter that she trusted him to make the right decision for her.

CHAPTER 3

Simon de Hale removed his sword from his side and laid it on the table. He indicated to the servant to pour him some wine and then sank into the chair at his desk in his room. His office was next to his bed chamber on the upper floor of the main keep of the castle and was richly decorated with tapestries on the walls. Opposite his desk was a large fireplace with a hearth that hadn't been used for many weeks now. To the side of him was a window with shutters on the inside which provided the only daylight into the room. The papers he had started to go through earlier were still laid out on his desk and he picked the closest one up, and started to read it, but found that he couldn't concentrate. His mind kept going back to the events of the morning; the discovery of the body of the monk who had been killed and not by accident, but intentionally and brutally. The thought weighed heavily on him, along with his belief that whoever committed the murder was not a drunken thug with a grudge against the abbey, but a man of some means and standing; at least that was what the jewelled pommel would suggest. He reached into his bag and pulled out the stone that he had found earlier and holding it up he could see it glint red in the sunlight. The spherical stone was held in place with four metal claws that were shaped like talons of a bird of prey. It looked very much as though it came from the pommel or hilt of a dagger, and whoever it belonged to, may not even realise that it had been lost yet. It wasn't an item that would have been part of a knife belonging to a peasant or serf; this came off the hilt of an expensive dagger. The type of dagger that would belong to a nobleman or knight. The only problem was that there were quite a few of them in the shire and he had no idea who it might be. The other clue was the grey hair from a horse. It was possible the animal had caught itself on a branch and would have a scar on it from the injury. He wondered if sending his men out into the city, to look for a grey horse with a cut on it, might help in his investigation. Other than that, he really didn't have that much to go on.

He got up from his desk and moved across to a wooden coffer that was at the rear of his room and opened it. Removing a cloth from the top of the coffer, he carefully wrapped the two items in it, before placing them in the chest and closing it. He turned around suddenly as he heard a knock on the door and, he saw one of the serving women bringing him a jug of wine and a clean goblet and placing it on his desk.

"Can you find Adam and tell him that I want to see him." He told the woman.

"Yes sire." She nodded to him and quickly left his room.

Adam de Burgh was Simon's deputy and the head of his men at arms, who supported the work that Simon had been entrusted to carry out in the Shire. He was a man who had been with Simon for a good few years now and although not strictly friends, the two men had a healthy respect for each other. Adam was a well-built man with a gruff appearance that allowed him to blend in well with the general population of the city. He was a trained soldier and fine swordsman, and Simon knew he could rely on him whenever he needed assistance.

"Sire." Adam entered the room and addressed Simon, who had now returned to sit at his desk.

Simon gestured for Adam to take a seat in the chair opposite him.

"Adam, I promised the Abbot that I would take personal charge of investigating this horrific killing. Murder is dreadful at the best of times, but when the victim is a monk; it makes it even more atrocious." He paused for a moment, as he tried to imagine what the poor monk must have felt; the fear and terror that must have overcome him when he realised the men in front of him were not there to befriend him. "I need you to do some work for me. You know the grey horsehair that you found at the place where the monk was murdered."

Adam nodded. "Aye sir."

"I reckon that the horse might have caught itself on the branch where we found it and might have a small cut or wound on it. I think it would be wise to see if we can find that horse and identify who it belongs to. I would like you to send your men out into the city, and to the manors beyond the city walls to see if you can find the animal."

Adam nodded. "Aye, best to do that today. The owner may not have realised yet what's happened or have noticed the cut. I'll get the men together and arrange for them to look through the stables in the city and beyond."

"Tell them to keep it discreet," Simon said thoughtfully. "I don't want to alert anyone to what we are looking for or why."

"They'll do as I tell them, sire. Do you want me to go with them?"

"No, I want you to come with me this afternoon. The Abbot told me that Brother Clement was returning from visiting Lady Maud de Mowbray at the manor at Overton. I thought we should pay her a visit. We'll go after our meal."

Adam nodded. "I'll make sure the horses are ready for us." He got up from the chair and nodded a small bow of respect to Simon, before quickly leaving the room.

Simon poured himself a goblet of wine and then leant back in his chair and sighed. It had been an eventful morning, to say the least; and one which had not gone anything like he had planned. His mind wandered back to the body of the murdered monk and how brutal the attack on him had been. He wondered what on earth had happened to provoke such a savage attack. Was it something personal about Brother Clement? Something from his past that had resurfaced now with a horrific outcome. Or was it a warning to the Abbey and the Abbot about something to which yet, he had no knowledge? His first visit would be to see Lady Maud as Brother Clement had been returning from her manor. After that, Simon concluded he needed to pay another visit to the Abbey and to speak with Abbot Robert to ask if there had been any other acts of violence against the Abbey. However minor they might be, they could be a clue to who had done this. But, for the moment that would have to wait, as he needed to make a written account of what had happened this morning. He glanced across at the pile of papers still awaiting his attention and sighed; he had hoped to work through those this morning, but they would have to wait a bit longer now. He shouted for his scribe to attend him at once and a short wily man duly entered the room and sat at a small desk. Gathering the parchment and a quill pen, he sat ready waiting for Simon to speak. It was only a short while though, before there came a knock on the door and his young steward entered.

"What is it, Richard?" Simon felt slightly annoyed at the interruption.

"Lord Fitzwarren is here to see you sire."

Simon inwardly groaned and dropped his head. He had totally forgotten that he had agreed to see William this morning to finalise the details of Katherine's marriage. However, he couldn't turn the man away now he was here; it would be seen as a snub, and he didn't want that. He dismissed his scribe and tidied away some of the papers from his desk.

Simon didn't know Lord Fitzwarren well, but his reputation was that of a good, solid man. He might be slightly older than Simon would initially have wished for his daughter, but that was probably a good thing. Katherine would need a strong and wise man to understand and 'tame' her. He wondered if that was the correct word to describe it, but his daughter was strong willed, and a man of weak character would be no match for her.

"Send him in, Richard and arrange some more wine and something to eat for both of us."

"Very good sire." Richard left the room and then a

moment later Lord William Fitzwarren entered. The door was closed quietly behind him.

Simon stood up from his desk and went across the room to meet him.

"William, it is good of you to come." Simon greeted him jovially, observing the man who would soon be his son in law. Apart from him being less than ten years his junior, he had to admit that the man would be a very suitable match for his daughter. He had made several discreet enquires about Lord Fitzwarren and it seemed that no-one had a bad word to say about him.

"Simon." Lord Fitzwarren smiled as he greeted him. "It is good to see you again and in such happy circumstances. I must tell you how pleased I am that you have agreed to my request for your daughter in marriage."

Simon gestured to him to sit down; the man nodded and followed Simon across the room to sit at the desk in front of Simon.

"I have asked for some wine and food to be brought to us, so that we might discuss the details in comfort."

"Thank you." Lord Fitzwarren paused for a moment. "I expect you have been busy this morning?" He looked at him inquiringly. "It's an awful business, about the murder of the monk."

Simon was a little taken aback at the words, he hadn't expected the murder to be common knowledge quite so soon, but then he supposed it would be hard to keep such news secret for long. "I take it that the news is well known throughout the city by now?"

"You know what it's like; news like that, spreads quicker than a fever. And it is very unusual that the victim is a monk."

Lord Fitzwarren was interrupted by a knock on the door. Simon called out to admit entrance and two servants came into the room carrying food and wine. After placing it on the table, they were dismissed and the two men returned to their conversation.

"I don't think I can ever recall when a member of the

abbey was the victim of such a heinous crime." Lord Fitzwarren added.

"It certainly isn't something that I've ever encountered before." Simon admitted, pouring a goblet of wine and handing it to William.

"Do you have any idea of who might have carried out the murder?"

Simon shook his head. "Not as yet. But it's still early; his body was only found just after sunrise."

"I can't imagine why anyone would want to murder an innocent monk. Do you think it could be one of the drunken louts on his way home from the ale house? Itching for an argument with someone and not aware of what he was doing?" Lord Fitzwarren looked thoughtful.

Simon shrugged. "It's a possibility."

Over his years in service as a lawyer and now sheriff, he had learnt to keep his own council and to never say more than he needed to. Gossip was the enemy of justice, and he was well aware that anything he said would be round the city quicker that he could whisper his own name.

"So, we are here to agree the details of your betrothal to my youngest daughter, Katherine." He added, changing the subject.

"Yes, and I have to say that I am honoured you have agreed to the union." Lord Fitzwarren smiled and appeared genuinely pleased.

Simon wondered if his guest was trying to be overly agreeable and he speculated that Lord Fitzwarren was probably aware that he might have some reservations about the match.

"It is high time that my daughter was wed." Simon admitted thoughtfully, then added. "I have already written to the King to ask for his approval of the match."

Lord Fitzwarren looked genuinely surprised at the statement and Simon added. "I realise that it is not strictly necessary, but I have been in the King's service since he ascended to the throne, and I think it only right, given my position, that I ask for his agreement to the marriage."

Lord Fitzwarren nodded and then took a sizeable gulp of the wine. He understood that Simon's position as Sheriff of Yorkshire was a personal appointment of the King and in effect, as Sheriff, he was the power of the King in the north of the country. But he had not expected the betrothal to be subject to the Kings approval. He felt slightly uncomfortable and wondered if he would have to wait very long for the approval of his marriage.

"Of course; I understand, and I can assure you that I am happy to await the Kings response." He acknowledged, hoping that Simon did not notice his hesitation. "Hopefully once that has been received, I may be wed to your daughter as soon as possible?"

"There is no reason for that not to be." Simon watched his guest carefully. "I expect to hear any day now from the King. But we can agree the dowry today and settle on a date for the wedding."

Simon wasn't sure why, but there was something about the man that unsettled him this morning. Lord Fitzwarren had not said anything to worry him; but he couldn't shake the feeling that something was not quite as it should be. Perhaps it was just that the man was not much younger than himself and Katherine only seventeen years of age. The age difference was certainly an issue, but not out of the question. William had a good estate and could provide well for Katherine. There would also be land and a dowry to accompany her into her new home.

The two men took a meal together and continued to discuss the details of both the dowry and the betrothal. When Simon was satisfied with all the details, he explained that he needed to get back to his work and wished William a good day. He had no sooner returned to his paperwork on his desk, when he stopped and remembered that Adam would be waiting for him in the bailey for their visit to Lady Maud de Mowbray. He stood up and was just fastening his sword onto his belt when Katherine bounded into his room.

"Father, I need to speak to you."

Simon stopped and looked up at his daughter. "And I need to speak with you too." He smiled as he began to usher her out of his office. "But there are things that I need to attend to first. Why don't we dine together this evening, and we can both speak freely then?"

He saw Katherine hesitate, her impatience evident and thought for one moment that she might refuse, but then she relented and nodded. "Very well."

She seemed in good spirits, he observed.

Adam was already mounted and waiting for him in the outer bailey when Simon appeared. The yard was dusty and there was a distinct aroma of animal dung and rotting food in the air. Simon wrinkled his nose and wondered if it was ever going to rain again, or if they were to suffer the impossible heat for yet more weeks. He mounted quickly and Adam moved alongside him as they rode through the large timber gates and out of the bailey. As their horses picked their way along the crowded road that led out of the city, Simon reflected on how quickly things could change. This morning, he had been expecting to sit in his office with a day full of paperwork in preparation for the arrival of the Royal Justice next week; and now he was riding out to see Lady Maud de Mowbray, the last person to see Brother Clement alive; apart from his killer that was.

As they passed out of the city walls, Simon urged his horse into a canter and Adam did likewise. They passed a creaking, overloaded cart with a hunched carter urging his poor, struggling pony onward. The sun was just past its' zenith now, but the heat of the day was still increasing, and Simon could feel the hot sun on his back as they rode northward. For a while he was lost in his own thoughts, considering his daughter Katherine and the marriage he had arranged for her. He doubted that she would be happy with it, since he hadn't consulted her about it; and he was well aware that his daughter liked to be consulted about such matters. Even though, as her father, it was his decision as to whom she should marry, he also knew that his daughter believed she too was entitled to have a say. He blamed himself for being too lenient with her when she was younger. He had allowed her to be educated in things other than dance, needlework and the psalms, which he had been assured was inappropriate for a lady of her standing. But Katherine had shown an aptitude for learning, especially in matters of the law and he had also encouraged her to voice her opinions on matters. All of which he had been told, was quite unacceptable and unmaidenly. His pride in Katherine's intellect, sometimes made him wish that she had been born a boy. She would make an excellent lawyer, but such professions were not suitable, or allowable for a woman. His daughters' life was destined to be as the Lady of a manor, to bear her husband sons and run the household well. He sighed heavily and hoped that Katherine would understand, otherwise he would have to face the consequences for his indulgence of his beautiful, head-strong daughter.

Simon had never been to the manor at Overton before and he was pleased that Adam knew the way, or he would have had to enlist one of the guards at the castle to ride with him instead. He preferred to have Adam accompany him; the man was stoic and trustworthy and had earned his place as his trusted deputy. Simon knew Adam was a good judge of people and situations as well; such as now, when he realised that Simon needed time alone with his thoughts.

The manor at Overton came into view beyond a small cope of trees and Simon noted that it was larger than he had expected. As they neared the entrance, he could see that some of the land around was under cultivation and there was a small flock of sheep nearby, which raised their heads in curiosity as they passed. The huge wooden gates to the manor were open and as they approached a well-dressed man emerged from inside and demanded to know who they were and what business they had there.

"I am the Sheriff of this County, Simon de Hale and this is my deputy, Adam de Burgh. We request and audience with Lady Maud de Mowbray."

The man nodded and then indicated for them to enter the courtyard. Simon and Adam rode in and then dismounted before leading their horses towards the stables. A young man came out and approached them to take the reins of their mounts.

"Can you tell me where I will find Lady de Mowbray?" Simon asked the young man.

"I will take you to her." A voice came from behind them. Simon turned to see a finely dressed young man in what appeared to be the latest fashion. He wore a tunic of expensive material which was shorter than usual, and it finished at mid-thigh with exaggerated side splits. It was richly decorated with embroidery and Simon noted that it was an expensive garment to be wearing on a normal day. It was more an outfit which would be worn for special occasions and even suitable for the Kings Court. Simon considered the young man liked to think of himself as being someone of some importance; though Simon doubted he actually was.

"I am Roger de Mowbray. The only son of Lady Maud." The young man announced, offering a hand in greeting. "May I ask what you want of my mother? As you may be aware, she is not well."

Simon shook the proffered hand in greeting. "I am here on official business. I'm not sure if you have heard, but there was a murder last night."

"Goodness! You can't think that my mother had anything to do with it." The young man exclaimed, almost jokingly.

He gestured for them to follow him and led them from the courtyard towards the solar building where stout stone steps led from the courtyard up to the first-floor entrance. The door led into a great hall with a solar at one end and what looked like another door leading to what could have been a private chapel.

"My mother is still in her bedchamber." Roger said. "If you wait here, I will see if she is well enough to receive you."

"It is imperative that we speak with her. I understand that she was the last person to see the monk before he was killed." Simon wasn't sure that he entirely trusted the flamboyant young man to relay the message or stress its importance.

Roger left them for a short time in the hall. Simon looked around himself at the lavish tapestries and beautiful furniture; the room was certainly well appointed. It seemed that the de Mowbray's were quite a wealthy family and Simon wondered why he had not come across them before. Surely, they must have had reason to come to the castle at some point since he had been Sheriff.

"My mother says she will see you," Roger said on his return, though did not appear to be happy with his instructions. As he showed Simon and Adam out of the hall towards an inner chamber, he caught Simons' arm. "I would ask that you do not tire my mother with questions. You must understand that she is not at all well."

Simon looked down at Rogers' hand gripping his arm and pulled himself away. He disliked the young man even more now. Adam watched what was happening and moved a hand to his sword, but Simon signalled for him to stop.

Lady Maud de Mowbray was sitting up in her bed, propped up on a number of pillows. She was a neat, blonde-haired woman with the appearance of a fragile bird.

"Come in Sheriff." She greeted him, her voice sounding as light as a song-thrush. "My son tells me that you need to speak with me as a matter of urgency."

"Yes, Lady Maud." Simon approached the large carved wooden bed with an ornamented canopy and heavy drapes. There was a chair near the bed and Simon pulled it closer, so that he could sit next to her.

Adam remained standing and kept his eye on Roger. It seemed that he distrusted the young man just as much as Simon did and wanted to ensure that the young peacock behaved.

"I understand that you had a visitor from the Abbey last night." Simon said, looking directly at Lady Maud.

"Yes, that's right. Brother Clement came to see me." She smiled. "Dear Brother Clement, he's such a wise soul. Have you met him, Sheriff?"

Simon felt uneasy at having to impart the news to such a frail woman. "I'm very sorry to be bearer of such bad news, Lady Maud, but I have to tell you that Brother Clement is dead."

What little colour there was in Lady Mauds' face seemed to instantly disappear and she became quite agitated.

"Brother Clement? Oh no, you must be mistaken. He was here just yesterday evening. He brought me some more poppy juice to help with my pain." She looked genuinely alarmed and distressed.

"I am so very sorry." Simon waited for her to become calmer. "It seems he was attacked on his way back from visiting you."

"Really. Oh, how awful!" Lady Mauds' hand flew to her face.

Both Simon and Adam watched as the peacock quickly moved to his mother's side. "Now mother, please don't upset yourself." Roger took hold of one of her hands and made a play of trying to soothe her. "Do you really need to ask her these questions, Sheriff? Can't you see how ill she is?"

"I apologize for distressing your mother. But, as she was the last person who saw Brother Clement before he was murdered, I do need to ask her a few questions." He turned to face Lady Maud. "I hope you understand."

She nodded and seemed to regain some of her composure, but Roger did not move from her side. "Of course I do Sheriff. Please excuse my son, he does tend to get a little overprotective." Lady Maud gave a weak smile and waved a hand to dismiss her son. "Now what do you need to ask me?"

The young man stepped back from his mothers' bed but remained in the room. He took a resolute stance, his face showing annoyance and his arms firmly crossed in front of him.

"When Brother Clement was here, did he seem anxious or worried about anything?"

Lady Maud shook her head. "No, he didn't seem at all worried. We talked quite a bit about things in general, and also my legacy to the Abbey." She smiled and beckoned Simon to come closer, so that she could speak quietly with him. "Brother Clement knew that I had agreed to leave a handsome legacy to the Abbey, when I die. The land and money are mine and not part of my husbands' estate, so I am free to give them to who I want; and I want the Abbey to benefit from them." Her eyes wandered to look at her son and narrowed. "No matter what anyone else wants." Her voice was barely above a whisper, but Simon heard her clearly. Then she leant back against the pillows and continued in a normal voice. "After we spoke, Brother Clement heard my confession and administered the communion. He left me another bottle of poppy juice to help with the pain and promised he would come back and see me in a few days' time." She paused. "I don't suppose he will now."

"I am very sorry."

"He was a very kind man, Brother Clement." Lady Maud reflected. "I know monks are generally thought of as being good men of God, but Brother Clement had a real kindness of soul. I'm very sorry that he was killed." She laid a frail hand on Simons' arm and looked at him intently. "Please find out who did this to him. He did not deserve to be killed."

"I promise I will." He smiled at her, trying to reassure her and hoping that this was a promise he could keep.

"Is that all?" Roger interjected. "Can't you see she's exhausted by all this?

"Just one more thing." Simon promised, then asked her softly. "Was it late when Brother Clement left?"

"It was evening when he left." She recalled. "I believe he stayed longer than he intended as I remember him saying that he was going to miss vespers and that he would need to seek forgiveness from the Abbot."

"Thank you, Lady Maud. I will let you rest now." He smiled softly at her, and she returned the smile. Then, getting up from the chair, he made his way out of the bedchamber, followed closely by Adam. In the great hall, Roger de Mowbray joined them, still strutting around like a slightly annoyed peacock.

"You shouldn't take much notice of what my mother says. All that poppy juice has addled her brain; I don't believe she knows quite what she's saying."

Simon looked surprised. "She seemed perfectly rational to me. But if you think there is something else that she hasn't told me?" He eyed the young man suspiciously, who immediately appeared to become flustered.

"No, no, of course not. I just mean that she gets confused at times. But today, as you say, she seems quite well." Roger backtracked. "I expect you will want to be on your way now?"

"Yes, we do need to get back to the castle." He gave the young man a hard stare. "But I may want to visit Lady Maud again. I take it that will be acceptable?" It was more of a statement than a question and didn't leave Roger de Mowbray much option.

He nodded uncomfortably. "Of course. Yes, that would be fine." He stumbled over the words.

"I will also inform Abbot Robert that your mother requires regular benediction. It seems she was quite fond of Brother Clement, and I wouldn't want his death to deprive her of a confidant." Simon held Rogers' gaze as he spoke, trying to make his point.

He couldn't get over the feeling of dislike he had for the young man and once they were back outside in the courtyard, he allowed himself a heavy sigh. He had his worries for the continued health of Lady Maud and wondered if he should pay a visit to the Abbot on his way back to the castle.

Neither Simon or Adam spoke until they were well outside the walls of the manor and on the road leading back to the city.

"What do you think?" Adam asked him.

"Of what Lady Maud told me, or of Roger de Mowbray?" Simon asked as they rode steadily down the road.

Adam huffed ironically, "I think I already know what you thought about Roger de Mowbray."

"Was it that obvious?" Simon almost smiled.

"I'd say he's a devious character that one, mark my words. I wouldn't trust anything he says or does." Adam added, giving his own opinion.

"I agree. And I wouldn't put anything past him." Simon paused thoughtfully. "Lady Maud did tell me that she is planning to leave a substantial legacy to the Abbey when she dies. I can see that being a motive for murder."

"Do you think the Abbot knows what she is planning to do?" Adam asked.

"I'm not sure. Perhaps, Lady Maud was sending a message back to the Abbot with Brother Clement last night. That could be a good reason for him being killed."

"I agree, it would stop the Abbot receiving the message." Adam nodded his head. "And I would say that Roger de Mowbray wouldn't blink an eye at the thought of killing a monk."

"Yes. Also, a man like him would certainly own a dagger as grand as the one we found the jewelled pommel for."

Simon thought about the matter for a little while. He had no doubt that Roger de Mowbray was a devious character and one with a love of money to furnish his fine lifestyle. The possible loss of such a legacy from the family in favour of the Abbey would certainly infuriate him.

"Do you want me to send a couple of men to check the stables for a grey horse with a cut on its' side?"

Simon shook his head. "No, I think our friend, Roger,

will have already hidden that particular mount. And, if he hasn't done so yet, then I think our visit just now will have scared him into doing so. By the time the men got there the horse would be well hidden." He paused before adding. "But I would like you to arrange for a couple of men to watch Roger de Mowbray; to see where he goes and what he does. If he still has the dagger, then he might try to get rid of it; and I want to know if, and when, he does."

"I'll make arrangements as soon as we get back."

"I was thinking that on our way back, we could call in to see the Abbot to let him know about our meeting with Lady Maud." Simon allowed himself a small smile. "That way there can be no denial of her wishes."

Abbot Robert was back in his room after None service when Brother Michael announced the arrival of Simon. Abbot Robert got up from his chair and went to meet him as he entered the room.

"Greetings Simon, peace be upon you. I didn't expect to see you again so soon." He gestured for Simon to sit down, before returning to his own chair. "Have you found out who might have done this heinous act?"

Simon shook his head. "Not yet I'm afraid." He didn't want to say any more at the moment. Any gossip was bound to run through the Abbey just as quickly as it would do in the city, and it wouldn't take too long before the news got back to Roger de Mowbray. Simon could envisage the man quickly disappearing abroad beyond his reach before he could do anything about it. "I did want to ask you something though."

The Abbot nodded. "Please proceed."

"I have just returned from a visit to see Lady Maud de Mowbray. As I believe she was the last person to see Brother Clement before he was killed."

"Ah yes, Lady Maud. Brother Clement had been tending to her over the last few weeks. She is a noble, devout woman and one of our most prodigious benefactors. She has seen it as her duty to endow certain bequests to the Abbey in the past and she will be greatly missed when she passes."

"And I understand that she is planning to leave a substantial bequest to the Abbey when that day finally arrives." Simon studied the Abbot. "Were you aware of that?"

Abbot Robert looked thoughtful and shook his head. "I did suspect that she might do. But I hadn't heard anything officially. Why?"

"Lady Maud told me in confidence that she intended to settle on the Abbey the land and money that she owns in her own right. But I have my doubts that her son Roger de Mowbray is happy about the bequest."

The Abbots face remained passive, but the tone of his voice told Simon all he needed to know.

"You do not surprise me. Her son, Roger, has been quite vocal in objecting to her previous bequests."

"I thought you should be aware that she freely told me her intentions, in case she passes before the bequest is made official. My deputy, Adam, was also there and will be witness to what she said."

"Thank you, Simon. I appreciate your concern." He paused. "Was there anything else?"

"I do need to speak with you about Brother Clement at some point. I need to find out more about him and who he was before he took up Holy Orders." Simon observed just how tired the Abbot was looking. It must have been an incredibly difficult day for him. "But I suspect you have had quite enough for today and it can wait until tomorrow."

"Yes, it has been a most distressing day for everyone here. You can imagine how it has troubled and saddened all the monks." He glanced upwards as if seeking reassurance from a higher power. "They are wondering if they are safe; and who might be next. There is a lot of speculation and gossip going around; and I need to put a stop to it, before it gets out of hand."

Simon nodded. "I understand. It must be very difficult for you. I just thought you should be aware of what Lady de Mowbray has said." Simon got to his feet and gave a small bow of respect to the Abbot. "I will take my leave of you now and visit you again in the morning, if I may? I have more questions for you, but they can wait until tomorrow."

Abbot Robert nodded in agreement. "Tomorrow morning would be a good time for me. I shall see you then."

Adam was waiting for him outside in the courtyard, holding the reins of both of their horses. He handed one pair of reins to Simon and both men mounted.

"Well," Adam inquired, "did the Abbot know?"

Simon shook his head. "No, not officially." He urged his horse forward out of the gates of the Abbey with Adam at his side.

"So, that could be a motive for Brother Clements' murder?"

Simon nodded. "If Brother Clement had been entrusted with a document detailing the bequest to the Abbey. He could have been killed to stop that document reaching the Abbot."

CHAPTER 4

When Katherine had finally managed to see her father, it had been early afternoon, and he was just on his way out of the castle. He appeared distracted and she surmised that it must be the events of that morning that were preying on his mind. His quick dismissal of her had been such a disappointment and then when he'd delayed seeing her until the evening, she'd felt even more upset. She had been on the point of insisting that she needed to speak with him straight away but then realised that she was being unreasonable and that a murder took precedent over her needs; especially when it was a monk who had been killed.

For the rest of the afternoon Katherine found that she could not settle to anything. She even tried to distract herself with some needlework which she hated, but found that her mind refused to focus, and she ended up throwing it across the room when she made yet another mistake. In the end she took to pacing up and down her chamber as she tried to work out what she was going to say to her father. Katherine knew that her father was anxious to see her married and, given her status, the fact that she was not even betrothed at her age was virtually unheard of. She knew that if she could plead her case for a betrothal to Alexander, then it would give both of them what they wanted. It was the perfect match and the perfect solution to her fathers' dilemma. He could then concentrate on the impending assize court and finding the murderer of the monk; and she would be happily distracted in planning her wedding to Alexander.

Smiling, she went to sit in the window embrasure and finally relaxed as she day-dreamed about her future with Alexander. A future where he would be the perfect man, a brave soldier and an attentive husband. Whilst she would be a beautiful wife, who would bear him the sons he wanted. She hugged her knees to her as she pictured Alexander standing next to her on their wedding day and thought about just how much she loved him. It was all so very perfect. He made her feel so loved and wanted. Katherine imagined that what she felt was the same thing her mother must have felt for her father. Although her parents' marriage was arranged by their families to the mutual benefit of both sides, she was well aware of the deep love that had grown between her mother and father. They may not have been in love at the start when they first married, but they very quickly fell in love. And now she felt the same way about Alexander. Katherine knew she needed to make her father see that her love for Alexander was the same as he had felt for her mother, and there was no reason to oppose the marriage. He could not object to Alexander by reason of his family not being good enough. It was true that he might not be the eldest son, but he was still a knight, and his father was the Baron of Helmsley Castle. Katherine was also sure that Alexanders' father would grant them a small manor to live in once they were married; either that or they would have apartments in the castle at Helmsley with his family.

The rest of the afternoon felt intolerably long to Katherine, and she wondered why time seemed to drag when she was waiting for something to happen, whereas the time spent with Alexander seemed to go past in the blink of an eye. No matter what else she tried to think of to distract herself, her mind kept going back to Alexander. She wondered what her wedding would be like, would it be at the castle chapel, or perhaps the minster, she wondered? She imagined that her father would want it to be in the private chapel in the grounds of the castle, as he wasn't one for grand gestures. But given his standing in the Shire there would be a lot of people wanting to attend, so perhaps a larger venue would be more appropriate.

Simon had arranged for Katherine to join him for dinner

in his chamber. Normally he would have taken his meal in the hall with his deputy, Adam, and the rest of his men. But the hall was far too open a setting for the conversation he needed to have with his daughter and there were too many people around who, he was aware, would listen into what was being said. He wanted this to be a private discussion between his beloved daughter and himself, before he made the official announcement of her betrothal.

He'd arranged for the servants to bring the food and wine to his chamber, and they were just leaving as Katherine entered the room.

"Katherine." Her father greeted her, taking her in his arms and holding her close.

He might be a stern soldier as Sheriff of the County and there were many that feared him, but when it came to his daughter, he was a different man and would let his guard down and his true self show through. He relaxed with Katherine, the same way he had done with his darling wife Ellen, and every time he saw her, it reminded him of just how much he missed his wife. Ellen would always know just what to say or do to take his worries away. He might have had a stressful day at Court, dealing with the vagaries of the King's demands, but as soon as he was in their apartments, Ellen would know just how to calm him and stop him brooding over things. Katherine had the same way with her and after today's terrible events, holding his daughter in his arms for just that brief moment reminded him that he had a life outside of his work. He also felt pleased that, after such a difficult day he had some good news to discuss with her.

"Come, let's sit," he said, letting go of her and indicating a chair.

"I heard the news about the monk this morning." She said, taking her seat and helping herself to some food. "They said that he had his throat sliced open. It seems such a wicked and evil thing to do to anyone, let alone a holy brother."

"I wasn't sure if you had heard." He noted, trying not

to sound surprised.

"Jennet told me early this morning that a monk had been killed." She relaxed in her chair. "And you know what it's like, father; the servants like nothing more than having something juicy to talk about. And a murdered monk is quite exceptional."

There was silence between them and Katherine studied her father's face, wanting to know if she should ask more.

"Do you have any idea who would do such a thing?" She asked at length.

He shook his head. "Not yet. I have a suspect, but nothing to actually link him to the crime. I have no doubt that the truth will come to light sooner or later."

"And have you found any evidence?"

"There were a couple of items found where Brother Clement was killed, which might prove insightful." Simon relaxed in his chair. If he was to share the details of what had happened with anyone it would be his daughter; she was the only person whose discretion he trusted without doubt; and, in the past, he had found that just talking through the facts with her, sometimes helped him to get a clearer perspective on the matter, he was dealing with.

"I know I can trust you to keep what I'm going to tell you to yourself." He watched her closely and thought that she looked even more beautiful today and wondered if she had also heard gossip from the servants regarding his visit from Lord Fitzwarren earlier. As Katherine nodded her agreement, he continued. "You were right when you said that Brother Clement had his throat cut, I suppose that detail was bound to get out from the carter who found him. The rest of this, only the Abbot and I are fully aware of."

As they continued to eat together, Simon told Katherine more details of what he had found at the site of Brother Clements death. Afterwards he told her about returning to the Abbey and seeing the body of Brother Clement and what he had noted when he had examined him.

"So, you believe there was more than one person

present when the monk was killed?"

Simon nodded. "Without a doubt. The bruises on his upper arms show that he was held by at least one other person. There may have been a third person there to hold his head back whilst his throat was cut, but I can't be sure of that. What I know for certain is that he was definitely restrained whilst another person cut his throat."

"And whoever did this you don't think is a serf or villein?"

Simon got up from his chair and went across to the chest to retrieve the two items he had found that morning. He had wrapped them in cloth to keep them safe and together.

"I doubt even a journeyman or squire would have the means to purchase a dagger of such extravagance as this came from." He unwrapped the items and passed the red jewel in its' mount across to his daughter. "I believe it's part of the hilt of a dagger, and a very valuable dagger at that."

Katherine took the item from her father and looked at it closely.

"I see what you mean; it really is quite exquisite and not from any ordinary weapon. It's more like something from a dagger or sword that one of the Barons or Earls would have. Or even you, father!" She teased him, a smile brightening her face even more.

He smiled. "Even my dagger isn't that impressive." He took his own dagger from its scabbard where it was attached to his belt and laid it on the table. By comparison his own weapon was quite modest with a circular metal pommel fixed onto the hilt of the weapon.

"But why would someone of such standing want to kill a monk?" Katherine asked perplexed.

"That's what I was asking myself too." He sighed as he sat down again. "Until earlier this afternoon, when I happened to pay a visit to Lady Maud de Mowbray."

"You can't think that Lady de Mowbray had anything to do with this." Katherine exclaimed teasing her father.

"She's not been well for some months now and I hear that she's not long for this world."

Simon smiled at his daughters' words. "No, not Lady Maud; but her son Roger."

"Roger?" She frowned as she tried to picture him, then added. "I know who you mean now. He's very full of himself, always boasting about something he's done. I can't say that I like him much, but I wouldn't have thought of him as a murderer."

"You would be surprised what the thought of losing part of your inheritance to the Abbey could make you do. It seems Lady Maud was going to give a large bequest to the Abbey on her death."

"Maybe, but even so," Katherine countered. "For all his bluster, he's a weak man; a coward really. I doubt he would have the stomach to cut the throat of a monk."

Simon considered his daughters observation and acknowledged that she had a point regarding Roger de Mowbray. The man was a strutting peacock, but when Simon had challenged him, he had conceded instantly.

"You might be right, but then perhaps he was the one who held the monk, whilst his accomplice slit his throat?"

"Maybe, but I've seen Roger turn green over the sight of offal being thrown out from the kitchens. I'm really not sure he'd have the stomach for watching a man's throat being cut." Katherine paused and looked at her father. "He really is just all show, you know. There's no substance and, absolutely no back-bone in the man."

"And all this you've gathered from seeing him at dinners and events?"

Katherine laughed. "I have eyes father; I've seen how he is. All the tall tales he tells and how he tries to impress the eligible ladies. Then afterwards, I've seen how he reacts when they rebuff him."

"I hope he hasn't tried to pursue you?" Suddenly he was a protective father again and not a Sheriff.

"He tried." She stressed the words and then laughed again. "But he failed to get anywhere. I saw through him straight away and gave him short shrift."

Simon smiled at the thought. He could just imagine his daughter coldly dealing with Roger de Mowbray.

"Apart from the fact that Roger might lose some of his inheritance to the Abbey, is there anything else to connect him to the murder of the monk?"

Simon took another sip of his wine and shook his head. "No, nothing yet. At the moment, all I have is this," he said holding up the jewelled pommel, "and a piece of hair from a grey horse. That is all that I have to go on." He turned the jewelled pommel around in his hand. "I've sent Adam out with his men to try and see if they can spot a grey horse with a bloodied scar on its neck and I told him to pay particular attention to the horses at the De Mowbray manor."

"Do you think whoever owns the dagger to which the jewel belongs will still have it?" Katherine asked. "If he knows it's damaged, wouldn't he get rid of it?"

"No, I doubt it. Whoever the owner is, whether it's Roger de Mowbray or not, I don't think that they would discard such a valuable item just because the pommel had come off. I believe that they will keep it safe until all the uproar has died down. Then perhaps they will get it repaired." He looked at the beautiful jewel thoughtfully. "They may not even have realised that it is damaged. Or that it happened when the monk was murdered." He looked across at Katherine. "At the moment only the Abbot, Adam, myself and now you, know that I've got this. I don't want anyone else to know, because whoever owns the dagger might still have it in their belt and be unaware that it's been damaged."

"But it's hard to imagine that the owner of the dagger wouldn't have noticed it was damaged; I mean you would only need to draw it from the scabbard to notice something was wrong. It wouldn't feel right."

"Very true. You would notice it was missing as soon as you took hold of the hilt; and then drawing it the dagger would feel unbalanced. But you never know, he may still have it on him and for the time being I want to keep this to myself."

"Find the dagger; find the murderer" Katherine mused thoughtfully.

"Precisely."

"I hope you find something," Katherine added. "Because, if you are going to accuse someone like Roger de Mowbray then you will need to be certain of your facts. He is not a man to take such a thing without question."

"I know; and all I have is a motive, but no evidence. What I need is something to link these two items to the perpetrator."

"And what if it isn't Roger de Mowbray?" Katherine asked him. "Do you have any other ideas as to why the monk might have been killed?"

Simon shook his head. "Not as yet. I plan to speak with the Abbot in the morning and find out more about Brother Clement and how he came to the order. I wondered if there might be something in his past that I'm not yet aware of."

"You mean it might be a personal grudge against the man himself and not a grievance against the Abbot or the Abbey." Katherine added thoughtfully. "But then, there are a lot of people who aren't happy with the Abbey and the Abbot. Don't you remember how it was last winter when the crops failed after the hot summer? There was a lot of resentment against the Abbey and the monks being well fed, whilst ordinary people were starving. I fear it will be the same again this year if this hot weather continues."

"You could be right. But then this," he held up the jewel, "belongs to a nobleman and not a peasant. Why would a nobleman have a grudge against the abbey? It's not as if they would be left starving?"

"No, I agree." She sighed and they were both silent for a moment before Katherine added. "Perhaps there is something that we are missing here. Maybe there will be something that the Abbot can tell you that will help."

"Maybe." He admitted as he poured himself some more

wine and offered the jug to his daughter. Katherine took it and filled her goblet too.

"I know you wanted to see me earlier. I take it that was on a totally different matter to the murder?" Simon said.

Katherine nodded and suddenly felt very nervous about what she had to tell him.

"Yes, there is something important that I wanted to speak to you about." She took a deep breath and tried to calm herself, though she could feel her heart beating incredibly quickly, making her feel even more nervous. "You know Baron de Ros of Helmsley?" She started slowly.

"Yes, I know him, we've met several times." He looked across at Katherine and saw just how anxious she was. "Why, does this have something to do with him?"

"No, not exactly." She paused gathering her thoughts. "As you may know he has three sons and I have been seeing the youngest of his sons, Alexander. We've been seeing each other for a few months now and yesterday he asked for my hand in marriage. He will be coming to see you, probably tomorrow, to request your permission."

There she had said it.

Her father was unusually quiet, and Katherine instantly started to worry. Every moment that past between them felt like an eternity, until eventually he placed his goblet down on the table. Simon felt as though he had been punched. He had been hoping the reason that Katherine was elated was because she had heard whispers of his plans for her betrothal to Lord Fitzwarren. He had not been expecting her to say that she was in love with another man.

"I'm so sorry my darling girl, but I'm afraid that just won't be possible."

Katherine tried to remain calm, but her heart was pounding as her brain tried to look for possible reasons why her father could object to Alexander.

"Why?" She asked eventually, her voice barely a whisper.

Simon looked at her and saw the distress etched on her

face. He felt as though the closeness they had been sharing barely a few minutes ago, had just been shattered. He'd had no idea that she was in love with someone; why on earth hadn't she told him? He would have understood; or at least tried to. It wasn't as if she had run off with the farrier or butcher, she'd fallen in love with a knight; the son of a Baron; and now Simon was about to break her heart by refusing her and telling her that she was going to marry someone else.

"Because I've already agreed a match for you. In fact, I met with him this afternoon to settle all the details."

Katherine suddenly felt her world starting to disintegrate.

"What...who?" She stammered, feeling the room starting to spin around her.

"Lord William Fitzwarren. I think you met him when all the Barons attended the assize court here at Easter."

Katherine opened her mouth to speak, but nothing came out, as her brain tried to process what her father had just told her. She desperately tried to recall who William Fitzwarren was, but for a little while, she couldn't picture him.

"He asked me a couple of weeks ago," her father continued, "and, after giving it due consideration, I thought it would be a good match for you. I realise that he is slightly older than you; and that he has been married before, but he is still relatively young and a good soldier."

Katherine suddenly realised the man to whom her father was referring. She remembered speaking to him after the dinner following the court sitting. He was tall, dark haired and not entirely unattractive; but as for his age.... slightly older than her, her father had said, well, that was an exaggeration. He had looked to be more of her fathers' age, than her own. She started to shake her head.

"No, this can't be true. Why didn't you tell me before, when he asked you? I would have told you then that I couldn't marry him; that I was in love with someone else."

"I'm sorry. With hindsight I should have; and I did

intend to, but then I got distracted by other things, and it didn't seem to matter. I am your father, after all."

"But you have to tell Lord Fitzwarren that I can't marry him." She pleaded. "You must tell him father!"

"I am so sorry Katherine, but I'm afraid it has all been agreed. I've written to the King to inform him of the match and ask for his approval. I am unable to go back on the agreement now."

Katherine couldn't believe what she was hearing. "No, no you must! I love Alexander and he loves me. He wants to marry me. Whatever you have arranged has to be unarranged!" She was angry and blindsided by what her father had just told her.

Simon hated seeing his daughter so distressed, but she had to understand that the betrothal was settled now.

"I'm sorry Katherine, truly I am." He added. "But you know how it is. Families like ours have to make good marriages. I have given my word to Lord Fitzwarren, and I have informed the King as well; this can't be undone." He paused, struggling to see his beloved daughter so unhappy. "William Fitzwarren is a good man, Katherine. I know he isn't your choice, but he will be a good husband to you; and he will be away quite a lot of the time in service to the King, so you will be in charge of the household and the estate. It will be a good life for you."

Katherine shook her head; this was not how she imagined it would be. "He might be a respectable man, father; but he isn't the man that I love. Surely, you can understand that?" Tears had started to well up in her eyes at the thought of her future happiness suddenly disappearing in front of her. "I know how much you loved mother; don't I deserve to know that same love that you both shared?"

She knew how to inflict pain and Simon felt her words cut deeply into his soul. He had loved Ellen so very much; perhaps not when they had first married, but he had very quickly fallen in love with her and still felt the pain of her death, even though it was many years ago. He had to admit that he wanted Katherine to know the same love he'd felt.

"I know and I can see that." Suddenly he felt overwhelmed by anguish for his daughter and his own memories of his darling Ellen. "But you know, my marriage to your mother was an arranged one too; neither of us had any say in it. We were lucky, we fell in love very quickly after we married; I'm sure that the same will happen for you too."

Simon looked at his daughter and the shock and distress on her face was evident. He hated to see her so unhappy. He thought back over the last few months and suddenly realised what had been happening.

"Do I take it, that all the times you have been sneaking out of the house in an afternoon with Jennet has been to meet with Alexander?" He asked, now putting two and two together.

Katherine nodded her head as tears streamed down her face. She had never believed that her whole life could change quite so quickly. This afternoon her world had been perfect and now everything was in tatters. She leant back in her chair and tried to blink away the tears as she struggled to take everything in. She supposed that there was no point in holding back anything from her father now. If he knew the whole truth about how she had fallen in love with Alexander, he might start to understand how much he meant to her. She hoped the facts might make her father relent.

"I first met Alexander when he came here with his father back in May. His father was in a meeting with you, and I ran into Alexander outside the stables." She tried to keep her voice level. "He was tending to the horse of his father, and I was planning to ride out with Jennet. We talked for a while, and then he asked if he could join me on the ride. I liked him straight away and I believe he felt the same. We used to meet up along the riverbank outside the city walls. We would sit and talk for hours; about our lives and what we enjoyed. But it was always very proper,

Jennet was with me; well at least to start with." She could see the look of concern run across her fathers' face. "Don't worry, nothing improper happened." She reassured him. "We would just sit and talk and laugh. Sometimes Jennet came and she would bring something to eat. We just enjoyed being together. Then, when we met yesterday, he told me that he wanted to marry me and said that he would come to see you to ask your permission."

Simon closed his eyes. It was a terrible situation, and he felt awful at making his daughter so unhappy.

"My darling child, I wish it could be different, but it can't." He tried to plead with her. "It's all been arranged now; it's too late to change it." He watched her as she cried, and he felt wretched at being the cause of her distress. "I understand it's hard but believe me you will get over him. I'm sorry it has to be this way; really, I am." He didn't know what else to say. "In a couple of days, I will arrange for Lord Fitzwarren to dine with us." He paused. "He is a good man, Katherine. I'm sure that, given time, you will learn to love him just as much as you believe you love Alexander now."

Katherine seized upon what her father had just said. "Believe I love him?" She shouted back angrily. "I don't just believe it; I know it!" The tears were streaming down her face, and the emotions were getting the better of her. "Father, it doesn't matter what you say, I will always love Alexander; nothing that you can ever say or do will ever change that." She sobbed loudly and shook her head. "I just don't understand. Why would it be so wrong for me to marry Alexander, especially as we're both in love?"

"I'm sorry Katherine. You should have told me earlier that you were courting him; then perhaps all this could have been prevented."

Katherine shook her head. "Don't try and put the blame on me. That's not fair and you know it!" Katherine stood up from the chair and looked defiantly at her father. "I don't care that you've told Lord Fitzwarren he can marry me; you can un-tell him. I want to marry Alexander and

I'm going to. I don't think that the King will care one little bit about who I marry. It's not as if I've been a regular at court – the last time I was there he didn't even know who I was."

He had to admit that she did have a point. Despite the King knowing him very well, he'd paid little attention to his daughter.

"Katherine, please; you have to understand that this is how it is; I am appointed by the King; I serve him, and I don't want anything to change his high regard for me." He paused. "It might not be entirely necessary to have the Kings approval for your betrothal, but it is done now. I'm sorry, but you will marry Lord Fitzwarren, I have given my word, and I see no reason to change that."

Katherine felt herself growing even angrier at him.

"And what if I refuse to marry him?"

"Katherine, please don't. You know that as your father I have the final say in this. If you refuse Lord Fitzwarren then your alternative will be to take the veil; you know that as well as I do." Simon was starting to feel very uneasy about the whole situation. He had never once considered that his daughter might end up in a convent rather than marry the man he wanted her to. "There is nothing else I can do. And, as your father, I should also reprimand you for meeting Alexander in secret and without my permission. I had no knowledge of how you felt about him. I'm sorry, but it's too late now to stop your betrothal to Lord Fitzwarren."

"Then you give me no option, I will leave!" She said defiantly, setting her gaze firmly on her father. "I will run away. I will marry Alexander, and we will make our own lives away from here."

Simon felt equally horrified at the thought of his daughter running away. A nunnery was bad enough to contemplate but losing her permanently was even worse.

"Don't be silly Katherine." He implored her. "You know you can't do that; you have nowhere to go." He tried to think of something more direct to say. "Besides, I know that Alexander's father will not let him marry you, once he knows that you are betrothed to Lord Fitzwarren."

"You wouldn't do that to me!"

"Katherine, you're not leaving me any choice." He shouted and then drew breath to calm himself. "You're not being reasonable. You can't run away; you know that I would send Adam and the guards after you to bring you back. And you can't marry Alexander, I'm sorry, but that's just how it is. You will marry Lord Fitzwarren. I know it's hard for you to accept, but I'm your father and I have the final word on this."

Katherine clenched her fists as she struggled to contain her anger and pain. She knew if she stayed any longer that they would both end up saying things that they would regret. Getting up from her chair, she turned quickly and walked towards the door without stopping. She knew that shouting at her father wouldn't solve anything. He wasn't the sort of man to respond to raised voices; he preferred reasonable debate instead and that was something she couldn't do right now. Leaving the room, she ran down the corridor towards her bed chamber and slammed the door behind her. She leant against it, breathing deeply as the tears fell down her face.

Jennet was sitting by the window sewing the hem on one of Katherine's dresses when she came into the room.

"My lady, what on earth has happened?" She put her sewing down as soon as she saw Katherine and got up from her seat.

Katherine shook her head, not trusting her voice as the tears streamed down her face.

"Oh, my lady! Come here." Jennet walked over to her and wrapped her arms around Katherine. "Now come and sit down with me; and you can tell me what has happened. There is no rush, whenever you're ready to talk, I will be here."

Katherine allowed herself to be comforted by Jennet as the tears continued to flow down her face; she cried silently at first and then uncontrollable sobs started to escape. Jennet sat next to her holding Katherine as she cried. She had never seen the girl quite so distraught before, but she could guess at the cause of it.

"So, he's told you then?" She said softly as Katherine's tears finally started to cease.

Katherine sat bolt upright in shock and wiped her eyes with the sleeve of her dress.

"You knew?" She looked directly at Jennet as a feeling of betrayal filled her.

"Your father did mention it a couple of days ago, that he was making arrangements for you to be betrothed."

Katherine couldn't believe what she was hearing.

"Did he tell you who it was?" She demanded, pushing Jennet away.

Jennet swallowed and felt uncomfortable at admitting what she had known. "He did mention Lord Fitzwarren's name. But he asked me not to say anything. He wanted to tell you himself." She knew her words had damned her in the eyes of Katherine, and she wished the master hadn't put her in such an impossible position.

Katherine had never felt quite so let down. The one woman she trusted and whom she thought of like a mother, had deigned to keep something as important as this from her.

"Jennet, how could you?" She implored, the feelings of betrayal and isolation welling up inside her. It seemed two of the people that she loved most in this world had conspired against her. "You of all people; you've been like a mother to me; and to deceive me so completely; how can you think that I will ever trust you again?"

"Oh Katherine, I am so sorry. I knew you would be angry; but your father forbade me from telling you and, after everything, I am still just a servant here and he is my master. I had no choice but to do as he'd asked."

"And what I want, means nothing to you?" She was shouting now, as the tears ran down her face again. "If I'd known what he was planning, then I could have spoken with him earlier and told him about Alexander. But now it's too late. Don't you see what you've done? You've sentenced me to a life with a man that I don't love and can never love; not so long as Alexander is alive."

"I wish I could undo what has been done." Jennet pleaded. "But your father is a good man, Katherine; he will understand if you try to explain it to him.

Katherine shook her head wildly. "No; no, he won't. He says it's too late now and that he's given his word and written to the King. I tried to persuade him; tried to reason with him, but he just didn't want to know." She turned away from Jennet as the pain of remembering what her father had said welled up. "I always thought that he would listen to me." She said, more calmly now. "That he would never force me into a marriage that I didn't want. I thought that he wanted me to have the same kind of happiness that he shared with my mother. But no, he's just gone ahead and arranged everything without even a word to me." She started to cry again. "Then, when I told him about Alexander and just how much we loved each other, he was unmoved. I pleaded with him to change his mind and allow me to marry the man I love; but he refused." She started sobbing again and Jennet came towards her and took Katherine into her arms. "I tried to talk to him, to make him understand;" Katherine gulped between the sobs. "I tried to reason with him; but he said it was too late and that he has already written to the King for his approval of the marriage and given Lord Fitzwarren his word. He said that there was nothing to be done; that it was all arranged now. Oh Jennet, what am I going to do? I can't marry Lord Fitzwarren; I love Alexander, and I want to marry him."

"Hush now child." Jennet soothed, gently stroking Katherine's hair, and grateful that their brief quarrel was over. "Cry all you want; I'm not going anywhere."

Katherine let herself be comforted by the security of Jennets arms and it was a while before she finally stopped crying and managed to regain some of her composure. Sitting down together by the window, she stared blankly out into the night. The sun had set a little while ago, but the sky was not yet totally dark, and ribbons of deep orange still streaked the sky in the west.

"What am I to do?" She asked softly. "Tell me Jennet, what am I to do?"

Jennet sat next to her and held Katherines' hands in her own.

"Oh, my love. I wish I knew. If I could talk to your father I would do; but he won't listen to me. I am just a servant after all."

"Even though you've been like a mother to me?" Katherine asked, but Jennet shook her head.

"I'm still just a servant."

"I understand." Katherine sighed. "And besides, I don't think father would listen to anyone right now. My marriage has been agreed with the King, and it seems nothing can be done to change it."

"I think if your father could stop the marriage, he would do. But you must see that he can't go back on it now without losing face."

Katherine supposed Jennet was right.

"Have you met Lord Fitzwarren?" Jennet asked. "You never know, you might like him. It might not be as bad as you think it is."

Katherine pulled a face. "I met him briefly once a few months ago, but I can't say that he left much of an impression. He was courteous and chivalrous and just what you would expect of someone of his standing; but nothing more." She shrugged. "And anyway, how can I ever like him when I'm already in love with Alexander?"

Jennet put a soothing hand on Katherines' arm. "I'm sure there will be some way of getting through this. But there is nothing more to be done about it tonight." She stood up and helped Katherine to her feet. "So, why don't you try and get some sleep now and we will talk about it some more tomorrow. You never know, with a good night's sleep, you might feel differently in the morning."

Katherine shook her head. "I don't think that I will ever

feel differently about it, Jennet. In the morning, I will still be betrothed to Lord Fitzwarren; and I will always be in love with Alexander."

Simon leant back in his chair and poured himself another goblet of wine. It had been one of the most stressful days he could recall. First a murder, then meeting Lord Fitzwarren to finalise the betrothal; and, to finish it all, an argument with his daughter, whom it appeared was in love with someone else. He drank the wine more quickly than he intended, hoping that it would at least relieve the headache that was starting to pound in his forehead.

Getting up from his chair he walked across to the narrow window hoping that the fresh air would help. It was late and the sun had disappeared beyond the walls of the castle as the darkness of night started to envelope the city. The breeze that came in through the opening was still warm. It had been another hot day, just like it had been for the last few weeks and there was no sign of the weather turning cooler at all. If there wasn't any rain soon then the crops would be no more than dust in the fields, and it would lead to another starved winter for everyone. There was so much for him to do at the moment and at the end of the week the Royal Justice would be coming to the city to hold the quarterly assize court. He needed to ensure that everything was ready for Sir Robert de Lexington when he arrived and, the last thing he wanted was a fight with Katherine on top of everything. If only she could see that Lord Fitzwarren was a good match for her. He wished that for once she would just do what he asked of her, instead of challenging him. He smiled to himself, realising that if Katherine didn't challenge him then she wouldn't be the daughter he loved so much, or remind him of his beloved late wife, Ellen.

At his manor house outside the city, Lord William Fitzwarren was dining in the main hall with a collection of his friends. He was in good spirits and wanted to celebrate his news with everyone. An impromptu dinner always went well with his close friends. He'd sent messages out this morning anticipating that his meeting with Simon would go satisfactorily and the response had been reassuring.

He felt so pleased that his marriage to Katherine was going ahead. He had been smitten with the girl from the first time he had seen her in the great hall at the castle. She was beautiful, with her wild red hair and her head held high. There was a spirit about her that had beguiled him, and he was totally entranced. He knew from that very first day, that he had to have her as his wife. Sitting at the top table in his large carved chair, he looked around at the gathering. It had been a good day, he considered.

William was in his late thirties, a tall man with blond hair and grey eyes. His first wife had died following a tragic accident when her carriage had overturned. He had thrown himself into knightly service to the King for a while, to help lessen the pain. But now he was to be married again; to have another chance at being a husband and a father. Although he could never deny that his first love was being a soldier, he also knew that he needed a son and heir to succeed him and inherit his title and lands. William considered himself a good swordsman and prided himself on training regularly, keeping himself sharp and fit; unlike, he considered, some of his guests whose expanding waistlines showed that they had different priorities. He would endeavour to be a good husband to Katherine and do everything he could to make her happy. He planned to have sons with her, and he would lavish her with gifts to show how proud he was of her. However, he knew his life as a knight in service to the King was not yet over and he would have to leave her at times and trust her to manage his estates and care for his children. Her father had said that Katherine was intelligent and had been taught to read, write and handle household accounts. He could see his dream of a good future coming to fruition and he was well pleased with how it looked. It made him happy to feel that his life was finally looking good again.

"Friends!" He called out, banging his empty pewter goblet on the table to get their attention. There had already been a substantial amount of wine drunk, and the gathering was quite loud with laughter and chatter.

"Friends!" He called out again, as the noise began to subside. "I have asked you here for a reason. And that reason is, that I am to marry again." A great cheer went up amongst the assembled guests and some comments were passed about it being 'about time'. He waited for them to quieten again, before he added. "Today I met with our Sheriff Simon de Hale, and he agreed with my request to marry his youngest daughter, Katherine. I will expect all of you, as my friends, to attend this happy event."

With this, another cheer went up, and goblets were raised in toast to him. William signalled to one of the servants to bring more wine and fill up his goblet. He intended to enjoy the celebration. It had been a really good day today, he considered.

CHAPTER 5

Simon was tired. He hadn't been able to sleep much, as his mind had been in turmoil for most of the night, going over the events of the previous day. As if he didn't have enough to deal with, with the murdered monk and the forthcoming assize court, now he had a rebellious daughter who was refusing to marry the man he had promised her to. He sunk into the chair at his desk and allowed himself a moment to gather his thoughts and clear his mind, before he summoned his deputy to his room. He was hoping that Adam might have found out something more about the murder. It had been so brutal and shocking that he would be very surprised if there was no gossip in the city taverns about it.

"Did your men find out anything yesterday." He asked, as Adam entered the room.

Adam shook his head as he sat down opposite Simon. "Nothing much. There's plenty of talk about what happened, and everyone seems to have a theory as to why the monk was killed, from a drunken altercation, through to robbery; though what a monk would have on him that was worth stealing, I don't know. The cooper even swore that the monk was up to 'unnatural' things with another man, and that his death was God's revenge."

Simon raised his eyebrows. "I hardly think that's likely." He smirked. "Did you hear anything that could be more realistic?"

Adam shook his head. "No, there's certainly no useful gossip about who it might be. I hung around in one of the alehouses for a while last night, listening to the talk; hoping that the liquor might loosen a few tongues." Adam leant back in the chair. "But there was nothing substantial; nothing I would want to investigate further."

"And what of your men? Did they manage to find a grey

horse with a cut on its neck?"

Again, Adam shook his head. "No. But I will send them out again today, to extend the search beyond the city walls and pay particular attention to any horses in the de Mowbray manor. I realise that we need to keep looking for the animal whilst any injury or scar is still fresh."

Simon nodded. "Yes, we do. And I want you personally to be the one to visit the de Mowbray manor again and have a look around there as well. I don't care if Roger de Mowbray objects, or thinks he's being persecuted. I just want to know for certain if he was involved in this."

"You still think it could have been him?"

"I don't know. I spoke with Katherine last night and she doesn't think that Roger would have the stomach for it. She thinks he's a weak man, who is all show and no substance."

Adam nodded in agreement and stroked his beard thoughtfully. "She has a point. I did think the same myself; but that's not to say that he wouldn't have had help. When we were looking at the area where the body had been found, there were more than one set of hoofprints in the dust."

"That's what I thought too, and I want to know who might also have been there."

"You mean if it actually was him."

"Roger de Mowbray has a real motive for murdering Brother Clement: to stop any message about his mothers' bequest getting to the Abbot; and so that he could retain her wealth as part of the estate. I'm not going to dismiss him as a suspect until we're absolutely certain that he wasn't involved."

"Very good, I'll go there this morning, and I'll get some of the other men to continue the search of other manors outside the city walls. Though I doubt we'll find the animal. If the owner knows it's been injured, then he's probably got it well hidden."

"I know and it does feel as though we're looking for a moving shadow, but we must give it our best efforts." He rubbed his face, trying to stave off the tiredness. "Meanwhile I have an appointment with Abbot Robert this morning to see what he can tell me about our monk."

"I'll leave you to it, then. Is there anything else you want me to do, Sire?"

Simon shook his head. "No, not for now. Just keep the pressure on Roger de Mowbray and keep looking for the horse. You never know we might just get lucky. We'll meet back here this afternoon."

Adam went to take his leave as Simon leant back in his chair and closed his eyes for a brief moment. However, his respite was short-lived as a young messenger boy came in with a letter that he handed over to Simon. He sat up again and took it from the boy, opening it quickly, he scanned the contents.

"Wait boy. I need you to take a letter for me."

Simon took a piece of parchment from the desk and quickly wrote on it, before sealing it with red wax and affixing his seal.

"This is to go to Lord Fitzwarren, can you do that? Do you know his manor?"

The boy nodded as Simon handed him the letter. "Quick as you can, mind." The boy nodded again.

Simon watched him leave. At least that was one thing sorted for today. The letter had been from the Kings advisors telling him that the King gave his approval for the marriage of Katherine to Lord William Fitzwarren. With the Kings approval, he saw no reason to delay the wedding, especially given Katherines' objection to the union. It would be better to get the marriage settled as quickly as possible, so that his daughter had little time to rebel against it. He didn't want to force her into the marriage, but he had no choice, and Lord Fitzwarren would be a good husband for her. The letter he'd sent had been to Lord Fitzwarren asking him to dine with them the following evening. It would give Katherine a chance to get to know the man and also to agree a date for the wedding.

The heavy wooden gates of St Mary's Abbey were closed as he approached on horseback. Simon dismounted and rang the heavy bell hanging outside. It wasn't long before the small door within the large gate opened, and a monk stepped out.

"Sheriff Hale. Peace be with you." Brother Michael greeted him. "I'm sorry about the gates, normally we would have them open, but under the circumstances..." His voice tailed off.

"Quite, I understand." Simon nodded, sensing the shock that was still present amongst the monks. "Abbot Robert agreed that he would spare me some time this morning."

"Of course." Brother Michael signalled for the main gate to be opened, and Simon led his horse into the courtyard. "Brother Francis will take your horse for you; and I will take you through to the Abbot's room."

Simon nodded as he unfastened the belt carrying his sword and handed it along with his dagger to another of the monks. He respected the tradition of no man bearing arms within the House of God and readily complied. Then he followed Brother Michael into the abbey buildings. He waited as the monk knocked on the wooden door of the Abbots room and then went inside to announce his guest. Moments later he emerged from the room and smiled at Simon.

"Please do go in," he gestured.

Simon entered the room to see the Abbot rising from his desk to come forward in greeting.

"Good morning, Simon. You are welcome to God's house." The Abbot gave a weak smile, as though he had the troubles of the world on his mind, which in a small way, Simon considered, he did have. "I wish I could believe that it actually is a *good morning*, but given the circumstances I don't feel that the sentiment is entirely justified."

"Good morning, Abbot Robert. I understand what you mean. I hope I am not disturbing your work?"

"Not at all. And we agreed that we would meet up this morning. Even if you were disturbing me, I think your visit is far more important." He gestured to another chair for Simon to sit down. "Do you have any news for me regarding Brother Clements dreadful death?"

Simon shook his head. "Nothing definite yet. I have one lead, but that is all."

"Might I ask what that is?"

Simon paused wondering whether it would be wise to divulge his thoughts to the Abbot.

"When I visited you yesterday, I mentioned that on my visit to see Lady Maud de Mowbray, I suspected that her son Roger, might not have been happy with the bequest she intended to make to the Abbey."

"Yes, I recall."

"I understand that Lady Maud was intending to send you a letter outlining her bequest and that Brother Clement might have been carrying it the evening he was killed. I do wonder if he was killed to prevent that letter reaching you."

The Abbot settled his head onto his raised hands and was silent for a while. "Do you have any proof of that?"

Simon shook his head. "No, not at the moment. It is just a theory, so I would be grateful if you didn't say anything about it, until I know more."

"Does Roger de Mowbray know that you suspect him?"

"If he doesn't now, then he very soon will do, as my deputy is currently at the manor looking for evidence."

"Please let me know if he finds anything."

"Yes, I will do."

Abbot Robert nodded in understanding and there was a silence between them for a moment, before he said. "When you asked yesterday if you could see me again you didn't mention the reason; was this it? Or was there something else?"

"Apologies Abbot, you are correct, I do have some questions which I was hoping you could help me with."

"By all means then, ask away."

Simon settled himself in the chair to try and stop himself from feeling the waves of tiredness that periodically seemed to engulf him. "I wanted to know a little more about Brother Clement; for a start you mentioned that you had sent word to his family, could you tell me a little more about them?"

"Indeed," Abbot Robert started. "As I mentioned, I sent word to them yesterday about his death…" He paused and corrected himself, "his murder, I mean; and they are due to arrive here later today to take his body for burial in the family plot. They don't live too far away."

"Family plot? So, they are of noble birth?"

"Yes, that's right, though not of high standing. I don't know the family well myself, but they are known in the area. You might have heard of them, the de Glanville's?"

Simon thought about it for a moment, then shook his head. "I've heard the name mentioned, but I don't know any more about them other than that. Did Brother Clement come to the order as he was the younger son of the family?"

Abbot Robert considered the question thoughtfully. "No; although he was the second son, I understand he had trained as a soldier initially."

"A soldier?" Now Simons' interest was piqued. As a soldier there would have been plenty of opportunity for him to make enemies. Perhaps, Brother Clement had been recognised by someone from his past.

"Yes, a soldier. I must admit that it surprised me too. It seems that after having had a religious epiphany, a calling you may say, he decided to leave his previous life and to take Holy Orders. He came to us about three years ago now, as a novice and, I must admit, that at the time, I had my concerns about his vocation. I thought he would find the rules of St Benedict too hard to adhere to. Not everyone is cut out to comply with the vows of obedience, poverty and chastity."

Simon was well aware that the monastic life was not for everyone, and it would not have been a life he personally would have chosen; but then, he had never felt the calling to Holy Orders, that it seemed Brother Clement had.

"Quite; but I take it from the fact that he was an ordained member of the order, that it turned out he was suited to a religious life?

"Yes, he was." The Abbot leant back in his chair and mused on the subject of Brother Clement. "He was quite a reverent man and quick to learn our ways and he showed a great aptitude for the herb garden. Brother Jacob, our apothecary, had taken him under his wing. And although, as I initially said, I had my doubts about whether this life was for him, I could find no reason to refuse him taking his final vows."

"And he never gave you cause to regret that decision?"

"Not once. In fact, he seemed determined to prove me wrong." The Abbot sighed, as he recalled the young man who had approached him to talk about his calling to serve God. He had been so certain in his conviction that his fervour had somewhat surprised Abbot Robert, especially in a man so young and well born.

"Of course, you know that his name wasn't originally Clement; he took that name once he joined the order. When he came to us, he was known as Hugh; Hugh de Glanville."

"I didn't know that, thank you." Simon replied, committing it to memory. "Is there anything else that you can tell me about him, or am I better speaking with his family?"

"The only other thing that I know about him is that he was betrothed to a girl when he came to us. Obviously, he broke off the betrothal but more than that, I cannot tell you."

"Thank you, that is very illuminating. I was intending to pay a visit to the family of Brother Clement; however, you mentioned that they were due to come to the Abbey to take Brother Clement...." He stopped uncomfortably, not sure by what name he should now address the late Brother. "I mean Hugh de Glanville, back to their manor for burial, I was wondering if I could speak with them whilst they were here?"

Now it was the Abbot who looked uncomfortable. "If this is not too impertinent of me to say, Simon, I would leave it until after they have buried him, to pay them a visit. The sadness of seeing their son and taking him home for burial will undoubtedly lay heavy on them."

Simon breathed deeply and considered his reply. "I know it's not an ideal situation, but if I am to catch the man who murdered their son, it's imperative that I speak with as many people who knew him as possible; and his parents are top of my list."

"I do understand Simon, but in the circumstances, I would advise you to wait, let them bury their son in peace."

Simon knew that this would only delay his investigation and might lead to the killer escaping; he shook his head. "I wish I had the luxury of time, but the longer I wait, then the further away his killer may get. If this was someone from Brother Clement's past life as a soldier, who just happened to see him that night and decide to elicit his vengeance on a sworn enemy, then the man could already be on his way out of the county."

"So now you think that his killer could be a soldier; an adversary he made in his former life?" The Abbot said firmly. "This morning you thought it was Roger de Mowbray; has that now changed?"

"No, it hasn't changed. I still suspect Roger, but it may well not be him; and at this early stage, as you might agree, I need to consider all the possible options and suspects."

The Abbot nodded. "Very well. But if you do come to see them, please be respectful and understanding. They have just lost their son!"

The Abbots words hung for a moment in the still air.

"Of course." Simon agreed. "I will let you speak with them first to see if they are happy to answer some questions. I find your concern for them quite understandable."

"Thank you, Simon." Abbot Robert sighed heavily.

"What I find so terrible is that a son who had survived his life as a soldier, must meet his end so heinously when he turns his life to the service of God."

"It would almost have been easier for them to bear if he had been killed in battle." Simon mused.

"Precisely. But then the good Lord has his plan for all of us, and none of us may question what He decrees."

Simon nodded understanding the Abbots meaning. For a soldier to be killed was somehow understandable, it was almost expected. But for a man to leave behind that dangerous lifestyle and then meet his end whilst a servant of the Lord, was somehow incomprehensible.

"If that is all Abbot, then I will take my leave of you and return tomorrow to meet the de Glanville family." Simon got up from his chair and gave a small bow of respect to the Abbot. "Thank you for your time. I can assure you that both I, and my men will do our utmost to uncover the truth behind what has happened."

"Thank you, Simon, I know that you will."

Simon left the Abbots room and walked down the covered walkway of the cloister and outside into the courtyard. Brother Michael noticed him instantly and quickly made his way across to Simon, carrying his sword and belt. Simon thanked him and, after affixing it, made his way to the stables where Brother Francis was watering his horse. He thanked the portly monk and quickly mounted, before leaving via the now open wooden gates.

The ride back to the castle was a short one and the day was already quite hot. The roads of the city were dusty and dry, and the stench of human waste and detritus hung in the hot air. The people in the city streets were selling their wares, shouting out to passers-by, or talking or arguing and paid little attention to him as he rode past. Simon wondered just how long this relentless heat would continue. The farmers prayed for fine weather to harvest their crops, but this had been unyielding and there was hardly anything left growing in the fields now. Initially, when the hot weather had begun, the castle had been a haven of coolness away from the heat of the day, but now the great walls had absorbed the unremitting heat and it seemed there was no escape from it; except, that was, for down in the dungeons; but he drew the line at some things, and this was one of them.

Arriving in the outer bailey of the castle, he had dismounted and handed the reins of his bay cob over to his stableman when his squire approached him.

"Sire, you have a guest waiting to see you in the great hall."

Simon furrowed his brows; he wasn't expecting anyone this morning. "Did he say who he was and what he wanted?" Simon asked. The news made him faintly annoyed as he had more than enough work to be getting on with. He had been hoping to go through more documents submitted to him ahead of the visit of the Royal Justice for the Assizes.

"He said that his name is Alexander de Ros and that he wishes to speak with you on a private matter concerning your daughter." For some reason, the squire looked faintly uneasy at imparting the news, as if he feared that Simon would be angry.

"Ah yes, I was expecting him." Simon lied and watched his squire visibly relax. "In the great hall, did you say?" The squire nodded. "Can you ask him to join me in my office and then bring us both some wine?"

"Yes sire. Of course."

The young lad was very capable Simon considered, if only he wasn't quite so nervous and eager to please. Still, there was time for him to learn, and Simon was sure that he would soon become more confident. He strode across the inner bailey and took the steps up to the first-floor, two at a time, eager to be back in his office. He was intrigued to meet the man whom his daughter was in love with, though he doubted very much that the meeting would be an easy one; given what he'd told his daughter the previous evening. In fact, he expected it to be quite difficult for both himself, and Alexander.

Simon had comfortably made it back to his office when there was a knock at his door and the young squire showed Alexander de Ros into the room.

"Good day Sheriff and thank you for seeing me." The young man did a small respectful bow as he came to stand in front of Simon.

Simon regarded him thoughtfully as he gestured to the chairs by the empty fireplace so that they might both sit down. The boy in front of him wasn't '*a boy*' as he had expected, but a fine-looking knight, worthy of his spurs. In truth, Simon could see why his daughter Katherine had fallen for him, but sadly that would not change what had been arranged. Simon felt uncomfortable having to break the news to Alexander but, as he'd told Katherine the previous evening, it was too late to change what had been arranged.

"Alexander, it is good to finally meet you. My daughter Katherine has told me about you."

Alexander looked up expectantly and a little surprised. "So, you know why I am here then?"

Simon nodded. "Katherine spoke with me last evening." He was about to continue when Alexander interrupted.

"So, you will know that I love her very much." He began eagerly, his blue eyes sparkling and clearly nervous. "I have spoken with my own father, and he is agreeable to the marriage. I can assure you that I will take care of her and provide for her. After we are married, we will live with my family to start with, but in time I am hoping to renovate one of the properties on my father's estate."

Simon admired Alexanders' enthusiasm, but he held up his hand to stop him from continuing. He had to put an end to this now, before it went too far. The last thing he wanted was to lead Alexander into thinking there was any chance of him marrying Katherine.

"Alexander, I appreciate everything that you are saying, and, in any other circumstances, I can assure you that I would be agreeable to your request." Simon paused. "But I'm afraid that you cannot marry Katherine." He added and watched as Alexander's face changed as he absorbed the news. "Katherine didn't know this until yesterday, which is why she didn't tell you, but I've already agreed to a betrothal for her to Lord William Fitzwarren. It is a match that I am in favour of and, due to my position, I have sought the Kings approval for it, which he has given."

Simon watched as the colour drained from the young man's face, and it took on a grey pallor. He felt genuinely sorry for Alexander; he was a handsome young man from a good family and normally he would have been happy to give his blessing for the betrothal, but it was too late for that now. Simon considered that Alexander must be aware that nothing more could be done by either of them. The King had approved the marriage, and an agreement had been reached with Lord Fitzwarren. It was far too late now for that to be changed. As Katherines' father he had made a good and respectable match for her. But looking at the young man in front of him he could see that Alexander's feelings for his daughter were true and honest; and Simon felt it wrench at his soul; he understood the heartache of loss all too well and wished he didn't have to be the bearer of such sadness.

"I wish she had told me earlier that you were seeing each other. If I had known, then I would not have made the arrangements for her betrothal." He tried to offer some solace to Alexander.

"And Katherine had no idea that she was to be betrothed?" Alexander breathed.

"As I said, she did not know about it, until last evening. I was awaiting a reply from the King to give his agreement to the match, before I told her."

He watched as Alexander nodded slowly, his head bowed, before he asked. "And there is nothing I can do to change this?"

Simon shook his head regretfully. "Nothing, I'm afraid." He could almost feel the young man's distress. "It has all been agreed and I am not in a position to go back on my word. I am sorry."

"I understand." He lifted his head to look Simon straight in the eye. "I will not lie and say that I do not wish it could be different. I would do anything for your daughter sire, and my feelings for her are true and honourable. I also believe that Katherine feels the same way about me, as well." He paused, trying to maintain his composure. He wanted to appear a tough, persuasive man, but it was hard to do, when it felt as though his whole world was collapsing around him. "Forgive me for saying this, but are you certain that Katherine will agree to it? As her father you are no doubt aware of what a strong character your daughter is," he added. "I admit that I find it admirable in her, though it does make me wonder if she will go quietly into a marriage that has been arranged for her and which she does not want."

Simon nodded and gave a small smile considering that Alexander knew his daughter better than he had expected. "I believe you are correct on that point, and she has already made her feelings on the subject quite clear to me. But I am her father, and she is duty bound to do as I ask of her." He paused recalling the argument of the previous evening. "Though as you so rightly say, I expect that I have not heard the last of this matter from her."

Alexander managed a weak smile. "I think you can be assured of that sire." There was silence between them for a moment, before he added. "You do know that I would put up a fight for her if I thought there was even the slightest chance that I could persuade you to annul the betrothal and allow me to marry your daughter." He drew breath and Simon could see that he was choosing his words carefully. "But I am an honourable man too, and I understand that as Sheriff of the county you have a duty to the King. I can understand why you sought his agreement to the marriage and why that makes it impossible to break the betrothal. I can assure you that I have no wish to invoke the Kings displeasure." He paused. "Though I will say that if there is even the slightest chance of the marriage not happening, or if Katherine comes to me of her own free will, then I will not turn her away." He looked directly at Simon. "I love your daughter sire, and I will not give up hope of being with her. Not yet, you understand."

Simon was surprised at how admirable the young man was. "I would not expect anything less from you, and I respect you for saying it. As you are aware my daughter means a great deal to me and, I believe that I am arranging a good marriage for her; one which she will eventually be happy with; and one with a man who she will come to respect and, in time I hope, love as well; just as I did with her mother. But I do understand your sentiments Alexander and I can see that you care for her a great deal. I just wish I had known about this before I arranged the betrothal."

"I know." He paused. "I suppose we didn't want to be hurried into a decision, but when I asked her for her hand two days ago, we both knew it was what we wanted. I need you to know sire, that I love your daughter with all my heart."

Simon could almost feel the weight of the young man's heartbreak.

"And believe me, I am very sorry that I have to turn down your request. But what is done cannot be undone. Not without greatly offending Lord Fitzwarren, or the King; and considering my position here is at the Kings behest, then the last thing I want to do is to offend him."

"I do understand that. I may not like, or agree with it, but I do, at least, understand." Alexander replied graciously.

Simon nodded, accepting what he had said. He found himself admiring Alexander greatly, both for his eloquence of speech and the strength of his character; and, although he hated to admit it, Alexander would have made a good match for Katherine; but that was irrelevant now.

Alexander got to his feet. There was nothing more he could say, except to take his leave. "Thank you for seeing me, I will bid you good day sire."

Simon got up from his chair. "Good day Alexander, I wish the outcome of our meeting could have been better for you. Please give my regards to your father."

"I will." Alexander made his way towards the door, then paused. "If you will excuse me for saying this sure, but I believe you will have a tough time ahead of you. As I've said before, I cannot imagine that Katherine will be easily convinced about her betrothal as you may hope."

Simon sighed and shook his head. "As much as it grieves me to admit it, I fear that you may be right about that."

Simon watched Alexander leave and felt a pang of guilt at the marriage he had arranged for his daughter. Alexander de Ros would have been a good match for her, and they were clearly very much in love with each other. Still, Lord William Fitzwarren was also a good man and, of higher standing than Alexander. Katherine would have more power and position in the county than she otherwise would have had. She would be the lady of a large manor and in charge of a big household with all the power and influence that position would bring, surely that must count for something.

CHAPTER 6

Katherine was sitting in the window embrasure in her bed chamber looking out over the bailey when she saw Alexander leaving one of the castle buildings. She realised that she must have missed his arrival earlier and she inwardly chided herself for being so remiss. She wondered if he had been to see her father to ask for her hand in marriage as he had promised, and her heart went out to him. If only she'd been able to tell him beforehand that it would all be in vain. Suddenly Katherine felt cross with herself for not being able to warn Alexander and she knew she had to see him to tell him that she hadn't known about the betrothal before last night and how miserable it made her feel. As she slipped from the window seat and ran quickly across the floor of her room, she wondered what she would have done if she had seen him arrive. Would she have gone with him to see her father, so that they could plead their case together? Or would it have made things worse, if her father was still angry with her?

"Where are you going?" Jeanette asked, looking up from her sewing.

"Alexander is outside. He must have been to see my father. I want to talk to him before he leaves." And without waiting for an answer, she had disappeared through the open door and ran down the stairs. Outside the sunlight blinded her for a moment as her eyes adjusted to the change from the dimly lit stairs.

"Alexander!" She called out, running towards him.

He had already mounted his horse and turned to look as soon as he heard his name called. On seeing her running towards him, his expression changed from indifference to a warm smile, which touched his blue eyes. He quickly dismounted and opened his arms as she flew into him, and he enveloped her in a hug.

"Oh, my love, it's so good to see you." Katherine breathed. "Please tell me that you've been to see father and that it went well?"

Alexander held her close for a moment enjoying what might well be, he considered, their last private moments. He took a deep breath, but Katherine had already pulled away from him. Around them the stable hands and servants busied themselves, ignoring the Sheriff's daughter and the young man.

"You did speak with him?" She asked again. "Tell me you did?"

"Yes, I did my love, but it seems that I was too late, and you are already betrothed."

She hung her head. "Yes, he told me last night that he had already agreed for me to marry Lord Fitzwarren." Katherine felt tears pricking at her eyes. "But I told him that I wouldn't marry him. I told him that I was in love with you; but he just wouldn't listen."

"Yes, your father told me that he has the King's agreement for your marriage and that he has already settled it with Lord Fitzwarren." He held her hands as she tried to pull away from him. She was shaking her head and there were tears in her eyes. "I'm sorry my love, but it seems there is nothing to be done."

"No, no... there must be something we can do. I don't believe my father would do this to me; I thought he loved me. I didn't realise that I was just another chattel to him." She pulled her hands away and clenched her fists in anger as she tried to keep her feelings under control.

"I don't believe that your father sees it like that." Alexander tried to soothe her. "I think he loves you a great deal. He told me that if he'd known about the two of us earlier, then he wouldn't have arranged the betrothal to Lord Fitzwarren."

"He told me the same thing. It was just such a shock." Katherine said. "This time yesterday, my life was perfectly wonderful and now everything is....." She started to cry, and Alexander put his arm around her to comfort her.

"I know my love. I wasn't expecting this either, but there is nothing we can do about it."

"But we have to try!" She protested. "I won't marry Lord Fitzwarren; I just won't, and my father can't make me."

"Katherine please. I know it's difficult, but there is nothing we can do." Alexander was becoming aware that some of the castle staff were staring at them.

"Nothing!" She shouted at him, raising her head to look him straight in the eyes. "I won't accept it. I will fight it; I thought you would feel the same? I thought you loved me."

"I do; I do!" Alexander tried to calm and reassure her. "I love you so very much. Please believe me." He held her away from him so that he could look at her. "You know that if I thought there was even the smallest chance that your father would relent on his decision, then I would never give up. But you must understand, it's not only your father that's involved; the King has given his blessing to your marriage, and not I, or anyone, can change that. I am so very sorry."

He glanced around him, noticing that the servants and guards were now taking a distinct interest in them and what was being said.

"Look, we can't talk here." He added, making her aware that they were being watched. "Meet me by the river, where we usually go, as soon as you can get away. I'll be waiting for you." He kissed her quickly on the cheek and then turned to leave.

She didn't want him to go and tried to grab at his sleeve.

"Katherine, please do as I ask." He told her softly and smiled. "We can talk more freely when we are alone." He watched as she gathered herself and nodded. "Besides, I want a chance to see you one more time."

Katherine looked up at him and smiled. Just looking at him made her feel so much better and then when he smiled at her she could feel her heartbeat faster.

"Yes, I want to see you too." She kissed him chastely on the cheek. "Until this afternoon."

Alexander smiled, then mounted his horse quickly and circled it so he could look back at her. "I will see you soon." He added, then spurred his horse forward.

Katherine watched him leave and felt rooted to the spot in the bailey. She stood there long after he had left through the castle gates and disappeared from view, unable or wanting to move from the spot. She could feel her breath coming in short gasps, as she thought about Alexander and how her life had suddenly changed within the space of one day. Katherine finally gathered herself and left the bailey with as much dignity as she could muster. She held her head high as she walked back across to the staircase and made her way to her room.

Alexander was all that she could think about as she climbed the stairs. She loved him so much and she wasn't ready to give up on him, or to stop fighting to be allowed to marry him. She had allowed herself to dream that Alexander would be able to convince her father that the betrothal to Lord Fitzwarren could not go ahead but it seemed that he had failed, just as she had. If he hadn't been able to change her father's mind about them marrying, then this afternoons' meeting could well be the last time she saw him and she couldn't imagine her life without Alexander. She brushed stinging tears from her face. Pushing open the wooden door she stepped dejectedly into her room.

Jennet was sitting by the window and looked up when her mistress entered the room. Immediately she put down the dress she was mending and went over to her.

"My love, what has happened?

Jennet stood up and opened her arms as Katherine began to sob uncontrollably once again.

"Alexander has been to see my father, but he couldn't persuade him to dissolve the betrothal and allow us to marry." She sobbed. "I thought, once Alexander had seen him, my father would understand how much we were in love and give us his blessing." She shook her head. "But he won't change his mind."

"Oh, my lady. I know this must hurt, but you must know how much your father loves you. He only wants the best for you, and he believes that Lord Fitzwarren will make you a fine husband."

"But can't he understand that I love Alexander, and I want him as my husband." Katherine protested. "I don't want to marry Lord Fitzwarren."

"I know, but sometimes it's just not possible to have what you want." Jennet sighed, as she comforted her mistress. "Katherine, you are a fine lady of high birth; your father is a man of standing; not just here in the county, but also in the whole of the country. You know that, as your father is in the Kings service, his position doesn't come without responsibility." She stroked Katherine's hair as she comforted her. "My dear girl, it's right for your father to arrange a marriage for you. It's how things are. You're a lady of position and your father must ensure you make a good marriage."

Katherine could barely speak. "But Alexander is from a good family."

Jennet nodded. "I know he is. I'm sure if you're father had known earlier that you were in love with him, then he would have agreed to your marriage to Alexander."

Katherine nodded. "Father did tell me the same thing; but it doesn't change things now." She sighed heavily. "I need to get out of here Jennet." She said solemnly. "I need to get some fresh air to clear my head and have some time to think." She didn't mention meeting up with Alexander, she didn't want Jennet to feel that she had to tell her father.

"You know that your father doesn't want you going out of the castle grounds."

"I know, but you must understand that I need some time to myself." She pleaded with Jennet. "Will you cover for me?"

Jennet saw the desperate look in her young mistresses' eyes. She knew she shouldn't let her go, not alone; Katherines' father had been quite firm on the matter. On the other hand, Jennet could well understand Katherines need to get out of the confines of her room and the castle and to have some freedom after what had happened. Then another thought crossed her mind.

"Are you planning to see Alexander?"

The look on Katherines' face told her that her suspicion was correct.

"No, don't tell me." Jennet said quickly holding up a hand. "If I don't know, then I can't lie to anyone."

"Then, I won't say anything." Katherine replied. "But I do need to have some time to myself, Jennet. You do understand, don't you? My whole life has been turned on its' head in the last day."

Katherine gave Jennet a hug and took a step back. Then she went to walk towards the door.

"I think I'll disappear now, while father is still in his office. Then I won't be missed for a while."

"Are you sure?" Jennet asked, concern evident in her voice.

Katherine nodded. "Yes, I'm sure, Jennet. Very sure."

Jennet was still uncomfortable at the deception she was now party to. Then, something occurred to her, and she caught Katherine's hand to stop her leaving. "You are coming back, aren't you, my lady? Your father would never forgive me, if you didn't come back."

Katherine looked at her and held her gaze for a moment. "Of course, Jennet. I promise you I will come back. Please don't worry."

Jennet didn't seem quite convinced by Katherines words. "Because if you were considering running away, then you must know that your father would search high and low for you in order to bring you back." She held Katherines' gaze. "He loves you very much. It would hurt him dreadfully if you left without him knowing."

"I used to think that he loved me." She whispered. "But at the moment, it doesn't feel like it."

"Maybe, but you must also know that your father is Sheriff of this county. If you disappear, then he will send so many men after you, that you will never be able to hide from him." Jennet still felt concerned about what her mistress might be planning.

"I know Jennet." She sighed. "I know."

"Just promise me that you will come back. Whatever happens; just come back here." Jennet looked at Katherine sternly. "Please don't run away and make your father angry. It won't help your cause, my love."

Katherine nodded slowly. "I know and I promise I will come back."

"Then I will cover for you, but you must be back before sunset. If anyone asks, I will tell them that you are too distraught after what's happened and don't want to see anyone. Just make sure that Alexander escorts you back here safely before sunset and the gates close."

"I will do; and thank you Jennet! Thank you so much!"

Jennet sighed heavily, already regretting her decision to cover for Katherine.

"Don't let me down, my lady. I can't help you if you do, you know that. And I can't lie to your father if he asks me outright."

"I know." She kissed Jennet on the cheek. "I promise I will come back; and I'll take Grenulf with me so I will be safe."

At the sound of his name the great wolfhound lifted his head from his sleep on the cool stone floor.

"Then go quickly and make sure that you're not seen." Jennet raised her hand to silence Katherine. "I know you've managed to get out of here unseen before and I'm not going to ask how you did it. I don't want to know, because then I cannot lie about it."

Katherine nodded quickly and hugged Jennet before dashing across to a coffer and taking a shawl from inside it. She signalled to Grenulf, who leapt up instantly, happy to be going out with his mistress once again.

Katherine put the shawl over her head to hide her noticeable red hair as she left the building and walked into the outer bailey. She stayed near the walls, in the shadows, trying to avoid the servants and soldiers that hustled and bustled around the bailey. Outside the castle walls, she kept her head down and walked quickly with Grenulf lolloping at her heels. Once she was clear of the city where there were less people to recognise her, she removed the shawl and broke into a slow run until she could finally see the trees and riverbank where Alexander was standing waiting for her. Normally she would have taken her horse, Lily, but she knew it would raise too many suspicions if she went out riding so soon after Alexander had left.

She was out of breath when she got to their meeting place. As she approached, she saw Alexander turn and he was just in time to catch her as she flung herself into his arms.

"Oh Alexander! I wasn't sure if you would be here, yet."

"I had nowhere else to go, so I thought I'd come straight down here to wait for you." He held her close and kissed her on the top of her head.

Grenulf circled them in a protective manner, ensuring his young charge was safe, before settling down on the ground at the side of them.

"It feels so good to be away from the confines of the castle." She sighed. "Jennet told me to be back before sunset, so we have some time to spend together."

"She's going to cover for you?"

Katherine nodded. "Although she did make me promise to return, and not to run away."

Alexander smiled. "She obviously knows you very well."

"I have to say that the thought had crossed my mind. But as Jennet pointed out, my father would send his men out after me."

Katherine sat down on the grass and looked out over the river. The water was sparkling in the sunshine and the sound of the river running low over the stones felt calming. Alexander joined her and the two of them remained silent for a while, until Katherine finally broke the spell.

"What are we going to do?" She asked. "I can't marry

Lord Fitzwarren."

Alexander looked at her and sighed. "I don't think there is anything we can do." He paused. "You know that if there was, I would move heaven and earth to make it happen. But I can't see any answer to it."

"Jennet may have a point; we could run away."

Alexander mused on the suggestion for a few moments before adding. "I suppose we could leave here and go to Wales or Scotland, where we would be beyond your father's reach."

Katherine sighed. "And Jennet also pointed out that we probably wouldn't get very far before my father sent his men out after us."

They both fell silent for a moment.

"Katherine, all I've done since your father told me that you were already betrothed, is try and think of a solution to our problem. But, as much as I've tried, I can't really see that there is one. Your father has given his word to Lord Fitzwarren, and the King himself has approved your marriage. I am sorry my love, but you cannot do anything but go through with the marriage."

Katherine shook her head and stared out at the river. "No, I won't marry him! No matter what happens, I won't marry him." She turned to look at Alexander. "Don't you understand I can't marry him because I love you. I want to marry you, and I couldn't bear to be without you." Her face was solemn and serious.

"And I feel the same, but you must see, it's a lost cause." He put an arm around her shoulder and pulled her close. "I'm afraid my love, that we have no choice in this."

"No, no. I will find a way. I won't give in."

Alexander admired her spirit and her will to fight, but he knew that there was nothing she could really do to change the outcome.

"I wish there was a way. But if you refuse Lord Fitzwarren, then your father will be disgraced in the eyes of everyone. The King would see it as a lack of power on your fathers' behalf, that he can't even get his daughter to do his bidding. Lord Fitzwarren would take it as a personal snub and the whole thing would bring your father's name and reputation into disgrace. Don't you see there is no option for you; either you marry Lord Fitzwarren, or you will have to take the veil."

"Into a convent?" Katherine looked at him sharply. "I could never do that."

Alexander looked at her and gave a wry smile as he thought about her taking a vow of obedience; somehow, he could not imagine that going down well.

"Would it be worse than marrying Lord Fitzwarren?" He asked. "I've seen it before with wealthy women going into a convent to avoid a marriage they are opposed to. I believe that it would be the only way for your father to keep face, by saying that you had a calling by God to serve him and would deny yourself all worldly things in order to fulfil your vows."

Katherine sighed heavily as the reality of her situation finally hit her. She suddenly shivered and felt cold even though the afternoon was still very warm.

"I don't think I'd ever realised just how futile this whole situation is." She breathed. "I really can't change anything, can I?"

Alexander said nothing for a moment as they both tried to accept the situation they were in.

"It's terrible, I know." He said eventually. "The likes of you and I, have little say in who we will marry."

"Not you!" She turned on him sharply. "You're a man, so you will get a say in who you marry. You can choose the person you want; but for me, as a woman, I get no say in the matter at all. I am nothing but a possession of my father's, to be disposed of as he sees fit." Katherine sensed the anger rising inside her. Suddenly, she felt as if the clouds had lifted and she was through with feeling sorry for herself. No longer was she going to bemoan her situation; her need to fight for her rights had surfaced.

"But..." Alexander tried to interrupt, but her fierce glance told him it was best to remain silent.

"Even my maid Jennet has the right to choose who she wants to marry, but it seems that I, as daughter of the Sheriff, am afforded no such luxury." She sat up straight. "Well, if my father thinks he is going to marry me off without my permission, then he has another thing coming."

Alexander felt wary. He knew his beloved Katherine was spirited, and he had also seen that look in her eyes before. He was suddenly concerned about what she was planning. "What are you going to do?"

"I am going to write directly to the King and ask him to give me leave to marry whoever I choose. I've heard of other women doing this; widows, obtaining permission from the King so that they would not be forced into another marriage that wasn't of their choice, so why shouldn't I? I am in love with a very respectable knight from a good family, so why should I be forced to marry someone whom I don't want."

"I'm not sure it's that simple." He admired her resolve and determination, but he knew it probably would do no good. Her father was the King's man and there was no reason for the King to go against what her father had already asked permission for. "But if that's what you want, then I will help you. I too will write to the King and plead my case to be allowed to marry you."

"Oh Alexander." Her voice softened as she looked at him. His words meant that he loved her just as much as she did him. She leant in and kissed him tenderly. "I do love you so very much and I promise that, if we are allowed to marry, I will be the best wife you could ever wish for."

"I should hope so." He teased, returning her kiss. "And you will promise to love and obey me at all times?"

She sat back and looked at him sharply. "Perhaps!" She smiled and kissed him again.

Simon didn't really expect to see his daughter for the rest of the day. So that, when he received word from Jennet that she was too distraught to join him at dinner, he accepted it without question. He knew she had been out that afternoon, as his squire had tactfully mentioned it to him, but he also knew that Grenulf had been with her, so she would have been quite safe. He assumed that she had now returned to the castle and was secure under his protection again; the fact that she didn't want to join him for dinner was a minor inconvenience. He had received word back from Lord Fitzwarren that he would be joining them for dinner the next evening and Katherine would then be summoned to join them, whether she wanted to or not. He just hoped his spirited daughter would at least remain civil, but that was never guaranteed.

Simon decided to dine in the hall that evening and asked Adam to join him, to discuss if his deputy had discovered anything further during his visit to the de Mowbray manor. Adam was in a jovial mood when he joined Simon at the table.

"Good day?" Simon enquired of his deputy, thinking that his good mood must be down to a productive day, however it seemed not.

"Frustrating." Adam replied, his smile turning to a grimace as he drunk thirstily at a mug of ale. But then he smiled again and Simon, following his gaze, realised that the reason for Adams' previous good mood had been a young serving girl, who was now blushing and smiling at him. It had nothing at all to do with his day's work.

"We spent the whole morning looking through all of the barns, buildings and stables at de Mowbray manor but turned up nothing." Then he grinned cheekily. "All we succeeded in doing was annoying that young upstart who struts around like he's already Lord of the Manor."

"Roger de Mowbray was there?"

Adam nodded and leant back in his chair. "Yes, all the time. He followed me around all morning, and he questioned everything we were doing."

"Did he look as though he was trying to hide something?"

"Possibly, I'm not sure. Maybe I'm losing my touch." Adam filled his mug up with more ale. "But there's definitely something very shifty about the lad." He thought about it as he took another gulp of ale. "If he isn't involved in this murder, then he's definitely up to something else. I'll warrant my best sword on it!"

"But you didn't find anything to link him to the murder of Brother Clement?" Simon asked, as he put some more fish on his plate.

"Not a thing." Adam replied, shaking his head. "It grieves me to say it, but we didn't find a single thing to link him to the murder of the monk. I had the men looking high and low for that dagger and they couldn't find it. Neither could I."

"And the grey horse?"

Again, Adam shook his head. "There wasn't a sign of a grey horse anywhere in the manor or in any of the surrounding barns."

"And none of the servants were forthcoming with any information?"

Adam shook his head. "None of them would talk. Either they genuinely don't know anything, or Roger de Mowbray has threatened them into not talking."

Simon sighed heavily, knowing that they had absolutely nothing to link Roger to the murder, but he was still certain that the young peacock was involved somehow.

"Make sure you have one of the guards watch Roger de Mowbray." He told Adam. "I want to know everything he does; where he goes; who he talks to. Sooner or later, he will slip up and then we'll be waiting for him."

"You're certain that it's him then?"

Simon shook his head. "I wish I could be certain that he is our man, but I can't. However, he's the only lead we've got so far." He paused. "And besides, I don't like him."

Adam laughed. "That makes two of us then."

"Was there anything else that your men heard? Any talk on the city streets, or in the ale houses?"

Adam stuck his knife in a piece of meat and dropped it onto his plate. "Nothing of any value. There's a lot of rumour going around, but nothing more." He took a bite of the meat before adding. "I also had the men search as many barns and stables in the city as they could, but there's no sign of the grey horse. I suspect it's long gone now; whoever owns it, probably has it well hidden."

They ate in silence for a while, before Simon added. "The Abbot told me that the family of Brother Clement are coming to the Abbey tomorrow to take his body home for burial. I'm going to meet them before they leave. I'm anxious to ask them about Brother Clement's life before he joined the religious order. The Abbot told me he was a soldier before he joined them."

Adam looked up. "That does put a different light on things. Do you think that it's someone from his past life who has a grudge against him?"

"I don't know, but it's something I'd like to investigate further. Perhaps there was someone who harboured a grievance against him."

"I take it the family are local?"

Simon nodded. "The de Glanville's, do you know them? Abbot Robert tells me they have a manor to the north of the city."

"Aye, I know them, but not well. So, our Brother Clement was a de Glanville before he took the cowl?"

"It would seem so. What do you know of the family?"

"Not much. Lord de Glanville and his wife keep themselves very much to themselves. I believe they had two sons, Arthur and Hugh. Arthur was the eldest, but he was killed in the baron's war, so I take it that our dead Brother was Hugh de Glanville?"

Simon nodded as he filled up their mugs with more ale. "Yes, Hugh de Glanville; and if he was a knight and soldier, then he would likely have met and known others of equal standing. Men who could easily afford a fine dagger with a jewelled pommel."

"And men who were trained to kill." Adam proffered.

"Yes, exactly. The neck wound that killed him was so precise, it couldn't have been done by just anyone. It would take a skilled man; a soldier, to know how to inflict such a fatal wound."

"Do you want me to come with you to meet the Glanville's tomorrow?"

"No, I don't think so. Abbot Robert was concerned that my being there would upset them even more, so I don't want to have more men with me than I must. I will go alone. Hopefully they will find a way through their grief to talk with me about their son. I need to find out more about him and his life before he took up Holy Orders."

"So, what do you want me to do tomorrow? I think we've exhausted the search at the de Mowbray manor; but as you say, I will make sure one of the men keeps watch there. Maybe if Roger de Mowbray thinks that we've finished with him, he'll do something that will lead us to the evidence we need."

"We can only hope." Simon mused. "I'd like you to continue searching for the grey horse though. Try the barns and stables outside the city, in the woods; ones that belong to local manors. If the owner knows that the horse has been injured, then he's likely to hide it away well out of sight."

"And a lowly squire would not be able to hide a horse in a stable without it being seen." Adam added.

"Exactly, the animal would likely be their only mount, and people would notice if they suddenly changed their horse. It's likely that the person who did this has more than one horse, so a missing one would not be noticed. Also, he is likely to have plenty of old barns and hovels on his land where he could hide the injured horse until the cut heals. Somewhere, very private, where hardly anyone would notice the animal."

Adam nodded in agreement. "Perhaps I would be more successful talking to some of the huntsmen or poachers. I could ask them where they thought the best place to hide a horse would be; rather than getting the men to search all the barns and buildings in the woods."

"That's a good idea. And see if any of them have noticed something different or odd, over the last few days." Simon leant back in his chair, trying to relax, but he still felt tense. The events of the last two days had made him feel decidedly uneasy. Not only the murder of the monk, but the argument with his daughter had both unsettled him greatly.

"Shall we meet up again tomorrow evening?" Adam asked.

"Yes, we should. I'm anxious to resolve this matter as soon as possible and certainly before the Royal Justice arrives for the assize court. I will have far too much to do then." Simon suddenly remembered his invitation to Lord Fitzwarren. "But best make it late afternoon; I have Lord Fitzwarren coming to dine here tomorrow evening, to make arrangements for the wedding."

Adam nodded his head. "I heard the betrothal had the King's approval. I take it your daughter is pleased with the match?"

Simon sighed heavily as he recalled the conversation and subsequent argument with Katherine the previous evening. "Not exactly," he admitted reservedly.

Simon knew he could trust Adam with a confidence. Simon rarely spoke of private matters with anyone, and he realised that the only person he actually unburdened himself to, was his daughter Katherine. He knew that if his darling wife, Ellen, had still been alive, he would have trusted her with his confidence; but without her, that responsibility had now fallen on Katherine.

"It seems my daughter is in love with another man and does not want to marry Lord Fitzwarren." He poured himself another large mug of ale, feeling the relief of being able to speak about the matter, and looking forward to the slight intoxication that another mug of ale would bring him this evening.

"Ahh..." Adam replied thoughtfully. "I did wonder. I'd seen her with a young knight in the bailey earlier today and they looked to be having a very intense talk."

"Alexander de Ros." Simon informed him. "Son of Baron Robert of Helmsley."

Adam nodded approvingly. "He's a good man; an excellent soldier, so I hear."

"I just wish she'd told me about him earlier." Simon protested. "The first I hear of it, is last night when she comes to tell me that Alexander will be visiting me to ask for my permission to marry her. And I have to tell her that it won't be possible, as I've already agreed for her marriage to Lord Fitzwarren."

"Ahh, I can see you have a problem." Adam had watched Katherine grow up. He had seen her develop into a beautiful, intelligent woman with a vivacious nature and strong will. He liked Simons' youngest daughter but also knew that she would not be easy to convince that a marriage to Lord Fitzwarren was worth giving up the man she was in love with.

"You are right there!" Simon exploded. "I've never known her be so angry or fight me so hard. Perhaps I've spoilt her too much; allowed her to be educated more than a woman should be. She has opinions, but I've always found her views interesting and considered. But now, she thinks she has the right to go against me, as her father, and choose her own husband."

"Simon, I know your daughter and, I know Alexander de Ros too." Adam paused uncertainly, wondering whether his words would make things worse. "I have to say that I think he would be a good match for her."

"That's not the point. The King has given his approval for the marriage to Lord Fitzwarren, and I cannot change it." He filled his mug up with yet more ale and pondered the statement for a while. "But much as I hate to admit it, I think you are right." He softened. "Alexander de Ros would be good for Katherine; and they are in love with each other. It was the one thing I wanted for her; to find a match that would bring her the same happiness as I had with Ellen."

"And I don't suppose Katherine was very happy when you told her that the betrothal couldn't be dissolved."

"To say she is unhappy with the situation, is a gross understatement. I just dread to think what she might do."

Simon pondered thoughtfully. He only wished that his dear Ellen had been there to advise him; she would have known just what to do. She would also have observed of the burgeoning relationship between his daughter and Alexander and informed him of it much earlier. Instead, he'd had to take the decision of Katherines' marriage solely on himself. Perhaps if he had asked Katherine prior to taking the decision and writing to the King, things might have been different. Yet he was her father, he reminded himself, and she should honour his wishes. But that had never been the way of his spirited daughter.

Simon mused that with the murder of the monk and the assize court next week he already had enough to deal with; and, as much as he loved her, the last thing he needed was Katherine being angry and awkward. It wasn't as though they hadn't had their run-ins in the past; she was a strong character and reminded him of himself at her age. But they had always been able to reconcile their differences. Yet this time, he had the feeling that it would be different.

CHAPTER 7

Abbot Robert had just finished taking the office of sext in the abbey the following day, when he was told that the family of Brother Clement were waiting to see him. He felt weary as he made his way out of the nave; the events of the past few days weighed heavily on his soul and the responsibility he felt, not just to the family of his departed brother, but also to the rest of his brethren, worried him greatly. It wasn't only the terrible murder of Brother Clement, but also the way it had been carried out; so viciously. The rest of the monks in the Abbey were unsettled and there was much gossip and speculation about what had happened, together with a lot of fear that it was a grudge against the abbey and speculation as to which of them might be next. Subsequently, there had been no willing volunteers amongst the monks to visit Lady Maud de Mowbray the previous evening and reluctantly the Abbot had asked Brother Michael if he wouldn't mind carrying out the task, just this once.

As he made his way out of the Abbey and down the steps, the strong sun blinded him temporarily until his eyes adjusted to the brightness. In the courtyard Lord and Lady de Glanville had just arrived. Lady de Glanville was just alighting from her carriage with her husband attentively helping her down, whilst the rest of the retinue were busy with the horses and the cart, which Robert imagined would be used to transport the body of their son. Lord de Glanville was a short and portly man with a round face and, what Abbot Robert supposed, would normally have been a jovial countenance; however, today, he looked understandably drawn and gaunt. Lady de Glanville was a small, thin woman with a pinched face, that was reddened from grief. As she stepped down from the carriage, she looked up and caught Abbot Roberts' gaze; the haunting, desolate look in her eyes made him feel her pain.

"Lord and Lady de Glanville." Abbot Robert greeted his guests. "Peace be with you, in your time of sorrow; we welcome you with open hearts to our abbey. May God's grace be with you." He paused and observed their small bows of respect to him. "May you find comfort in the prayers of this house. Please know that you are in our prayers and may God's mercy be upon the soul of our departed brother."

"Thank you, Lord Abbot." Lord de Glanville bowed his head again to the Abbot. "It has been such a dreadful shock to both of us. As you can imagine, my wife is distraught over this terrible news."

"I can assure you that the events of the past few days have caused all of us great distress. Brother Clement was a well-liked member of this House." He watched as Lady de Glanville bent her head to hide her quiet weeping. "Would you care to join me in the guest lodgings, to rest a while and take refreshments before I show you to your son?"

"Please, I just want to see my son." The thin, frail voice of Lady de Glanville was barely audible, as she took a step forward towards the Abbot and reached out a hand to him.

Abbot Robert looked at her and saw the distress in her eyes; then he nodded and gestured for them to follow him. "Then that is what we shall do." He assured her. "One of the brothers is with him now, praying for his soul. Please be assured that he has not been alone since he was returned to us. We have prayed for his soul continually and we have been most careful in our care of him." Abbot Robert tried to reassure them but could see that no words were going to comfort them. "I will take you to him now. We will hold the service in the Abbey when you are ready."

"Thank you, Abbot." Lord de Glanville nodded his head.

"After the service, several of my monks will ride with you back to your manor and preside over the burial."

Abbot Robert was beginning to escort them back towards the main door of the abbey when the sound of another horse arriving at the abbey made him look up. He saw that it was the Sheriff, Simon de Hale and, for a moment, wished that he had seen fit to leave his questioning for another day. But he also knew that apprehending the man who had carried out such a heinous act was also paramount, and no more so than for Lord and Lady de Glanville.

"If you would excuse me for one moment." He stopped walking and turned to face them. "I would like to speak with the Sheriff before I take you to your son."

They both nodded and Lady de Glanville turned to look at the visitor who was walking towards the Abbot.

"Simon, peace be upon you." Abbot Robert greeted.

Simon gave a small bow. "And also with you, Abbot. Do I take it that those are the family of Brother Clement?" He nodded towards the waiting couple.

"Yes, you are correct in your assumption. I am about to show them to the sacristy to have some time alone with their son before the service. As you can imagine they are quite distraught. Once they have seen their son, I have suggested that they retire to the guest lodgings for some refreshments until the service begins. Perhaps that would be a good time if you want to speak with them?"

Simon nodded. "I understand. I don't want to distress them further, but it really would be better if I could speak with them whilst they are here." He could tell that Abbot Robert wasn't at all happy with the situation.

"You are already aware of my concerns about your speaking with them in their time of grief. I would ask you again if this could wait until another day?" His voice was stern.

Simon lowered his head for a moment. He had no wish to antagonise Abbot Robert, but if he was to find the murderer of Brother Clement, then he needed to gather as much information as he could, as quickly as possible.

"I'm afraid it cannot wait, Abbot. Not if I am to find the man has done this."

Abbot Robert sighed heavily. "Yes of course, very well.

I do understand. I have been praying that you will find the murderer of dear Brother Clement swiftly; as, I am sure, are his family. I am certain they will understand the need for you to speak with them when I explain it." Abbot Robert paused. "Brother Luke will take you to the guest lodgings, you can wait there until we return from the sacristy."

"Of course."

Simon waited as the Abbot summoned one of the brothers to attend him.

"Brother Luke, please take Sheriff de Hale to the guest lodgings and bring him some refreshments."

The Brother nodded and gestured to Simon to follow him away from the abbey and towards a stone lodging house to the west of the courtyard.

The guest lodging was a separate building within the precinct of the abbey and apart from where the main cloister and dormitories where located. Simon gazed on the building as they approached, he'd never taken that much notice of it before. The building was quite grand, even by the standards of St Marys, Simon observed. Brother Luke showed him into the main hall, where stunning tapestries hung from the walls and there was even glass in the small windows. The chairs and table in front of the large empty fireplace were ornately carved and adorned with embroidered cushions. Simon settled in one of them alongside the table while Brother Luke enquired if he would like some wine. Everything was expensive and high quality and not exactly true to the Benedictine life of poverty, but then Abbot Robert appeared to follow every other Benedictine rule as a pious and obedient servant to God's teaching. He was not one of those power hungry, acquisitive clergy men that Simon was all too well acquainted with. Yet, the Abbey of St Mary was as rich as Croesus. Even if Abbot Robert managed not to delight or gloat in the wealth he commanded, the obvious display of prosperity somewhat jarred with Simon. Yet he knew the Abbot to be a shrewd, thoughtful man who also wielded a lot of power too. Simon had seen how much Abbot Robert obviously cared about the monks in his charge and the reason someone would want to murder one of them had obviously upset him. It vexed Simon too; the thought that a monk with seemingly no enemies should be so brutally killed, had shocked him as well.

It was some time before Abbot Robert returned to the guest lodgings with Lord and Lady de Glanville. Simon rose as they entered the room. It was apparent to him straight away that he needed to give Brother Clements parents a little time to compose themselves. Lady de Glanville, in particular, appeared very distraught, and Simon stood up to offer her his chair, as her husband gently guided her towards the table. Simon watched the grieving woman; she looked frail and inconsolable, her reddened eyes standing out in a pale face. Suddenly, he recalled the death of his wife Ellen, and the pain of her loss surfaced within him, giving him an understanding of what Lady de Glanville must be going through.

Abbot Robert followed the couple into the hall and quietly summoned one of the lay brothers to him, instructing the young man to bring refreshments for all of them. Simon took a step back and let Lord de Glanville comfort his grieving wife and observed the pain and anguish also present in the man's face. He wondered for a brief moment, whether he should leave and visit them at a later date, once they had had chance to bury their son. But he reminded himself that the longer the murder went unsolved the less chance he had of finding the murderer. Abbot Robert settled himself in a chair opposite Lady de Glanville and spoke to introduce his guest.

"Lord and Lady de Glanville, I would like to introduce Sheriff Simon de Hale. He is the man entrusted with discovering the identity of the murderer of your son." Simon moved to the front of Lord and Lady de Glanville and gave a nod of respect to both of them. "Whilst I realise that this may not be the best time for either of you to speak with him," the Abbot continued, "I do beseech you to be strong and try to answer his questions. The more information you are able to give him, the more chance he will have of apprehending the man responsible for this."

Lady de Glanville could barely speak and looked up at Simon with eyes full of sorrow and tears.

"Can't this wait?" She breathed, her pleading gaze looking directly at Simon.

"Madam, if that is what you wish...." Simon started, but Lord de Glanville stopped him and turned to his wife.

"No Margaret, we must do this. I know it is hard my dear, but we want the Sheriff to find the man who did this as soon as possible; and if there is anything we can do to help, then we must do it." He took his wife's hand in his own and tried to comfort her. "We have to do it for Hugh."

Simon watched as Lord de Glanville reassured his wife and after a little while, she nodded in his direction. "I promise I will be as brief as I can," he assured them.

As he spoke, the lay brothers returned and began to lay the table with fish, bread and fruits along with a jug of wine and pewter goblets.

"I am sure that Simons questions can wait until we have had a little sustenance. Let us sit and eat first." Abbot Robert suggested. "I find that the food and wine that our Lord gives us is always restorative."

Simon took his lead from the Abbot and followed him around to the other side of the table facing Lord and Lady de Glanville. He turned his chair at a slight angle away from them, not wanting to feel imposing, or as if he was about to interrogate them. He waited until the wine had been poured and watched as the Abbot paused to say Grace before they commenced their repast. He observed the lusty way that Lord de Glanville enjoyed his wine, while Lady de Glanville barely sipped at it, nor did she take of any food. Grief, he noted, was an unpleasant emotion to observe and even worse to bear.

"Are you able to tell us what you have found out so far?" Lord de Glanville asked and looked at Simon earnestly.

"There isn't much I can tell you at the moment." Simon

was guarded against saying more than he had to. "There are a couple of things that my men are investigating, but I have nothing certain at the moment. I was hoping that you would be able to give me some idea of what kind of man your son Hugh was." He glanced at the Abbot, "The Abbot has graciously told me of the man who was the Benedictine monk here, but I would like to know about what he was like before he became Brother Clement? I understand he was a knight?"

Lord de Glanville nodded. "He was; and he made us very proud. He left us when he was just a boy to become a squire and earn his spurs with a family in Derbyshire. When he was a young boy it was all he ever wanted. He used to watch his elder brother Arthur train, and he wanted nothing more than to be like him. Arthur fought on behalf of the King in the Barons war, you know. We were both distraught when he was killed in service of the King. It was then that Hugh became more determined to be a knight. He was anxious to prove himself as good a soldier as his brother had been, and he did it admirably. When he finally returned to the manor.... well, we were so very proud of him."

Lady de Glanville sobbed quietly on hearing his words and Lord de Glanville put out a comforting hand to soothe her once more.

"As a knight he must have made some good friends; but also, some enemies." Simon observed.

"I suppose we all do at some point in our lives." Lord de Glanville replied and sighed thoughtfully. "I can imagine that you have made a fair few yourself, Sheriff."

Simon nodded, knowing that it was true. There were quite a few men who would be happy to see him with his throat slit. "Given my position, I believe that would be a certainty." He tried to make light of the situation but realised that it wasn't helping. "I was hoping that you might recall anyone who could have been an enemy of your son. Someone he might have had a quarrel or fight with; or an opponent from a tournament with a grudge to bear?"

Lord de Glanville shook his head. "He didn't really talk about that sort of thing." He paused thoughtfully. "He arrived home one time with a couple of men, who he said were friends he'd met on his travels. They stayed with us for a couple of days. They seemed to be good sorts. But, other than that, he never really talked about his life as a soldier and certainly never mentioned anyone who might have a grudge against him."

"And these two men you mentioned, do you know anything more about them?" Simon asked curiously.

"I remember their names; one was called Geoffrey Devereux and the other was Nicholas Montague. But I don't know where they are from."

"So, they weren't local?"

Lord de Glanville shook his head. "No, I think they were both from south of here. They were just heading through and stopped off on the way back to their own manors."

Simon sighed, realising that he was very unlikely to be able to find either of these men. "And what about his friends? Was there anyone who he was close to and that he might confide in?"

"He was close to Peter Beaumont," said Lady de Glanville. She spoke quietly but the sound of her voice still managed to surprise Simon.

"Ah yes, Peter Beaumont." Lord de Glanville added. "Hugh and Peter were friends from being young. They trained together as squires. I suppose if anyone would know more about Hugh's life as a soldier, or if someone had a grudge against him, then it would be Peter." He looked across at Simon. "Do you know the family?"

"I do." Simon replied, as he conjured up an image of Peter Beaumont in his mind. He felt satisfied that at last he had a lead for his investigation. "I will arrange to pay him a visit."

"Apart from that, I can't think of anyone else that knew Hugh."

"I have to ask; I was told that Hugh was betrothed before he took Holy Orders? I can imagine that as a knight, he would have women set their hearts on him. Can you tell me more about this?"

Lord de Glanville smiled, as he recalled. "Aye, he was betrothed. He'd known the lass since he was young; and his mother and I were in the process of arranging the wedding." Lord de Glanville stopped speaking and dropped his head.

Simon could see that whatever he was about to say brought him anguish.

"When Hugh decided that he wanted to take Holy Orders. Well, it was a bit of a surprise."

Lady de Glanville started to sob again, and her husband placed a comforting hand on her arm once more. "It was a shock to everyone when he told us what he wanted to do. It broke his mother's heart; and the lovely lass he was seeing was so distraught. But he told us that he had heard the voice of the Lord calling to him, and that he couldn't deny what he was being asked to do. He just wouldn't be moved." Lord de Glanville sighed heavily and hung his head. "There was nothing either Lady de Glanville or I could do to dissuade him. We just had to come to terms with it."

"And what of the girl he was supposed to marry? What happened to her?" Simon was curious now.

"I don't know. She refused to talk to us after it happened. She just cut herself off from everyone. I don't believe she ever saw him again." He tried a faint smile. "I expect she is happily married now, with a couple of children around her skirts."

It seemed a logical conclusion to Simon. "I expect you're right. Thank you for your time. I am so sorry to have to ask you these questions on what is, such a terrible day for you."

Lord de Glanville nodded in understanding. "All we want, is to know who did this to our son."

"I assure you, I will do everything in my power to find

out who killed your son."

Lady de Glanville raised her head to look directly at Simon. "It's all we ask." She murmured. "Find the man who did this and see to it that he is punished for what he has done."

"I promise you that I will do my best." Simon stood to take his leave of the Abbot and his guests. "If you will excuse me now, I will trouble you no more."

As he took a step to the side, he nodded in respect to Lord de Glanville, before turning to the Abbot and giving a small bow. "Thank you, Abbot Robert for your kindness in allowing me to come here today."

"Peace be with you Simon. We will speak again soon."

With that, Simon went to leave the hall. The meeting had at least given him something to follow up. Hopefully, Peter Beaumont would know a little more about Hughs life before he took his vows and might give him some information about anyone who might have a grudge against the poor fellow. He couldn't help but feel the sadness for Lord and Lady de Glanville and was acutely aware of their grief. However, he knew if he felt that for everyone, he would never be able to do his job. Yet there were some events that happened which affected him far more than the general everyday lawbreaking he dealt with.

Roger de Mowbray stood over the bed and looked down at the frail woman lying there and scowled. Even though it was another warm summer's day outside, his mother had insisted on a fire being lit in the grate, so that the room felt hotter than ever. As she lay there, barely awake under the blankets, she didn't appear to notice the heat or to acknowledge the presence of her son.

Roger grimaced and shook his head as he stood there. All these years he had lived in their shadow, not just his mother but also his father. They had looked down on him, constantly belittled him, and had never seen him as the son either of them had wanted. Roger had been made to feel that he could never, ever be good enough. He was not the big strapping son and capable soldier that his father had desired, nor the consummate Lord, capable of furthering their social standing, that his mother had hoped for.

When his father had tried to tutor him with as sword as a young man, Roger had recoiled at the violence of it; preferring instead to indulge in books and learning the latest poems and stories. As he had grown into a man, he liked to adorn himself with the latest clothes and finery and to indulge in courtly pursuits, which incensed his father even more. Neither was he the obedient and compliant son his mother would have liked; one who had made a good marriage to a Duke or Earls daughter and made her proud of her son through his achievements; though Roger knew it wasn't for lack of trying on his part. He had attended court as much as was allowed, being from a minor, provincial family; and he'd tried his best to woo the most eligible and prettiest women, but they had looked down on him with disdain and brushed off his advances. He had lost count of how many times he had been rejected and also, how many times he had subsequently been told he was a disappointment by his parents. The sense of inadequacy he felt, had festered and transformed into resentment and bitterness as an adult, and now Roger hated both of his parents. He hated his bullying father and his compliant, socially climbing mother. He had never been good enough for either of them; and now he had a plan to be rid of them both.

Roger gazed down at his mother without feeling or compassion. She was ill and had been so, for some months now. Her condition was gradually worsening and the monks from the abbey visited her regularly to administer poppy juice to ease her pain. Her death was unlikely to be remarked on by anyone and would probably be seen as a blessing, that she was at last, free of pain. No-one would question an overdose of poppy juice given to help with the pain when she cried out one night. His father's demise had been a little more difficult to arrange, but he had seen how the two events might tragically combine. A message would be sent to his father, who was visiting his brother in Durham, to inform him of his wife's death; and, as he travelled back to his manor in Overton, a terrible accident would befall him. Everyone knew that the roads could be treacherous and there were all sorts of ne'er-do-wells and cut-throats out there. His father bore the appearance of a well-dressed nobleman, one who would not travel without enough silver pennies to ensure his comfort where-ever he stopped on his travels. There were plenty out there who would be only too happy to relieve him of some of it and Roger had arranged for a known band of these cut-throats to assist him in his plan. He had paid them well, but it was money that he knew he would be amply recompensed with, when he inherited the manor and his parents' wealth.

The terrible loss would be a tragedy that Roger would be happy to play his part in as the grieving son. He would be inconsolable when being told that such a dreadful accident had befallen his father, and especially whilst he was travelling home following the death of his wife. Roger pictured his reaction when the news was delivered to him about his father's murder. He imagined himself sitting down to dinner, when a breathless messenger would arrive to inform him of what had happened; and how he would perform his act of the devastated son so convincingly to all around him.

Roger sighed, looking down at his mother as she slept peacefully and considered the first part of his plan which he intended to enact this evening. His mother had considerable wealth in her own right. Her first marriage had ended when her husband had been killed in battle, and she had been left a young childless widow. With wealth and land as part of her widows' dower, she had been very desirable and when she had married Lord Mowbray, she had retained all of them in her sole ownership. But recently, she had spoken of her intention to bestow this wealth on the Abbey of St Mary, citing her wish to reward those who had cared for her and wanting to ensure their prayers in the future, for her soul. Roger had seen this as yet another snub to him by his mother, and it had made him angrier than ever. Those lands and money were his birthright, they were due to him, and he intended to make sure they remained with him.

Roger had watched as his mother entrusted a letter to the monk who had visited her and knew he had to act quickly. Fortunately, he had managed to relieve the kindly monk of the letter that she had intended to send to the Abbot; and now he needed to be sure that she didn't have time to summon the Abbot when she realised that her letter had not been delivered. He had also been there when his mother had confided her intentions to the Sheriff, which had annoyed him greatly, but he had been unable to prevent it and chided himself over the matter. However, without any document confirming the bequest, her words meant nothing. They were only the ramblings of a very ill and dying woman, whose thoughts were muddled and impaired by poppy juice.

Roger looked down at his mother and felt nothing, she was no more than an obstacle between him and his rightful inheritance, and his place as Lord de Mowbray. He had planned this for so long. He gave a sly smile and walked away. Later that night, he would ensure that he was the one to take his mother her bedtime drink and lace it with poppy juice. That, together with the normal dose administered to her nightly, would be ample to see she passed away peacefully in her sleep. The first part of his plan would then be enacted and all he needed to do afterwards, was to wait patiently for the rest of his scheme to fall into place. Soon, he considered, he would be Lord of this manor and then, with wealth and position, the young eligible noblewomen of this county would not dismiss him quite so casually.

CHAPTER 8

Katherine spent the day in her room planning just how she could escape with Alexander. She considered that, since her argument with her father and Alexanders failed request for her hand in marriage, she had a good reason not to take part in the normal daily events of the castle. If her father was unaware of just how displeased she was with his choice of husband, then her absence from the normal routines would just serve to remind him. Besides, there was no way that she could pretend everything was fine, when her heart was breaking over his decision, and the choice he was forcing her to make. Either she acquiesced to her father's wishes and agreed to be married to Lord Fitzwarren, or she would have to find a way to escape with Alexander and break with her family forever.

Walking across to the window she sat on the padded window seat and leant her head against the cool stone of the surround. Katherine had not been able to get the thought of running away with Alexander out of her head. Jennet had been the first to mention it, as a fear that Katherine would not return home the previous day; and, at the time, Katherine had dismissed the thought. Then, when she had briefly mentioned to Alexander, they had both agreed that it wouldn't work as her father would send his men out to find her as soon as he knew she was missing. But what if he didn't know, at least not for a while? She stared out at the bailey below without really seeing anything, as ideas ran through her mind. It was such a difficult decision to make; she loved her father with all her heart, but she also loved Alexander too and being asked to choose between the two of them was tearing her apart.

Katherine thought of Alexander once again and recalled his touch and how his eyes sparkled when he smiled. She remembered the look on his face when he'd asked her to marry him and knew that the memory of it would stay with her forever. He was her future, and she could not imagine her life without him. But was it enough of a reason to leave her father and her sister behind? Whatever the future held for her now, it was not the one that she wanted or had dreamed of.

When Jennet came into the room to see if Katherine wanted something to eat, she found her mistress deep in thought and believing it to be sadness after saying farewell to Alexander, she didn't press the matter further when Katherine refused.

Katherine managed a small smile at Jennet and then went back to staring out of the window to hide any slight expression on her face that might hint at her inner thoughts. An idea was beginning to take form in her mind and, although excitement started to bubble inside her, she managed to keep her countenance unaffected. She had finally reached a decision that she could not face the rest of her life without Alexander. The price she was going to pay would be high, but the thought of a life without him in it, was far worse. Katherine knew that even if she was married to Lord Fitzwarren, it would be Alexander that held her heart and her love. It would be him, that she dreamed of when she closed her eyes. He would be in her heart forever; and that one thought had reinforced her decision.

It was mid-afternoon when Jennet returned to the room and this time it was to pass on a message from Katherine's father. The reaction she got was not quite what she had expected. Katherine leapt down from the window seat straight away and gave her maid a small, restrained smile.

"Your father has asked that you attend him for dinner this evening." Jennet told her.

"Yes, I suppose I will have to show my face at some time and there is no point in delaying it." Katherine sighed heavily.

"I understand that your father has invited Lord

Fitzwarren to dine with him and that he is going to announce your wedding tonight."

Jennet watched her mistress carefully, almost expecting an outburst at the statement, but it wasn't forthcoming. Katherine did feel the need to shiver with revulsion at the request, but she managed to stop herself just in time, so that Jennet saw nothing.

"Very well. I will attend him as he wishes."

Jennet continued to watch her mistress. "And you have given up all hope of marrying Alexander?" She asked cautiously.

Katherine tried a small smile, but it didn't touch her eyes. "My father wishes me to marry Lord Fitzwarren and, as I have no say in the matter, then there is nothing I can do about it."

She was careful not to lie to Jennet, but she could not hide the slight tone of anger creeping into her voice.

"My lady, your father is doing this for you." Jennet tried to soothe her mistress, acknowledging her resentment. "Your father loves you; he only wants what is best for you."

"I know he does. But he also knows that it is not what I want either."

"Lord Fitzwarren is a good man, Katherine. I know he is not the man that you love, and he is a little older than you, but you will want for nothing as his wife."

Katherine almost snorted at the words but stopped herself. She had no wish to argue with Jennet and neither did she want to confide in her about her plans to run away. For the moment she knew that she had to play along with her fathers' proposal.

"Yes, you are probably right."

"So, you will attend the dinner tonight, as your father wishes?"

Katherine nodded in agreement, even though she clenched her fists at the thought. "Yes, Jennet. Tell my father I will be there."

"Oh, come here, my lady." Jennet took a step towards

Katherine and enveloped her in a hug. "Your father will be so pleased to hear that."

Katherine allowed herself to be enveloped in Jennets embrace. She was the closest thing to a mother that Katherine had known and part of her felt uneasy at keeping her plans from someone who loved her so much. But she was also aware that the less Jennet knew, the less she could tell anyone.

Jennet leant back and put a hand gently on Katherines' face. "I realise this isn't what you wanted Katherine, and I know just how much Alexander means to you." She paused. "Letting him go, cannot have been an easy thing for you to do." She smiled softly at Katherine. "You've shown such a strength of character, and I know your mother would have been very proud of you."

At the mention of her mother, Katherine felt the emotions well up inside her.

"Your father will be so proud of you as well." Jennet told her. "His youngest daughter is showing just what a strong, dutiful and devoted woman she is."

Katherine caught her breath and found herself unable to speak. She so wanted to tell Jennet that it was a deception and part of a bigger plan where she would not marry Lord Fitzwarren, but she managed to keep her silence.

"I will put out your new gown for you tonight, so that you will look your best. I know you will make your father so incredibly happy." Jennet continued.

"Thank you, Jennet. I will do my best not to let my father down."

"I know you won't." Jennet let her go. "And Lord Fitzwarren will be a very fortunate man to have you as his wife."

Katherine took a deep breath as she stood at the entrance to the great hall, taking a moment to compose herself. She was determined to put on a show tonight and she ran her hands across her new crimson gown to ensure that she looked her absolute best. Jennet had combed and dressed her hair so that it fell down her back in ripples of auburn and was held in place by the latest fashionable barbette. She intended to be the centre of attention tonight and not to give anyone present at the dinner, the slightest impression that she had any reservations about her betrothal. Her father might believe that her destiny had been decided, but she had quite a different plan in mind. She lifted her chin and put a false smile on her face as she walked into the room.

Simon watched his daughter enter the hall. He had half expected her to refuse to come down to dinner this evening as he was well aware of her strength of feelings about being betrothed to Lord Fitzwarren. He had anticipated having to summon her to attend the meal, but instead she was here of her own accord, and looking so beautiful that it made him catch his breath. His daughter looked so much like her mother at the time when he had first met her. He recalled the evening so vividly and felt a stab of pain in his heart as he wished that his wife was there with him tonight. He was aware that the chatter around the room had quietened as all eyes watched his daughter approach the main table. She looked so magnificent and every part the noble woman that it made him fill with pride. Katherine stopped in front of him and gave a small curtsey, as she rose, she looked directly at him; it was only then that Simon saw the emptiness in her eyes. Anyone else would have missed it, but, as her father, he knew her far too well not to be able to see it.

"Katherine, I am pleased that you could join us this evening." His voice almost choked with emotion on the words. "May I present Lord William Fitzwarren." He paused as William got to his feet. "Lord Fitzwarren, may I present my daughter Katherine."

Katherine turned her attention to Lord Fitzwarren and gave another small curtsey to him. Although she had seen him before at the banquets her father had hosted, they had never been formerly introduced.

"Lord William it is good to meet you." She maintained her composure.

Lord Fitzwarren gave her a small bow. "And it is good to finally meet you, Katherine. Please do come and sit next me." He smiled as he left his chair and walked towards Katherine to escort her to the seat next to him.

Simon watched Katherine as she graciously accepted Lord Fitzwarren's hand and raised her gaze to look up at her future husband. It was then that he was certain it wasn't just a figment of his imagination; there was a definite, distinct coldness in his daughters' manner.

Katherine sat down to the left of Lord Fitzwarren with her father to the other side of him. She maintained her composure, but her father noticed that she was looking straight ahead without interacting with anyone else. Katherine had vowed to keep her emotions in check and not to show just how angry and distraught she really felt. Smiling falsely, she allowed one of the servants to pour her wine and waited for the food to be served, but other than that, she did not speak. Katherine looked around the hall and noted quite a few people that she knew. For one brief, terrified moment she wondered if Alexander might be there with his father, but as her gaze swept the room, she was relieved to see that neither were present. Either her father had not invited them, or they had not accepted the invitation, for which she was grateful.

Katherine glanced to her side at Lord Fitzwarren, she was determined to dislike him, but it seemed that he was resolute to make it difficult for her. He was kind and attentive to her throughout the dinner and, as she stole a brief glance at him later, she could not deny that he was attractive, but nothing compared to Alexander. Suddenly a vision of him invaded her thoughts and made her draw breath as she disappeared back into her own private thoughts.

"Are you alright my dear?" Lord Fitzwarren enquired.

"Yes, I'm sorry, I think I just drank the wine too

quickly." Katherine smiled at him dismissively, then remembered she was supposed to make a good impression on her future husband. "Please, tell me more about yourself Lord Fitzwarren." She smiled at him again. "If we are to be married then I need to know more about the man who is due to be my husband."

He returned her smile and Katherine listened attentively as he told her about himself. He recounted stories about his life growing up, and as a soldier. He also told her about his first wife and how she had died in an accident when the horses drawing her carriage had become spooked and it had overturned. Katherine had to admit that the more she spoke with him, the more she found it hard to dislike him. He came across as a good and kind man and she realised that he would have made a good husband if things had been different. Katherine was forced to admit that her father's choice of husband would have been acceptable to her; if it wasn't for the fact that she was already in love with someone else. And nothing about the evening, or anything else, could change the fact that Alexander was the man she intended to marry and, as much as she might learn to respect William, she could never love him.

"My lady, you look sad." William observed. "Is there anything the matter?"

Katherine hadn't expected him to be quite so perceptive. She found herself surprised and her brain quickly scrambled to find an excuse.

"Forgive me, Lord Fitzwarren. I was just thinking about my late mother; and how much I would have loved her to be here tonight." She lied convincingly.

"That is a lovely sentiment, my dear. I'm sure she would be very proud of you."

"Thank you, Lord Fitzwarren."

"William please. There is no need to use my title if you are to be my wife."

"William." She corrected herself and managed a small smile. "As you may know my mother died when I was quite young, but I like to think that she would approve of our betrothal."

"I am sure that she would have been very happy to see you wed."

Katherine had to admit that he was very caring in his attitude towards her, and she almost wished that he wasn't. At least that way, she would have something to dislike about him but, at the moment, she couldn't find any reason to hate him.

"William." She paused inquiringly. "As my mother is no longer alive, I was hoping you would allow my personal maid, Jennet, to help me with the arrangements for the wedding. She has been with me since I was born and has been like a mother to me." She looked at him, giving him her sweetest smile.

"Of course, my dear. I see no reason why that should be a problem." He leant in towards her. "I will tell you now, that I would like to be married as soon as possible. I have mentioned this to your father, and he has agreed with me that there is no reason to wait." He waited for her reaction but took her averted gaze as a mark of respect. "To that end, I have already made enquiries about having the wedding at the minster." He beamed with pride.

"But isn't there building work going on at the minster?"

"Yes, but it will not affect our nuptials." He smiled at her with genuine affection.

Katherine felt her heart falter, she had always imagined her wedding taking place in a small private chapel; the one at her father's manor in Northampton, or here at the castle in York. Never had she ever imagined that it would be in somewhere as grand as the minster.

"I understand." She paused. "However, I wonder if it might be appropriate at the moment, surely a smaller venue would be better?"

"Ah yes, you mean the murder of the monk. Such a dreadful thing. But you are a lady of great standing. After all, your father is the Sheriff of the County, and you should have a wedding befitting your position." He smiled at

Katherine.

"Thank you, my Lord."

"What shocks me, is why on earth anyone would want to murder a lowly monk?" William added.

"I have no idea. It's quite dreadful and a real puzzle."

"And does your father have any clue as to who was responsible?"

"No, I don't believe so, as yet. But if anyone can find out who did this, then it is my father." Katherine gave nothing away and wasn't sure whether Lord Fitzwarren was trying to probe her for more information or not. A heavy, uncomfortable silence fell between them for a short while, before it was interrupted by Katherines' father standing up.

"Can I have everyone's' attention!" He waited for the sound of talking to cease and the hall fell into an expectant silence. "I would like to explain, that I have asked you to join me this evening to announce the betrothal of my youngest daughter, Katherine." He gestured towards her, and she found herself blushing as everyone turned to look at her. "It is my greatest pleasure to say that Katherine will be marrying Lord William Fitzwarren, who is also here tonight."

There followed a great deal of cheering and banging of tankards on the tables and Katherine felt very conspicuous in the room, but William placed his hand over the top of hers in reassurance. It was a small gesture and took Katherine by surprise. Her instinct was to snatch her hand away quickly, but she realised that it would be seen as inappropriate in the circumstances. She breathed deeply and forced herself to remain calm and play the part of the happy bride to be. If she was true to herself then she could admit that Lord Fitzwarren was not the enemy, and she should not take her anger and frustration out on him. She found herself appreciating his kindness; he was not a bad man, but neither was he Alexander. No matter what happened she couldn't stop her feelings for Alexander surfacing every time she looked at Lord Fitzwarren.

"I hope you are looking forward to our wedding." William said, once the cheering in the room had subsided. "I would like us to set a date for next week if possible. I am sure your father would have no objection to it. Does that give you enough time to make preparations?"

Katherine felt herself blanche at his words. She had thought that she would have more time to plan her escape.

"Not too soon, I hope." She stuttered, her mind racing. "I would very much like my sister and her husband to be at the wedding. I have sent word to them, but they will be travelling from Northamptonshire, so I must allow them time to get here."

"I did not know that you had a sister."

"Yes, Angharad. She's two years older than I am, and lives with her husband, not far from our family home." Katherine realised she was starting to ramble, but William didn't seem to notice. "We are very close; and I can't imagine getting wed without her being here."

"Of course, of course. I will wait to arrange the date of our wedding until you know how soon she can make it here." He paused for a moment. "I had a sister too once. I was very close to her, so I do understand."

William suddenly looked thoughtful, and Katherine noticed that he had referred to his sister in the past tense.

"Will your sister be joining us for the wedding?"

"No, unfortunately, she died tragically a few years ago." He suddenly looked bereft, and Katherine watched as he stared down at his wine goblet. For some reason she got the distinct feeling that the subject of Williams sister was not something that he wanted to talk about. The mood between them had suddenly changed and Katherine was at a loss for anything to say.

After a short while, William seemed to regain his composure and returned to his previous jovial mood, and the uneasy moment appeared to be quickly forgotten. Katherine watched him as he once more entered into the good-humoured mood of the celebration and the brief dark interlude was forgotten. Katherine continued to play her charade as the dutiful daughter, the last thing she wanted was for anyone to guess that she was less than happy at her forthcoming marriage.

It was late when the last of the guests finally left the hall. William was one of the last to leave and in saying goodbye, he kissed Katherine on the back of her proffered hand.

"I look forward to meeting you again soon. I hope that we might spend some more time together before our wedding so that we may get to know each other better." He smiled kindly at her.

"I am sure that can be arranged." She replied chastely. "But my maid Jennet will have to accompany me to prevent any..... impropriety."

"Of course, I would expect nothing less."

Katherine gave a small curtsey to him and Lord Fitzwarren moved on to give his thanks, and say his farewells, to her father. After that, Katherine found herself alone in the hall with her father. He had watched her carefully throughout the evening and had been impressed with her countenance at the dinner.

"I am glad that you are giving Lord Fitzwarren a chance. He is a good man. And I saw how agreeable you were with him tonight."

Katherine gave him a small sideways glance and spoke curtly. "I am merely being the dutiful daughter as you instructed me to be. Do not think for one moment that anything has changed!"

"What do you mean?" He was genuinely taken aback.

"I still love Alexander," she told him angrily. "I will play the dutiful daughter, as you want me to, for the moment. But don't think that I intend to go through with the wedding. I would rather take the veil than marry Lord Fitzwarren."

Simon felt his mood deflate. He should have known that it was too good to be true. Katherine had never given in so easily before to his requests and he had fooled himself into thinking that this time would be different. His daughter had always challenged him and his decisions in the past, and he now realised that this occasion was just the same. If he admitted it, it was something that he loved about her; her spirited attitude had always made him proud in the past. However, sometimes it could be a little trying, and this was one of those times.

"You *will* go through with the wedding!" He countered her. "I will ensure that you do. Even if I have to stand over you in the church." He breathed deeply and allowed himself to calm down. "Lord Fitzwarren is a good man and, even if you do not care for him now, I am sure you will grow to like him."

"I don't doubt that he is a good man, and, in any other circumstances, he would be a good choice as a husband." Katherine was determined to remain rational in her argument. "But he is not the man for me; not now and not ever. I love another man who, I might remind you, is equally as eligible as William is."

Simon found his patience was being tested. "You must try to forget Alexander. You are to marry Lord Fitzwarren, and that is non-negotiable. I know that you don't love him now, but I hope that, given time, it will change. Just like your mother and I fell in love after we were married." He sounded more forceful than he had intended, but he was beginning to feel exasperated with Katherine.

Katherine was not going to give in, quite so easily. "As I said, I will be the dutiful daughter and I will do as I am told, for the moment. But please do not think that I will ever forgive you for doing this; or, that I will ever forget Alexander." She stood before him; her chin raised in defiance.

"Damn it, Katherine; as if I don't have enough to deal with, following the murder of the monk, I do not want to be at war with you as well. Please do not fight me over this marriage, it will not change anything, and you will not win."

"We will see about that." Katherine turned and stormed out of the hall in a rebellious mood.

Behind her, her father slumped into his chair with a sigh of resignation. This was the last thing he needed. Being at war with his daughter could not have come at a worse time for him. Not only did he have a brutal murder to solve; he also had the Royal Justice due imminently to hold the quarterly assizes in the county. It wasn't what he had expected; he had thought the marriage would be a joyous time, instead it was quickly turning into a nightmare. Simon was conscious that there was a part of him which didn't want to push his daughter into a marriage she didn't want; but as it had already been arranged, there was little that could be done. Katherine would just have to accept it now. Though, if he knew his daughter, it wouldn't be the last that he heard of it. For now, he needed to concentrate on things he could resolve and finding out who had murdered the monk, was his priority.

Simon was still bothered by the argument with his daughter the following morning when he met his deputy Adam in his room, and he found it difficult to focus. He needed to follow up on the friends of Brother Clement, or Hugh de Glanville, as he was known before he joined the Benedictine order at St Marys' Abbey. There was something nagging in Simon's mind that told him the murder was connected to Hugh's previous life. He couldn't put a finger on it, or give any reasonable explanation as to why, it was just a gut feeling; and if his many years of work had taught him something, it was to trust his gut instincts.

"It was a good evening last night." Adam said, as he sat down opposite Simon, then sensing hesitation. "Didn't you think so?"

Simon sighed heavily. "And Katherine was as stubborn as always." He replied gruffly.

Adam chuckled slightly. "Well, that goes without saying. But you must admit that she did play her part last night. She looked every bit the happily betrothed daughter, even if it was done just to please you."

"Was it that obvious?"

"Probably only to those who know her well."

A silence fell between them for a moment and Adam realised it was wise to change the subject.

"How did your meeting with the family of Brother Clement go yesterday?" He asked.

"Yes, sorry." Simon was aware his personal problems were starting to interfere with his work, and he was not about to let that happen. "Hugh's parents were able to give me the name of a man that he was friends with before he took Holy Orders. They thought that he might have some more information about any enemies that Hugh might have made in his life as a soldier."

"Who is the man?"

"His name is Peter Beaumont."

Adam nodded. "I know the family; they have an estate to the north of the city towards Huntington."

"Well then you can come with me. I thought we could go there this morning."

Adam nodded. "Yes, very well."

"But before we leave; tell me how you got on yesterday. Is there anything more to report on Roger de Mowbray?"

Adam pulled a face. "There's nothing more to report. But I have a distinct feeling that he is up to something. He's not done anything solid to incriminate himself in the murder of the monk, but I know there is more going on there. He is guilty of something and I'm going to find out exactly what."

"Keep watching him, whatever he is up to; I want to know about it." Simon stood up and reached across for his sword before fastening it onto his belt. "Right. If we set out now to pay Simon Beaumont a visit, then we should be back before it is time to eat."

Adam followed Simon out of the room and downstairs into the bailey. It was fresher outside than it was in the castle and, as they waited for the groom to saddle their horses, both men relaxed for a brief time in the cool shade.

A BROTHERLY DEVOTION

The constant heat of the last few weeks seemed to have permeated everywhere in the castle now. It was as if the very stones of the building had become saturated with all the heat of the last few months and were now radiating it outwards, even during the night. It was refreshing to be outside in the slightly cooler air of the morning.

Simon looked around and was grateful to see that there was no sign of his daughter in the bailey. He hoped that she had given up her daily ritual of escaping from the castle to ride out into the surrounding fields. Even if she had Grenulf with her, it was not right for her to be riding out alone and she could easily be attacked or killed, for no other reason than she was the daughter of the Sheriff. Simon reminded himself to speak with Jennet about it. He needed to make sure that Katherine did not do it again and, if anyone could persuade her not to, it was Jennet. For now, he was grateful that he didn't have to face another run in with her, like the one they'd had the previous evening.

The ride out of the city to the north did not take long. It was an opportunity for Simon and Adam to talk more about the murder and discuss what they had found out so far which, other than their suspicions about Roger de Mowbray, wasn't much. Simon had been hoping to have found out who the owner of the grey horse was; or even find the dagger with its' missing pommel, but neither had transpired so far. He was still at a loss to know why anyone would have wanted to murder Brother Clement, or Hugh de Glanville, as he formerly was. He couldn't imagine why anyone would have a grudge against a penitent monk; and that made him more certain that it was something to do with Hugh's past. Either that or the monk had just been an innocent caught up in a grudge against the Abbey. It was no secret that the Abbey of St Mary's was incredibly wealthy and there was always unrest against the monks who supposedly pledged a vow of poverty, but had everything they needed. There was resentment as to how the monks grew fat in winter, whilst the peasants struggled to feed their families.

"Was there any more gossip in the city about the murder?" He asked Adam.

"Nothing that I would give any credit to. Though there is a growing number of people saying that the monks had it coming. Perhaps not that monk in particular, but the monks in general."

"I was just thinking that the only other reason for the murder could be disquiet against the Abbey in general. If someone were trying to send a message to the Abbey and, in particular, to the Abbot, then perhaps Brother Clement was an easy target."

Adam considered it for a moment. He had his reservations where the religious organisations were concerned. He was a reverent man, who believed in the word of the Lord, but did not view this as an excuse for the wealth of the church. "And if it were to do with the Abbey, do you think they are listening?"

Simon shook his head. "I'm not sure. The Abbot certainly doesn't think it has anything to do with them in general, and he seems blind to the people's feelings of discontent."

"But he must be aware that the disquiet is growing?"

"If he is, then he does not recognise it, or it doesn't worry him." Simon then added. "Don't get me wrong, Abbot Robert is a good man, and I have a lot of respect for him. But sometimes I think he is a little too wrapped up in monastic life and unaware as to what is going on outside the walls of the Abbey. Perhaps he thinks that it's the likes of you and me that will prevent anything untoward happening to him and his monks."

"He may have a shock to learn what the people are actually saying then."

"I fear you may be right."

"And it's going to get worse," Adam observed. "The people barely got through last winter and this spring; and now it looks as though there will be very little to harvest this year as well. The fields are like dust, the river is running low, and the animals are starving too."

"I know. I can see it." Simon observed as they rode past another field where the crop was withering in the heat.

The landscape around them was quite flat, and the grasslands and ridge and furrow fields stretched out on both sides of the track, so that they could see for miles in every direction. Everywhere around them, the ground looked parched and the grass brown, whilst the crops were withered and stunted. The small manor house was easy to see, rising up from the flat landscape away to their right. As Simon and Adam rode in through the open outer gate, a man looked up from his work mucking out a stable. He put his pitchfork down and wiped his hands on his shirt as he approached the two visitors. He was a young man, big and muscular and from his tanned appearance, it was clear that he spent most of his time outside.

"Can I help you sire?" He asked approaching the two men.

"I'm Simon de Hale; Sheriff of Yorkshire and I'm looking to speak with Peter Beaumont. I understand that he resides here." Simon dismounted and held on to the reins of his horse as Adam joined him.

"Aye sire, he does that. But he's not here right now." The man approached the horses and stroked the muzzle of Simon's mount.

"And when do you expect him to return?" Simon asked.

As they were speaking a well-dressed gentleman came out of the main door of the manor and strode towards them.

"George, what's happening?"

Simon and Adam turned their attention to view the approaching gentleman. Simon could see from his attire that he was likely to be the owner of the manor and from his age, that he was probably the father of Peter Beaumont. But it wasn't Simon that the man was looking at, it was Adam.

"Adam de Burgh, well I never!" The man exclaimed. "My apologies, I didn't recognise you." He came over and exchanged a large bear hug with Adam; the two men obviously pleased to see each other.

"Lord Beaumont," Adam greeted him, "it's good to see you again."

"And you. When did we last meet? It must be several years ago now; Christmas the year before, wasn't it?"

"Yes, I believe it was," Adam smiled and gestured towards Simon. "Lord Beaumont, can I introduce you to Sheriff Simon de Hale."

Lord Beaumont turned his attention to Simon. "Sheriff de Hale, it is good to finally meet you. Your reputation precedes you." The man smiled and held out a hand to Simon, which Simon shook in welcome.

"Lord Beaumont, we were hoping to speak with your son Peter." Simon said. "Is he at home?"

Lord Beaumont shook his head. "No, I'm sorry he is away at the moment. He's down at my brothers' place in Derbyshire. Why don't the two of you come inside, the least I can do is offer you some refreshments and we can talk some more."

Simon, looked across at Adam and then nodded his head. "Aye, thank you, that would be good."

"George, take the horses." Lord Beaumont instructed his servant. "And you two, please come with me."

Simon and Adam followed Lord Beaumont across the courtyard towards the stone stairs leading up to an open door. At the top of the steps the door led through into a large, airy hall. The room was lavishly appointed, with fine carved furniture and beautiful wall hangings. The discreet outside of the manor belied the sumptuous internal decoration and Simon noted this approvingly.

"Now, why do you want to speak with my son?" Lord Beaumont asked as he indicated chairs set around the empty fireplace.

"You may have heard that a monk was brutally murdered in the city a few days ago."

"I did, but you can't believe that Peter had anything to do with that?" Lord Beaumont sounded shocked.

Simon shook his head. "No, it's not that. We have no reason to suspect Peter was involved at all. But we understand that he was a friend of the monk who was killed. Before he took the cowl the monk was known as Hugh de Glanville, and I understand from his parents that Peter and Hugh were good friends and served together." Simon told him as they sat down.

"Hugh de Glanville." Lord Beaumont mused. "Well, that's a name from the past. I didn't realise that the monk who was killed was him, dreadful business. But you are correct, Peter and Hugh were good friends and served together as soldiers. So, that is why you want to speak to Peter?"

"Yes, I wondered if his murder might be connected to something in Hugh's past, and I thought that Peter might be able to help."

"My son and Hugh were good friends, but Peter never spoke of what they faced in their travels. Yet, I can easily see that there might have been an encounter at some point, where someone might have borne a grudge against Hugh."

A servant arrived at his masters' side to inquire whether they would require refreshments and Lord Beaumont asked him to bring them some ale and fruits.

"I spoke with Hugh's family yesterday and they thought that Peter might be able to give me some insight into Hugh's friends; and also, his enemies, if he had any." Simon added.

"Yes, I see. Well, it really is Peter you need to speak with then. I'm afraid there's nothing I can tell you that would be of any help." Lord Beaumont paused as a servant arrived with refreshments for all of them. "I know Hugh stayed here on several occasions and I have to say that we all liked him. He was a very amiable man and a good soldier, from what I hear. But apart from that I don't really know anything more about him."

"When do you expect Peter to return?"

"He is due back in a couple of days."

"Could you ask him to send word to me when he is

home. I do need to speak with him."

"I will ensure that he does."

"Thank you, I appreciate your help."

Simon was slightly deflated that the meeting had not yielded anything, and felt thwarted in his endeavours to bring the murderer of the monk to justice. But he knew he should have more patience. If there was anything he had learnt in his time as Sheriff, it was that he needed patience. But he was a driven man and needed to resolve things and see justice prevail. It annoyed him when he couldn't achieve it.

CHAPTER 9

The wooden gates of the abbey were open, and the monks were busy unloading provisions in the precinct. Merchants were coming and going through the gate, and it was another busy day at the abbey. The monks did not hear the approaching noise until it was too late, and by that time, they were unable to close the gates to keep out the angry mob. The already anxious monks were terrified as the men stormed past them into the abbey precinct. The angry men were armed with pitchforks and axes, and a few of them were pulling carts behind them. All were shouting, and some were uttering obscenities as they confronted the scared monks. Others manhandled the monks, pushing them out of the way and sending some of the Brothers falling to the ground. Suddenly there were shouts from one man at the head of the group.

"Do not harm any of them. We are not here to kill anyone. We just want to take back what is ours."

"To the stores!" The yell went up and the mob started to move together towards the buttery, pantry, and store buildings. The men hauling the carts were pushed through to the front and directed to the doors of the pantry and buttery.

The monks tried to stop the men, but they were pushed away and threatened with pitchforks. The lowly monks who were used to more gentle employment, in prayer or writing of manuscripts, were very unprepared for such a hostile invasion. The men before them were rough and threatening, taking their anger out on the monks, and forcefully manhandling them when the monks tried to object. In turn, the monks were terrified and scared and eventually huddled together to evade persecution.

The Abbot was in his room working on the abbey accounts. He heard the commotion, but didn't think too much of it until there was a knock at his door, and Brother Michael entered the room looking flushed and concerned.

"What is it?" Abbot Robert enquired.

"We are being attacked!"

Abbot Robert stood up straight away. This wasn't right; not right at all. Not only had one of his brethren being brutally murdered, but now he had to deal with the abbey being attacked. He had not expected this to happen, and he intended to put a stop to it at once. He quickly followed Brother Michael from his office and around the cloister, to the precinct in front of the abbey. As he stepped out on the stone steps of the abbey in front of the west door, he was shocked at the sight before him.

"Stop this at once!" He yelled, but his voice was lost amongst the melee in front of him. "I forbid you to take anything. How dare you defile the house of God!"

It was quickly obvious that there was nothing he could do to halt the onslaught of the angry mob.

"Brother Michael, I need you to go to the castle at once and bring Sheriff de Hale here. Tell him what is happening."

Brother Michael nodded and managed to find a way around the baying mob and slip out of the gate. He quickly made his way as fast as he could, whilst still maintaining some decency, towards the castle to fetch the Sheriff and his men.

Simon was in the bailey with Adam, having just returned from their visit to Lord Beaumont when they heard the shouting and saw Brother Michael arrive, looking exhausted and quite dishevelled.

"What is it?" Simon asked, approaching the monk.

"It's...the.... Abbey." Brother Michael managed between gasps for breath. "Men.... broken in... threatening the Abbot." The slightly rotund monk bent over as he tried to catch his breath. "Please.... you need to go quickly."

Simon patted him on the back and turned to face Adam.

"Get as many men as you can together; we ride out

there straight away."

With that he was striding out towards the stables, where the stable-boy still had his horse in hand. Adam nodded and shouted at his men to mount up quickly. Simon was already astride his horse and waited for Adam to return and join him. Once Adam and the rest of the men were ready, he spurred his horse forward and rode out of the castle gates. The group of armed soldiers followed the Sheriff and his deputy out of the castle and went along the road through the centre of the city to the west. The streets were busy with people doing business or talking and they moved quickly out of the way as the horsemen rode past them at speed. The people stared after them with curiosity and then started to gossip as to what was going on.

When Simon pulled his horse to a stand-still outside the gates of the abbey, he could see men running towards him, their arms laden with all manner of provisions. The men seemed intent on quickly making their escape with their ill-gotten gains and Simon directed his men to stop them. Then he pushed his horse into the crowd inside the abbey precinct and seeing it was worse than he had imagined, he turned around to address his men.

"Close the gates and guard them." He ordered his men, then turning to Adam he barked out instructions. "Take some of your men and secure the stores. Make sure everything that's been taken is returned." Simon then rode through the crowd to the front and brought his horse to a standstill at the bottom of the steps up to the main Abbey building. He remained mounted, knowing that it gave him a height advantage over the mob in front of him and that, in these circumstances, it was all about maintaining a position of power. Being seated on a lofty horse gave him an advantage and he did not want to lose it just yet. Simon pulled his horse around so that he could face Abbot Robert who was, at that moment, growing angrier with the crowd.

"You are defiling the house of God!" The Abbot was shouting. "Your actions are blasphemous. It is against all

Holy law to steal from Gods House."

"And where is the vow of poverty that you are supposed to have taken, Abbot?" Came the voice from the front of the mob.

Simon looked around and quickly identified the man who he had previously seen issuing orders to the mob. He noticed straight away that the man wasn't dressed as a serf, peasant or yeoman, but a merchant with a fine tunic and stout leather boots; not the sort of man who he had expected to be at the forefront of such a disturbance. Simon didn't recognise him but could see instantly that he had the mob following his every word; and he knew that the man was probably the one responsible for whipping up the resentment amongst some of the city folk and inciting them to come here this morning.

"You and your monks grow fat, whilst everyone else is struggling to find enough food to live on." The man shouted again. "Your stores are overflowing, whilst ours lie empty. Where is your Christian charity now, Abbot?" The crowd behind him roared in agreement, and there was shaking of fists and pitchforks in the air.

The mob were in no mood to be placated or calmed, and Simon could sense the anger rising once again amongst them. Whipped into a frenzy by their leader, they were intent on exacting their version of justice. It was obvious to Simon that the man in front of him had traded on peoples' fears and grievances and kindled the unrest that had now manifested itself in this riot. Simon knew that these things did not happen quickly, and the discontent had been building within the city for weeks now. He had heard rumours, but there had been nothing to prepare him for the angry mob he now found in front of him.

"We are the people who work every day to provide for our families, and then the church takes part of our harvest so its brethren can feast whilst we starve. Even when we have nothing to eat, there is no compassion from the church. You say that you pray for our souls; well, how about feeding our bodies as well? That way we can continue to provide our tithe for you in the future?"

A cheer rose from the crowd and the man at their head raised his hand to silence them.

"What do you say Abbot?" He demanded. "Will you not take care of your flock? Or is the church indifferent to the suffering of its' people?"

The spokesman for the mob, buoyed by the support of his peers, made to move up the steps to confront the Abbot. As he moved, Simon caught sight of a dagger tucked into the side of his belt and he rounded his horse to prevent the man getting any closer. He managed to manoeuvre his horse in between the Abbot and the man, the horses head knocking the man to the side.

"There will be no drawing of blood today. Simon shouted down at the man, pushing his horse further against him, so that he was knocked off balance. He looked up and quickly signalled to two of his armed men to attend him. As they came forward, he indicated to the man in front.

"Seize him! Make sure you get that dagger off him and keep hold of it." He said, then turning on the man he added. "And you will now answer to the law of the land for threatening the Abbot and inciting this riot."

The man struggled and tried to resist being held by the guards, but they were burly men and quite used to restraining belligerent felons.

"Don't you understand." He addressed Simon. "The people have had enough. We won't be silenced any longer."

As they saw their leader being restrained, the momentum behind the mob started to dissipate and they backed away slightly, unwilling to be the next to be arrested.

"This isn't the way to do it." Simon replied. "Threatening the Abbot will not help you. And as for the rest of you." Simon turned his horse to face the crowd. As he moved, the unsettled horse snorted and side-stepped agitatedly. "Unless all of you want to be arrested and spend some time in the dungeons at the castle, then I suggest you leave here this instant, and do not *EVER* threaten the Abbot or the abbey ever again. If you do, I will personally see to it that you are found and publicly whipped for your insubordination."

There were murmurings of discontent amongst the crowd, who had visibly taken a step back after their leader had been seized.

"It seems that the Sheriff is on the side of the Abbot and not for the people!" Their leader shouted as he struggled with the two men holding him, then turned to address Simon. "What do you know about the reason for us being here? You have no idea what it's like to wake up every day feeling hungry and to watch your children beg for scraps. You live a privileged life." The mob were buoyed again and cheered in agreement. The man could see he still had the momentum. "The people of this city are living hand to mouth with no certainty as to where their next meal will come from. There will be little to harvest in the fields next month and the cattle and pigs have grown thin or died because there is too little to feed them."

"And as a merchant, I doubt you will suffer the same as the farmer or a villein." Simon retorted looking down on him.

The man clearly felt offended by the comment, he stopped struggling and tried to raise himself to stand at his full height. "I speak for the people. They need someone; a man of position and reputation to speak for them."

"And what do you personally gain from this?" Simon asked, being well aware that very few people did something for nothing. There was usually some reward for their endeavours.

The crowd were waiting in anticipation for the man to defend himself against the accusation.

"I do this for my family and my friends. Surely that is as good a reason as any. And certainly, a more charitable reason than the church can admit to."

"You defile the abbey grounds and the word of the Lord." The Abbot shouted.

"And didn't the Lord say that 'the generous will themselves be blessed, for they share their food with the poor?'"

Simon realised then that the man they had restrained was a learned man, capable of reading and understanding scripture.

"How dare you quote the Lords words to me." The look of anger on the Abbots' face told Simon that the confrontation needed to be diffused as quickly as possible.

For a short while, neither man moved, both standing firm. Then Simon, kicked his horse forward; he had had enough of this now. He turned towards the crowd.

"Leave here now." He instructed them. "My men will arrest you, if you are not gone from the abbey straight away."

At first the crowd didn't move, but then slowly, one by one they started to retreat and leave the grounds of the abbey by the west gate. As they left, Simon noticed Adam coming towards him. Along with more of his guards, they were escorting two men who were none too happy about being seized and held.

"These two were beating the cellarer and another monk." He said roughly. "Not content with taking food from the kitchen, it seems they were spoiling for a fight as well."

"Are the monks badly hurt?" Abbot Robert asked with concern.

"They've been badly beaten, but they will live." Adam replied to the Abbot.

Abbot Robert shook his head. "This is most shocking. How dare these people come into the abbey and assault our brethren. It is unbelievable that they would do such a thing."

Simon could clearly see how the events had frightened him. The fear and alarm were evident on the Abbot's face. Simon knew this event must have caused him more consternation, coming so soon after the murder of Brother Clement. The Abbot and his monks were now living in fear, and it was up to Simon to ensure that they were safe.

"Take those two, along with this one, back to the castle and I will deal with them later." Simon said, finally dismounting from his horse and approaching the Abbot on the steps of the abbey.

The crowd were starting to disperse, and calm was slowly being restored to the abbey grounds. The threat had been quashed, at least for the moment.

"Close the gates." Simon ordered his men; then turning to the Abbot. "I suggest that it may be prudent to keep them closed for a while, Abbot Robert."

"Yes, yes of course. I agree." Abbot Robert was clearly shaken by events. "I can't believe that this has happened; so soon after the dreadful murder of Brother Clement." Abbot Robert tucked his hands into the opposing sleeve of this vestment and shook his head as he spoke. "I have never, in all my years, seen such a display of anger and malice against the church."

Simon could understand how stunned he must be at two terrible incidents, happening so close together. Were these just isolated events or the start of something more worrying, that would manifest itself increasingly over the rest of the summer? Simon couldn't help at being more than a little bemused by the Abbots reaction though. Did he really have no idea what was going on in the fields beyond the abbey? Was he so insulated by the running of the abbey and the daily offices, that he couldn't see what was happening to the people on the land and in the villages around the city?

"Let's hope that this is the end of it." Simon tried to reassure him, but even as he spoke the words, he didn't believe it.

"I do hope so." Abbot Robert paused. "Thank you for your assistance in dealing with this matter."

Simon nodded and wondered if he should broach the

subject on his mind. "You do understand that the people are scared that there will be no harvest again this year?" He tried to remain unbiased in his words.

"I do; but this is not the way." The Abbot protested. "Is that what this is all about? Is that why Brother Clement was murdered?"

"It may be." Simon restrained himself from saying what he wanted to. "I will know more, once I have questioned the men we've arrested."

Abbot Robert nodded understandingly. "Please report back to me on what you find out? If these men were responsible for the appalling murder of our dear Brother, then I need to know."

Simon nodded. "I will do." He looked around as Adam assembled the men and their captives ready to leave. "As I said earlier Abbot, it would be a good idea to keep the gates closed; at least for the immediate future."

He went to mount his horse and then indicated to Adam that they should leave. "I will call on you once I have found out more."

Simon's mind was occupied by what had happened at the Abbey. It disturbed him that events had escalated quite so quickly. First the murder of Brother Clement and now the riot; he only hoped that things were not going to get worse. He had no idea if the two incidents were connected at all, but it was impossible to ignore the possibility. As much as he admired and respected the Abbot, his seeming obliviousness to the plight of his flock worried Simon. He didn't doubt that Abbot Robert was a good and Holy man of God, but he was a man whose life did not seem to extend beyond the reaches of the abbey precinct and out to the people he was supposed to serve. As Simon rode through the city following Adam and the arrested men, he looked closely at the people they passed along the way. Busy buying and selling goods they stopped and fell silent as the Sheriff and his deputy went by and looked on the men in their custody. Simon could sense the heightened feelings of the people and the murmurs of discontent as they rode past. He found himself observing things that he would normally have paid no attention to, but today seemed to have more importance. The woman carrying the basket of vegetables that would have been full to overflowing but now was half empty. The man walking towards the market leading a cow that looked thin, and half starved. The more he looked; the more he saw the effect that the endless weeks of summer heat and lack of rain, were having on the people of the city. It was a pity that the Abbot couldn't see it too.

Once back at the castle complex, he went straight to his office where Adam joined him.

"Not quite the morning we were expecting." Simon said.

"I know." Adam replied, shaking his head. "It's not good."

"Have any of the men said anything yet?"

"Other than curses and promises of what they will do to me once they're released; nothing else useful."

Simon poured them both a tankard of ale and handed one to Adam. They both sat down either side of the desk in Simon's office and Simon leant back in his chair.

"Do you think these men are the same ones that might have killed the monk?" He asked.

Adam shook his head. "No, they're just local lads, who have whipped up this frenzy amongst the city folk. I don't see them as murderers."

"Do you know who any of them are?"

"Aye, I know John of Askham; the one who was challenging you and the Abbot. He's a wool merchant and full of himself. He's always got something to say, but he's not a threat. He's the sort of bloke who's got a big chip on his shoulder about everything."

Simon nodded in understanding. "Doesn't sound like you think much about him?"

"He can be a bit of a hot-head and a troublemaker; but a murderer: no."

"And the others?"

"They're just local men. I've seen one of them around, but neither of them has been in trouble before." He paused. "I think they were just motivated by the cause. There is a lot of unrest out there, everyone can see that the harvest this year won't be a good one. The people are scared and worried." He took a drink of the ale. "Can't the Abbot see that?"

Simon sighed heavily and shook his head. "I don't think he has any idea."

"I know you have a lot of respect for the Abbot, but he needs to see what is going on outside the Abbey precinct."

"I agree, but there's nothing we can do to change that. We just have to deal with this mess." He paused for a moment. "Let them all sit in the dungeons for a while; it will give them a taste of what they might be facing. And it will also give me some time to get on with the rest of my work."

"Shall I leave them down there all day?"

"No, just until later this afternoon, give them some time to consider their actions."

It wasn't yet noon and Simon felt had already had enough to deal with. He gave up a silent prayer that the rest of his day would be more trouble-free.

The first thing that alerted Roger de Mowbray to what had happened, was the raised voices of the servants. He was finishing putting on his tunic and ensuring his hose looked perfect, when there came a knock on the door to his room. He paused for a moment before going to open it, not wanting to appear too eager.

A flustered maid addressed him. "Please sire, you need to come at once."

"Why?" He inquired. "What's happened?"

"It's your mother sire. You need to come at once."

"What is it this time?" He appeared exasperated. "Has she refused to take the poppy juice again?"

The woman did not reply but scuttled along, ahead of Roger, leading him to the room that his mother occupied.

The bed-chamber was still quite dark with the shutters closed and the candles giving the only light. It felt eerily quiet, and Roger felt the hairs on the back of his neck prickle as he walked in. The servants remained at the door as Roger went inside and he felt a sense of apprehension as he approached his mother, lying motionless in the bed. He reached out a hand to touch his mother's and the cold firmness of the skin, told him that she had died. It was just as he had planned. He steadied himself, ready to play the next part of his charade.

"Oh no. Oh mother!" He exclaimed, then turning to face the assembled servants. "Send someone to the abbey, as quickly as you can. I can't believe this has happened. She must receive their offices and find mercy and blessing from the Lord on her final journey." He sank to his knees at the side of her bed and leant his head on the coverings and appeared to weep in reverence for his deceased mother.

After the events of the morning, Abbot Robert had shut himself in his room trying to regain some composure and understand what had happened over the last few days. He closed his eyes and offered his thoughts and prayers to God, asking that he be guided to understand the trials he was being subjected to. He could not help but question if the two events were related and it made him feel uneasy to think that more danger may await both him and his monks in the coming days and weeks. There was nothing more that he could do, other than to offer himself and the care of his monks to the Lord and ask that they be kept safe. He was deep in contemplation when there was a tentative knock on his door, and he hoped that it was not to inform him of further unrest within the abbey grounds. He summoned the person outside to enter and a young monk, who he was not overly familiar with, hesitantly entered the room.

"Forgive me father for disturbing you," he greeted the abbot and bowed deeply in front of him. "I did not want to interrupt you; only the messenger did say it was urgent, and I didn't think that you would want to refuse them, considering where they had come from."

The young monk was clearly nervous at being in the presence of the Abbot.

"What is it Brother...?"

"Brother Eustace, Abbot." The monk informed him.

"Ahh yes, Brother Eustace." He now recognised the young monk. "Now, where is the messenger who wishes to see me?" He kept his voice calm, trying to reassure the anxious young monk. It seemed that the events of the morning had made them all very uneasy.

Brother Eustace looked vaguely surprised for a moment as he processed the words. "Oh yes, the messenger. He's outside; shall I show him in?"

Abbot Robert breathed deeply to conquer the faint irritation he felt. He knew it wasn't Brother Eustace's fault; he was young and unused to being in the presence of his superior.

"Yes, I think that would be a good idea." He gave a small smile to the monk, who then nodded and walked back out of the room. A moment later he reappeared, this time accompanied by another young man.

"This is the messenger, Lord Abbot. He's come from the manor of Lord and Lady de Mowbray."

"Thank you, Brother Eustace." The Abbot signalled that he was to remain in the room. "How can I help you?" He asked the visitor.

The man gave a small nod of respect. "Roger de Mowbray has sent me, Abbot. It seems that his mother, Lady Maud de Mowbray, died during the night, and he has asked that you might send one of the Brothers to attend her."

The news surprised the Abbot a little. He was aware Lady Maud had been unwell, but he hadn't expected her to pass away quite so quickly.

"Yes of course, we will." He nodded and turned to address Brother Eustace. "Brother, will you go and find

Brother Michael and ask him to join me here."

The monk nodded and quickly left the room.

"I am very sorry to hear the news of Lady Maud. She was a good woman and a benefactor of the abbey. I imagine that her son is quite distressed at her sudden death?"

"Indeed, he is, Lord Abbot." The man was quite articulate and spoke well. "His father, Lord de Mowbray is away visiting his brother in Durham at the moment as well, so he is alone at the manor to deal with this."

"Then we will ensure that he is supported in his grief," the Abbot reassured him.

At that moment, Brother Michael appeared at the door.

"Come in Brother Michael." The Abbot summoned his most trusted monk to him.

Brother Michael approached and gave a small bow to the Abbot. He was still looking somewhat dishevelled and exhausted from his earlier run to the castle to summon the Sheriff.

"This is a messenger from the De Mowbray manor at Overton." He indicated the young man in front of him. "It appears that Lady Maud died during the night, and we have been asked to attend her. I would like you to be the one to accompany him back to the manor and to perform the necessary rites over her."

"Very well, Lord Abbot. I will prepare and leave immediately." He gave another small bow to the Abbot and then indicated for the young man to follow him.

The Abbot looked up and realised that Brother Eustace was still there.

"Was there something else? He inquired.

Brother Eustace paused for a moment, then shook his head. "No Lord Abbot."

The Abbot maintained his gaze and Brother Eustace suddenly realised that he was being dismissed. He left the Abbots room and then realised that he had not closed the door and returned to hastily pull it shut.

The Abbot shook his head and sighed. The young monk

meant well, but he was a simple lad and not destined to be one of the great characters, or spiritual leaders of the Abbey.

CHAPTER 10

Roger de Mowbray sat at his desk and tried to compose the letter he needed to send to his father. In his mind, he had gone over the words many times as he planned the events which were now unfolding, but when it actually came to writing it, the words would not come. At the fourth attempt he managed to finish the letter and waited for the ink to dry before folding it and affixing his wax seal on it. On the front he wrote his father's name and then got up from the desk and shouted for a servant to attend him.

"I need you to arrange for a messenger to ride out to my uncle's manor in Durham," he told the man who appeared at the entrance to his room. "I must get a message to my father as soon as possible to inform him of my mother's demise."

"Of course, sire." The man accepted the letter from him.

"Can you tell the man to make all possible speed. I don't want my father to be away any longer than is necessary."

"I understand. I will ensure the messenger is instructed." He bowed and went to leave the room, then asked. "Is there anything more I can do for you, sire?"

"Thank you, but no." He gave a small smile. "I would like some time alone now."

"Of course, sire."

"Oh, but do let me know as soon as the monk arrives from the Abbey. I want to be with him when he performs the rites for my mother."

The servant nodded and closed the door behind him.

Roger went back to his desk and sat down in the chair. Then, pouring himself a goblet of wine, he leant back and put his feet up on the desk. He congratulated himself on the first part of his plan being implemented so smoothly. To everyone at the manor, he was now the grieving son, and it pleased him that no one there suspected anything was awry.

After the servants had informed him earlier that morning of his mother's death, he had gone to see her and played the part of the distressed son. At her bedside he had wept, letting the tears fall readily. The servants who had accompanied him into the bedchamber had respectfully retreated from the room to leave him alone. But, as he knelt at the bedside, he looked at her and was surprised to see her appearance. With her face no longer lined with pain, she looked younger than he recalled and there was a peaceful countenance that surprised him. For a brief moment he wondered if he had done the right thing, but then he chided himself for being so weak.

Roger had waited at the bedside for a little while, until he was sure none of the servants were around or spying on him. Then he quickly retrieved the small vial of poppy juice from the chest at the side of his mother's bed and slipped it into the front of his tunic. He would make sure that the vial was suitably disposed of, and then there could be no chance of him being questioned about just how much of it had been used. After a short time, he had risen and made his way to leave the room. Taking a deep breath, he made sure that he looked suitably bereft as he opened the door to the hall. Outside, the servants had congregated and took a step back as he emerged.

He had instructed one of them to go immediately to the abbey and summon the Abbot, or one of the monks to attend his mother and say prayers for her. Then he told a servant to keep the shutters in the room closed and the candles lit. He wanted the room to remain like that until after the monk had attended his mother and said prayers for her soul. Following that, her body would be moved to their private chapel where she would remain until his father returned.

Except that Roger knew his father would not be returning. He had ensured that this would not happen. Leaving the manor the previous evening to ride out, he had given payment to a group of mercenaries. A small payment to each of them now and the rest once he had been informed that they had succeeded in their undertaking. They had been instructed to follow the messenger he would send to his uncle's manor near Durham and then to wait until his father, and his party, left on their journey back to York. They were to waylay the party on one of the wooded roads along their journey home and to attack and rob the group. Roger had given them explicit instructions that his father was not to survive the attack. By the time the alarm was raised, the men would be long gone with their rewards. Roger had arranged to meet them later with the remainder of their payment, once he knew that his father had been killed.

Roger smiled to himself as he drank the wine from his goblet and mulled over the plan. Everything was going exactly as he had envisioned. Relieving the monk of the letter his mother had written to the Abbot, had been unfortunate. He hadn't expected his mother to put her intentions in writing and send it quite so quickly. But he had dealt with that efficiently and, other than his mother telling the Sheriff of her intentions, there had been nothing else to concern him. Roger didn't allow himself to worry greatly over the sheriff being told about the bequest. He would find her words easy to dismiss as the ramblings of an ailing, drugged woman. The sheriff had probably paid no attention to her words either, as he had visited specifically to inquire about the monk who had been murdered and would likely have paid no heed to anything else. The death of the monk had been unexpected, but it would prove useful, and there was nothing to connect him to the murder.

Roger was still in his room when the servant came to announce the arrival of Brother Michael and Brother Julius. It pleased Roger greatly that the Abbot had seen fit to send two monks to pray for the soul of his mother. It was a mark of their importance in the city and of her previous, overly generous gifts to the Abbey. He gathered himself and tried to think of sobering thoughts to make himself look suitably downcast and sorrowful, instead of the joyous sense of freedom and anticipation that made his heart leap.

"Good day, Brothers," he nodded in sombre greeting.

"Good day sire. May God look down on you and bless you at this time of great sadness." Brother Michael said reverently.

"Thank you, your thoughts and blessings are appreciated. I shall take you to my mother. We have left her, as she was found, asleep in her bedchamber." He indicated for the monks to follow him.

Brothers Michael and Julius walked behind him across to the main solar where the bedchamber of Lady Maud was located. The room was dark compared to the brilliant sunshine that flooded the great hall. The candles that had been lit around the room sent eerie shadows across the walls and a ghostly calm required all speech to be in hushed voices.

Brother Michael approached the bedside and leant down to touch the exposed hand of Lady Maud; it was quite cold and stiff. From the calm look on the woman's face, it appeared that her passing had been very peaceful. The Lord had called her, and she had gone to him with Grace. He gave a small nod towards Brother Julius, who started to carefully unpack the small leather bag he was carrying over his shoulder. In it there were oils for anointing the dead and incense for burning. He had also brought herbs from the abbey garden in order to lay alongside the body once it was washed, shrouded and prepared for burial.

"My father is away at my uncle's manor near Durham," Roger said in a hushed voice. "I sent word to him first thing this morning, so that he might return straight away. I thought we could lay my mother in the private chapel until he arrives."

Brother Michael nodded. "We will say the mass for her soul now and then perhaps some of the maid servants could wash her. Afterwards, we will anoint your mother's body and then wrap her in the shroud."

Roger nodded, uncertain whether they wanted him to fetch the maid servants now, or to wait until they had finished their prayers. He decided to wait and stood resolutely at the bottom of the large wooden bed as the two monks stood either side reciting their Latin prayers for the dead. Roger had never learnt Latin and although he could understand a couple of phrases, the vast majority of what was being said by the monks was entirely unknown to him. The chanting appeared to go on for a very long time and, for all he knew, they could have been condemning her soul to hell, instead of heaven. He knew he had to trust in them, and the Church. He waited patiently until Brother Michael indicated that they had finished and both he, and Brother Julius, moved away from the bedside.

"It is time to let your maidservants prepare her now." He walked slowly towards Roger. "Come, we will wait outside until they have finished."

Roger nodded and for a brief moment met the gaze of the monk. The calmness of the older man was soothing, and also a little unnerving. It was as though he could see straight through Roger's façade and into his soul. Roger looked away and then turned to leave the room. Outside the servants had gathered and a couple of the younger maids were tearful. Roger approached the housekeeper and asked her to arrange for his mother to be prepared.

"It's no matter sire." The woman replied. "I know what it's about. Done a few of these in my time. We will take care of her sir, don't you fret."

"After you've finished, will you arrange for some of the men to carry her to the chapel. I've decided that she should lie there until my father returns." Roger managed a half-hearted smile at the woman.

"Of course," she assured him.

He then showed the two monks through to the great hall.

"Can I offer you refreshments?" There was a jug of ale together with bread and cheese left out for them on the table.

"Thank you." Brother Michael replied accepting the proffered mug of ale. "I will return shortly to the Abbey, but Brother Julius will remain here in the chapel with your mother and say prayers for her soul."

"Thank you, for offering your devotions to her." Roger walked over to a chest positioned against one of the side walls and retrieved a small leather pouch from inside. "Here," he said giving it to Brother Michael. "Payment for the masses that my mother wanted said for her soul." He paused for effect. "She was an incredible woman and, although we knew that she was not long for this world, in the end her passing came as a shock to everyone." Roger lied effortlessly.

Brother Michael nodded serenely. "Thank you, I know the Abbot had a particular affection for your mother; she was a very pious and god-fearing woman. She will be greatly missed."

Not least because of the large amounts of money she gave to the Abbey, Roger thought, but kept his opinion silent. At least the payment today would be the last one she made. After that, all her monies would revert to his father; and then once his father had been tragically killed on his way back from Durham, it would all belong to him.

Brother Michael watched Roger de Mowbray carefully. He wasn't entirely sure what it was about the man that unsettled him so. Roger had done nothing to suggest there was anything wrong, and the monk knew it was ungodly of him to feel so suspicious, but he couldn't get away from the feeling that something here was amiss. A little voice at the back of his mind was shouting at him, but he wasn't certain if it was the voice of an angel trying to warn him; or the voice of the devil trying to provoke him.

Simon had spent the remainder of the morning in his office instructing his scribe to write out the account of what had transpired earlier that day at the abbey. The charges against the men were something that could be dealt with by himself and did not need to form part of the assize court proceedings when the Royal Justice would attend. But, if one of the men had been the killer of Brother Clement, then that would be a different matter altogether. Simon looked at the papers for the other cases he was due to hear in the assize court. There were a lot to get through before the court was due to sit and he was still no further along. Every day there were more requests from disgruntled landowners to settle disputes, or fines to issue for theft or poaching. Most of them he could deal with himself, but the larger disputes would be referred to the assize court.

It was late afternoon when Adam returned to Simon's office and knocked on the door. Simon looked up from his desk as his deputy stepped into his office.

"Do you want to see the man who was at the head of the riot this morning?" He asked.

Simon nodded and dismissed his scribe. "I think so. He's had enough time in the cells to consider his actions, so let's hear what he has to say for himself."

"Very good." Adam made his way to leave, before Simon stopped him.

"Has he said anything more whilst he's been in the gaol cell?"

"Nothing, other than telling me the Abbot had it coming."

Simon shook his head. "It just doesn't make sense to me; why would a merchant get involved in a revolt against the abbey? It isn't as though he is the one starving." It had been bothering him since they'd left the abbey earlier in the day with their prisoners. He could have understood a farmhand or peasant as leader of the riot, but for a seemingly affluent merchant to be involved, struck him as totally illogical. There had to be more to it; and that made him wonder if there was a connection between the riot and the murder of Brother Clement.

"No, I don't think John of Askham has ever wanted for food." Adam grinned. "But I understand what you mean; I thought the same myself. What motive could he have for risking his business, his reputation and his life for this cause?"

"Then I think it's about time we asked him that very question."

When Adam returned, he was accompanied by a guard and John of Askham who was shackled between his hands and feet, so that he walked at a slow, shuffling gait. The guard roughly held on to the arm of the prisoner and once they were inside the Sheriff's office, took his leave of them and closed the door behind.

Simon looked more closely at the prisoner, John of Askham. In the morning's melee, he had taken little notice of him, being only concerned with the need to ensure that no harm came to the Abbot, or any of the monks. He observed that John was quite smartly dressed in an outfit befitting a cloth merchant, but after time in a gaol cell, he now looked quite dishevelled, his clothes dirty and stained. He was a middle-aged man, with a leaning to a slight portly appearance, which agreed with Adam's earlier observance of him not going hungry. He looked quite reticent and nervous as he stood before Simon.

"I understand from my deputy that you are John of Askham?" Simon stated.

The man appeared to stand up straighter as his name was spoken. "Yes sire." His voice was quiet.

"Well John, do you want to explain to me what you were doing this morning and why you were threatening the Abbot with this knife?" Simon held out his hand and Adam passed the knife to him.

"I was not threatening him." The statement was said with force. "I never drew any weapon against the Abbot and had no intention of doing so."

Simon sat back in his chair and looked up at the man before him, intrigued.

"Then what were you doing?"

"We merely wanted the Abbot to understand that the people are going hungry whilst he and his monks live a life of plenty. The people of this city are good Christian people and deserve better from the monks who are supposed to care for their souls. Pray and eat! That is all the monks of the abbey do. They take the tithe from people who have little to give, but never once think of giving charity back to those in greater need." He paused for a moment to draw breath. "You know as well as I do Sheriff, that the abbey is a wealthy place. They have fishponds, flour mills and farms a plenty; all to serve their needs. They seem to be increasingly concerned about their own welfare and not that of the people of this city. It is time that they were made aware of what was happening outside the walls of the abbey."

"And inciting a riot was the way to do it?"

John of Askham sighed heavily and hung his head. "In hindsight, perhaps not. But what other way was there? The people go to the abbey for food but are turned away."

Simon gave a slight nod at the man's honesty.

"What intrigues me is why you are a part of this? You are a merchant, not a farmer or a peasant and, forgive me for saying this, you do not look as though you have missed many meals."

"No, that is true," he admitted. "I have not. The reason I took their cause is because I've seen what is happening all around me in the manors and cities that I visit as part of my work as a cloth merchant. I've seen the gaunt look in people's faces, the sunken eyes and swollen bellies; and the children dying because their mothers cannot feed them."

"So, you took it on as your personal crusade?"

"Not exactly a crusade. But I could see that the people needed someone to speak for them. Someone who could talk with the Abbot and explain their plight with words which might move him and get him to agree to help."

"And the knife?" Simon held it up, so the man could see

it, and also looked at it more closely himself. It was a large knife, but it wasn't a dagger; it wasn't as fine as the blade that had slit the monk's throat. It was only sharpened on one edge and not both edges, as it would have been with a dagger. The handle of the knife was carved bone, but it wasn't an expensive knife and there certainly was no missing pommel on it.

John suddenly turned very pale in understanding of what he was being accused of. "I... I wasn't going to hurt him. No, no, not at all." The man stumbled over his words. "I just wanted to make him understand what is going on and to see that we were serious about this. I wasn't planning on using it." He protested.

"No?" Simon questioned. "It didn't look like that when I saw you with it this morning. In fact, it looked as though you had every intention of using it on the Abbot."

"No, no! I would never hurt anyone; I couldn't."

"And you expect me to believe this?" Simon narrowed his eyes to look at the man before him. He was articulate, and well spoken, but that wasn't to say that he wouldn't be moved to violence if pushed enough.

John of Askham raised his head and looked Simon straight in the eye. "It's the truth, I swear. I thought that if there were enough of us at the abbey, we could persuade him... that he would be forced to listen to us. Then, the Abbot would see that it wasn't just one person with a grievance, and that there were many people who felt the same way." He paused and swallowed nervously. "It is true, we planned to take food from the stores to help the families who are starving; and I had planned to make the Abbot promise not to take the tithes from us this year, so that the people might have enough food to last them through the winter. But that was all it was. I promise. I was never going to do anything more than that."

The man stood before him quaking and Simon was silent as he watched him squirm.

"And what about the monk who was killed? Was that also you, trying to send a message to the Abbot?"

The man looked instantly confused. "The monk?"

"Yes. Surely even you have heard about the murder of the monk, out by the river the other day."

"Yes, sire. Yes, I heard about what happened, but I swear that I had nothing to do with it." John looked flushed in the face, but Simon wasn't sure whether it was from guilt or fear.

"And I am supposed to take your word for that?" He demanded.

His prisoner went quiet, and Simon watched him closely.

"If truth be told, I was at the ale house all that evening." He replied eventually. "I was with some of the men you saw today. We all had too much ale, and I got very drunk. Anyone who was at the ale house that evening will tell you I was there; and my wife will tell you how drunk I was when I got home. She is still angry at me for it."

Simon gave a long sigh. It was true the man had threatened the Abbot, but he couldn't see him as a cold-blooded killer. The riot earlier in the morning was no more than a crowd being whipped up into a frenzy for a cause they believed in. Whereas the murder of Brother Clement, was cold, calculating and vicious. Simon knew that the two were very different. However, John of Askham was still responsible for what happened at the abbey that morning and Simon couldn't let him go unpunished for that.

"I will be confirming what you've told me about the other night. And, if you are lying to me then I will want to know why." Simon watched the man carefully for a moment. "Even if you weren't responsible for the murder, you were still responsible for what happened this morning and for that you will face court and be tried." He watched as the man before him blanched. "But you will not hang for your deed." Then, he turned his attention to Adam. "Take him back to the goal."

Adam moved forward and took hold of the man's arm and escorted him out of the room. As he did so, Simon sunk further back into his chair and sighed. He had stopped the uprising this morning, but he still needed to speak with the Abbot about it. If it happened again then it could end up being far worse. Simon knew that he had to make sure that this was not the start of something dangerous, and he couldn't do that on his own; he would need the help of Abbot Robert if he was going to accomplish it. The dissent had to be quashed straight away, and he would need the Abbot to see what was going on outside the confines of the abbey precinct, if he had any hope of succeeding in this. There was a lot of unrest in the city, the hot weather still hadn't relented, and in another month, the farmers would be going into the fields to bring in the main harvest of the year; however, there would be almost nothing there for them to gather in. The laws of the church asking people to give one tenth of their harvest as tithe, along with one tenth of their livestock, would mean there would be a lot of starving people this coming winter. The ill-feeling against the Abbot and the monks was only going to get worse, and something had to be done before there were more deaths of monks to contend with. Simon knew he would have to broach the subject with Abbot Robert soon but, for the rest of today, he had other more pressing matters to attend. He would arrange for a couple of his men to stand guard outside the abbey gates for now, to ensure there was no repetition of the riot.

He was as certain as he could be, that John of Askham had nothing to do with the murder of Brother Clement. He was an articulate man with a cause he believed in and not a cold-blooded killer and his knife was not the murder weapon. Simon considered that John might not have owned the dagger but could have been given it and then disposed of it somewhere after the killing, but that didn't seem plausible and did not sit well with him. Who would give a middle-aged cloth merchant an expensive weapon in order to carry out a murder for them? Besides, he claimed to have been in the alehouse all evening, before going home drunk. Simon needed to confirm this, but he was certain that it would prove to be correct. Over the years, Simon liked to think that he had become a good judge of character, and the way that John had reacted when he was questioned about the murder, told him that he wasn't the man he was looking for. But that still left him no nearer to finding the murderer of Brother Clement.

Katherine finished the short letter and waited for the ink to dry before she folded it and then sealed it with wax. She had not planned to write to Alexander, but she knew that he wouldn't come back to the castle without her asking and, now that she had finalised her plan to escape, she needed to see him again. Throughout the morning, she tried to put all thoughts of Lord William Fitzwarren out of her mind. He wasn't a bad man, she considered, and she felt a pang of sorrow for him; but there was no way that she could ever love him or marry him, no matter what everyone else wanted.

When Jennet came into her bedchamber, Katherine hid the letter in the sleeve of her gown. It wasn't that she didn't trust Jennet, but she knew that her maids' loyalties were split between herself and her father. Katherine wanted to be seen as the dutiful daughter in her father's eyes, one who was complying with his command that she should marry Lord Fitzwarren. In order to maintain the appearance of preparing for her wedding, Katherine had already written to her sister Angharad to tell her of the impending nuptials and ask her to travel north to York as soon as possible. Katherine knew that she had to be careful to make everything appear as normal as she could; and continue to arrange things for the wedding as if it was going to happen. If she was to run away with Alexander then no-one, absolutely no-one could know about it.

Katherine slipped out of her room and made her way down to the stables, looking for young Alfred, one of the stable hands. She needed someone she could trust to deliver the letter to Alexander, and who wouldn't talk about it with anyone, especially her father. Katherine knew Alfred would do her bidding without question. The young lad had a soft spot for her and with a silver penny for his troubles along with a chaste kiss on the cheek, Katherine knew he would not let her down. He was brushing down her father's horse when she found him.

"Alfred," she whispered.

He looked up from what he was doing. "Mistress Katherine, are you wanting to ride out? I can saddle Lily for you if you want?"

She shook her head. "No, I don't want to ride out just now. I was hoping you could do something for me." She smiled coyly, putting her head on one side.

Alfred blushed. "Of course, mistress. Anything for you. What do you want me to do?"

"I want you to deliver a letter to a friend. I want to make sure that it gets there, and I know I can trust you to deliver it." The horse Alfred was grooming whinnied, and Katherine stroked the neck of the animal.

"Of course, mistress, I can do that for you."

"But you must promise me not to speak to anyone about it. This must be our secret, do you understand?" She smiled sweetly at him.

Alfred blushed again. "You can trust me, mistress. I will do it straight away."

"That would be wonderful, if you could."

She removed the letter from the sleeve of her gown and pressed it into his hand. "It's for Sir Alexander de Ros at Helmsley castle. Do you think you can get it to him as soon as possible? Take one of the horses, so that you get there quickly."

He nodded.

"When you get there if anyone tells you that they will take it to him, then you must refuse and tell them that you've been asked to deliver it to him in person. Do you understand?"

"Yes mistress. I know the castle and I know Sir Alexander; I've seen him here before and I will make sure that I give the letter to him."

"Thank you, Alfred. You've always been so kind to me." Katherine said leaning forward and giving the boy a chaste kiss on the cheek.

If Alfred could have turned any redder than he did, he would have looked as though he was having a heart attack. Katherine watched as he tucked the letter into his shirt and smiled at him as she left. She almost felt like skipping back across the outer bailey. It was another hot July day, and the heat was already starting to feel a little stifling, but she didn't care; not today. She had sent a message to Alexander to meet her this afternoon, down by the riverbank where they had met so many times before; and nothing else mattered to her now. She was being the dutiful daughter as far as her father and everyone else was concerned; but she was also going to see Alexander and that made her heart sing.

The idea had been more of a fanciful dream to start with, but the more she had thought about it, and considered how it could work, the more it had moulded itself into a definite plan. She had thought of little else over the last day and now her plan, for how she and Alexander could be together, was fully formed. They would run away together. In a few days her father and his men would all be engaged with more important matters when the Royal Justice, Robert de Lexington, came to the city to hold the quarterly assizes. In addition, Katherine was known to go out of the castle grounds most days and no-one would think anything more of it. It would only be, when she didn't return in the evening, and the gates were being closed at sunset, that the alarm would be raised. By that time, Alexander and her, would be well away from York and on their way to a new life.

Katherine almost skipped up the steps back to her room and was smiling to herself as she walked through the door. Jennet looked up from her sewing and smiled.

"You look happy, my lady." She observed.

"I am. I feel that everything is going to be alright now."

"Oh, I'm so glad that you feel like that. Lord Fitzwarren

is a good man, and he will make you a good husband." Jennet smiled and went back to working on the gown in her lap. The silver and gold embroidery on the bodice of the blue gown, for Katherine's wedding, sparkled as it caught in the sunlight.

"Do you know where the wedding is to be held?" Jennet asked.

"Lord Fitzwarren sent word to my father that he has arranged for the wedding to be at the minster."

Katherine was still smiling with the joy of knowing that she would soon see Alexander. But Jennet saw it as the happiness of the girl finally giving in to her father's wishes.

"Oh, the minster. Well, that will be so grand. I'm so pleased for you, my lady. But then with your father's position, that's just how it should be. I suppose I'd better get on with finishing your dress."

Katherine knelt down at the side of Jennet and looked at the dress her maid was working on. It was beautiful fabric and the embroidery that Jennet had done was exquisite. Katherine imagined herself walking down the aisle of the minster in the dress, alongside her new husband; except that it wasn't Lord William she saw at her side, but Alexander; and that made her smile even more.

"I'm so glad that you've come round to your father's point of view. Lord Fitzwarren will make such a good husband for you." Jennet paused. "Not that Alexander wouldn't have, I mean, but this is all for the best."

Katherine kept the smile on her face, even though it felt so false once she started thinking about Lord Fitzwarren. If everything went to plan then there would be no wedding at the minster for her, just a merciful escape from a marriage she didn't want, and a reunion with Alexander. She considered that if they met just after the church bells sounded at noon; then they would have a considerable head start on any men that her father saw to send out after her. By the time she was missed at sunset, both she and Alexander would be safely on their way towards Wales, where her father's jurisdiction didn't reach. Once there, they could make a life for themselves without worrying about her being seized by her father's men. Perhaps her father would come round in time and welcome her back, but if he didn't, then she would understand. It was the most difficult decision she'd ever had to make; choosing between her family and the man she loved, but it was going to be worth the sacrifice. She was aware that her life would be quite different to the one she had now. There would be no servants or maids, as she had grown up with; and there would be less money to spend on clothes or entertaining. But they would probably be able to afford a house or a small manor, if Alexanders father was lenient with them. Katherine was also aware she wouldn't have Jennet, or anyone else she knew. In effect she would be cutting herself off from the life she now had. However, none of it mattered if she could be with Alexander. She would give up everything she had, just to spend the rest of her life with him.

"I'm sure it will be fine." She said smiling at Jennet.

As much as it hurt her to remain silent and not tell Jennet everything, she couldn't be certain that her maid would remain loyal to her. Jennet had a loyalty to Katherine's father as well and had been with him since before Katherine was born. Katherine ached with the need to confide in someone but was so very wary of trusting anyone with her plan. She wanted nothing more, than for her plan to work out, and if that meant keeping everything to herself and trusting no-one, then that was how it had to be.

CHAPTER 11

It was late morning when Katherine received word back from Alexander. She had gone down to the stables, hoping that Alfred might have a message for her, and he carefully placed it in her hand; anxious that no-one would see it.

"You know I am grateful for what you have done for me, Alfred. I will not forget your loyalty." She whispered.

"You know I would do anything for you, mistress." Alfred blushed.

Katherine smiled, knowing how much the boy really liked her, and it was good to know that she had friends like him. She might need his help again quite soon. Katherine was conscious that she didn't want to take advantage of the boys' good nature and devotion to her. She tucked the note into the sleeve of her dress and calmed herself by stroking the neck of Lily, her favourite horse, and the grey mare nudged her playfully. Alfred tended one of the other horses in the stables, trying to hide his embarrassment by concentrating on his work. Katherine loved being in the stables, the horses had been her friends since she had moved to the castle with her father. When she had arrived, she had known no-one, other than Jennet and her father, and she had found herself taking comfort in being with her horse Lily and the others. It was a place where she always felt at home. The calmness of the horses around her made her feel safe, and they seemed to react to her in the same way. Lily had been a gift from her father a few years ago, when she had outgrown her small pony and was tall enough and strong enough to ride a fine horse. Jennet had been horrified at her young charge riding such a large horse, but Katherine had loved the beautiful mare from the start and would not be deterred from going out riding on her. It hadn't taken long for Katherine to form a close bond with the grey mare.

"Alfred, I think I will ride out this afternoon; after I have eaten. Can you have Lily ready for me then?"

"Of course, mistress."

Katherine smiled at him and left the stables to go back to her room. It was likely that her sister, Angharad, would arrive soon, and she was aware that once her sister was around, escaping the castle to meet Alexander would be far more difficult. If she already had a daily routine of going out riding in the afternoon and taking her wolfhound, Grenulf with her, to make sure that he was exercised; then when it came time to escape with Alexander it would not raise suspicion. She couldn't believe that she would see Alexander again later that afternoon. Although it was only two days since she had last seen him, it felt like a lifetime; and so much had happened during that time. Now that she had finalised the details of her plan, she needed to tell him how they were to escape and be together. Once they had crossed the border into Wales, then her father could not get to them. His men would have no jurisdiction there and would be less than welcome on Welsh land. She smiled happily at the thought she would eventually be with Alexander, and no-one would be able to separate them. It was the thought of this that allowed her to smile and keep a good countenance when Jennet later asked about the preparations for her wedding. Jennet added how pleased she was for her mistress and just how well suited she and Lord Fitzwarren were. None of it was true. They weren't well suited; not when she was in love with someone else; and Katherine wasn't pleased that her father had declined to listen to her and refused to change his mind about the betrothal.

She opened the door into her chamber expecting that she would be alone in order to read the letter that Alfred had given her. But she was disappointed to find Jennet still working on the gown she was supposed to wear on her wedding day. The maid was concentrating on the fine needlework and, at first, didn't hear Katherine come in.

"Oh, my lady." Jennet exclaimed startled. "I was wondering where you had got to."

Katherine smiled. "You were so busy concentrating on your needlework, and I didn't want to disturb you. I've just been down to the stables to tell Alfred that I will be taking Lily out this afternoon." She looked across at her dog snoozing in front of the empty fireplace. "Grenulf is getting lazy, and he needs a good walk." She turned her attention back to the gown Jennet was working on. "It's beautiful." She observed, kneeling down next to Jennet.

"Only what you deserve, my lady. I promised your mother I would take care of you, and this is my way of honouring that promise."

Katherine suddenly felt incredibly guilty. Jennet had been as good as a mother to her and was really, the only mother she could remember. Deceiving her felt very wrong; but Jennet was also a servant to her father, and Katherine was well aware, that if she confided in Jennet, then it would leave her maid in a terrible situation. One where her loyalty was torn between Katherine and her father, as her master. It was a decision that Katherine didn't want Jennet to have to make. It felt so hard for her to do this, as Jennet had been her confident for so many years as she was growing up, but her love for her maid, made her realise that she couldn't put Jennet in this situation.

She felt the letter against the skin of her arm and knew that she needed to have some time alone to read it. She expected that Alexander would tell her he could not wait to see her that afternoon; but what if he had written to say that he was unable to meet today? What if he didn't want to see her again? The very thought left her cold, and she knew that she had to read it as soon as possible.

"Is it too early to have something to eat?" She asked Jennet.

Jennet looked up from her needlework. "If you want my lady, then I will go down and organise it."

"That would be lovely, Jennet. All this talk of the

wedding has got me quite excited," she lied.

Jennet smiled. "You don't know how good it is for me to hear you say that, my lady. I was worried that you were going to do something silly over that boy Alexander, and I am just so relieved to see you happy at the thought of marrying Lord Fitzwarren."

Katherine smiled, even though it riled her to have Alexander described as 'that boy'. The letter was now burning into her skin, and she was glad when Jennet put down her needlework and left the room in search of something for them to eat. As soon as the door closed behind Jennet, Katherine slipped the letter from her sleeve and unfolded it. Her eyes quickly scanned it, and, in her head, she could hear Alexander's voice speaking to her.

"My darling Katherine. I had hoped to hear from you, but didn't dare think about it until I received your letter. I don't know what else there is to say about the betrothal that hasn't already been said, but if you want to meet; then I will agree to that. Let it be this afternoon at our spot by the river."

Her heart leapt at reading the words. It was exactly what she had hoped to read, and she felt reassured that Alexander still wanted her. The need to take Grenulf for a walk was a good excuse, and her beloved wolfhound was always happy to oblige. In the meantime, she needed to start planning how she was going to secrete items out of her room over the next few days, without them being missed by Jennet. Katherine had surmised that she would need to take a change of clothing and also a cloak to hide behind, even though wearing it in the hot summer sun would be near impossible; but the hot summer would not last forever and it would still come in useful once the weather changed. She also needed to take some jewellery with her, the items that had been left to her when her mother passed away, and some pieces that had been given to her by her father as presents. Even if she didn't want to keep the jewellery, they would have a value, and they could use them as payment in exchange for lodgings. Katherine's plan was to secretly take things from her chamber and hide them in a specific place near where she met with Alexander, so that she could collect them later when the day came for them to escape.

When Jennet returned to the room, Katherine was sitting in the window embrasure reading a book of psalms. She had put the letter back into the sleeve of her dress and had already taken a couple of items of jewellery from her coffer. They were small pieces, and wouldn't be noticed as missing, and they fitted easily into the alms purse that hung from her girdle.

"The servants will bring some food to us shortly." Jennet said, sitting back down in the chair and picking up the dress to continue with her work.

"Thank you, Jennet." Katherine replied. "It feels so stuffy in here, I'm looking forward to going out riding this afternoon down by the river." She looked across at her maid as if sensing her reluctance to let Katherine go out alone. "And don't worry Jennet, Grenulf will keep me safe."

"I know, my lady. That animal is devoted to you."

Katherine turned her attention to looking back out of the window. "It seems so odd that we are complaining about the hot weather now, and earlier in the year, when the snow was on the ground, we were wishing for it."

Jennet nodded but didn't lift her head from her work. "It seems we are never happy, whatever the weather is."

Alfred had Lily ready for her when Katherine went down to the stables in the afternoon. Grenulf followed his mistress a few steps behind and busied himself sniffing around the stables as Katherine mounted her horse.

"I'll be back later this afternoon." She smiled at Alfred. "I thought I would take Grenulf out for a long walk along the river. We both need to be out of this stifling atmosphere, and he could do with some exercise, he's getting rather lazy." There wasn't a need for her to say anything to Alfred, but if anyone should ask him where she had gone, then it would not be a worry.

Katherine intended to keep doing this every day, so that when the time came for her and Alexander to escape, they would not be missed for quite a while. By then, they would be well on their way towards Wales and if they stayed away from the main citys, then she hoped that they wouldn't be noticed.

The streets of the city were dirty and no better than open sewers. The smell was even worse that day than Katherine had expected, and she put her arm and sleeve across her face to stop her breathing in the foul odour. The river wasn't much better either, as the water level had dropped considerably over the last month and the concentrated smell of human and animal waste was horrendous. At least she was heading out of the city walls and into the fields to the east.

The sun shimmered off the water as Katherine rode Lily down the side of the city walls and along the track down to the river. The water level was low, and the banks of the river were hardened into cracked bare mud. Swarms of flies hung over the water, no doubt attracted by the concentrated open sewer that was once a fast-flowing deep river. Katherine noticed that the trees along the river were already starting to shed their leaves, and the barren look of the fields beyond was more like late September rather than July. Katherine relaxed as she rode slowly along the river with Grenulf following on behind. Occasionally, he would stop and sniff at a bush or shrub and then run back after his mistress, before she got too far out of his sight.

Alexander was already waiting for her when she got to their special place. He took the reins of Lily to steady her and then helped Katherine down.

"I never thought I would see you again after the last time." He said, as he held Katherine close and kissed her tenderly.

"And I didn't think I would see you either. At least not until after I was married and then perhaps only at gatherings at the Castle." She paused. "I'd imagined that seeing you again then, would be so awful to bear."

"Yes, I didn't think I could face it either." He stopped and looked down at her. "To be honest, I planned to go away from here, to my father's lands in the north, so there was no chance of my accidentally seeing you again. Your note this morning arrived just in time."

"Going away to the north?"

"Yes, I was planning to ask father about either, going up to his lands in Northumberland, or perhaps over to France; he has land in Normandy as well. And I thought that either of them would be far enough away from you." He gave her a half smile. "I didn't think I would be able to cope with the possibility of seeing you again; especially once you were Lady Fitzwarren."

"I know, I understand and believe me I have no desire to become the next Lady Fitzwarren. Even though everyone keeps telling me that he is a good man, I cannot bear the thought of being with him and not being with you."

"But you will be: And soon, so I hear."

She looked up at him. "The wedding is planned for next week. But it's not going to happen."

The statement took Alexander by surprise, and she took his hand in hers and guided him to walk with her along the riverbank.

"I know that there is nothing my father can do to stop this betrothal." She told him. "I know that he loves me, but I did think that he would allow me to choose my own husband. However, it seems that I was wrong. I know it's different for you; you are a man, and you have more say in your life than I do. But still, I thought that my father respected me and understood that I could never be happy with someone I didn't love." She sighed as they walked, then turned to Alexander. "So, I knew it was down to me to find an alternative and I think I have come up with a plan for us."

"A plan?" He stopped walking and looked down at her.

"Well, you did say that you were thinking about leaving here. And I know I could never bring myself to marry Lord Fitzwarren, no matter how good a man he is. So, I thought that we could run away together." She paused for a moment and then continued without giving him chance to reply. "We could leave here and make our way towards Wales. If we met like this, just after noon, then no-one would miss me until nightfall; they would just think that I was out with Grenulf, as usual. By the time anyone suspected something was wrong, we would be well on our way west towards Wales. And, once we are there, my father can't get to us; he has no jurisdiction in Wales, so we will be safe." She paused. "I know you mentioned you were thinking of going to Northumberland, or Normandy, but those are both places where your father would know where we were, and he would feel obliged to tell my father; and then we would be split up again."

"Not if we had already got married."

The statement took her totally by surprise. "Married." She whispered.

"Why not? We both know that we want to; and, if it wasn't for your father obtaining the Kings permission for your marriage, then we would be planning to do so."

"That is true, but how would we?"

"I'm not sure yet," Alexander sighed. "I hadn't really given it much thought, up until now. Probably in a city far away from here where nobody knows us, and we could have the bans read quickly." She nodded happily as he continued. "I was thinking that we could head up towards Northumberland and stop at a church along the way. Once we are married, then there is nothing your father, or mine, can do to stop us."

Katherine beamed with happiness. It seemed that Alexander had been thinking about this just as much as she had.

"Oh Alexander, that does sound perfect." She kissed him tenderly on the mouth and they lingered together before sitting down on the grass.

"There is one thing, though," she said cautiously. "If we remain in England then my father has the authority to capture us and take me back. That's why I thought if we went west, and into Wales then he couldn't get to us."

"I know, my love." He leant towards her and kissed her on the forehead. "But I also know just how much your family means to you. And escaping to Wales would mean that we would have to break with our families forever." He drew back and looked down at her. "I don't want that for you, or for either of us. My father has lands at Wark-on-Tweed in Northumberland. If we travel there and get married along the way, then neither your family nor mine would be able to do anything about it. We could make the manor house at Wark our home; I know my father would not mind; he often complains that he has no-one to administer the area. And then, in time, I am sure your father would come to accept it too."

His plan to escape was even better than hers, and Katherine sighed with relief that he, not only wanted to run away as well, but had also thought of a way for how they could do it.

"Oh Alexander, it sounds absolutely perfect! I don't really care where we go, just as long as we're together."

He smiled and kissed her tenderly on the mouth. "As long as I am with you, then I know everything will be well."

Katherine felt tears begin to sting in her eyes, but they were not tears of sadness. "I can't tell you how much this means to me," she breathed. "I thought about escaping into Wales only because I knew we would be safe there, and my father could not do anything. But I also knew I would have to leave my family behind and sever all contact with them. That was the part I wasn't looking forward to." She smiled as she looked up at him. "Your plan is so much better. We can be together without having to break with our families."

"Now, all we need to do is to make arrangements for when we are going to do this." He smiled at her. "Obviously it needs to be before your wedding."

She laughed softly and leant into him. "Yes, and I had thought about that too. As you know, the Royal Justice is due in a few days' time, and my father will be occupied by the court duties. He will have no time for me, or to notice that I am not around."

"But your maid will still miss you."

"Not if I go out riding most days and take Grenulf with me, like today. No-one will realise that I am missing, until they come to close the gates at sunset."

"You really have thought about this." He smiled at her.

"Yes," she looked up at him lovingly, "it's all I've been thinking about. Making plans for how we might be together. The thought of being married to Lord Fitzwarren was just too much to bear. I know how everyone tells me that he is a good man; and, in a way, I do feel sorry for him. He has done nothing wrong. But I could never have married him; I could never have loved him; not as I love you."

"Oh Katherine." He leant forward and kissed her passionately. "I was all set to leave here and go as far away from you as I could. My father's lands in France were looking very appealing I must say. I just couldn't have borne the thought of seeing you on the arm of another man; but going with you to the north, would be even better. You know how much I love you."

"And I love you too, my darling."

Katherine stopped, as Alexander wrapped her in a tight embrace.

"There was one other thing that I thought of," she said at last, pulling away from him. "I thought we might need some things to take with us. Clothes and such, as well as things that we could sell to provide for lodgings along our way. I've brought a few things with me today." She retrieved the jewellery and showed him. "I was going to hide them somewhere near here, but it may be better if you keep them with you. They're pieces that I don't wear, so they won't be missed. My father gave me some of them as presents and the rest I inherited from my mother." She pressed the jewellery into his hands.

He looked down at them. "Are you sure?"

Katherine nodded.

"Then I will look after them for you." He took them from her and put them into his bag. "But if we go up to my father's manor in Northumberland then we won't need much. I will bring some money with me to pay for lodgings on our way there. The journey will take a couple of days at least; and if we stop along the way to get married, then we will need some money to pay for lodgings whilst the bans are read. But after that I'm sure my father will see that we're well provided for." He said reassuringly. "And besides, he's been on at me for some time to earn my keep and manage one of his estates. This way he gets what he wants, and we will be able to start our married life, away from both of our families. I will tell him this evening that I plan to go north to manage the estate. He will be pleased that I've finally made a decision."

"But you won't tell him anything about our plan?" She suddenly tensed with worry.

"No, of course I won't. My father knows that I had asked for your hand in marriage and that I failed in it, as you had already been promised to Lord Fitzwarren. So, I expect that he will understand the reason why I've decided to leave here and to travel north to make a new start for myself. I will suggest to him that I make the move straight away." He paused thoughtfully. "I will tell him that I want to be away from the city when your wedding is due to be held. I can tell him that I will journey north on my own and then send for my things once I have got settled. That way he will not suspect anything, and there will be no servants to travel with me."

"As soon as the Royal Justice arrives, and my father is occupied with the assize court, I will ride out after the noon bells sound, and we can meet somewhere along the route. Then we can continue our journey north together."

"Yes, I suppose it will be the same as today and everyone will expect you to go out riding. We could agree somewhere heading north from here and then, after a day's ride, when we were sure no-one was following us, we could stop somewhere for a while and get married."

"Oh, my darling, that would be so wonderful." She beamed up at him. "A few hours ago, I was dreading the thought of telling you. I didn't know what you would say. But now, I'm looking forward to it. In fact, I can't wait for us to be together."

"And neither can I," he smiled. "I wanted to be with you so much, but I just couldn't see a way to get around your betrothal. However now, I am so glad that we have a future together."

He kissed her again and Katherine felt herself melt into his arms. Then Alexander leant back and looked at her more seriously. "I know we have to keep this a secret, and we can't speak to anyone about what we're planning, but there is one person I need to tell, and that is my man at arms."

"Your man?" Katherine was suddenly worried.

"Yes, his name is Stephen and he's very loyal to me. He's a good man; you'll like him." Alexander said smiling. "You see it wouldn't be right for me to travel anywhere without him, and it would certainly arouse suspicion if I left to travel to my father's manor in Wark on my own. Besides, he can be our witness at our wedding, as well as a fellow man at arms, should we encounter any trouble along the way."

"Are you sure you can trust him not to say anything?"

"I've known him nearly all my life and I trust him completely; you don't have anything to worry about, he won't tell anyone what we're planning."

"So, it will be the three of us travelling?"

"That's right. To all intents and purpose, it will look as though you are a lady travelling with her two men at arms."

Katherine paused thoughtfully. "I'm not sure if it's a

good thing for me to look like a lady; I mean, my father is going to send men after us and they will be looking for a lady. I think it would be better if I were dressed more like a servant. After all, it's me that they will be looking for, they won't be looking for a knight travelling with a servant girl and a man at arms. I will get one of my old gowns that I was intending to give away and an old cloak to hide under, so I will look more like a servant."

"You're incredible!" He exclaimed. "You think of everything; and you're right, no-one will question a servant girl riding with a knight."

"But for the next few days, I'm going to come out here with Grenulf every day, so that everyone is used to me going out."

"Then I will get to see you again."

"Of course," she told him. "It all feels a little surreal, rather like a dream. This morning, I had a plan to run away with you to Wales, but now I can see that your idea of heading north, is so much better. As long as we are together, I don't care where we go."

"And not only that, but we will be man and wife before they get chance to stop us."

"Once we are married there will be nothing my father can do to keep us apart." She leant forward to kiss him and Alexander enveloped her in his arms and returned her kiss passionately.

It was barely daybreak; the morning light was beginning to change the darkness of the night into the half-light of early morning. The long, dark shadows were starting to take shape and form in the dawn light. The young boy had escaped from the stables at the manor to sit under the oak tree outside the walls. He was safe there, away from the harsh stable-master, and the stillness of the morning air and the tree calmed him. Soon it would be time to make his way quietly back to the stables, before he was missed; but he had a little more time yet before the servants would start their daily chores, and the horses would need feeding.

The tree was his sanctuary; it was the one thing that was steadfast in his world and offered him solace. As long as he could escape to sit beneath its sheltered canopy, then he could face anything that might happen to him under the harsh stable master.

In the darkness, the boy blended in with the gnarled trunk of the old tree and the man coming out of the manor gate, had no idea that he had been seen. The boy watched with curiosity as the man walked around the corner of the manor walls towards the midden, where the spoil from the kitchens was dumped. It was away from the main entrance of the manor, and out of sight for any arriving guests; and where the aroma of rotting food would not impinge on the main house. The boy wondered why someone should be going around to the midden at dawn, and his curiosity was piqued even more as he watched the man take something out of his cloak and bury it in the depth of the midden. The man stopped and looked around himself, but the boy was well hidden in the shadows of the night. He watched as the man quickly made his way back along the wall and then disappeared inside the wooden gate into the manor complex.

The boy waited for a while to make sure the man wasn't coming back and then stole quietly from his place under the tree and walked across the grass to where he had been standing at the midden. He was intrigued to know what the man had concealed beneath the scraps of waste and peelings. It took him a little while of digging into the pile of waste before his hand felt the cold sharpness of what had been hidden. His fingers grasped around it, and he pulled it out so that he could look at it in the increasing daylight. The dagger was beautiful, with its ornate carving on the blade. The boy turned it around in his hands; he had never seen anything like it before and now it was his. The boy decided he would hide it in the barn where he slept, burying it deep in the hay, so no-one else would find it. It was a treasure that he didn't want anyone else to see.

A BROTHERLY DEVOTION

CHAPTER 12

The Abbot was just leaving the abbey after the office of terce the following morning, when he saw Simon dismounting in the abbey precinct. Instead of heading straight back to his office, he changed his direction and went down the steps of the abbey to greet him. Brother Francis was leading Simon's horse into the stables and Simon was removing his sword to leave it in safe keeping whilst he was there.

"Good morning, Simon," Abbot Robert greeted him. "May God be praised that it is a calmer morning today, than it was yesterday."

"Good morning, Abbot Robert. Yes, indeed," Simon replied, turning to gesture at the entrance. "I have arranged for a couple of my men to stand guard at the abbey gates for the time-being, until we can be certain that there isn't going to be a repeat of yesterday."

"Thank you, I appreciate that. But I have the feeling that ensuring there isn't a repetition of yesterday, isn't the only reason you are here?"

Simon smiled. "No, you are correct, may we talk somewhere?"

The Abbot nodded. "Walk with me to my room."

Simon fell into step alongside the Abbot as they walked through the abbey grounds. The place was a hive of activity as monks worked in the herb garden and around the kitchen, but unlike the previous day, the place was calm. The Abbot walked along one side of the cloister and then stopped to open the door to his office. Simon followed him inside.

"So, what can I do for you?" The Abbot asked as he sat down at his desk, indicating for Simon to sit in the chair opposite.

"I wanted to inform you that I have spoken to the man

who was the ringleader of the riot yesterday. His name is John of Askham; and, although he has admitted to being the head of the rioters, I do not believe that he had anything to do with the murder of Brother Clement."

"So, the killer of our dear Brother is still out there."

"He is, I'm afraid. But I am confident that it is only a matter of time before I find him." Simon paused, uncertain as to whether he should say more, but decided that it would help. "I am waiting to speak with a man who was close to Brother Clement, before he took Holy Orders; and I think that will give me more insight into who might have killed him."

The Abbot nodded contemplatively and there was silence between the two men, before the Abbot said. "I have a feeling that this was not the real reason you've come to see me today."

A small smile crept across Simon's face; the Abbot was a very astute man. "No, you're correct, there was another matter that I wanted to talk to you about."

"And that would be?"

"The riot yesterday," Simon began, "I'm sure you are fully aware of the reasons why it happened."

"The people think that they don't have enough food, so they thought they would come and take what we have here at the Abbey." Abbot Robert replied, more sharply than he had intended.

Simon sighed to himself, this was clearly going to be more difficult than he had anticipated, and he knew he needed to choose his words carefully.

"It's not that the people don't *think* they have enough food; they really do not have enough," Simon explained, keeping his voice calm and level. He paused for a while before continuing. "The harvest was bad last summer, and people only just made it through the winter and spring. And now, it looks as though the harvest this summer will also fail, and they have nothing left. Their animals are starving; that is, if they haven't already died, or been killed. The people literally do not have anything left. There are going to be a lot of people starving to death, this winter."

The Abbot did not respond but instead pressed his hands together in front of his face and rested his chin against them.

"What made the men come here yesterday was that they feel you do not understand their plight," Simon continued. "What they did was wrong, I know; and they will be punished for what they have done. But they feel they have no other way of making you aware of their predicament. If the people are forced to give up one tenth of everything they have to the church, then many of them will not survive the winter. The tithe may well be the difference between life and death for a lot of people this year."

The Abbot paused thoughtfully and dropped his hands onto the arms of his chair. "I realise that there are problems out there. My lay brothers tell me how things are on our own lands, and I am aware that our harvest will not be good this year either. I have a duty to ensure that my brothers here are taken care of first. As you well know, Simon, the abbey has a duty of prayer to God for the souls of those in our city. The tithe that the people give us is their payment for our prayers and salvation of their souls."

Silence fell between the two men, as Simon wondered how he was going to explain the severity of what was happening to the people. He watched as the Abbot tapped the arm of his chair with his fingers as though he too was contemplating the problem. Then the Abbot spoke.

"I know you said that the leader of the riot was not responsible for the murder of Brother Clement, but do you think that what happened here yesterday is connected to it?"

"I cannot say for certain. But it would be foolish to ignore the fact that they might be connected." Simon paused and sighed heavily. "Abbot, you must see that the people are angry with the abbey, and with you. I cannot rule out that Brother Clement was murdered to send a message to you that the people are not happy. They see themselves struggling to put food on the table, whilst you and the monks here want for nothing." Simon did not mention the dagger and that it was likely a possession of a nobleman and not a disgruntled peasant.

"That is utter nonsense." Abbot Robert was incensed and slammed his hands down on the arms of the chair. "How dare they! We take care of all their spiritual needs; we are there for them when they require our benefaction and absolution; we tend them when they are sick, and we deliver alms to those that need it. Do we not deserve some small reparation for our intercessions and doing His work? The peasants always believe that they have nothing, and we have everything, but I tell you Simon, it is simply not true. We give our lives to the service of our Lord, and we pray every day for those who toil and work hard to sustain their lives. We deny ourselves, for the benefit of others."

Simon could see that it was not going to be easy to convince the Abbot.

"Forgive me for being so direct Abbot, but the situation outside the walls of the abbey is far worse than I think you realise. When was the last time you actually went out into the fields around the city, and looked at what is really happening out there?"

"Simon, we have known each other for a while now and I think we have respect for each other, so I do not mind you being direct with me." The Abbot gave a courteous nod. "As you well know I do not often go out beyond the walls of this sacred place, and I realise that things outside, may be different to what I see within the walls of the precinct. But I am not blind or deaf; I hear what my lay brothers tell me, and I see how much less they bring in from our farms. But this abbey is foremost a house of God, and my first responsibility is the religious welfare of the brothers here and our faithful patrons. I like to think I take my duty as Abbot very seriously and I want the abbey, under my stewardship, to be a place of religious piety and devotion. As you know the previous Abbot was quite lax in his religious duties and was what I consider to be quite frivolous. My fellow brethren have dedicated their lives in the service of God and, I feel that I owe them a duty of being a good and faithful shepherd to my flock."

"And does your flock not include those outside the walls of the Abbey?" Simon could feel himself getting angry.

"Yes of course it does."

"Then you must be aware of their suffering?"

"I don't like to think of it as suffering Simon, but that the Lord is testing his people to see who is worthy and who is not." The Abbot sounded very resolute in his belief.

"Either way, it does not alter the current circumstances, I'm afraid." Simon paused and drew breath. He believed that even though the Abbot was a God-fearing and pious man, he must also be able to see what was happening around him. If God was indeed listening to the prayers of the Abbot, then He must see that it would take a miracle to change the shrivelled crops into a bountiful harvest. "I do not want to tell you what to do Abbot. I just need you to see that all is not well in the land. I beg you to go out into the villages and see what is happening for yourself. If you insist on the people paying their tithe to the abbey this year, then you must have satisfied yourself that it is what God would want. I doubt that even He would want his children to die just because the Abbot cannot bring himself to be informed of their plight."

The Abbot drew breath sharply and Simon realised that he had probably overstepped the bounds of friendship he had with Abbot Robert. But then, if he couldn't be the one to tell the Abbot of what was happening, then who could? The monks that served him would probably never dare to raise their concerns with him.

"Simon, I understand that we are friends, and I will allow your plain speaking this once. But I tell you, that if this is God's decree of how things should be, then I am not one to change His will. If He wanted it to be different, then I am certain He would make it so. The tithe that is paid to this Abbey, is the charge that the people pay for us to pray to God for his merciful blessings upon them, and I can only say that myself and the brethren under my care here, have done our utmost to ensure that our prayers have been heard. We have never shirked in our duty Simon, and I know that you would never doubt that."

Simon knew that he could say no more without offending the Abbot further and losing his friendship. In one way, it was hard to find fault with Abbot Roberts' virtuous words, but Simon was a practical man, and he saw every day what was going on, both inside and outside the city wall, even if the Abbot did not.

"Abbot Robert, with great respect, all I am saying is that you need to be aware of what is going on outside the confines of the abbey precinct. You were lucky this time with the rioters. Next time, I might not be able to stop them before one of the monks is seriously hurt or killed; and I know you wouldn't want that to happen. Please give some thought to what I am saying."

"I understand Simon," the Abbot's voice had calmed a little. "And you have given me cause to contemplate your words and to add the plight of the people to my prayers. I am sure that He will be benevolent in His blessings."

Simon realised that there was nothing more for him to say. It wouldn't matter how much he stressed the importance of understanding the troubles faced by the people of the city and the surrounding villages, the Abbot really believed that his prayers to a benevolent God would make the situation resolve itself.

"I am sure He will." Simon smiled and went to get up from his chair. "And with that, I must take my leave of you."

"Yes, I am sure you have much to do. I understand that the Royal Justice is due in a few days. I expect your time will be taken with court duties."

"Indeed, they will Abbot."

"It has been good to see you, Simon." Abbot Robert rose from his chair.

"And you too." Simon gave a small respectful bow to the Abbot before he took his leave.

The short journey from the abbey back to the castle gave him little time to think, but Simon was certain of one thing, and that was, that the riots of the previous day had absolutely nothing to do with the murder of Brother Clement. If only now he could find some evidence as to who actually murdered the monk. Simon was aware that, as much as he might want to head up the investigation into the murder, he had other things that needed his attention. Firstly, the arrival of Robert de Lexington, the Royal Justice for the quarterly assize, would take up most of his time over the following few days; and after that there would be the wedding of Katherine to Lord Fitzwarren. He was only grateful that, after her initial outburst and objections to the wedding, Katherine now seemed to have come to terms with it and was behaving as a devoted daughter should. He also hoped that the arrival of his older daughter, Angharad, would also ease the tension between himself and Katherine. He disliked the animosity between them; they had always been so close. But in the last few days she had tested his patience more than once, even though he hated to admit it.

The large wooden carriage arrived at the castle in the late afternoon. Five mounted guards accompanied it: three riding at the back, along with two at the front. Bringing up the rear was a smaller open cart, laden with chests and boxes. Two servants sat at the rear of the open cart, and they quickly dismounted once it came to a halt. The castle servants were quick to rush forward and attend to the guests, whilst one also disappeared into the buildings to find the Sheriff and announce the arrival of his eldest daughter.

Angharad waited for her husband to attend her, before she moved to step down from the carriage. She was wearing a plain green dress, which was not belted so it hung loosely on her and her fair hair was covered with a fine coif and delicately embroidered padded band. Her husband held out his hand to assist her as she alighted carefully onto the hardened ground of the outer bailey. His eyes watched his wife devotedly as she stood before him. However, their attention was quickly diverted by the arrival of Angharad's father.

"My darling daughter." Simon said as he approached, then stopped with a small start of surprise as he observed his daughters swollen belly, evident now beneath the loose dress she was wearing. "Oh, my love, why didn't you tell me?" He beamed with pride that his daughter was pregnant, and he was to be a grandfather.

Angharad smiled at her father lovingly. "I wanted to be certain. And then when I got the letter about the wedding, I thought I would wait and make it a surprise." She walked towards him, and he embraced her. She was smaller than her father, with fine delicate features in an oval face that gave her an almost angelic appearance.

Simon realised that he had missed his eldest daughter. It seemed only a little while since she had been a small child, learning to walk and it had been his wife Ellen then, who had been pregnant, with their second child. Now time had moved on, and that small girl had grown into a beautiful woman who was now expecting a child of her own. Life had moved on by a whole generation and he felt as though it had happened without him really noticing. Simon considered that he also missed the calming influence Angharad had been on Katherine too; it had been easier for him to keep his youngest daughter in check with the more sensible Angharad at home to provide guidance; even though the two girls had often fought terribly. Over the last year there had been times when he'd found it difficult to know just how to deal with his headstrong youngest daughter.

Simon released Angharad and gazed on her again; pregnancy seemed to be good for her, and she looked radiant. He turned towards his son-in law.

"Richard, I am so delighted to see you again and so

pleased to see that you are taking good care of my daughter." Simon could imagine how proud the man must be to finally be on the brink of fatherhood. He may be twenty years older than Angharad, but that age difference appeared to have manifested itself in a true devotion to his young wife.

"It is good to see you too Simon." Richard smiled warmly as he looked between his father-in-law and his pregnant wife.

"Come into the hall, both of you. You must be exhausted after your travels; come and rest a while." He took his eldest daughters' hand and began to escort her. "I'm sure your servants can sort everything out for you. I have arranged for you to stay in the rooms next to your sister and Katherine will join us in the hall shortly, so that the two of you can discuss her wedding plans and decide how to spend even more of my money." He laughed genially.

Angharad leant lovingly against her father, holding onto his arm as they walked across the bailey towards the new castle keep building. Richard followed them, happily resigned to be taking second place behind his wife and her father.

Katherine had not long since returned from her ride along the riverbank. She would have stayed longer with Alexander if she could, but she didn't want to raise suspicion. As well as the jewellery she had given to Alexander, she had managed to take a cloak and conceal it within the hollow of an oak tree. It would be safe there until she went to collect it when the time came for both of them to leave. She was hot and dusty and was changing her gown when Jennet came to tell her that her sister had arrived. Forgetting all etiquette, she raced down the stairs from her room and across the bailey towards the great hall. Katherine didn't care that the servants were watching her and shaking their heads with despair, as her manner was not appropriate for a daughter of one of the most important men in the country. It was expected that ladies of her standing, should behave in a more restrained manner, and Jennet kept telling her that a proper lady should walk or glide everywhere. But Katherine, unlike her sister, struggled to keep her natural enthusiasm in check. Her pure joy and excitement in a particular moment would always override what she knew was expected of her. Today, the excitement and joy of seeing her sister again could not be contained. Even though the two sisters were completely different in character, they shared a deep love for each other and a bond that was borne out of losing their mother when they were both so little.

Katherine arrived in the great hall quite breathless and with her cheeks burning from the exertion. Her father was standing near the head of the high table with Angharad and Richard in front of him. Angharad turned when she heard the commotion from the entrance and Katherine rushed towards her sister.

"Oh Annie!" She cried as she saw the swelling of her sister's pregnancy. The two sisters hugged each other with delight. "I didn't know. Why didn't you tell me when you last wrote? When's it due? How are you feeling? Do you need to sit down? Shall I get you a drink?"

Angharad laughed and raised her hand to calm her enthusiastic sister. "My darling Katherine. You never change. I'm just fine, but to sit down and have a drink would be wonderful. The carriage ride was far more uncomfortable than I expected."

"Oh, of course; you must sit down and rest straight away. Come with me." She took her sisters hand and led her around the high table to where the chairs were placed. "Father, can you get Annie something to drink?" She looked at her father for his agreement and he instantly summoned the servants to attend them.

Simon smiled as he watched his two daughters conspire together and was glad, at last, that Katherine had stopped fighting him over her intended marriage to William Fitzwarren. The last couple of days, things had been much calmer between the two of them and she finally appeared to have forgotten all thoughts of marrying the De Ros boy. Katherine now appeared to be genuinely happy with his choice of husband. He sighed with gratitude that it was at least, one of his problems, that had been resolved. He just hoped that the matter of the murdered monk would also resolve itself as easily.

"So, tell me about it." Katherine said as they sat down together, far enough away from her father and Richard, so that they could talk in private. "When did you know you were with child? When is it due to be born?"

"I have about four months to go until the baby is due." Angharad replied, smiling at her sister's enthusiasm. "I wasn't certain at first if I was with child, or if it was something else. But then I saw one of my women staring at me one morning and she told me that I was definitely with child. Richard and I were beginning to think that we would not be blessed with children; you know how it is. So, we are both delighted now. Of course, Richard is sure it's going to be a boy, but I don't care whether it's a boy or a girl, as long as I get through this." Suddenly both of the girls' minds turned to their mother and there was a brief silence of unmentioned fear between them. Then Angharad continued breezily. "I was so worried at first how it would be, as I'd heard such tales from some of my maid servants, but so far, everything has been fine. There has been very little sickness; only for a few weeks. But I didn't want to tell anyone until I was certain the pregnancy was safe. I am so blessed with how things have been so far; but I don't want to bring ill fate on it by saying too much."

"You look amazing Annie. Having a child really seems to suit you."

"Thank you. But this isn't the reason I am here." She put a protective hand over her swollen belly. "I am here to help you with your wedding. You must tell me everything about it, and what you have planned."

"My wedding." Katherine felt a little reticent. "Yes, I

suppose it would have been a surprise for you. It certainly was for me. I don't feel like the preparations are something which I'm really a part of; it just seems to be happening around me." She tried to keep her countenance as normal as possible, determined that Angharad would not suspect anything was amiss. But her sister knew her better than that.

"Father isn't trying to take control, is he?"

Katherine shook her head. "No, he's far too busy to be bothered with the wedding. He's got enough to worry about with the Royal Justice coming for the assize court; as well as the murder of a monk to look into."

"A murdered monk?" Angharad looked surprised. "You must tell me all about that, but first you need to tell me what has been organised for your wedding and what you need help with. Then I will do everything I can, to make sure it goes perfectly."

Katherine gave a small sigh and was grateful that Angharad had not asked directly about Lord Fitzwarren. She was relieved that she had managed to avoid speaking of him, as she was worried her sister would perceive that she didn't want to marry the man. She also found it difficult to talk of Lord Fitzwarren and not to think of her love for Alexander; and her sister could never, ever know about Alexander or what she was planning.

"It has seemed strange not having you here with me," Katherine said changing the subject and leaning over to hug her sister again, "but Jennet has been helping with the plans for the wedding. She has been making me a new gown for the day, as the ceremony is to be held at the minster?"

"That's incredibly grand, how did father manage that?"

"Oh, it wasn't father, it was Lord Fitzwarren who arranged it. And I'm not quite sure how he did it, but I suspect he used our father's name and also how the King has agreed to our wedding."

Angharad laughed. "That's something you have to deal with little sister, which I didn't. Our father wasn't the

Sheriff of Yorkshire, or quite so grand, when Richard and I got married."

"Is it really two years ago?"

Angharad nodded. "And eighteen months ago, since you moved here with father."

"I have missed you so much since we left," Katherine admitted to her sister. "But I know that you've had Richard to look after you." It was a strange thing that, even though when they had been together, she had found her sister impossible to live with; but when they were apart, Katherine missed her dreadfully. They were so different, but at the end of it all, they were sisters and no matter what happened they would always be there for each other. They were silent for a little while; both lost in thought until Katherine finally spoke.

"How did you feel when you were getting married? I was expecting to feel excited and happy, but I haven't, not yet."

"If I'm honest, I was terrified," Angharad admitted thoughtfully. "I hardly knew Richard; we'd only met twice and both times with other people present, so we couldn't really talk. I knew he was an important man, and I wanted to be worthy of him. I wanted to be the best wife, to run the household well, and to be a good companion to my husband. But I also wanted to please him in the bedroom too, however I had no idea what was expected of me. Mother was gone and Jennet has never married, so she wasn't really much help to advise me on the more personal aspects of being married. If you understand what I mean."

Katherine blushed; it was something that she had never considered before. In her mind she could not countenance it happening with Lord Fitzwarren; but with Alexander, just thinking about his touch made her body come alive.

"I do understand," she said carefully. "Jennet has always been wonderful to me, but she's not our mother and has never spoken of such womanly things." She sighed heavily. "I do wish mother was still here. I have absolutely no memories of what she was like, so it's difficult to say how much I miss her."

"I understand, I was only two when she died, and I hardly remember her at all either. I have just the odd image of her in my mind and sometimes I can recall the sound of her voice singing to me. I wish she was here to tell me what to expect with this little one." Angharad placed a hand on her swollen belly again and Katherine could see tears stinging in her sister's eyes. "I hope she would be happy for me; for both of us."

"I know she would be overjoyed for you." Katherine put her hand over her sisters to comfort her. "I wish that we'd both had more time with her."

She couldn't help but wonder, if her mother had still been around, whether she might have had more influence over her father's decision when it came to choosing whom Katherine would marry.

From across the hall, Simon watched his two daughters chatting happily together and mused on the fact that they had never got on quite so well, when they had been younger and living together. Angharad had always been the more serious and reserved of the two girls, whereas Katherine had been the more spirited, and strong willed. He considered that Angharad had never questioned his choice of husband for her, whereas he had a nagging feeling that he still hadn't heard the last from Katherine about her impending marriage to Lord Fitzwarren. Even though, in the last day, she seemed to have resigned herself to the fact that it was going to happen. Simon noticed that his eldest daughters husband Richard, looked slightly lost and superfluous as he watched the two sisters talk, and Simon could see how much the man doted on Angharad.

"I see you are taking good care of my daughter," Simon smiled and gestured for them to sit in the chairs at the opposite end of the table to his daughters.

"I am, sir." Richard replied taking a seat next to Simon. A servant came to fill up their goblets and he was silent for a while, before adding. "Your daughter has brought me more joy than I can say. And now, we are to be blessed with the greatest gift. I was beginning to think that we were not to have children, and then... Well, as you can see, God has seen it fit to bless us with a child, which is everything that I could wish for." He smiled proudly. "To have a son and heir is everything that a man could want."

Simon studied his son-in-law carefully. He was only a little younger than Simon was, and was known for being a deeply religious man, but Angharad seemed to be very happy with him, and that was all that mattered.

"Then, I hope for your sake that you have a son." Simon replied. "For me, I wasn't so blessed, but my two beautiful daughters are a special part of my life, and I am grateful every day for their presence."

Richard blushed with slight embarrassment. "Of course, if it is a girl then she will be just as welcome. But a son, would carry on my name and my estate."

Simon understood the need for a son to carry on a lineage, but it had never happened for him. After Ellen had died, he had been encouraged to marry again to provide the two small girls with a mother figure. But his grief at losing Ellen had been all encompassing and he hadn't been able to even consider the thought. Instead, he had buried himself in his work and service to the King. Now, he considered himself too old and set in his ways to start trying again with a second wife, even if the thought of having a son to pass on his estates to, would be an appealing proposition.

Simon leant back in his chair, trying to relax, as the servant's brought food and wine to the table. He watched as Richard gazed across at Angharad with love and pride; and Simon hoped that Lord Fitzwarren would show the same devotion to his younger daughter, though he had to admit he doubted it. Lord Fitzwarren was a stronger character and more assertive than Richard; and Simon mused that he would need to be quite forceful to deal with the spirited nature of his daughter Katherine. Simon had never been sure whether he had done the right thing in allowing his daughter to be fully educated. She could both read and write in French and Latin and was more fluent than even he was. Her interest in his legal work had endeared her to him and he had happily indulged her interest in the law, although he knew Katherine would never be allowed to use it. His daughter was an intelligent and self-confident woman; and he was well aware that it would take a strong individual to keep her in line and not to let her have everything her own way. Simon had realised that since he had come to York, under instruction of the King to become the new Sheriff of the county, he had not been as strict in keeping his youngest daughter in check. She had had things her own way for quite a while now, as his work as sheriff had been his priority. He was aware that she still went out riding on her own, even though he had instructed her not to. His only consolation was that Grenulf was with her; the dog doted on his mistress so much, that he would never allow any harm to come to her. Simon also doubted that Lord Fitzwarren would indulge his daughters' escapades once they were married, and she was lady of the manor.

"I hear that you have a busy week ahead of you." Richard said, distracting Simon from his thoughts.

"Indeed; I have the Royal Justice arriving tomorrow for the assize court; and then there is the wedding at the end of the week." He gave a small grin. "Though I doubt I will have little say in that, other than paying for it."

Richard nodded. "I'm sure Angharad will make sure everything runs smoothly. My wife is exceptionally good at organising events and I'm sure she will enjoy overseeing everything."

"I am also hoping that her being here will help Katherine accept this marriage as well."

"Katherine is not happy with your choice of husband for her?" Richard sounded genuinely surprised.

"Not exactly. In fact, she was very angry about it when I told her." Simon recalled their argument. "Although, in the last couple of days, she does seem to have resigned herself to it."

"But she must accept your decision. You are her father." Richard stated, quite bemused.

Simon knew that Richard was correct. But then the man didn't know Katherine as well as Simon did. "Yes Richard, I know."

"Do I get to meet your future husband before the wedding?" Angharad asked her sister.

"Father has arranged for a dinner to be held here at the castle the evening before the wedding." Katherine told her. "The Royal Justice will be here too, so I think father wants it to be a great banquet."

"So, our father will be busy this week with the assize court. I'm surprised that you didn't want to wait until afterwards, to hold the wedding."

"I would have, but this is what Lord Fitzwarren wanted." Katherine said with a resigned voice, and wanted to add that she would have been happy to wait, even if she was waiting for months, or years.

"What is he like, this William Fitzwarren?" Angharad seemed oblivious to her sister's tone.

"Oh, you know, he's older than I am; more fathers' age than mine. A little like Richard and yourself." She paused thoughtfully. "I suppose he's quite handsome."

"You don't sound very happy about him?" Angharad was now curious.

"I didn't have a say in the matter," Katherine replied firmly. "The betrothal was all done and sorted before I could object." She bit her lip to stop herself from saying any more.

Angharad put out a hand to reassure her sister. "But you know, that is how it is for women in our position. We do not get a choice. We are obedient to our fathers, and then our husbands, wishes."

Katherine put her head on one side as she looked at her sister. "Annie, when have you ever known me to be obedient to anyone?"

They both started to laugh, and Simon looked up and smiled. It was good to hear Katherine laugh again. He hadn't heard much of it lately; there had been more angry words and tears rather than laughter.

CHAPTER 13

Simon left the castle early the next morning with his deputy, Adam, at his side. They were riding out to see Peter Beaumont, who had sent word that he had now returned to his parent's manor. The journey gave Simon time to reflect on what had happened. It was now five days since Brother Clement had been killed, and he still had no more information about who might have committed the heinous crime, as he did on the first day. He was conscious that he needed to try and resolve this murder quickly and it bothered him that he seemed to be no closer to finding out the truth. He only hoped that Peter might be able to help with his investigation.

As they rode, he discussed the matter with Adam, in the hope that his deputy might have some more information, or insights into the murder. But Adam was just as much at a loss as Simon was.

"I can't see it being John of Askham," Adam mused, "and as far as any of the other rioters are concerned, none of them would have it in them to kill a monk. And there's also the matter of the dagger that we found; none of that rabble would own, or ever hope to own, something so grand."

"And what of Roger de Mowbray?"

"Ahh, now that's a different story. Roger is a man that I don't trust and who would be rich enough to own a dagger like the one we found; in fact, I would say that it would be just his sort of thing; very flashy and grandiose. But, on the other hand we have nothing, other than our own suspicions, to say he carried out the murder, or was in any way connected to it."

"Other than the fact, that Brother Clement came to see his mother that evening," Simon reminded him. "And we know that his mother was a benefactor of the Abbey."

"*Was*, being the operative word," Adam noted. "As I hear that she passed away two days ago."

"Really?" Now Simons' interest was piqued.

"Of course, it was expected," Adam continued, "as she's been ill for a while now."

"But very convenient, wouldn't you say?"

"Aye, I would. But then, Lord de Mowbray will be returning from the north for the funeral, so there isn't much more we can do. It's not right to go disturbing a family when they're grieving."

"Very true," Simon concurred. "But let's not take our eyes off that young man. Roger de Mowbray is definitely hiding something and sooner, or later, he's going to slip up."

It wasn't long before they arrived at the manor. The steward was already waiting for them as they rode in through the main gate and the stable hand took charge of their horses as they dismounted.

"If you would be so good as to follow me," the man invited. "Lord Beaumont and his son are waiting for you in the main hall."

Simon nodded to Adam and they both followed the steward across the courtyard and into the main hall. Peter Beaumont was waiting for them just inside the entrance, together with his father.

"Welcome Sheriff de Hale. My father wrote me a letter to say that you wanted to speak with me, so I came straight home."

Simon clasped the outstretched hand in a warm greeting. Peter Beaumont was a young man, tall and sturdy, such as would be befitting a knight of his age.

"Peter it is good to meet you. May I introduce my deputy, Adam de Burgh, though I believe you two already know each other."

Adam stepped forward and the two men greeted each other warmly, clapping each other on the back.

"Adam; it's been two long. How are you my old friend?"

"I'm good Peter; and I can see that you are doing well

for yourself."

"Yes, I ride out for the Earl of Chester now." Peter smiled and then turned his attention back to Simon. "My father told me that you wanted to speak to me about Hugh," he said, indicating that they were to follow him.

"Yes, that's right," Simon replied, as they were shown to a table. He took a seat opposite Peter, with Adam next to him and Peter's father opposite them. "I'm trying to find out who might have murdered him and why."

"It's absolutely dreadful. I couldn't believe it when my father told me what had happened." Peter shook his head in disbelief. "I mean murder is a terrible thing anyway; but the murder of an innocent monk is unconscionable."

"Yes, I agree and we're trying to find out more about Brother Clement and who he is or was. I believe you knew him well before he decided to take Holy orders?"

"Yes, that's correct; I've known him since we were young boys," Peter confirmed.

"You see, I cannot find any reason why anyone would want to murder Brother Clement as a lowly monk, and the manner of his death suggests that this wasn't just a random, drunken act. So, I have to wonder if his past life as a soldier might have some bearing on this. His family told me that you knew Brother Clement, or should I call him Hugh de Glanville, well; and I thought you might be able to tell me more about him; what he was like before he took Holy Orders and whether there was anyone who might hold a grudge, or ill-will against him?"

"You're right, I did know him well when we were younger. We trained as squires together and then fought in the Barons war ten years ago." Peter sighed heavily. "He was a good friend; we were very close, and we always had each other's back."

"So, was there anyone who might have harboured a grudge against him?"

Peter shrugged. "Not that I can think of, and no more than they would have had for me. He was a good soldier, but he also had a solid sense of fair play too. In some ways,

I can see why he took Holy Orders, the injustice of war never sat quite right with him. In the end, I believe he was just tired of fighting and that's why he decided to take the cowl."

"But there was no-one in particular who might have taken against him?"

Peter paused thoughtfully for a moment before he spoke. "No, I'm sorry. I've given it a lot of thought since my father told me you wanted to speak with me, and there is no-one I can think of."

Simon nodded understandingly. It was not the answer he had wanted. He had hoped that there would be something about Hugh's service as a soldier that would have given him a clue as to who might have wanted to kill him in such a brutal manner. He needed to find out who had done this, and he was still no closer to knowing who it could be.

"His parents mentioned that Hugh was also betrothed to be married before he entered the Abbey." Simon said after a while.

"Yes, that's correct," Peter replied, "Lady Isabel. She was beautiful, and the two of them had known each other for years. They were betrothed when they were just children, but it was a good match, and they were well suited."

"I can imagine that Hugh deciding to take Holy Orders must have come as a great shock to her?"

Peter nodded. "Yes, Hugh told me she was distraught. I believe she tried everything she could, to try and persuade him against it. But he was a very focused and single-minded person, and once he set his mind to something, there was no moving him. Isabel came to me and told me that nothing she said could dissuade Hugh; and asked me to intervene. I tried to talk to him as well, but he assured me he knew what he was doing. He really did believe that he had heard the voice of God calling him. He said that God wanted him to leave behind his previous life as a soldier, and to live a life of prayer; to atone for his past offences." Peter shrugged and gestured with his hands. "There was nothing I, or anyone, could say that would stop him."

Simon nodded. "Do you know what happened to Isabel after Hugh entered the order?"

"Now, that was tragic." Peter added. "She tried again and again to see him and talk to him whilst he was a postulant, but he was resolute about his calling. He just wouldn't change his mind, and, in the end, he refused to see her anymore. Isabel asked for my help, to try and persuade him to see her, and also for me to try and sway him, but he said the same thing to me; that God had called him and that he had found peace and had no doubts that this was what he was supposed to do with his life."

"And Lady Isabel, what happened to her? Hugh's parents thought that she had married."

Peter shook his head and took a while before he spoke. "No, that's not right. Isabel didn't get married. She was so distressed by Hugh leaving her; she would never have looked at anyone else. She loved him so very much you know, and I think, in the end, it must have all been too much for her. I believe that she just couldn't face her future without him and ended up taking her own life."

Simon found himself a little shocked by the news. His instincts were peeked at the information Peter had just given him.

"She killed herself?"

Peter nodded. "Yes, she drowned herself in the river, one winters night, a couple of years ago." He said solemnly. "From what I know, she placed stones in the hem of her gown and cloak and then walked into the river one night after a rainstorm when the water was high. It was such a shock to all of us."

"Indeed, it was." Lord Beaumont added. "No-one had expected her to do that."

"That is very sad," Simon stated. "I gather that Hugh must have been told what had happened?"

"Yes, he was told," Peter continued. "I visited him to

tell him the news myself. He looked sad, but said that she had gone against all the Holy laws by taking her own life. He told me that her soul could not be saved because she had taken her own life, which is against the teachings of God."

Simon drew breath as he considered the importance of what he had just been told; that the Lady Isabel would have been denied a Christian burial in consecrated ground. Her burial would have gone unmarked, and her family would have been tainted by the deed.

"I imagine that her family must have been very upset about it?"

"Yes, they were. Fortunately, her parents were both dead and were therefore spared the anguish. But I know her brother was distraught by the news. He was very angry at Hugh and blamed him for driving his sister into taking her own life."

Finally, Simon thought to himself, a possible motive for the murder of Brother Clement.

"And this brother, can you tell me who he is? And does he live locally?" Simon tried to hide his impatience.

"Yes, he still lives around here. In fact, I believe you are acquainted with him."

Robert de Lexington rode at the head of his men as they approached the castle in York. It was late morning, and it was already incredibly hot. There was very little breeze, and the air was heavy with the stench of human waste and decay. Robert was a tall man of almost fifty years of age with greying hair, and he had a strong face which was lined from spending many years in the saddle. He had a presence that went with the confidence of his position at court and of being a Royal Justice for seven counties in England. His appointments kept him constantly on the move around the country and his visit to York was just the latest stop in his travels. The county was the second most important judicial area in the country and its sheriff, Simon de Hale, had done an excellent job in administrating the area since his appointment at the beginning of the previous year. Robert knew Simon well from their time at court together and had a healthy respect for the man. As Royal Justice, Robert, was there to oversee the assize court for the most serious crimes in the county; everything else, all the petty squabbles between local landowners and tenants; charges of theft or poaching, were left to Simon as sheriff, and local smaller hundred courts to deal with.

He watched as the castle gates opened to him and his retinue, as they approached the walls. He appreciated it when those in charge of the county were organised, and he was given the respect that was due him; and knowing Simon de Hale as he did, he expected nothing less. It made everything run more smoothly, and his time was not wasted unnecessarily on insignificant items. It was less stressful for everyone involved. He was anticipating that Simon would be there to greet him and, after refreshment, they would adjourn to his office where the two of them would go through the cases he would be hearing at the assize court. The next few days would be taken up with preparing and hearing the cases at the assizes, before he took his leave and then moved on. He had a few days in between his work at York, and his next assize court, and was anticipating he would take the time to rest away from the city.

Simon was waiting for him as he dismounted and came to greet him.

"Robert, it is good to see you again." Simon greeted his guest happily. "How was your journey?"

"Not too arduous. I stopped over at Pontefract castle last night, I had some business with John de Lacy." Robert smiled at his friend. "So, the journey this morning was quite acceptable. He sends his regards, by the way."

Simon nodded as they walked towards the great hall. "John is a good man. I'm afraid I have lost touch with so many people, as I haven't been at court for quite a while."

Robert smiled. "I hear that you have been busy since I

was last here."

"Yes, but I enjoy the challenge as you well know. And, saying that, we have a busy few days in front of us. I have all the documents ready for you to go through, but first I thought we could have something to eat."

Robert smiled and nodded as he followed Simon up the staircase into the great hall.

"I also hear that your youngest daughter is to be married later this week."

"Yes, that's right. I am surprised that such news has reached you. She is to marry Lord Fitzwarren at the end of the week. If you are able to stay on, you would be most welcome at the wedding."

"I think that could be arranged. I have a few days to spare before my next assize court." Robert said, as they entered the hall. "Do I know this man, Lord Fitzwarren?"

"He's a local nobleman; a good man. I think he will be a good husband for Katherine. He's arranged for the wedding to be held at the minster, as he believes it to be appropriate to my daughters standing," Simon said with irony. He was still unsure as to why Lord Fitzwarren had insisted that the minster should be the venue for the nuptials. He would have been happy to see his daughter married at the castle chapel, more modestly and quietly. Simon was never one for an overly display of position.

Robert laughed companionably. "I think I get the measure of this Lord Fitzwarren, already."

"You will see Katherine at dinner tonight, and my eldest daughter Angharad is also here; she arrived yesterday with her husband."

"You have a lot to deal with at the moment my friend; assize court, a wedding and also, a murdered monk, I hear?"

"It seems that nothing escapes your knowledge," Simon joked. "Indeed; a lowly monk from St Marys Abbey was brutally murdered a few days ago and I still need to find out who the killer was."

Simon was pleased that Robert had agreed to stay on

after the assize court. It would be good to spend time with his friend, and also to speak with him about the murdered monk and get his view on the matter. Following Simons' meeting with Peter Beaumont earlier that morning, his mind was now in a quandary. The information that he had been told, would give the man in question a motive to kill Brother Clement, but he had nothing else to link him to the actual murder. The man Peter had implicated, had never given Simon any indication that he would carry out a cold-blooded murder. Simon was reluctant to question him about it, given that at the moment, he had nothing else than Peter Beaumont's word to back up the information. He had the predicament of wanting to resolve this matter as soon as possible but, equally, the last thing he wanted to do was to give the man in question advance warning. Simon believed that the dagger might still be in the man's possession, and if he knew Simon suspected him, he might quickly decide to discard it. At the moment the information was inconclusive at best, and Simon knew he needed something more. He only hoped that he would be able to find it to either prove, or disprove, his suspicions while Robert de Lexington was staying in the city.

"May I present my eldest daughter Angharad and her husband Lord Richard Payne." Simon said as his eldest daughter and her husband approached Robert de Lexington at the dinner that evening. "They have joined us for Katherines' wedding."

"I am pleased to meet both of you." Robert greeted them as they stood in front of him. Richard gave a small bow and Angharad curtseyed in front of Robert before exchanging pleasantries with him.

"And this, as you already know, is my daughter, Katherine." Simon added as she approached and curtseyed graciously in front of Robert.

"Katherine, it is good to see you again," Robert greeted her warmly. "Will you do me the honour of sitting beside me this evening?"

Katherine glanced across at her father for approval and he gave a small nod.

"Yes, Sir Robert. That would be most agreeable."

Katherine had taken particular care with her appearance that evening, wearing one of her best gowns, and her hair was neatly dressed and held in place with a wimple and barbette.

Robert smiled at Katherine and offered his arm to escort her to the table. She was a true beauty, he considered, though she had the demeanour of an unbroken horse, half wild and half trained. She would be a handful for any man to control as a wife. From what he had heard, even his good friend her father, appeared to be struggling to keep her in check at the moment. He had only been in the castle a few hours but had already found out from the servants that attended him, that Katherine liked to go out riding most days. But what they found most unacceptable was that she would not take any men to guard her, only that great dog of hers. Robert had found that it was usually the servants who knew most about what was going on in a castle, rather than anyone else.

It wasn't until after the dinner that Robert finally had chance to speak more with Katherine. She intrigued him; since his last visit in the spring, she had changed suddenly into a beautiful young woman, as opposed to the tall girl who looked as if her long limbs weren't quite within her control. But she had also lost, or was it merely controlled, that spirited character of hers. Normally, she would have talked endlessly with him. Inquiring about his work and the other assize courts he had presided over; but tonight, she was quieter and more reserved. He was curious to know what the reason for this might be and wondered if it was to do with her forthcoming wedding. When Simon had told him about her betrothal to Lord Fitzwarren he had been surprised. The man was unknown to him, but from what he had heard from the servants, Fitzwarren was not a good match for Katherine.

"I hear you are to be married soon?" He inquired, turning to her as they finished their meal. "Your father has asked me to stay on after the assize for the wedding. I hope that you find that acceptable."

"Yes sire, whatever my father wishes." Katherine kept her voice calm and soft. She liked Robert de Lexington greatly. When he had attended previous assize courts, he had always found time to talk with her and was happy to answer all the questions she flung at him, with good grace. But she knew that he had a reputation as a strong man, and one who was not to be crossed on any terms.

"But what do you wish, mistress Katherine?"

Katherine raised her head to look at him and momentarily had to stop herself from telling him everything that was on her mind. His gaze had a way of drawing out unspoken truths from people and she could feel its power encouraging her to tell him her secrets; but she managed to stop herself just in time.

"Do you not wish to be married to Lord Fitzwarren?" Robert asked sensing her hesitation. "Does he displease you?"

"No, he is a good man." She told him truthfully, then hesitated before adding softly. "But I am in love with another."

"Ahh..." Robert nodded his head, so now he understood. "Does your father know this?"

"Yes, sire; he does." Again, she paused, not sure just how much to tell him. "But he said that it was too late as he had already sought the Kings approval for the marriage."

"And this man that you are in love with, is he of noble birth?"

"He is sire"

"Do I know him?"

"He is Alexander de Ros, the third son of Baron Robert de Ros of Helmsley."

Robert nodded thoughtfully. "I know his father quite well, and his elder brother William. As you say they are a noble family." He leant towards her, almost conspiratorially. "I take it that if your father hadn't already arranged this betrothal, then you would be marrying Alexander in a few days' time instead." He studied her carefully. "I hope you are not expecting me to intervene on your behalf mistress, because you know that I cannot."

Katherine blushed with alarm; it had not occurred to her that Sir Robert would think that. "No sire, I would never be so bold as to ask that of you."

Robert nodded. "I know that." He looked at her carefully and realised that the quietness was actually a deep sadness. "But it grieves me to see you unhappy about your wedding, Katherine." He added. "I have two daughters of my own, although they are both older than you; and their mother and I did try to make good matches for them. I like to think that, even if at first, they did not love their husbands, that they have now grown to love them." He turned to look at Katherine's sister. "Your sister and her husband appear to be very happy together."

"They are." Katherine observed.

"And I believe your father arranged your sister's marriage too?" Katherine nodded, she could see where this was leading. "So, there is no reason that you too could not have a marriage as devoted as that." Robert smiled as he spoke to her.

"But Angharad wasn't in love with another man when she married Richard." Katherine countered. "How can I be expected to love Lord Fitzwarren when my heart belongs to someone else?"

He put his hand over hers in reassurance. "You will find a way my dear Katherine."

CHAPTER 14

Katherine woke up early the following morning. She hadn't slept well, being kept awake by thoughts of her conversation with Sir Robert. Then, when she had finally fallen asleep, it had been fitful and punctuated with dreams of Alexander and their impending escape to the north. There had been horsemen following them and they had been trying to outride them; but these horsemen were not guards, but soldiers all dressed in black. When she awoke, as the dawn light was coming into the bedchamber, she wondered if it could all be an omen; and not a good one. Trying to put it out of her mind, she slipped out of her bed and wrapped a shawl around her shoulders. Sir Robert had been very kind to her the previous evening. He had listened to her speak of her unhappiness about her betrothal to Lord Fitzwarren, and he hadn't judged; he hadn't taken sides. Katherine knew that he would never back her against her father and she would never ask it of him, but there was a part of her which was glad that she had told him, and that he'd understood.

Katherine found herself actually enjoying her sisters' company since Angharad's return yesterday. For some reason she had imagined that she and Angharad would be sharing a bedroom, just like they used to do when they lived together at the manor in Earls Barton. Katherine had pictured them lying together in bed, talking into the early hours, but she wondered if she would have told her sister about Alexander? She had told Sir Robert, but she trusted his discretion more than she did her sisters. When Katherine had asked her sister, after the banquet had finished, if she would be joining her in Katherine's bedchamber, Angharad had laughed and told her that, as a married woman, she was expected to retire to the same bedroom as her husband. Katherine had blushed with embarrassment at the words from her sister and realised just how naïve she had been. Sitting by herself in the early morning sunlight, Katherine couldn't help but feel slightly upset that everything around her was changing. Angharad and her father were her family and her last connection to her mother. They were the only ones who remembered her mother and were her link to that early part of her life. But now she was planning to give it all up for a life with Alexander, the man she loved. Katherine knew that once she had run away with Alexander, and broken with her family, then there would be no going back; there would be no more happy conversations with her sister, or sharp sparring with her farther. But equally the thought of spending the rest of her life with Alexander as his wife, and mother of their children, was worth more than the loss of everything else she held dear.

Katherine was just finishing dressing in a light blue gown when Jennet came into the room with a letter for her. Initially, Katherine was excited and almost grabbed the letter from Jennet, thinking that it was from Alexander. But, as she opened it and started to read, she realised that it was not from him, but from Lord Fitzwarren. She tried to hide her disappointment, as she noticed Jennet watching her.

"It's from Lord Fitzwarren." Katherine said, eventually. "He asks if I would like to visit him at his manor this morning; to see the house I will be living in once we are married."

"Oh, that will be good." Jennet beamed at her. "You will get to meet the servants and see the place where you will be living."

"Will you come with me?" Katherine asked, suddenly feeling nervous at meeting Lord Fitzwarren on her own.

"Do you mean this morning? Or when you are married?"

Katherine considered it. She hadn't really thought about what would happen once she was married, because in her heart she knew it wasn't going to happen. But she still needed to maintain the illusion that everything was going to plan.

"Both," she smiled, "you know I couldn't manage without you Jennet; and I will need a friendly face once I am married. Somehow, I just assumed that you would come with me, to help me settle in and teach me how to run the house." Katherine watched as Jennet beamed with happiness, and she felt a little wrong at deceiving her maid so badly. "I would also love you to come with me this morning; I'm sure Lord Fitzwarren won't object. Then we can both see the manor where we will be living."

"Do you want your sister to come too?"

Katherine shook her head. "I don't think it would be good for her in her condition, and I don't want Lord Fitzwarren to think that I've invited the whole family to come with me. Besides, I could tell she was very tired from the journey yesterday and I think she will want to rest."

Jennet nodded. "Very well, I will go down and tell the stable master that we will be riding out to Lord Fitzwarren's manor this morning. Will you tell your father?"

Katherine shook her head. "No, he's going to be busy with Sir Robert and the court hearings all day; I don't want to disturb him."

Jennet left and Katherine went to brush her hair. When Jennet returned, she was still sitting on the chair trying to decide what to do with her unruly locks.

"I thought I would tie it back and try to get it covered properly, as I had last night. But I don't seem to be able to manage it on my own."

Jennet nodded and smiled as she took the brush from Katherine. "You want to look your best for Lord Fitzwarren, I understand. I will make sure you look so beautiful that he will be speechless when he sees you."

Katherine sat patiently as Jennet brushed and tied up her hair to go under the simple wimple and barbette. She knew that as long as Jennet believed she had finally reconciled herself about the marriage to Lord Fitzwarren then she wouldn't question her when she took Grenulf out for a walk later that afternoon. Then, when she planned to leave with Alexander, she wouldn't be missed for quite a while; and by that time both she and Alexander would be well on their way north from the city.

The manor of Lord Fitzwarren was to the east of York and as Katherine rode there with Jennet and one of her father's guards, she tried to look as noble and important as she imagined her new husband would expect her to be. When the manor house and surrounding buildings came into view, Katherine found herself surprised at just how large and imposing the buildings were. Lord Fitzwarren had certainly managed to establish himself as an important man in the county. The main gates were open to receive them, and Lord Fitzwarren appeared almost immediately to greet them as they entered the courtyard.

"Katherine, I am so pleased to see you." He greeted her smiling.

Katherine couldn't deny that he was a good-looking man and even though he was older than she was, he did not appear so. She returned the smile and dismounted from her horse Lily. Katherine found that she couldn't help feeling a little sorry for Lord Fitzwarren. He had done nothing wrong and yet she was planning a life, which he wouldn't be part of.

"Lord Fitzwarren, it was so good of you to invite me. I hope you don't mind, but I wanted to bring my maid, Jennet, with me today. I hope you will be willing to agree for her to stay in my service after we are married?" She smiled and tried her best to look demure in his sight.

"Of course, my dear. I would be pleased for you to bring your maid with you. Anything that makes you happy." He said, as he took her hands in his own to greet her.

He looked at her with such devotion that it made Katherine feel terrible at the way she was planning to deceive him.

"Let me show you my home," he added. "I hope you will be very comfortable here."

"I'm sure that I will be." Katherine looked back to Jennet to check that she had dismounted and was ready to accompany her.

Lord Fitzwarren led Katherine into the main hall of the manor house. It was well appointed and lavishly decorated with large wall hangings and beautiful pieces of furniture. Katherine found herself admiring it and oddly imagining herself dining in the hall as mistress of the manor. William introduced her to his steward and to the other staff, including his housekeeper, an older woman called Margaret, who seemed to take an instant dislike to her future new mistress. Katherine felt the woman's eyes boring into her, questioning and examining her and seeming to find her wanting, in some way or another. Katherine felt uneasy in the sight of the woman but then reassured herself that she would never actually have to deal with Margaret, as she never intended to be mistress of this household.

"Take no notice." Jennet whispered, observing the other woman's attitude towards Katherine. "Just remember you will be mistress here once you are married, and she will have to answer to you."

Katherine gave a small nod and looked towards William to see if he had registered his housekeeper's animosity, but he appeared to be totally oblivious to it.

The main solar was up a stone spiral staircase leading off the main hall and was just as lavishly appointed as the hall. There were heavy curtains around the enormous beautifully carved timber bed. Katherine involuntarily shivered at the thought of her lying there, next to William, even though she knew it wouldn't actually happen. Jennet noticed her hesitation and reached out to touch her mistress in reassurance, believing there was a different reason for Katherine's reaction.

Lord Fitzwarren was a gracious and proud host showing off his manor to his intended future wife. Everything, and every room of the manor, had been cleaned and prepared to show it off to its' best to

Katherine. As they finished their tour of the manor, Lord Fitzwarren smiled and turned to Katherine.

"I have something that I would like to show you." He gently took her hand and guided her out of the manor buildings. "I thought your maid would like to stay and acquaint herself with the rest of the manor, such as the kitchens and servants' quarters, whilst I show you something that I have bought for you as a wedding present."

He glanced across at Jennet, who nodded her head and then left them in order to acquaint herself with the other staff. Lord Fitzwarren led Katherine down the spiral staircase and outside across the courtyard to the stables.

"I know you are very fond of your own horse, but I thought you might like to have this fellow as well."

He led her down to the end stable where there was a fine bay horse with a white blaze down his face. Katherine was immediately drawn to the horse and went up to stroke his head.

"His name is Tiberius," Lord Fitzwarren told her. "I think it is a very fine name for such an impressive horse."

"He is beautiful." Katherine stroked the horse as he nuzzled her. "I would still like to bring Lily with me though. If that would be acceptable to you?"

"Of course, my dear. Anything to make you happy. You know I used to have a grey mare as well, she was a fine horse; but I let her go quite recently. If I had only known you had a grey mare too, then I would have kept her, and they could have been stabled together."

Katherine started to feel quite terrible at the way she was behaving towards Lord Fitzwarren. He was a good, thoughtful and kind man and didn't warrant the way she was treating him. Her mind pictured a scene of him standing alone at the entrance to the minster waiting for her to arrive and then receiving the news from her father that she had run away, and there would be no wedding. It made her feel terrible; but the thought of being married to William and not Alexander was an even worse proposition.

She was lost in her thoughts as they walked along the stables looking at the rest of the horses.

"Here," Lord Fitzwarren said. "This is my horse, Titus, isn't he a magnificent animal?"

"Oh yes." She replied, reaching up to stroke the horse in front of her. "He's quite beautiful."

As Katherine stroked the muzzle of the horse, there was sound of a commotion elsewhere in the courtyard and a servant suddenly arrived at Lord Fitzwarren's side and whispered to his master.

"My apologies Katherine. I have to leave you for a little while. Will you be alright here?"

"Yes, of course." She watched Lord Fitzwarren walk away, leaving her on her own at the stables, then went back to find Tiberius in the corner stall.

She was happily stroking the horse, when she heard a noise within the stable building. At first, she thought it was just one of the other horses moving around its' stall; but then she became acutely aware that the noise was not that made by another animal, but a person.

"Hello?" She called out, stepping forward. Tiberius had also registered the noise, and his ears lay flat against his head and his eyes widened. Katherine remained alongside Tiberius, stroking him to try and calm the nervous horse. From inside the stable there was no answer.

It struck her as odd, that Tiberius was the only horse to be disturbed by the noise. If there was someone moving around the stables, then the other horses were not at all frightened by them. There was no alarm or whickering from the horses, that might suggest fear. Whoever was there, it was someone that the other horses knew and felt safe with.

"Hello?" She asked again, leaving Tiberius and venturing into the stables to look around. "It's alright; please don't be afraid; I won't hurt you."

Quickly looking around the stables, Katherine could not see anything amiss. Then, she looked more carefully in each of the stalls, petting the horses as she passed by and trying to see if there was any movement in the bedding. It was in the end stable that she noticed a small movement in the corner. It looked as though someone had been sleeping in the stable, alongside one of the horses, which would be a dangerous thing if the person was not well known to the animal, and even then, not what she would expect to happen in a fine stable such as this.

"Hello, whoever you are," she asked softly. "I'm not here to scold you. I just came here to see my new horse. His name is Tiberius; you might know him; he's a very fine mount." She paused, hoping for some acknowledgment, but there was none. "Please won't you tell me who you are. I would like to be your friend." She paused sensing the fear of whoever was hiding from her. "I would like you to look after Tiberius for me. Is that something you can do?"

She waited patiently, her senses working overtime as she tried to detect the smallest sound, or movement in the stables. Eventually she heard a small rustle and caught sight of a mop of black hair emerging from the hay.

"Are you alright?" She asked softly.

The mop of hair was followed by the face of a small boy, who looked straight at her and nodded.

"I'm sorry, I didn't mean to scare you," she added. "Lord Fitzwarren brought me here to show me a horse that he has bought for me. He's quite a fine animal; have you seen him?"

The boy nodded his head.

"Do you work here?" The boy nodded again, and Katherine took a step towards him as he emerged from the hay. "What's your name?"

"Edward, mistress." He couldn't have been more than ten or eleven years old, she thought.

"Hello Edward, I'm Katherine."

"Pleased to meet you, mistress." He stood up and did a small bow in front of her.

"Well Edward, have you met Tiberius? He really is a fine horse, and your master has told me that he is to be mine." She walked slowly along the stables until she reached Tiberius, and started to stroke the bay horse, as the boy approached her.

"But don't you have your own horse?" He asked, reaching out a hand to pat the horse's muzzle with great tenderness.

"Indeed, I do. Her name is Lily, and she is the grey mare that is tethered up outside."

She watched as the boy turned and then stepped warily out of the stable building to go towards Lily, and Katherine followed him.

"She's very beautiful, mistress." He said stroking Lily and seeming to grow in confidence. "They tell me that you are to be the new mistress of the manor. Will you let me take care of her once you come to live here?"

"Of course. In fact, I shall insist on it," Katherine said, smiling. She had taken an instant liking to the young boy, who seemed to have such affinity with horses. Edwards' face lit up at her affirmation. Katherine watched him and then suddenly saw his demeanour change from being totally calm and at peace with the animals; to becoming quite agitated. Then Katherine saw what she could only have described as a look of fear on his face.

"I'd better get back to work," he stammered and quickly disappeared into one of the stables.

Katherine wondered what on earth she had done to make him suddenly seem so frightened. But it wasn't long before she realised that it wasn't anything she had done. As she looked to her side, she saw a burly man striding across the courtyard towards the stables. Katherine remained stationary next to Lily, with the horse half-hiding her from the view of the man, who quickly disappeared into the stables after Edward. Instantly, she heard shouting and then the whinnying of the horses, followed by a cry of pain.

Katherine felt a sense of anger rising inside her, as she left Lily to walk over to the stable entrance. There, she saw the burly man who had just walked past her, with his arm raised and a leather strap in his hand. In front of him, lying on the straw of the corner stable was Edward.

"I told you boy, to finish grooming the horses. And what do I see? I see you outside talking with the new mistress; that is my job to do. How dare you disobey me. How dare you! You're a useless good-for-nothing piece of dirt. I'll teach you not to disobey me."

Before Katherine could stop him, the man brought down the strap onto Edward and the boy cried out in pain.

"Stop that at once!" She yelled, mustering as much authority in her voice as she could manage. "If you hit him once again, I will call for Lord Fitzwarren."

The man turned quickly, shocked that he had been seen and especially by the future lady of the manor.

"My lady, I didn't see you there."

"Obviously not."

Katherine watched as the man raised himself to his full height and turned to face her.

"With respect my lady, I would suggest that you leave now. This is none of your business," he replied angrily, then turned back towards the boy.

"I disagree. I think it is very much my business." Katherine could feel herself trembling but was determined not to show it. She watched as the man stopped again and turned to face her.

"With respect, you know nothing about our ways here." He took a step towards her, and she could smell the stench of alcohol on his breath. "If you know what is good for you, you will leave it alone."

Katherine felt intimidated but was determined to stand her ground. In the stable, Edward had retreated into one of the stalls, where he slunk into the corner half-hidden by the straw bedding.

Katherine drew herself up to her full height. "I will remind you, that I am to be married to your Lord later this week; and, once I am mistress of this manor, I will not tolerate such unacceptable behaviour. How dare you speak to me this way."

"Katherine, is something wrong?" She turned to see

Lord Fitzwarren almost running towards her. It seemed the raised voices in the stables had brought the rest of the servants to a standstill.

Katherine gathered herself. "I'm afraid it is, my Lord." Her voice calmed and she tried to become more respectful. "I have witnessed your man here, beating the stable-boy Edward with his belt. The reason for this appears to be, that I have spoken with the young boy about the care of my horse, Lily, once I am your wife." She lowered her eyes demurely in reverence to her future husband, knowing that she was playing a game here.

"Is this true man?" Lord Fitzwarren sounded incensed.

The burly stable master seemed to visibly shrink in front of his Lord.

"It was just a misunderstanding, my lord." He protested.

"But did you beat the stable boy in front of my future wife?"

"I did not realise that she was there, my lord." He was almost trembling now; the bully quickly reduced to a coward.

"That is no excuse man!" William bellowed. "I will not tolerate that sort of behaviour; and especially not in front of my future wife. You will take your things and be gone from this manor. I saw how you spoke to Lady Katherine, and I will not tolerate that sort of behaviour from anyone. Go now; do you hear me? Go!"

Around them the servants in the courtyard whispered quietly amongst themselves. The man looked as if he was going to protest, but the look on his master's face told him it was not a wise decision. Instead, he bent his head in submission to his Lord and master, but gave Katherine a sly, hateful glance as he walked away without a further word.

William turned to face Katherine with regret etched on his face. "I am so sorry my dear. He had no right to speak to you as he did. I can only apologise."

Katherine bowed her head in respect for her future

husbands' defence of her. She could not deny that he was a good man and appeared to care very much for her. If only she could feel the same for him.

"Thank you for intervening." She said, and then went across to stroke Lily, to calm the horse. "I only wanted to assure myself that Lily would be taken care of. Edward, the stable boy and I, were talking together about it, when your man took exception."

Lord Fitzwarren shook his head. "There was no need for him to speak to you that way and I am sorry that you had to witness him beating the boy."

Katherine sighed heavily. "There was no reason for him to treat the boy like that. He had done nothing wrong," she replied, trying to keep her voice calm. "And I did wonder that if he treated the stable boy like that, then what was he like with the horses." She paused, stroking Lily, who now calmly nuzzled into her. "I could never trust Lily to the care of someone that I thought might beat her. I do hope you understand my Lord."

Lord Fitzwarren looked momentarily shocked. "Of course, and I do understand." He smiled at her. "I want you to be completely happy here Katherine, and if there is anything I can do to ensure that, then I will do it."

Lord Fitzwarren's steward arrived at his side and spoke quietly to his master.

"Katherine, please excuse me, but the earlier matter that took me away still requires my attention. I promise you I will not be long. Shall we meet again in the great hall?"

Katherine nodded. "By all means."

She watched him leave and then heaved a sigh of relief. The incident had shaken her, more than she liked to admit. After a brief moment, she managed to gather her composure. Lord Fitzwarren had been nothing but kind to her, but the confrontation with his stablemaster had greatly unsettled her. She instantly felt concerned for the young boy, who had quickly disappeared from view, once Lord Fitzwarren had appeared. She patted Lily and decided to leave her and go and look for Edward. Walking out of the bright sunlight into the dim shadows of the stables, it took a moment for her eyes to adjust to the subdued light; but then she caught sight of him huddled down in the far corner of the end stall, close to where she had first seen him.

"Edward, are you alright?" She asked as she approached him and sank to her knees in the hay. "Please don't be afraid. I promise you; that man will never hurt you again."

Edward looked at her with fear and then with a little suspicion. Katherine quickly realised that this wasn't the first time that he had been beaten by the stablemaster. In fact, he looked as if he lived in daily fear of it happening. Her heart went out to him. If she ever thought this would happen in her fathers' stables, she would ensure that it was eliminated at once, but she had to remind herself that this wasn't her manor.

"Edward, I will make sure that Lord Fitzwarren never lets anyone treat you like that again. And I want you personally to look after both Lily and Tiberius for me; will you do that? If you are happy to do that for me, then I will settle it with his Lordship today." She realised that she should not make promises that she knew she couldn't keep; but she guessed that Lord Fitzwarren would be more than happy to accommodate her wishes.

Edward nodded at her, his eyes staring into hers and his hand grasping at the straw bedding to each side of him. Katherine paused for a moment and then saw a glint in the straw near to Edwards right hand. Curious, but not wanting to alarm him she settled further down in the straw in front of Edward.

"Are you sure you are alright?" She asked him.

"Yes mistress," Edward said softly.

"That's good then. I'm very sorry that I got you into trouble." She smiled at him and watched as he started to extract himself from the hay bedding. As he did so, the glint of metal hidden in the hay caught her eye again, and she looked down at the object next to Edward's hand. "What is that?" She asked softly.

"Nothing." He said defensively and tried to pull more straw over the object.

Watching Edward carefully, she moved her hand towards the glint of metal hiding beneath the bedding, but Edward was quicker, and his hand grasped the handle and pulled it away from her.

"It's alright Edward, I don't want to take it from you." She reassured him, holding up her hands. "I just wanted to see what it was."

"It's mine. You can't have it!" He protested and looked at her fearfully.

"Don't be frightened. I can see that it's something very precious to you and I promise I won't tell your master about it."

"You promise?" Edward eyed her uncertainly.

"Yes, I do." She said firmly. "Edward, I will make a bargain with you. If you promise me that you will personally look after my horse Lily for me, then I promise not to tell your master about this."

She looked at him hopefully and he paused for a moment before nodding at her. "I promise, I will look after Lily for you."

"Then you have my word that I will not tell Lord Fitzwarren about what you have here. Can you show it to me?"

He nodded and slowly pulled the item out of the straw. Katherine almost gasped when she saw the dagger.

"That's a fine dagger you have. Is it yours?"

He nodded. "I found it. It was thrown away; no-one wanted it, and I found it."

"Can I look at it please?"

Edward passed the dagger across to her and Katherine took it gently. It was a beautiful piece with a well-polished blade and a leather grip with engraved metal ends. As she held it, Katherine felt her heart begin to beat more quickly; the dagger was missing its' pommel end.

Carefully she moved it around in her hands looking at it. She drew breath as she realised that the pommel end appeared to have been broken off, and pictured the jewel, that her father had shown her some days ago; the one which had been found near the body of the murdered monk. It looked as if it would fit the dagger exactly.

"It is a fine piece." She told him calmly, anxious not to alarm him. "You should be very proud of it. You said you found it, because it had been thrown away. Where was that?"

Edward suddenly looked frightened again and grabbed the dagger back from Katherine.

"I'm sorry," she told him. "I didn't mean to upset you. I was just curious, that is all. I give you my word, that I will not tell Lord Fitzwarren about this." She looked at him pleadingly.

She waited patiently as Edward thought about it.

"Please will you tell me how you came to find it?"

"It's mine!" Edward said defensively.

"I understand that. And I know you didn't steal it. But will you tell me the story of how you came to find it?"

Silence fell between them as Edward looked down at the dagger and turned it around in his hands. "I was sleeping under the oak tree outside the walls," he said eventually. "No-one could hurt me out there."

From what had happened earlier Katherine understood all too well what he meant.

"It was a couple of days ago, at dawn; I was awake and watching the sun rise over the hills. I saw a man come out of the manor and walk around the walls to the midden. I watched him as he buried something deep inside it and then afterwards, he walked back to the manor gate and disappeared inside. I was curious to know what he had put into the midden, so I got up and walked over there to find out. I had to search in the rubbish for quite a while until I found it." He indicated the dagger to Katherine. "I don't know why he wanted to get rid of it; it's very fine, isn't it?"

"Yes, it is. It's very fine indeed." She touched the dagger

again. "Did anyone see you find it?"

He shook his head. "There was no-one else around, mistress."

"Do you know who the man was? The one who put this into the midden?"

Edward nodded and Katherine drew breath knowing the implications of what she was about to ask.

"Can you tell me who it was?"

He nodded and then told her the name of the man, whom he had seen at dawn disposing of the dagger in the kitchen midden.

Katherine felt as if she couldn't breathe. Her mind started to race with the implications of what Edward had just told her.

"Edward, will you promise me to keep this safe?" She indicated the dagger and tried to keep her voice calm as she spoke. "Hide it again, like you had done before, and don't let anyone else see it."

He nodded and immediately crawled back to the corner of the stable and buried the dagger under the straw bedding.

"It will be safe there, mistress," he told her.

Katherine smiled and placed a reassuring hand on his shoulder. "Will you be alright here now?"

He nodded. "Now that *he's* gone. I will be alright."

"And you will look after Tiberius for me?"

Again, he nodded.

"I will come back tomorrow and bring my father with me. Will you tell him about the dagger and what you saw?" Edward instantly looked frightened, and Katherine reached out a hand to reassure him. "You're not in any trouble at all, I promise you. In fact, quite the opposite." She watched him relax a little. "My father is a good man. He will make sure that you are safe and nothing bad happens to you." She smiled trying to calm him.

Standing up, Katherine realised that Jennet and Lord Fitzwarren were probably waiting for her in the hall." I have to go now Edward, but I will come back tomorrow."

He nodded and got up from the hay to give her a small bow as she left.

Katherine was correct in her assumption that everyone was waiting for her in the hall. Jennet looked a little alarmed when she saw her mistress, and the pieces of straw that clung to the bottom of her gown.

"I apologise for keeping you, Lord Fitzwarren." Katherine bowed in front of him. "I was concerned for the stable boy, Edward. He was very upset by what had happened and I wanted to assure him that none of it was his fault."

"I am very sorry that you had to witness such a thing, Katherine. I do hope that it hasn't upset you too much." Lord Fitzwarren looked genuinely perturbed by the incident.

"Thank you, my Lord, it hasn't. But I must tell you that I have asked the young stable boy Edward, to look after Tiberius for me. He has a way with horses, and I hope that is agreeable to you?"

"Of course it is. I will ensure that it happens." He smiled at her warmly and Katherine had to admit once again, that he was quite a handsome man.

"Now, if you will excuse us, my Lord; it is time that we returned to the castle."

She gave him a small curtsy and then nodded to Jennet to follow her.

Down in the courtyard, Edward already had Lily and Jennets' mount saddled and waiting for them. Katherine noticed that he seemed less nervous now and even gave her a small smile as she mounted her horse.

"I look forward to seeing you again, Lord Fitzwarren." She smiled, as she spurred Lily to walk forward.

"And I you, Katherine."

The ride back from the manor was quiet. Katherine was very reserved and even when Jennet tried to speak with her, she gently dismissed her maid. She needed to be alone to think about what she had learnt today and what she was going to tell her father.

"Did you have a good time?" Angharad asked as she met the returning party in the inner bailey of the castle. "Is the manor very grand?" She asked, going up to Katherine.

"It's a very nice manor and Lord Fitzwarren is a very nice man." She told her sister vaguely.

Angharad looked surprised at her sister's bland description and then realised that something must have happened, because it was obvious to her that something was very wrong with her sister.

"Katherine?" She called out, as her sister walked away from her. Then she turned back to face Jennet. "What happened?" She demanded.

Jennet shook her head. "I don't know. She hasn't spoken to me since we left the manor. I know there was an incident in the courtyard, with the horses; but I couldn't tell you what happened."

Angharad and Jennet stood together as they watched Katherine storming off towards her room, and they both acknowledged that there was definitely something amiss.

CHAPTER 15

It was early afternoon, and Katherine had remained thoughtful and reticent since her return to the castle. She had retreated into the safety of her room and sat in the window embrasure, staring out into the distance but not looking at anything in particular. She wanted to go straight to her father, but she knew that he would be in the middle of preparations for the assize court with Robert de Lexington and would not welcome the intrusion. She would have to wait until she saw him this evening at dinner.

Both Jennet and her sister had tried to engage her in conversation but neither had been able to get any explanation or reason out of Katherine, for her current demeanour since her return from Lord Fitzwarren's manor. It therefore came as no surprise to them, when Katherine eventually got up from her seat and told Jennet that she was going out for a ride and would take Grenulf with her.

"Perhaps that will help clear your mind." Jennet told her, still at a loss to know what at happened earlier on their visit to the manor. It had been plainly obvious since they had left that something was quite amiss.

Katherine nodded silently.

"Is there anything I can do to help?" Angharad moved towards her sister and reached out a hand to her. "Is it something that Lord Fitzwarren has said to you?"

"No Annie, it isn't anything that he has said. This is just something I need to sort out for myself." Katherine gave her sister a half reassuring smile.

"Perhaps a ride will do you good then." Angharad nodded in agreement and then turned to look at Jennet in despair.

Katherine summoned Grenulf as she walked past them

towards the door, and the hound instantly obeyed his mistress and trotted happily behind her as she left the room.

The slight breeze in the hot air helped to calm her thoughts and the animated sound of the river soothed her troubled mind. Grenulf trotted on obediently behind her and Katherine hardly noticed his presence. Her mind was troubled by what she had found out that morning. In one respect, it offered her an opportunity that she could never have hoped for and was something she had only dreamed of. But on the other hand, she wondered how she could have been deceived so badly; and not just her, but her family too. What troubled her most was that she couldn't work out the reason for it. Why would he had done such a terrible thing? The thought bothered her greatly and she wasn't sure just what she should do next. She didn't want Edward to get into trouble either. He was a good lad and had a true love for horses which she could see was reciprocated by the animals. But how was she to handle the situation and let the truth be known without him getting hurt in the process?

Alexander was waiting for her by the riverbank, just as he always was; and he got up from his repose as he saw her approach.

"I wasn't sure whether you would come here today." He said, helping her to dismount.

She greeted him with a kiss. "After what happened this morning, I needed time away from the castle to be able to think."

He looked at her with concern, as Katherine moved away out of his arms. He knew instantly that something was wrong, as she had lost her normal joy and happiness at seeing him and it had been replaced with a cool distance, that he had never seen before.

"My darling, what is wrong?" He asked.

Katherine pulled away in distress and walked towards the riverbank. "I've found out something this morning that changes everything."

"What is it? Please tell me."

Alexander was suddenly afraid of what might have happened to change her demeanour towards him and followed her as she walked. Eventually Katherine stopped and turned to face him, before shaking her head.

"I can't tell you, not yet. There is someone else I must speak with first. Please believe me, I would tell you if I could."

Alexander felt a coldness seeping into his body and he hated to see her so distressed. "You're starting to worry me, Katherine."

She shook her head again and sighed heavily. "Please don't ask me anything more. Not now." She paused. "I will tell you everything, once it's all resolved, but at the moment I just can't."

"Very well, but you must promise to tell me everything when you can." He came to stand in front of her and tenderly stroked a stray lock of hair away from her face. "But whatever it is, please tell me that it will not affect our running away together tomorrow?"

Katherine looked at him and saw the pain in his eyes. She wanted so much to reassure him and tell him what had happened, but she knew she couldn't. It was the dilemma she had been wrestling with, all the way from the castle; and the conclusion she had come to, was that she had to tell her father first. He would know exactly what should be done, and then after that she could tell Alexander, but not before. She couldn't risk him saying something, and the news becoming common knowledge before her father had had chance to act.

"I'm so sorry Alexander." She started but he quickly interrupted her.

"No Katherine, no, you can't do this. I love you and I thought you loved me too."

"I do Alexander; I promise. But I need you to trust me, just for a little while. I can't tell you what's happened, but only to say that because of it, I can't leave with you tomorrow as we had planned." It broke her heart to say the words, but she knew she had to.

Alexander looked instantly bereft at the news and Katherine could almost feel his heart starting to break. He took a step away from her and looked at her suspiciously. To Katherine, the distance he put between them felt as cold as a winter's day and she watched as he shook his head in disbelief.

"I can't be hearing this. We agreed that it was the best thing to do. To run away to a place where we could be together. What happened to change your mind?"

She took a step towards him, but he backed away from her as if her coming any closer would endanger him.

"Nothing has changed my mind. But please Alexander, you must trust me. I love you and I want to be with you more than anything. I wouldn't be doing this unless I really had to. Try to understand that what has happened has changed a lot of things, and I need to resolve it before I can leave with you. Once it's done, I promise you, we will be together and no-one will part us." Katherine reached out to him, but he backed away. "Alexander, I love you. I love you more than anything. And I promise you; I want to spend the rest of my life with you. When this is all over, you will understand the reason why I can't tell you about it. But for now, I must ask that you trust me. Please, if you really love me, then trust me on this."

"Really?" He sounded a little scornful.

"Yes, I promise you; my feelings for you have not changed." She reached out and this time he let her take his hands in her own. "I love you more each day," she reassured him. "And I want nothing more than to be with you. This is not the end of our love, merely a little problem that I have to resolve; but once it is done, then we will be together for the rest of our lives. I give you my word on that."

"But we are not going to leave here tomorrow?" Alexander still couldn't understand why she could not leave with him.

"No, not tomorrow, but hopefully soon." She reached out a hand to stroke his face and he let her. "I know you have made plans and told your father you will be riding north to his manor in Wark. But just tell him that you will be delayed by a day or two. That's all I need, my love. I promise you. Give me two days to sort this out and then we will be together."

Alexander sighed heavily and took her hands in his before softly kissing each palm. He felt as though he didn't really have a choice in the matter.

"Very well, if you promise me that we will be together at the end of this." His voice sounded resigned. "I love you so much my darling Katherine. I just can't imagine my life without you in it."

"And I love you too," she said, looking at him tenderly. "I promise you that we will be together, but you have to trust me, for the moment."

He nodded and kissed her again, this time on the cheek.

"As long as I know we will be together. That's all I ask."

"We will be." She kissed him again this time on the mouth and more passionately. "I will leave you now, but I will send word to you soon, I promise. And when this is all over and you know the full story, then you will understand why I can't tell you more."

Katherine called Grenulf to heal and then went back to where Lily was contentedly grazing, on what was left of the grass on the dry riverbank. Taking the reins, she led her horse toward a fallen log and then stepped up on it in order to mount Lily. Her heart was almost breaking for the love of Alexander, and the sadness at having to leave him again; but knowing that they would soon be together, soothed her troubles. She knew that whatever happened, she would always love him.

The messenger arrived just before sunset. He was tired and his horse was exhausted. He had ridden hard that day, in order to make it to the manor before dark. On his arrival, he was shown into the great hall where Roger de

Mowbray was enjoying his meal and had already consumed a considerable amount of wine. Roger was relaxing at the table, feeling quite comfortable in his role as current head of the household, when his steward approached to inform him that there was a messenger to see him.

"Send him in, man." Roger replied loudly, the effects of the wine now evident.

The steward gestured for the man who was waiting at the entrance of the main hall to approach. The dishevelled man came to stand in front of Roger and bowed before his superior.

"Sire, I've come from your uncle's estate with news of your father." He spoke breathlessly.

"What is it man?" Roger sounded annoyed, even though he already knew what the news was. He then reminded himself that he wasn't supposed to know and needed to play the part of the son grieving the loss of his mother, if his plan was to succeed. "Bring him some ale and something to eat." He instructed a servant, as he saw the messenger approach and remembered his place as host. "Now tell me man, what news you have of my father. Is he on his way home?"

"Sire, I am very sorry." The messenger took a letter out of his pouch and offered it to Roger.

"Do you know what is in this?" Roger inquired, taking the letter from him.

"Sire, I know what has happened; so, I can guess what the letter tells you."

Roger also knew, but didn't want to show it. The messengers' words confirmed that the second part of his plan had now come to fruition. He opened the letter and read the words his uncle had written with great care. It seemed that his father had been returning home, following the news of the death of his wife. He had left his brothers' estate and was in the early part of his journey when he, and his guards, had been attacked by a gang of cut-throats. They had stolen his father's money and jewellery. But in the skirmish, his father had been wounded. The guards had brought his father back to his brother's manor, but by the time they had arrived; his father was already dead.

Roger knew that this was the time for him to once again play the part of the grieving son. He shook his head and put his hand over his eyes.

"I can't believe this. How could this happen?" He asked, of no-one in particular. "My mother is dead and now my father has been brutally killed whilst on his way home for her burial. This is just too much to bear!"

He started to sob false tears, but the messenger and Roger's steward were alarmed by his reaction. His steward stepped forward to try and reassure his master.

"Sire, this is truly dreadful news. I am so terribly sorry." He looked up and quickly dismissed the messenger. He disliked seeing his new young master so distressed. "Please sire, if it is your wish, then I will ensure that your uncle is informed that your fathers' body must be brought back to the manor, so he can lie here and then be buried alongside your mother."

"Yes, that is what I want." Roger managed between sobs. "I am unable to believe that something so terrible as this could have happened. First my mother and now my father. What am I to do?"

"Sire, this must be most distressing for you. Please allow me to write to your uncle straight away on your behalf, giving your instructions and you can then sign the letter." His steward suggested.

"Yes, do that." Roger feigned his distress. "I cannot bear this. Please make all the arrangements you need to. I will sign the letters. I just want my father home."

"Of course, sire. I understand." His steward assured him.

The steward signalled for the servants to take the messenger away and to leave the young master, now Lord of the manor, to grieve the terrible loss of his father, which had come so soon after the death of his mother.

Once the servants had left the room, Roger raised his head and glanced around himself to make sure that he was truly alone. Then he poured himself a large goblet of wine and leant back in his chair placing his feet up on the table. He smiled; he had done it. His plan to be rid of his parents, and take control of the manor and its' lands, had worked. Now he was a rich man and could indulge himself as he saw fit. He would no longer be bound by the restrictions his parents had put on him. He could buy new clothes in the latest fashions; enjoy the finest wines; and he would be one of the leading men in the county. He smiled, pleased with what he had achieved. Lord Roger of Overton; he was well pleased.

Outside the manor one of Adam's men, who had been keeping watch on Roger and the manor, saw the messenger arrive and the flurry of attention that went with it. He was curious and after the initial excitement had died down, he moved closer to the main gate, waiting for someone to come outside. It didn't take too long after the sun had set, and dark was beginning to fall over the land, before he saw a young serving girl emerge, that he'd spoken to a few times over the last few days. He liked the girl, and she seemed to take his being there, as an overture to a courtship.

"There's a lot going on tonight, Gwen." He said falling in step beside her as she left the manor.

Her eyes looked wide at him. "I know; and such terrible news as well." She said as she linked her arm through his. "The messenger came from the north; from the manor of his uncle." She told him. "It seems that his Lordship has been killed. Attacked by thieves on his way back here for her Ladyships funeral. How terrible is that?"

"Yes, it is terrible." He said, his mind working. "So, the young master is now his Lordship?"

Gwen nodded. "Yes, he is Lord of Overton now; but how awful for him. To lose both his mother and father so close together." She paused. "The steward, Philip, who was there when the messenger delivered the news, said the young master was so very distraught when he heard it." She shook her head. "I can't imagine how difficult it must be for him."

"Hmmm... yes I can imagine." He said, knowing that his master, Adam, would be very interested to hear the news when he saw him in the morning.

It was evening before Katherine managed to see her father. Simon had been in his office all day with Robert de Lexington and several scribes, going through the forthcoming petitions before the start of the assize court in the morning. It had been an intense and busy day, but he was pleased that everything was in order for the start of the court hearing in the morning. Simon leant back in his chair and rubbed his eyes. He was tired and was looking forward to relaxing over dinner when he could forget about his work, at least for a few hours. He had just dismissed the scribes for the day and was talking with Robert, when there came a knock at his office door. He wasn't expecting anyone and was even more surprised when Katherine entered his room. From the glance she gave towards Robert, he could tell that she had hoped to find him alone, but what concerned him more was the look of worry on her face. Both men stood up as she entered.

"I'm sorry to disturb you father." She nodded her head in respect to Robert de Lexington. "I was hoping that I might speak with you. There is something of great importance that I need to discuss."

"Will it wait?" Simon asked her. "We will see each other over dinner in the hall shortly?"

Katherine shook her head and closed the door behind her. "No, I'm afraid it won't wait." Her voice sounded very determined. "And I don't think this is something that should be discussed in front of everyone."

"Then I will take my leave of you both. I will see you again at dinner." Robert told them getting up from his chair.

"Actually, Sir Robert. Would you stay?" Katherine asked, turning to face him. "I think this might concern you, as much as it does my father."

Robert looked at her and she met his gaze with pleading.

"Of course. If that is what you wish." He returned to his chair, but instead of sitting down, he offered it to Katherine, which she accepted.

"This all sounds very intriguing Katherine." Her father said and moved to bring another chair up to his desk. "Why don't we all sit down, and you can tell us what is so very important."

Katherine waited as Sir Robert sat in the chair next to her. She felt unusually nervous, and her heart was beating so loudly that she felt sure both her father and Sir Robert could hear it.

"It is concerning the murder of the monk, Brother Clement," she said, "I think I might know who killed him."

The look on her fathers' face told her that he was now very interested in what she had to say.

"You have our undivided attention." Sir Robert told her, sensing her nervousness and trying to reassure her. "Is there something you have heard that might help your father with his investigation?"

"Not something that I've heard, although that is part of it; but more something that I've found." Katherine turned to look at her father. "Do you have the jewelled pommel that you found at the place where the monk was murdered?"

Her father nodded and, rising from his chair, went over to the chest at the side of his desk. Opening it, he removed the two pieces of evidence he had recovered from the place where Brother Clement had been murdered.

"May I look at the pommel end again?" Katherine asked.

She wanted to be sure that her memory of it was correct, and that it was likely to be the missing part of the dagger that Edward had in his possession. Her father passed it to her, and she turned it around in her hands, before looking up at him.

"I think I know where the dagger is, to which this belongs."

Both her father and Sir Robert were now fully alert to what she was saying

"Really?" Her father was intrigued. "Are you sure?"

Katherine nodded. "Yes. Earlier today, I met the person who found the dagger after the owner tried to get rid of it."

"This is very serious." Sir Robert interjected, looking at Katherine with a penetrating gaze. "Are you absolutely sure about it?"

Katherine turned to look at him and nodded. "Yes, I'm very sure. That is why I wanted to see the jewelled pommel. I needed to be certain. Now, I am sure."

Katherine passed the jewel back to her father and he returned it safely to the chest before locking it.

"Then you must tell us both what you have found out," he said.

Katherine explained her visit to the manor of Lord Fitzwarren that morning and meeting Edward in the stables; and how the stable master had beaten the boy because he had been seen speaking with her. Then she told them both about the dagger and how Edward had found it. When she finally told them about the man that Edward had seen disposing of it in the midden, Sir Robert looked surprised, but her father appeared more sanguine.

"I told Edward that I would return tomorrow and that I would bring you with me, father."

Simon nodded. "Yes, there is nothing more we can do this evening without raising suspicion. I think it would be good for you to be there with me as well, Katherine. I believe you have the trust of this young boy, Edward, you called him. I can imagine that he will be more than a little anxious at the presence of the Sheriff, so, it would be better for you to be there, and we can talk to him together." Simon glanced across at Sir Robert who nodded in agreement, then Simon added. "What neither of you know yet, is that yesterday I met with a man called Peter Beaumont. He was a close friend and fought alongside Hugh de Glanville; that was before Hugh took Holy orders and became Brother Clement. What he told me, led me to a theory about the identity of the person who may have murdered Brother Clement. However, up until now, what I was told by Peter Beaumont was purely hearsay. I had no actual proof to link the man I suspect with the terrible deed. Now, with what you have told me Katherine, it seems I have the evidence to support my theory." He turned to look at Sir Robert. "I think we need to act on this straight away, before the man in question begins to suspect what we know."

Sir Robert nodded. "Having heard what you have both said, then I would agree."

"But you have court sessions all day tomorrow." Katherine added.

"That is true." Sir Robert interjected. "But this is a matter of great importance. Any murder is reprehensible; but the murder of a monk is even more appalling. I think I can spare your father for a little time tomorrow, so that he might apprehend the man who has carried out this heinous crime." He turned his attention to Simon. "I suggest that when we break for something to eat at noon; you leave with your daughter and a couple of guards. Afterwards, I will sit for part of the afternoon session with your deputy, Adam. I know it's not an ideal situation, but this is something that needs to be resolved."

"Thank you, Robert." Simon added. "I appreciate your assistance in this."

"You need to arrest and punish the perpetrator of this murder, Simon. No murder is good, but something like this needs to be resolved as quickly as possible; no matter who the killer might be."

CHAPTER 16

The dinner that evening was more subdued than expected. Katherine kept herself to herself, but she could not avoid noticing her sister glancing across at her with a worried look on her face. However, Angharad didn't get to speak to her until afterwards and the guests were leaving.

"Please tell me what is wrong?" She asked Katherine.

"Nothing." Katherine replied. But she knew from the way that her sister was looking at her that she wasn't believed. Katherine realised that she wouldn't be able to get away with keeping the secret from her sister for long.

Angharad took hold of her sisters' hand and pulled her away from the group of people.

"You don't fool me, Katherine." She said sternly, guiding her sister into a quiet corner of the hall. "What is going on with you?"

"It's nothing." Katherine told her, anxiously looking around her and hoping that her father would see what was going on and come to her rescue.

It was her father who had instructed her not to say anything to anyone until the matter had been resolved the following day; and Katherine had agreed with his reasoning. Neither he, nor Sir Robert, wanted any information to get out, fearing that if it did, the man they suspected might make a run for it; although Katherine very much doubted he would. With Sir Robert, the Royal Justice, currently residing in the city, the man would not get very far or would ever be safe, no matter where he went. It had been agreed that Katherine would ride with her father to the manor house the next day. Katherine would then bring Edward to speak with her father and recount his story, as to how he found the dagger. It seemed such a simple thing to do, but thinking about it over the last couple of hours, Katherine was now very worried. She was concerned Edward would be too frightened to speak; and that if they met him within the grounds of the manor, then it would raise suspicion. What reason could there be for the Sheriff to be at the manor and speaking with a mere stable-boy? Katherine had thought long and hard about the problem and had concluded that it would be better to speak to Edward outside the walls of the manor. She had been putting together a plan where she could request his help without raising any suspicion; and it was this that had led to her being distracted all evening.

"If you are worried about marrying Lord Fitzwarren," Angharad began, "or even because he has arranged for it to be at the minster; then please tell me. I will help you as much as I can." She tried to reassure her sister.

Katherine felt oddly grateful for her sister's concern. But the fact that her sister believed her uneasiness was about wedding preparations and nothing more, also reassured her. She was so worried about keeping the identity of the killer of Brother Clement a secret, but it seemed, for once, that the castle rumour mill had failed in its usual bounty of gossip and information.

"Perhaps." Katherine lied as she smiled at her sister. "The wedding is a huge thing and, so far, I don't really seem to have had any part of it." She sighed and took her sisters arm in solidarity, as they walked together out of the hall. "It seems that Lord Fitzwarren has arranged everything, and father has allowed it, which is very unusual to start with." She sighed. "There are times when I wish mother was here, she would understand."

Angharad visibly relaxed, believing she finally understood her sister's hesitation. "Well, I should be able to help with that. But it is good news that that is all that is bothering you. For a moment, I thought you were having second thoughts about the wedding," she replied. "I thought you were so cross with father, for arranging the marriage without your involvement, that you might do something terrible, such as run away. But, of course, I would have understood if you had done. You forget that

I'm your sister. I know what you're like Katherine, and I know that you have always fought playing by the rules." She smiled at her sister. "I also know that father has somewhat forced you into this marriage, but I am glad to see that you aren't fighting him over it anymore."

Katherine smiled at her sister's words; how little did she know.

"I do know how it feels though," Angharad continued. "I remember how I felt just before my wedding. I was so nervous that I could barely speak. Our mother wasn't there, and Jennet didn't tell me anything about what to expect, so I was very scared about my wedding to Richard."

"But you never said anything at the time."

"Of course not. I didn't want to worry you." Angharad started to lead her sister towards their rooms. "I am your big sister; the last thing I wanted was for you to see me being afraid of getting married."

"You hid it very well." Katherine admitted, happy that she had her sister with her. They had fought so much as young children, but it was good to know that they were now close friends.

"I'm glad you didn't realise. But suffice to say, I do understand what you're going through."

The two sisters walked together towards Katherines' room. Jennet had been in the great hall with them, but had not been seated with the family, and she now obediently followed them at a respectful distance. She was pleased to see the two sisters finally getting on with each other. It had been difficult sometimes, when the two of them had lived together before Angharad's marriage, and the subsequent move of Katherine with her father to York. Katherine was the one who would challenge what was expected of her as a woman, whereas Angharad would happily comply to her father's wishes. At least they seemed to have put their past battles behind them now.

Back in her room, Katherine sat down by the empty fireplace, opposite her sister. She glanced across at Jennet who had followed them into the room.

"If that is all, my lady. I will leave you now." Jennet said taking the visual hint from her mistress.

Angharad waited until Jennet had left them before she spoke.

"I know Jennet brought up both of us, but I never quite got used to her trying to take the place of our mother."

"I don't think she ever really tried to." Katherine replied. "She was very fond of our mother and wanted to honour her memory. And father needed someone to look after both of us. I don't suppose he was in a position to do it; and we were both so young." She sighed and leant back in the chair. "I was just a baby, and you were barely two years old at the time. Poor father, I believe he was so distraught that he didn't want anything to do with us, so, he had Jennet look after us. She has been rather incredible really," Katherine mused. "I mean, when you think about it, she's given up her life for the two of us. She's never married and never had children of her own. That's quite a sacrifice."

"I suppose," Angharad admitted. "But probably because of that, she hasn't any idea of what is required from a wife, and so she didn't say anything to me about what to expect once you are married."

Katherine blushed feeling embarrassed. She knew what her sister was implying, but it was something that they had never spoken about. "Do you mean being alone with my husband?"

Angharad nodded; and Katherine instantly felt even more awkward; it wasn't an easy subject to speak of, especially with her elder sister. The thought of it happening with Lord Fitzwarren made her almost shiver with dislike and horror. But then, the thought of being alone with Alexander on their wedding night, elicited quite another type of feeling. Angharad must have registered the look on her face.

"I'm sure Lord Fitzwarren is a good man. I can imagine that he will be very gentle with you."

Katherine could feel herself blush with embarrassment,

as her sister described what to expect and how she should please her husband. Her wedding day was still several days away, and she really didn't want to think of it. If everything went to plan, then it wouldn't happen, and she would be with Alexander instead. However, that was something that she couldn't tell her sister, no matter how much she wanted to; instead, for the moment, she had to play along with the ruse.

The two sisters sat companionably together into the late evening and talked easily. The groups of candles, which lit the room, sent warm shadows across the walls and the heat of the day finally seemed to be subsiding. Katherine relaxed in the company of her elder sister and wondered why they had never talked like this before. Since Angharad had got married, and then Katherine had left with her father to come north to York, the sisters had not seen each other as much; and their previous bickering now seemed to have disappeared. It had been replaced with a genuine affection that had probably been there all along, just never acknowledged by either. Angharad seemed satisfied, that the reason for Katherines worried look at dinner was concerned with her forthcoming marriage, and nothing else.

Katherine woke with a start, the following morning, suddenly feeling anxious. Her dreams had been interspersed with battles and men fighting; and she was in the midst of the affray trying to find her way out of it, but everywhere she turned she had been blocked by angry soldiers. She shook her head as she rose from her bed and hoped that her dreams were not an omen for what was to come that day. Rubbing her eyes as she stood up, she walked across the room and then recalled what was planned for the day and suddenly felt even more worried. Katherine found the gown that Jennet had left out for her the previous night and dressed quickly before going to sit in her favourite place at the window. In the bailey below, the day was just beginning, and the servants were starting their daily duties at the castle. They had no idea what the day was going to hold, and they were content, or so it seemed, in their daily work. Katherine thought about the young stable boy, Edward, and felt nervous and worried for him. He had been suddenly thrust into the centre of the murder inquiry when he had found the dagger, and although Katherine had assured him that nothing bad would happen to him; she just hoped that she could fulfil her promise. She was still sitting at the window staring out into the bailey when Jennet came into the room, humming to herself in a cheerful manner.

"Not long now, my lady. Only a few days until your wedding." She smiled. "I should have your gown finished today, and all the other arrangements are set. I must say that Lord Fitzwarren has been very gracious, and nothing has been too much for him. You are to have the best of everything."

"Yes, he has been very kind." Katherine replied as she got down from the window seat.

Jennet looked at her, sensing that something was amiss, but believing that it was nothing more than nerves ahead of the wedding.

"What have you planned for today? Are you spending more time with your sister?"

Katherine nodded. "I think I will do so this morning, and then I'm meeting father at noon."

"I thought your father would be busy all day with the Royal Justice and the court hearings?" Jennet sounded surprised and Katherine realised that she had said too much.

"He is, but he said he would see me. Sir Robert agreed to his doing so." Katherine tried to explain her way out of it, but knew she was only making things worse.

"That all sounds a bit odd. Has it got something to do with your wedding?"

Katherine paused and gave a silent prayer of thanks that Jennet hadn't suspected anything more, than the meeting with her father being to do with the wedding.

"I believe so," she mused. "Sir Robert was very kind to allow it."

"Sir Robert is a good man" Jennet observed. "He holds your father in very high esteem." The fact that Sir Robert de Lexington thought well of her master, gave him great worth in Jennet's regard. "Have you thought about what you want to wear for the dinner this evening?"

Katherine shook her head.

"It will be quite a banquet and everyone will be there," Jennet added. "Your father has invited all the local Lords and Barons. I know that he usually invites them when it is the assize court, and Sir Robert is here; but this time, it is also a prelude to your wedding. Everyone is going to be there for you and Lord Fitzwarren, as well as for Sir Robert. What about the green gown, it goes so well with your hair colour, and you always look so beautiful in it?"

Katherine nodded, barely noticing what Jennet was saying. Her thoughts were still focused on young Edward, and what she could do to help him and to ensure he was safe.

"You will want to look your best tonight," Jennet carried on without noticing Katherine's disinterest. "I thought I could make a flower circlet for your hair; everyone is going to see you, so it does no harm to look your best. And it's going to be such a grand event. Did I tell you that your father has made provision for the best food and wine to be served tonight?"

Katherine shook her head at Jennets words. Then a sudden thought hit her, and she felt as if her stomach had fallen out of her body. If all the local Lords and Barons were to be at the dinner tonight, then that would also mean that Alexanders father was likely to be there too. In fact, he almost certainly would be. Sir Robert de Ros was one of the main noblemen of the county and she knew he had been present at the previous banquets held for the Royal Justice. In the past, he had been accompanied by his three sons as well, which meant that Alexander would be there too. Katherine felt a little dizzy. It would be hard to see Alexander tonight and know that she couldn't speak to him or go to him. But keeping up the illusion of being a happy bride on the eve of her wedding was just something that she had to do.

When Angharad came to see Katherine that morning, she appeared to be just as excited as Jennet had been. She greeted Katherine excitedly and ushered her to the chairs set out by the fireplace.

"Richard has gone out hawking this morning, so I thought that we could have some time together. How are you feeling? You must be so excited?" She said as they sat together.

Katherine managed a small smile and thought that being excited, was the last thing she was feeling at the moment. She had so much more on her mind and none of it could be spoken about, much as she wanted to confide in her sister. Katherine felt more anxious and worried as the time past, she just hoped that her sister didn't notice; and if she did, Angharad didn't question what the real reason for her anxiety was.

"I spoke with Jennet yesterday and made sure that she had everything ready for you," Angharad continued. "I must say that she has done an amazing job with your gown. I also made sure that she would make a new barbette for you to wear on your head, and that she has also arranged flowers for the day; though she did say with the flowers, it had been difficult to get all that she wanted, due to this impossible heat. I don't think, I've ever known a summer quite like this; although last year was hot, I don't remember it being quite as bad as this."

Katherine let her sister talk and tried to smile and nod, at what she hoped was the correct places. Her mind was instead running through everything that had occurred the previous day and what would happen when she accompanied her father later, to meet Edward. By the time of the banquet this evening it would all be over, and it certainly wouldn't be what everyone was expecting. She could imagine the topic of conversation in the great hall, being quite different from what was normally anticipated.

Suddenly, she realised that Angharad was trying to get her attention.

"Are you alright?" Her sister asked with concern. "You were miles away then. I doubt you heard anything that I've said."

"I'm sorry." Katherine apologized. "I think I'm just nervous." Which was true, but it was not about the wedding as Angharad thought. Katherine was worried about what would happen later that day when she rode out with her father to apprehend the killer of Brother Clement. She was just glad that her sister didn't know about it, especially given Angharad's condition; Katherine did not want to be the cause of any stress for her sister.

"You mustn't worry," Angharad assured her. "Everything will be fine. I know the match isn't one that you would have wanted, but I know you will be happy with Lord Fitzwarren."

Katherine looked at her sister sharply and knew that her colouring must have given her secret away.

"Oh Katherine. Didn't you think I would know?" Her sister asked. "I can see that Lord Fitzwarren is not your choice. He's father's choice, but I believe he is a good match for you."

"I thought I would have more say about who I was to marry."

"I know; and I can tell that he is not the man you would have chosen." Angharad softened her voice. "My darling sister, I know you wanted a love match, but women in our position don't get a say in who we marry. And, you never know, you might come to love Lord Fitzwarren." She paused. "You do know that mother didn't love father when they married, but she grew to love him over the years. In the end, they were so very much in love." Angharad reached out a comforting hand to her sister. "I didn't like Richard very much when we were first introduced; but now I can see that he is a good man, and he loves me very much."

"But you didn't tell me how you felt about Richard. Do you love him now?"

"Of course I do." Angharad sounded surprised. "Of course."

Simon summoned Katherine as soon as the assize court broke at noon. Katherine had made her excuses to her sister in the late morning, citing that their father needed to see her when the court was in recess. Instead, she had made her way to the stables and ensured that she was ready to go with him. She was already mounted on Lily and waiting for him when he arrived.

As Simon walked towards the stables, Adam managed to catch up with him and told him what his man, who was watching the de Mowbray manor, had discovered the previous evening.

"Well, well," Simon mused. "The sly young man. I can see what he's done now." He looked at Adam. "Walk with me. I have something I need to do whilst the court has broken, and I don't have time to waste. I take it that the new Lord de Mowbray will be at the banquet tonight?"

"Yes. His father was invited, but I can't see that Roger will let this opportunity pass to make his presence as the new Lord de Mowbray to be known to everyone."

"Quite!" Simon exclaimed. "Make sure he is seated close to the top table. I have an idea."

Adam nodded. "Yes, I will ensure that the servants know he is to be seated close to you. I am sure that he will not object to such a prominent position."

"Good. Now Adam, I need you to do something for me." He put his hand on the shoulder of his deputy. "The matter I have to attend now, cannot be avoided. Sir Robert is aware of it and, should I be delayed in my return, he has asked that you will sit with him for the afternoon session of the court." Adam nodded, feeling quite gratified that he was being asked to take such a position at the court hearings. "Good man," Simon clapped him on the back. "I will be as quick as I can, and I will relieve you as soon as I return."

Simon looked across the bailey and saw his daughter already mounted and waiting for him to join her. He ordered three of the castle guards to mount and to ride out with them. Very soon they were all on their way out of the castle heading north.

Katherine had given a lot of thought already, as to what they were going to do once they arrived at the manor, and she had put together a plan which she believed would work. If her father was in agreement with it, then she could ensure that young Edward remained safe. As they rode, she turned to her father to tell him what she planned.

"Father, I want to make sure that the stable-hand, Edward, is protected and that we can get the dagger away safely; so, I had an idea as to what we could do when we arrived at the manor."

"I thought you might have a plan." Simon smiled appreciatively at his daughter.

"I don't want to alarm Edward. He's just a boy and he's been badly treated by people. I don't want him to think that it's going to happen again." She turned to look at her father. "I fear that it will alarm him, if the Sheriff and his men ride into the manor in order to speak to him."

Her father nodded, happy to hear what his daughter thought. "And what do you plan to do instead?"

"I thought that we might stop a little way before the manor," Katherine began. "There is a small cope of trees nearby. If we stop there and you wait with the men, then I will walk to the manor alone and speak with Edward."

"And what do you plan to say to him?"

"I thought I would tell him that Lily has gone lame and that I have had to leave her outside the manor. I will ask him to come with me and take a look at her. He will do that, I'm sure; he trusts me. Then we will return to the cope, and you can speak to him about the dagger, and what he saw." She sighed as she thought of the scared boy. "I just don't want him to be afraid. He needs to know that he can trust us and that he isn't going to be punished for telling us what he saw. I think, if he was still inside the manor and knew he was being seen or heard by anyone else there, then he wouldn't tell us what he knows."

"And the dagger? Does he have it?"

Katherine nodded. "He does and I will ask him to bring it with him. If I tell him that Lily has caught something in her hoof and gone lame, then he will need to bring some tools to hook it out, so he could hide the dagger with them."

Simon looked at her and smiled. He had always known that his daughter was intelligent and sharp, but now he saw just how astute she actually was. He couldn't help but admire her; however, it also served to remind him as to why they were currently fighting over his choice of husband. She was a woman of great character, and one who would never accept what she was told but would challenge it; and there was a part of him that deeply respected her for it. As they approached the cope of trees, Katherine reined in Lily and dismounted.

"I think you should wait here with Lily." She told her father. "Let me take one of the men with me to walk the rest of the way, and then it will not raise any suspicions. Everyone will expect me to have an escort, and no-one will be surprised to see me, given that I will be their mistress in a few days' time."

"You really do have it all sorted out." Her father added, as he dismounted and took hold of Lily's reins alongside his own horse. "Do I need to be afraid that you are going to usurp my position as Sheriff?" He teased.

Katherine gave him a sideways glance. "Really father!" She chided him. "Can I please just start as your deputy first?" She added laughing.

Katherine summoned one of the guards and asked him to walk with her to the manor house. Simon watched his daughter walk away and couldn't help but feel a sense of pride at her resourcefulness and confidence. She really was something, and he did wish that her life could be different. He had seen lawyers in London with less intelligence and savvy than she had. He mused that it would certainly have been easier for her, and she would have had a lot more opportunities than she had now if she had been a boy.

Katherine felt a little nervous as she approached the large wooden gates of the manor house. But was grateful as they opened at her arrival.

"Mistress Katherine," the steward greeted her. "It is good to see you again; although we were not expecting it."

"I wanted to come and see my new horse Tiberius again." She smiled at the man. "But Lily has gone lame, and I was hoping that the stable boy, Edward, would be able to come with me and have a look at her. Is he here?"

"Of course, my lady." The steward went to guide her towards the stables.

Katherine followed him with her guard behind her. Once at the stable entrance, she saw Edward, grooming a horse in one of the stalls.

"Boy," the steward announced. "You are needed to go with the mistress to see to her horse."

Edward looked up and Katherine saw a brief look of panic in his eyes.

"My horse Lily has gone lame," Katherine explained. "I think she has picked up a stone in her hoof and I need you to come with me and see if you can help her." She tried to keep her voice as strong and authoritative as she could. Then turning towards the steward, she smiled. "There is no need for you to stay with me." She dismissed him. "I'm sure that Edward will be able to assist me now, and I don't want to take you away from your work. I'm sure you are very busy." She smiled sweetly at him.

"But my lady, Lord Fitzwarren would want me to ensure your safety." The steward protested.

"There is no need, I have my escort with me, so you can assure Lord Fitzwarren that nothing terrible will happen to me."

"Of course, my lady." He replied and looked across at the hefty guard who had arrived with Katherine. "If you are certain, then I will leave you here."

"I am certain," she replied, then added. "And please don't tell Lord William, I wouldn't want to disturb him; I am sure he is very busy. I was hoping to visit my new horse without causing a scene, but it seems that I haven't managed to do that." She tried to invoke all her best feminine wiles on him.

"Very well, my lady. I will leave you with the stable-boy."

Katherine watched the steward depart and waited until she was sure that they were not being overheard. Edward had stopped grooming the horse and had walked over to the side of the stables where the tools were located and was selecting a hoof pick and small knife from the assembled tools.

Katherine walked up to him and put a reassuring hand on his shoulder.

"Edward, Lily isn't really lame," she whispered to him. "I said that, because I wanted to get you away from here without raising any suspicion. My father is waiting for us outside." She felt him flinch in fear. "It's alright Edward, my father is a good man, he will not hurt you; you have my word on that." She reassured him. "Now can you bring the dagger with you? The one that you showed me yesterday?"

"But it's my dagger. I found it. He can't have it." Edward protested.

"It's alright, I know it is." Katherine bent down so that she was at his eye level. "And I promise you that no-one will try and take it from you." She realised that the dagger had a monetary value to Edward. To a person who had nothing and slept on the straw in a corner of a stable, the dagger had a significant value, and Katherine could understand why he wouldn't want to lose it. "Please don't worry, I will make sure that it is safe and that it is returned to you. I give you my word."

Edward still looked uncertain.

"Edward, I assure you that my father is a good man, and I will personally make sure that you are safe. We will both take care of you, I promise," she told him softly and watched as he visibly relaxed. "I have told my father everything about how you found the dagger and he knows it to be true. He believes you; and he will ensure that nothing bad happens to you."

Edward looked up at her with trusting eyes and Katherine felt the weight of having another person's life in her care.

"Do you still have the dagger safe?" She asked him and Edward nodded. "Then please fetch it and wrap it in this cloth along with the tools." She indicated a torn piece of sackcloth on the bench. "No-one will see it and, as you are expected to leave with me to come and tend Lily, then nothing will appear out of the ordinary." She smiled at him. "It will all be just as everyone expects, and no-one will stop us."

It was far easier than Katherine had anticipated. As she left, no-one questioned or even looked at her, or her escort and the stable hand as they left the manor. They were nearing the cope of trees when she finally allowed herself to relax. But it was too soon, as when Edward saw her father waiting for them and recognised who he was, he stopped and went to run away. The guard was quick to move and managed to stop Edward before he could escape.

"Edward please." Katherine knelt down in front of him anxious to reassure the boy. "My father is not here to arrest you. I promise, nothing bad will happen to you. You have my word, and I will stay with you."

She looked pleadingly at him and after a short while, he relaxed. Katherine looked up at the guard and he released his grip on Edward. Then, Katherine stood up and put a reassuring arm around the boys' shoulder and guided him towards her father.

"Edward, this is my father, Simon de Hale." She told him. "I realise that you already know he is the Sheriff of Yorkshire; but I can tell you that he is a good and fair man, and he will listen to you justly." She reached out to take the free hand of the boy and bent down so that she could look Edward in the eyes. "I promise you that I am not going anywhere; I am going to stay with you." She looked at him and smiled to reassure him.

"Edward?" Her father said softly, also crouching down in front of him, so that he met the gaze of the young boy. "My daughter tells me that you found a dagger, may I see it?"

Edward hesitated and glanced at Katherine, then he nodded and carefully unwrapped the bundle that he was carrying. Inside it, the dagger lay glinting in the summer sunshine.

"May I have a closer look at it?" Simon asked gently, and again Edward nodded.

Simon picked it up and turned it around in his hands. It was, as his daughter had supposed, a fine, expensive dagger that was missing a pommel end. It was easy to see how the jewelled pommel that Simon had found at the scene of Brother Clements murder, would clearly fit onto the end of the dagger. There was no doubt that this had been the murder weapon.

"Edward, my daughter tells me that you saw the man who threw this away in the midden. Can you tell me what you saw?"

Edward nodded and started to tell Simon the story of what he had seen at dawn a few days ago. He told of how he had been sleeping under the oak tree as the stable master had been angry and beaten him the previous evening; and he had escaped to a place where he was safe. Edward said that he had awoken just before dawn as the growing light had stolen across the sky. He had seen the man come out of the gate in the walls of the manor house, and walk around to the kitchen midden, where he had placed something within the depth of the rotting food waste. Edward told how he had watched the man return into the gate of the manor house and then, when he was certain he was alone again, he got up from where he was sitting and went to find what he had seen being hidden in the midden. He told Simon how it had taken him some time to find it and, when he had done so, he had been surprised at why the man would throw away something so fine. He looked at Simon straight in the eye and added.

"But it is mine now!"

Simon nodded. "I know and I won't take it from you."

A small smile appeared on Edward's face.

Katherine watched her father and felt a sense of pride, that a man of such power and strength could also be so kind and understanding with the boy.

Her father stood up and looked at her.

"I want you to take Edward and the dagger back to the castle," he told her. "I want to ensure that he is safe, and nothing happens to either him or the dagger. The guard will go with you." He nodded towards the man who had accompanied them to the manor.

Katherine nodded. "And what will you do?"

"Apprehend the murderer!"

Katherine had Edward sit with her on Lily as they rode back to the castle. The guard had offered to take the boy on his horse. But as Katherine pointed out, that wasn't logical, because if they were attacked, then the guard would need to defend them, and it would be far easier to do without the encumbrance of a small boy riding with him. Katherine felt strangely protective to the young boy. He was probably only six or seven years younger than she was, but the sense of responsibility and care that he elicited within her, made her connection to him feel more like he was a younger brother. She was already formulating a plan in her head of what would happen next. In her mind, Edward could not return to the manor, and she had decided that she would find a place for him within the castle staff. He could work in the stables there and be in charge of her beloved Lily, if that was what he wanted. But she also had an idea of giving him a chance to make something of his life, as a reward for his bravery. He could start as a servant and work his way up to being her steward. Of course, he would have to learn to read and write, but that was something she could arrange. By the time she arrived back to the safety of the castle, she had already decided what she would do.

"Come with me." She encouraged Edward as she dismounted and waited for him to get down. Then she offered him her hand and the two of them walked together towards her private room.

The look of surprise on Jennet's face when Katherine walked into her room hand in hand with Edward, was something to behold.

"Who is this?" Jennet asked, her eyes wide in disbelief.

"Jennet, this is Edward. He's going to be staying here for the time being. He will stay here with me for the rest of the day, but can you find him a room to sleep in for tonight."

The look of surprise on Jennets' face was something that Katherine had rarely seen.

"Are you sure about this?" Jennet whispered as she walked towards Katherine indicating that she wanted to speak with her mistress in private.

Katherine let go of Edwards hand and joined her maid, out of earshot of the young boy.

"I'm not sure this is a good idea." Jennet said. "He looks like he belongs out in the streets."

"He probably does; but he is my friend Jennet, and I owe him a lot." She wanted to add that Jennet would never know just how much she owed the boy but stopped herself just in time. "He has done this city a great service and I know my father would agree. Now, I'd like you to make sure he is bathed and find him something better to wear."

Jennet remained still and just stared at Katherine.

"Jennet?" Katherine prompted.

"Are you sure?"

"Yes, entirely sure." Katherine replied sternly. "Now, Edward will stay here with me until you have made arrangements for him."

Jennet finally regained her composure and went to leave the room, leaving Katherine alone with Edward. She walked back to the boy who appeared captivated by the opulence of the room and was staring around him at the embroidered wall tapestries and large bed with heavy drapes.

"It's alright," she reassured him. "You are my guest now and I will make sure that you are well looked after."

He suddenly looked wary. "What do you want from me?"

"Nothing more than you've already done." She reassured him. "Just to repeat what you told my father earlier, to another man who is also staying here."

Edward narrowed his eyes as if he didn't believe her. "And I can keep the dagger?"

"Yes, I promise." She smiled at him.

He was very trusting with her, despite having been so badly treated by his previous master. Edward nodded but retained a firm grip on the dagger wrapped in the piece of sackcloth. Katherine went over to the table and poured him some small beer from a pitcher and also picked up some bread and cheese from the platter which had been laid out.

Edward grabbed the food from her hungrily, and devoured it. Katherine could see that he probably hadn't eaten well in quite some time.

"Who is the man I need to speak to?" Edward asked at length, as he drunk from the tankard.

"His name is Sir Robert de Lexington," she told him. "He is the Kings Royal Justice, and he is here at the castle to hold the assize court. Sir Robert is a good man, like my father, and he will make sure that you are treated fairly." She sighed before adding. "He is also staying on to be present at my wedding on Friday."

"You're getting married?" Edward raised his head in surprise.

"Yes, I am supposed to be," Katherine told him.

"Who to?"

"To your master; Lord Fitzwarren."

CHAPTER 17

Once Katherine was sure that Edward was settled and Jennet was caring for him, she made her way towards her father's room. She had heard him arrive back in the castle grounds a little earlier and listened to the commotion outside and the sound of his voice carrying on the air. What she could not understand was that she didn't hear him issue any instructions to the guards regarding their prisoner, and this made her worried. Had something gone wrong? Had there been a logical explanation for the dagger that Edward had found? She had so many questions and she knew that none of them would wait until she saw her father that evening. Anxious to know exactly what had happened, she knocked on the door of her father's office.

"Enter." Simon's voice was quite clipped with annoyance. He had gone straight to his room after his return, to collect some documents and was about to leave to take his place alongside Sir Robert to complete the assize court for the day. He was not expecting any visitors.

"What happened?" Katherine asked as she entered his room.

Her father signalled for her to come in and to close the door behind her so that they were alone.

"He wasn't there," he told her. "His steward said that he had gone out and I didn't want to alert anyone as to why I was there. So, I told the man that I wanted to speak with Lord Fitzwarren, but didn't give a reason. And, as I really needed to get back here to finish the assize court, I wasn't able to stay and await his return. Don't worry, he's not going to go anywhere, and he has no idea that we know that he killed Brother Clement. His steward probably thinks that my presence has to do with the wedding, rather than anything else."

Katherine shook her head. "When I went to fetch Edward, the steward was going to go and tell his master, but I stopped him as I didn't want him to know I was there. So, he was at the manor then, but not when you returned. How unusual?"

"He might have gone out in between your being there and my visit," Simon ventured. "Or he might already have gone out and the steward wasn't aware."

"I doubt it." Katherine didn't sound convinced. "You know as well as I do father, that the servants in a household know far more about what is going on, than anyone else."

"So, you think he might have been avoiding me?"

Katherine shook her head. "No, I can't see that happening either." She sighed. "What do you intend to do about it now? How are you going to apprehend him?"

"Right now, I'm not going to do anything." He picked up a handful of documents from his desk and started to make his way towards the door. "Right now, I'm needed in the assize court. However, it did occur to me that our Lord Fitzwarren is due to attend the dinner tonight and that might give us an opportunity. I think I might have a plan as to how we can deal with this; but, right now, I really must go."

Katherine nodded as her father guided her out of his room and closed the door behind him.

"Is the boy safe?" He asked, as he turned to leave.

Katherine nodded. "He's in my room with Jennet. He's been bathed and she has found him some better clothes to wear. So, he looks quite presentable now."

"Good. Now I really must go." He smiled at her before leaving to walk quickly back towards the great hall.

Adam was pleased to see Simon arrive for the afternoon session of the court. It had only just started, and there wasn't much information to pass on to Simon. Adam rose from his seat, grateful that he was able to relinquish the position back to Simon. Sitting in judgement on court hearings wasn't something he was comfortable with. He much preferred to be a man of action, rather than one of letters. As Simon sat down, Adam leant over and quietly told him what he had planned for the remainder of the day. It concerned Roger de Mowbray, and he was anxious that Simon should be fully aware of what he was intending to do. Simon listened intently to what Adam was telling him and then nodded in agreement, before acknowledging Sir Roberts indication that they were ready to continue with the court hearing.

Katherine spent the rest of the afternoon in her room. Edward looked so much better now he was washed and dressed in clothes that weren't torn and dirty. Angharad was surprised to see a boy in her sister's room when she entered.

"Who is he?" She asked.

"His name is Edward," Katherine told her. "I'm looking after him as a favour to our father. But don't ask me anything more, as I promised father I would keep the rest of the story, and his reason for being here, to myself."

Angharad was wearing a beautiful golden gown with blue trim and her hand rested protectively across the swelling of her belly. She looked resignedly at Katherine before adding. "Well, if father has asked you to look after him, then I understand. But really Katherine, it's only a few days to go until your wedding. You're supposed to be preparing yourself and not doing favours for our father, and he should know better than to ask you. I must speak with him about this."

Angharad sat down carefully in one of the chairs and made herself comfortable. Katherine looked at her sister and saw there was a definite glow about her complexion. Pregnancy really did seem to suit her; she just hoped that everything went well for her sister. They were both aware of what had happened to their mother after Katherine was born; child-bed fever was a terrible thing, and both knew that it could happen again; but neither of them spoke of it.

Katherine didn't want to worry her sister and Angharad didn't want to tempt fate by speaking about it.

"It's only temporary." Katherine told her, indicating Edward who was stroking Grenulf. "By the time of my wedding, it will all be sorted. Now, no more questions on this." Katherine reassured her sister, holding up a hand to state that the matter was closed. "What shall we do this afternoon? I was going to suggest a walk, but I don't want to overtire you before the banquet tonight."

"You're right, I really should rest. Richard is fussing around me like a mother hen and, to be honest, it's driving me mad. That's why I thought I would come to see you, for a little bit of peace and some sensible conversation."

Katherine laughed at the analogy. "He really does think the world of you."

"I know and I should consider myself lucky. But he goes on and on about *his son* and the plans he has for him; I dread to think what will happen if the baby is a little girl. And I also worry about things well…. Things going wrong. Everyone tells me that there is nothing to worry about; but I know that childbirth is not easy and…." Her voice stopped and they both looked at each other knowing what she wanted to say but couldn't. Katherine could see tears forming in her sisters' eyes and she knew that Angharad was thinking about their mother.

"You can't think like that, Annie. There are far more women who don't have any problems giving birth; and I can assure you that Richard will make sure you only have the very best care." She knelt down in front of her sister and took hold of her hands to try and give her sister some comfort.

"And father gave our mother the best care he could too, but it didn't stop her dying." Tears began to fall down Angharad's face. "I know Richard will do everything possible to take care of me, but I can't help being afraid. And the closer the time gets, the more frightened I feel."

Katherine enveloped her in a huge hug. "Please don't upset yourself. I promise that when your time gets near, I will come and stay with you, so that you will not be on your own. I know you will have other women with you for the birth, but I am your sister, and I will make sure everything goes well for you. I will make certain that everything is done properly."

"Thank you. You don't know how much that means to me." Angharad leant forward and hugged her sister back, giving her a small smile. "I know we didn't always get on when we were younger, but now that we're both grown women, I am so pleased that we are finally such good friends."

"We were never *not* good friends," Katherine reminded her. "We were just very different, that's all. But at the end of it, we're family and although we might fight sometimes, it doesn't mean that we don't love each other." She tried to wipe the tears away from her sisters' face. "I mean, you should have been here for the argument I had with father when he told me I was to marry Lord Fitzwarren. I think the entire castle must have heard it! But, at the end of it, we're still family and that means more to each of us, than any petty squabble."

Katherine was warmed by the feeling of love for her sister and the need she felt to honour her promise to be with her for the birth of her first child. She was suddenly pleased, that her plan to run away with Alexander might not happen now. Running away would have broken the ties with both her father and her sister. It would mean that she couldn't be with Angharad at the birth of her niece or nephew, and she doubted whether she would even know it had happened. Suddenly, being an outcast from her family felt a terrible thing, and Katherine could see now just how much her sister and father really meant to her.

Roger de Mowbray made sure he was wearing his best tunic, and his hose and boots were new as well. He was determined to look his best and make a statement at the banquet at the castle this evening. It was the first time he would attend such an event as Lord Mowbray of Overton, and he wanted to ensure that everyone knew exactly who he was. He preened his dark hair before placing the hat on his head. It was the latest style from Spain, with a feather set at a jaunty angle on the side and Roger knew that it was good enough to be seen at the Royal court, never mind a mere county event. But it was a start; he was determined to work his way into the proper social circles and ensure that his name was mentioned amongst the right people, so that he would soon have an invitation from the King to attend his court.

The banquet that evening, was an event held every time there was an assize court. It was a time to acknowledge the visit to the city of the Royal Justice, who for the past couple of years had been Sir Robert de Lexington. It was also a time for all the local Barons, Lords and landowners, to gather together by invitation, to mark the occasion. However, this time it was also a joint celebration to mark Katherine's forthcoming wedding.

The great hall in the castle was full of trestle tables which were laden with pies, fruit, fish, meat, sweetmeats and every extravagance possible. Her father had left nothing out. Katherine had been to a few of these events over the last year, but none of them had been quite as grand as the one this evening. She was wearing her best gown and Jennet had put her hair up under a new barbette with a fine, gossamer thin wimple, so that the auburn colour of her hair still showed through. She entered the hall following behind her sister and Richard; and sat together with them at the top table. As she took her seat, Katherine looked around the room and noticed that Lord Ros was there; alongside him were his three sons, including Alexander. Katherine found her eyes drawn to him and as much as she tried not to look, she found she couldn't help her gaze being drawn back to him. At one point, he looked across at her and their eyes met for a moment. Katherine felt a jolt of energy surge through her body and her heart started to race. She just hoped that no-one else noticed, especially her future husband, Lord Fitzwarren, or her sister; but both appeared to be thankfully oblivious to it.

It was Angharad's first time at the assize banquet and she seemed suitably impressed, even a little over-awed by the event; and Katherine, who was seated next to her, sought to reassure her sister. Angharad's husband, Richard, however, suddenly appeared to preen himself like a peacock and was eager for everyone to note that he was seated at the top table in a prominent position. Angharad looked at her sister and rolled her eyes, at which Katherine had to stop herself laughing.

It was a little while before Katherine noticed Lord Fitzwarren, who was seated at a table immediately to the right of her. He raised his goblet in acknowledgement, to which she responded the same. She then turned her attention to look at her father who was seated at the centre of the table alongside Sir Robert. The two men were deep in conversation, and she had a good idea of what they were discussing. Katherine wondered how they intended to manage the situation, and she didn't have long to wait before she found out. After a short time, her father turned to her and spoke quietly. Once he had finished, she looked at him and nodded before getting up from the table. As she did so, she gave her sister a reassuring glance before she left.

Within a short time, Katherine had returned, and once comfortably seated again, she caught her fathers' eye and gave a brief nod. Her father then stood up and banged the table, to illicit silence from the rest of the room.

"My Lords, thank you for attending the dinner tonight. As you know, this is to honour the presence of our guest, the Royal Justice, Sir Robert de Lexington." He paused whilst there was much banging of knives and goblets on the tables as a mark of respect, before he quietened the assembled guests. Simon had found it best to get any speeches and matters of business done at the beginning of the banquet, prior to everyone consuming large amounts of wine and being rendered intoxicated. "However, this banquet is also to celebrate the forthcoming marriage of my youngest daughter to Lord William Fitzwarren." Again, there was much banging and cheering at the announcement. "Lord Fitzwarren, would you mind coming here to join me." As he spoke Simon moved around to the front of the table to meet his guest. Simon put a friendly arm around his shoulder. "Lord Fitzwarren is due to marry my daughter Katherine at the minster later this week; an event which I know most of you are due to be in attendance at."

Once more, there was much cheering in the room at the statement, but Katherine started to feel increasingly nervous. She glanced behind her to see if Jennet was there; she was. Angharad reached out and put a hand on top of hers. "Are you alright?" She asked.

Katherine nodded and smiled. "Yes, it's nothing." She lied and tried to smile acknowledging the good wishes that were sent to her and her future husband.

Simon had released Lord Fitzwarren to return to his seat, and the man was part way there when Simon started to speak again. Both of his daughters turned their attention back to their father, as did the rest of the guests.

"However tonight, there is also one amongst us who has committed the most heinous crime of murder." There was much muttering amongst the assembled guests. "There is someone here who has taken a life; someone who harbours such hate inside him, that he saw fit to carry out a monstrous act of violence." Simon paused and awaited the reaction of the crowd.

Roger de Mowbray, moved uncomfortably in his seat. He felt slightly nauseous and was certain that everyone around him must sense his anxiety. He cleared his throat and raised his head in defiance. He felt as though everyone was looking at him, but no-one could possibly know what he had done; he was certain of that. No-one could possibly know!

"I have spoken with the Royal Justice, Sir Robert,

about this matter." Simon continued. "And we have agreed that, as you are all present here this evening, you will act as our witnesses on what I am going to tell you, and the evidence I am going to present."

There was a nodding and agreement from the assembled guests.

"I'm afraid my good friends, that this is not a matter to cheer about." Simon walked across the room and stood before the man whom he knew had murdered Brother Clement.

The man looked genuinely startled. He tried to speak, but no words would come. In front of him Simon paused and looked around to ensure that the guards were positioned where he had asked at the doors into the great hall. The crowd had fallen silent as they waited for Simon to speak.

"Lord Fitzwarren, I have found evidence that you are the man responsible for the murder of Brother Clement."

There was an audible gasp from the assembled guests and Lord Fitzwarren visibly paled, before starting to laugh.

"I take it that this is a joke, Simon? You cannot seriously imagine that I had anything to do with the murder?"

After a short time of whispered chatter amongst the guests, they finally fell silent, and the hall had an almost eerie hush on it. Katherine noticed that Lord Fitzwarren looked pale and there were small beads of sweat starting to form on his forehead.

"But I do." Simon replied coldly to him.

Lord Fitzwarren stood up again and stared at Simon, before looking at Sir Robert and then back to Simon.

"This is totally unacceptable Simon! Explain yourself. What reason could I possibly have for murdering a man of God?"

Simon turned to look at Sir Robert who was still seated at the top table and gave a slight nod for Simon to continue. He was already briefed about what was to happen, and after hearing the evidence from both Simon and what Katherine had discovered, he had made his decision. He had suggested that the banquet may be the ideal situation to ask the Lords and Barons to determine the guilt of the accused.

"I would like to hear what Lord Fitzwarren is accused of." Sir Robert said, his voice booming loudly around the quiet room. "I would ask that all of you listen carefully to what is being said. I am charging you all with giving your verdict at the end of this."

Simon nodded at Sir Robert, accepting his authority, before continuing.

"Lord Fitzwarren, I would like to recount something that I was told by Peter Beaumont, a close friend of Brother Clement, who knew him before he took Holy Orders." He paused so that he was certain he had the attention of the rest of the assembled guests. "My story starts a number of years ago with a young man called Hugh de Glanville. Hugh was a soldier and, from what I've been told, a good man. He was also in love with a girl called Isabel Fitzwarren, whom I believe was your younger sister."

William nodded. "All of that is true, but I don't see how that has anything at all to do with the murder of the monk."

"Don't you?" Simon prompted him, but William remained silent. "Well, if not, then I will continue the story. Hugh de Glanville and your sister were betrothed to be married, but when he heard the calling from God to devote his life in prayer and service; he broke off their betrothal so that he might take Holy Orders. From what I've been told, by Peter Beaumont, your sister Isabel was distraught over Hugh's decision. It seems that, no matter how much she tried to talk him out of it, he would not change his mind. Even after he took Holy orders, she did not give up on him and tried to convince him of just how much she loved him. But it was all in vain. In the end, there was nothing your sister could do to persuade Hugh otherwise. I was told that following Hughs final rejection of her, your sister was so deeply distraught over the matter, that she decided she could not go on living and ended up taking her own life. Drowning, I believe it was."

William looked very pale. "Yes, my sister Isabel took her own life." He struggled with the words. "She loved Hugh so much that she couldn't live without him. So, what of it?"

"And because she took her own life, she was denied a proper burial in consecrated ground by the Church. Isn't that correct? And you've never forgiven either Hugh de Glanville or the church for treating your beloved sister in such a terrible way?" Lord Fitzwarren looked very uncomfortable as Simon continued. "As I said, you've never forgiven either Hugh de Glanville or the Church for what they did to your sister, and you've harboured that anger for years, knowing that one day you would exact your revenge."

"I don't understand the relevance of this," Lord Fitzwarren spluttered. "Or why the matter should be brought before your assembled guests." He turned to face the top table. "Sir Robert, I ask you to intervene here. The sheriff seems to have some personal grievance against me, which I do not understand, especially since I am due to marry his daughter later this week."

Sir Roberts' expression remained impassive. "I am curious to hear the rest of this tale; as, I am sure, are the rest of our assembled guests."

Simon acknowledged Sir Roberts words before continuing.

"Hugh de Glanville became Brother Clement upon taking Holy Orders." Simon stated, and there was an audible gasp around the room. "I would suggest that, even though several years have passed; you never forgave Hugh de Glanville, or should I say, Brother Clement, for what he did to your sister; and the anger that you felt against him has festered within you for all these years. Until that was, one evening about a week ago, when you saw him down by the river, and you became so consumed by that anger, that you could not stop yourself from exacting your revenge. That was when you killed him."

"This is sheer conjecture!" Lord Fitzwarren exploded angrily.

Angharad looked across at Katherine whos' face was set in a stony expression.

"Did you know this?" She asked her sister, her voice barely above a whisper.

Katherine looked across at her sister. "Not until yesterday."

"So that is why you have seemed so out of sorts." Angharad added.

They both turned their attention back to their father and Lord Fitzwarren.

"Sir Robert, I ask you again to intervene." Lord Fitzwarren walked forward from the table to stand in front of the Royal Justice. "This is just folly and there is absolutely no evidence to prove that it was I who was involved in this heinous crime."

There was a chatter of voices around the room and Sir Robert held up his hand to silence them, before stating. "I was told when I arrived, that a terrible murder of a monk had occurred in the city. This is a very serious matter. One which I hope can be resolved." He looked across at Simon. "I take it that you have evidence for your accusation?"

"Yes, Sir Robert, I do." Simon knew that Sir Robert was already as familiar with the evidence as he was; but it was the assembled court now in front of them, that needed to know the facts and evidence. "When the body of Brother Clement was discovered on the banks of the river and taken to the abbey; the Abbot summoned me to attend. To begin with, the Abbot told me about what had happened, and we returned to the site where the body had been found. It was there that my deputy, Adam and I, found two items of evidence." He paused for effect and also to ensure that he had everyone's attention. "The first was some horsehair that was caught on a thorn bush. The horse was a grey and there was blood mixed in the hair to suggest that there would be a wound on the horse. The second was this." He reached into his tunic and then held aloft the red jewelled pommel end. "This was found on the ground near to where the body had lain. Abbot Robert was also there when this was found and will vouch for the fact that it was covered in blood from the murdered monk when it was discovered."

"But what has that got to do with me?" Lord Fitzwarren sounded ready to explode.

"Because it was broken from the end of the dagger which you used to cut the throat of Brother Clement." Simon looked directly at him as he spoke.

"This is preposterous. How dare you accuse me!" Lord Fitzwarren was growing red in the face. "You have nothing; nothing at all!" He exploded. "That bauble could come from any number of objects, why should it belong to a dagger? And then why would that dagger belong to me? Look," Lord William was now shouting as he took his dagger out of its' sheath. "It looks nothing like my dagger." He held it aloft so that everyone could see it. "I used to have a lot of respect for you Simon; as Sheriff you are a man of high regard, but this is all quite mad." He turned round to face the rest of the assembled guests who were unusually quiet. "Your Sheriff has gone quite mad!" William stated, then turned back to face Sir Robert. "Sir Robert, do you not agree? He makes these accusations with absolutely no proof. As Royal Justice to the King, I beg of you to intercede here and stop this nonsense."

Robert de Lexington pursed his lips and pressed his hands together in front of him in thought. He knew all the evidence, but he needed to ensure that the assembled Lords and Barons knew everything as well. "Simon; Lord Fitzwarren is quite correct that the evidence you have presented so far does not tie him to the murder. Do you have any other proof for what you have said?"

"Indeed, I do, Sir Robert." Simon looked around for Katherine and then nodded to her where she was now standing by the main door into the hall.

In the heated discussion between her father and Lord

Fitzwarren; no-one, apart from her sister, had noticed that she had slipped away from the table to stand with Jennet at the door. It was just as her father had asked her to do. He would lay out the facts before their assembled guests and then she would slip away to ensure that Jennet had brought Edward, and the dagger to the hall. On his summons, she walked across and handed him the dagger wrapped in cloth.

"Do you recognise this, Lord Fitzwarren?" Simon asked unwrapping the dagger.

Lord Fitzwarren remained silent but visibly paled at the sight of the dagger.

"I believe this was your dagger?" Simon said, holding aloft the blade so that everyone in the room could see it. "Now, what is interesting is that I can show you, and everyone here, that the jewelled pommel end, found at the place Brother Clement was murdered, fits perfectly on to this dagger." He held the two items aloft again and showed the guests how they fitted together. Then he turned to face Sir Robert and walked over to his table, to place the two pieces of the dagger in front of him.

Sir Robert picked up the dagger first and looked at it carefully. Then, retrieving the jewelled pommel end from the table, he brought the two together. They were a perfect fit. It wasn't the first time he had seen both of them, but he wanted to show everyone in the room, that he was looking at all the evidence with great care.

"Even if this dagger was the one used to murder the monk, do you have any proof that it belonged to Lord Fitzwarren?" Sir Robert asked Simon.

Simon nodded and turned to look at Katherine. She was standing by the door with the young boy Edward. He gestured for them to come forward.

Lord Fitzwarren looked at the boy with curiosity, but did not recognise the smartly dressed boy, with neat hair and a clean face, until Simon introduced him.

"This is Edward, your stable hand."

Lord Fitzwarren visibly paled once again. "Have you

resorted to stealing my servants now?"

Simon ignored the jibe. "As you already know, my daughter visited you yesterday and you showed her to the stables where you had kindly bought her a new horse as a wedding present."

Lord Fitzwarren shrugged. "Am I to be accused of stealing horses now too?" He joked and a ripple of laughter went around the room.

"Whilst she was there, Katherine witnessed the stable master beating Edward, and I believe you intervened to remove the man."

"That much is true. I will not deny that I do not like to see violence within the bounds of my home."

There was a murmur of agreement around the room.

"Afterwards Katherine stayed in the stables and met the young boy, Edward, who the stablemaster had beaten. He was still understandably frightened; and it was whilst she was with him, that she noticed he had this dagger in his possession." He turned his attention now to Edward and, bending down in front of him, he softened his voice. "Edward, you're not in any trouble, I promise you. But could you tell my friend Sir Robert here," he gestured toward the top table, "where you found this dagger."

Edward stared blankly at him for a moment before he nodded and started to speak, but his voice was barely audible.

Sir Robert shook his head. "Come here boy. Come closer and tell me."

Edward looked instantly frightened at being taken away from the one person in the room he knew to be his friend. He moved forwards slowly towards Sir Robert, and was quite relieved that this took him further away from Lord Fitzwarren, but also nervous at speaking with the imposing man in front of him.

"It was three days ago sire." He began, again quite softly, so that Sir Robert had to lean forward to hear him. "I spent the night sleeping under the oak tree outside the walls of the manor. It was too hot in the stables and the stable master didn't like me very much." His voice grew stronger as he spoke, so that the rest of the room could now hear him. "I was awake as the dawn came, and I noticed a man come out of the gate of the manor. He made his way around the outside of the manor walls to the kitchen midden. I saw him place something deep in the midden before he left and walked back to the manor."

"Did he go back inside the gates of the manor?" Sir Robert asked.

"Yes, sire he did." Edward nodded.

"And then what did you do?"

Edward looked down nervously. "I was curious to see what he had placed in the rubbish pile. It's not usual for someone to hide something in the middle of the kitchen waste, so I went over to take a look. I wanted to know what it was."

"And did you find what he had placed there?"

Edward nodded his head. "Yes sire. It took me some time, but I found it after a while."

"Please tell me what you found?"

Edward turned around and pointed at the dagger which Simon was holding. "It was this dagger sire."

Sir Robert nodded. "Now listen very carefully to me. Did you recognise the man that went out to the midden that morning?"

There was silence in the room as everyone assembled there strained to hear what the boy had to say.

"Yes, sire I did."

"Tell me Edward, is the man here in the room tonight." Sir Robert tried to keep his voice level.

The boy nodded. "Yes, sire he is."

"Can you point him out to me?" Edward looked directly at Sir Robert, and the fear in his eyes was visible. "It's alright boy, he can't hurt you." Sir Robert reassured him.

Edward then turned and raised his hand to point directly at Lord Fitzwarren.

The hall instantly erupted with noise and commotion. Men stood up from their seats and started shouting and cursing at Lord Fitzwarren.

Lord Fitzwarren looked around him for support, but there was none.

"The boy lies!" He cried out in despair; and there was angry shouting at him from the room in reply.

Sir Robert stood up at the table and banged on it heavily until quiet was restored to the hall. "And why should the boy lie?" He asked of Lord Fitzwarren

"Because I am his master, and he resents me!" The explanation was simple and one that he knew most of the assembled Lords would understand. But there was a shaking of heads amongst the seated guests.

Then Simon interjected. "But my daughter, Katherine, tells me that you were the one who saved the boy from a beating by the stable master. So why would he resent you? If anything, he should be grateful to you."

"Because all servants resent their master!" There came a murmur of agreement. "And your daughter Katherine's word, is worth very little. Everyone knows that she is marrying me under protest and that she is actually in love with another man." Lord Fitzwarren's voice was full of malice.

There was a distinct intake of breath, and everyone's gaze suddenly switched from Lord Fitzwarren to Katherine. She felt distinctly uncomfortable with everyone's attention on her. Even her sister looked at her in surprise.

"I fail to see what relevance that this has here?" Sir Robert interjected.

"Then that is only because you do not know the full story." Lord Fitzwarren now saw that he was in control of the hearing. "The Sheriff here, has told the boy to say such things to make me appear guilty."

"And why would he do that?" Sir Robert was starting to lose patience with the man before him.

"Because, as I said, his daughter does not want to marry me, and he wants to find a way out of the union without losing face with the King! So, getting the boy to discredit me is an easy way out for him."

Simon shook his head. "Sir Robert, I can assure you that my only interest is to find the killer of the monk and see that justice is served. I am not the only one who heard the boy's story though; as well as my daughter, this man also heard." He pointed towards one of the guards standing behind the tables in the background.

The man stepped forward at his masters bidding.

"Is this correct?" Sir Robert asked. "You have also heard the boys' story?"

"Aye sire, I did, every word. I was with the Sheriff and his daughter when they went to the manor of Lord Fitzwarren, and I heard what the boy told them. It's all true." He nodded and then took a step back into the shadows.

"There is one more thing, Sir Robert, if I may," Simon concluded. "The final piece of evidence that I have, though it is not in this room, is the horse that was injured that evening. At the scene of the murder, I also found some horsehair, and this suggested that the animal was a grey and would have a scar, possibly on its neck. When I asked young Edward here, if he had seen this horse; after all, he did work in the stables of Lord Fitzwarren, he confirmed that there was a grey horse that had a cut on his neck. He also told us that Lord Fitzwarren had ordered him to take the horse away from the manor and to keep it in a barn located in the woods of the estate. This afternoon, I instructed two of my men to go and take a look in this barn and sure enough, we found a grey mare there with a scar on its neck. That horse is now safe in the stables here, and you can see it for yourself, if you so wish."

Lord Fitzwarren was now looking distinctly uncomfortable and glanced around himself nervously.

"So, I give you the evidence against Lord Fitzwarren." Simon spoke to Sir Robert and then turned to face the rest of the guests in the hall. "Firstly, the recollection of Peter Beaumont, who was a close friend of Hugh de Glanville before he took Holy Orders. He spoke of Hugh's betrothal to Isabel Fitzwarren and of how she subsequently took her own life after Hugh ended the betrothal in order to take Holy Orders; and how in doing so, she was denied a proper burial by the church. The jewelled pommel found at the scene of the murder." Once again, he held the jewel and the dagger aloft so that everyone could see them. "You can all see that the jewel found at the site of the murder, precisely fits the dagger which was disposed of by Lord Fitzwarren in the midden belonging to the manor. Unbeknownst to him, he was seen that morning getting rid of the dagger by the young stable boy, Edward. Then finally, I have found the grey mare with a cut on its neck, which on the instruction of Lord Fitzwarren, was hidden in a concealed barn on the estate. I set all this evidence before you, Sir Robert; and in front of these assembled Lords and Barons; and request judgement from you on this matter."

In the background, the guards silently and unobtrusively moved into position around the edge of the hall. There was nowhere for Lord Fitzwarren to go, all of the exits out of the hall were blocked. Anxiously he looked across at the table where the Royal Justice was contemplating the situation. Sir Robert de Lexington sat in silence for a while, his hands together in front of his face, with his fingers resting against his chin. There was a short pause before he spoke, and the rest of the hall was equally quiet and still, as it waited on his verdict.

"Simon, what has happened here this evening is highly unusual and not part of the official assize court. However, what you have laid before me is irrefutable and cannot be ignored. So, I will ask those assembled here, whether or not, they will accept any decision made this evening as though it were part of the assize court."

There was a clamour of agreement at Sir Roberts suggestion, after which he nodded before standing up to address everyone. He looked around the hall at his so-called assembled jury. "My friends, you are independent noble Lords, and you have heard what your Sheriff has told you and the evidence he has shown you. What is your verdict on the charge of the murder of the monk known as Brother Clement which is laid before Lord Fitzwarren? How say you?"

"Guilty!" Came the shouts from around the hall.

There was much shouting and threats levied against Lord Fitzwarren and Sir Robert held up his hands to silence the assembled guests.

"It is a decision that I also agree with, so let it stand." He turned to face Lord Fitzwarren. "Lord William Fitzwarren, you have been found guilty of the murder of the monk known as Brother Clement by the men assembled here in this room. Do you have anything to say?"

Lord Fitzwarren looked suddenly very old and pale as he shook his head. "No, I do not." He said quietly. His earlier bluster quite gone now.

Sir Robert summoned the surrounding guards. "Take Lord Fitzwarren down to the dungeons. My decision is that he will remain there, until he is taken to the gallows and hanged for his crime of murder."

The cries of Lord William Fitzwarren were guttural and echoed around the hall as he tried to fight the guards who took hold of him.

Katherine looked at him and suddenly felt a deep compassion. His love for his sister had been so great that it had clouded his judgement, and the anger he had felt against Brother Clement had never been forgotten. He was a brother who was so devoted to his sister and her memory, that he had been driven to avenge her sad death. Katherine had to admit that she felt sorry for Lord Fitzwarren. He was a good man, and he had never shown her anything but kindness.

Once Lord Fitzwarren had been removed from the hall, the chatter between everyone started again, and grew much louder. Ale was poured into tankards, and it quickly felt as though the previous events had never occurred.

Sir Robert turned to speak to Simon, as he sat back down again.

"Simon, I charge you to produce all the paperwork tomorrow, before we conclude the assize court."

"I will do that, I assure you." Simon replied.

"Now perhaps we can all continue with this banquet." Sir Robert announced to the assembled guests. "I know that all this has made me extremely hungry."

A large cheer went up in the room as everyone started to indulge themselves in the fine food and drink laid out before them.

Katherine went to meet with Edward and ensured that he was alright, before she put him into the care of Jennet and watched as they left the hall; then she returned to her seat at the table. The events of the evening had made her even more resolute that the boy would remain in her charge. She was determined to give Edward a better life than just being a stable boy. He had done her such a great favour, and he had helped her, more than he would ever know. As she sat down in her seat at the table, Sir Robert leant to his side to speak with her.

"Katherine, I am so sorry that there will be no wedding for you now. I know how distressing and difficult this must be for you." There was a twinkle in his eyes.

"Thank you, Sir Robert, for your concern." She smiled, maintaining the ruse. "It is certainly not how I was expecting it to resolve itself."

Sir Robert took a drink of wine and looked at her quizzically. "I have to ask you something though." He said seriously.

For a moment Katherine became quite worried, and unsure of whether to reply or not.

"Is the man that you have given your heart to, present this evening?"

Katherine looked nervously across at her father; the last thing she wanted was to say anything that would upset him. Then she looked across the room at Alexander, who was already looking in her direction and watching her intently.

Sir Roberts gaze followed hers. "Ahh, I see, that's the

de Ros boy." He winked conspiratorially at Katherine. "I don't think that now is the time to discuss this further, but I would ask that you come to meet with me tomorrow morning. For now, I want to enjoy the rest of this banquet. This has not been quite the evening I was expecting!"

CHAPTER 18

Katherine found it difficult to believe that, in a short space of time, her whole world had changed once again. She had known the facts and the evidence that was put against Lord Fitzwarren, but she hadn't given much thought as to how it would end. It was only yesterday that she had started to suspect him, and then earlier today, when she had journeyed with her father to speak with Edward; she had known for certain that he was the one who had so viciously murdered Brother Clement.

The banquet in the hall now felt quite surreal. She looked around at the rest of the guests, who had gone back to feasting and drinking at their tables, as though nothing had just happened. Yet, for her, everything had changed once more. Just a couple of days ago, she had been expecting to run away with Alexander in order to avoid marrying Lord Fitzwarren; and, up until yesterday, she had intended to keep to that plan. She had come to terms with having to give up everything; to lose contact with her sister and to disobey her father, in order to be with the man she loved. After sitting back down at the table next to her sister, she felt quite light-headed and reached out to pour herself a goblet of wine. She needed to consider, just what she was going to do next.

"Well, that wasn't what I expected!" Angharad exclaimed, leaning over to her sister. "You knew, didn't you?" She questioned Katherine.

"Not everything, and not finally until earlier today," she admitted. "But even then, I couldn't tell you. I hope you understand. Father needed to keep everything quiet, so that Lord Fitzwarren wouldn't get to know."

"This explains why you have been so distant. I still can't believe that the man you were due to marry was a murderer. That's quite a revelation." Angharad leaned back in her chair. "So, why did it happen here tonight, at the banquet?"

"We went to Lord Fitzwarren's manor earlier today to get Edward to safety and for father to arrest Lord Fitzwarren; but he wasn't there," Katherine told her. "Father didn't want to raise any suspicion. And, as he knew Lord Fitzwarren would be here tonight, he agreed with Sir Robert that this evening would be a good opportunity to present the case against him."

"Did father know before then, that Lord Fitzwarren had killed the monk?"

Katherine thought about it carefully. "He had spoken with Peter Beaumont and found out about Lord Fitzwarren's sister, so I think he had his suspicions. But he had no proof, and that was the main thing." Katherine took a drink of wine and relaxed back into her chair with a sigh of relief. "None of us were certain, until yesterday when I met Edward, and he showed me the dagger. Up until then, it was just a story father had been told by Peter Beaumont, who was a close friend of Hugh's. One about how William's devotion to his sister had been so consuming; and how she had taken her own life rather than live without the man she loved. That man was Hugh de Glanville, who became Brother Clement when he took Holy Orders. In Lord Williams eyes, the church took away his adored sister and then denied her a burial in consecrated ground. His grief and anger must have festered away inside him ever since her death, and become sort of twisted. Then last week, and quite by chance; he came upon the man who had been the cause of all his sadness." She took another sip of wine before continuing. "It was an accidental encounter as, from what father has told me, I don't believe Brother Clement left the walls of the Abbey much. Lord Fitzwarren must have thought it was divine intervention, and he was being given a chance to mete out his own kind of justice."

"So, he killed him?" Angharad stared at her.

"Yes, in order to avenge his sister." Then, Katherine

added more thoughtfully. "Such was his devotion to her."

"And to think you were so nearly his wife."

"I know, but he was never anything other than kind to me." She paused for a moment, then added. "I suppose I can tell you this now, because it doesn't matter anymore; but I wasn't going to marry him." She watched as the look of surprise crept across her sisters' face.

"So, what he said about you being in love with someone else, was actually true?" Angharad's expression was reflective, as she went over the last few days in her mind. "I knew it. I knew something wasn't quite right."

Katherine nodded. "Yes, but I couldn't tell you. I'm so sorry. I'm in love with Sir Alexander de Ros, son of Baron de Ros of Helmsley, and he loves me too. But, when I told father that Alexander wanted to marry me it was too late, as father had already got the Kings permission for my marriage to Lord Fitzwarren. So, there was nothing to be done about it."

"And you would have accepted that?" Angharad knew her sister all too well.

Katherine shook her head. "No, I was planning to run away with Alexander instead."

The look of shock on her sister's face assured Katherine that her secret had been well kept.

"Run away? But you couldn't have! What would father have said?" Angharad sounded genuinely surprised.

"He'd probably have had quite a lot to say and would have been extremely angry," Katherine admitted and looked across at her sister. "But I couldn't have gone through with the wedding. I hope you understand. I was, and I am, in love with someone else."

Katherine watched her sister as she assimilated the information and then realised the implications of what she had been told.

"Oh, Katherine, but if you had run away with Alexander, then you would have become an outcast. Father would have had to disown you; and I would never have seen you again." Angharad looked distressed. "You know it would have broken father's heart. He's already lost our mother, and I don't think he could cope with losing you as well." She paused regaining her composure. "I don't think you realise just how much our father loves you. You were always his favourite; I could never hope to come close in his affections."

Now it was Katherines' turn to look surprised.

"No, father loves us both." She shook her head. "He is so proud of you. You are the model daughter; with the perfect marriage to the man of his choosing; and now a baby on the way which will be his first grandchild."

"Perhaps I have been a little more accepting of my life. But I have always envied you; you have such spirit and you're not afraid to fight for what you want and what you believe in."

"And I suppose you'll tell me that's why I am willing to fight to be with Alexander." Katherine sighed. "I know that my plan to leave here with him, would have meant breaking with father and you. And I can tell you, that it was the one thought that I hated more than anything. But you must understand that I love Alexander so very much, and it seemed a price worth paying. Besides, we were planning to go to Alexanders father's manor in Wark-on-Tweed in Northumberland and live there; so, we would not have been too far away. I did hope that, once the shock about what had happened had died down, then I could be reconciled with father and also with you. Can't you see just how strongly I feel about this, and how much I love Alexander?"

"Yes, I can see that you really do love him," Angharad observed, smiling at her sister.

Katherine reached over and the two sisters hugged. There was a closeness between them that hadn't been there for a very long time.

"Tell me, is he here tonight?" Angharad asked as she let go of her sister.

Katherine turned and looked around the hall until her eyes alighted on Alexander. He smiled across at her and she now felt free to smile back at him.

"Yes, he's over there." She said, pointing him out to her sister.

Angharad looked in the direction her sister indicated. "He's very handsome," she observed. "Tell me more about the man who is to be my brother-in-law."

Angharad smiled and the two sisters sat together conspiratorially for the rest of the evening.

Simon had risen early to ensure that he had transcribed all of the evidence and charges against Lord William Fitzwarren for the murder of the monk known as Brother Clement. It was the last day of the assize court, and he wanted to make sure that everything was in place before Sir Robert de Lexington departed. He was also aware that Lord Fitzwarren hadn't been alone on the evening of the murder and that at least one other person had been with him. It had been obvious when he had inspected the body that there had been another man present, who had restrained Brother Clement while Lord Fitzwarren slit the monk's throat. He had summoned Adam to his office and instructed him to question all the men in the pay of Lord Fitzwarren and to find the name of the accomplice, before arresting the man. When they had finished speaking, Adam brought another matter before him.

"Roger de Mowbray," he said, as he stood before Simon. "I have it on good authority, that he paid men to rob and kill his father, whilst his father was travelling back from Durham for the burial of Lady de Mowbray."

Simon shook his head. He felt drained by the events of the past few days. Initially, dealing with Katherine's objection to his choice of husband for her, had been quite enough; but then finding out that the man who was due to be his son-in-law was responsible for the murder of Brother Clement, had shaken his faith in his judgement of other men; and that included Roger de Mowbray.

"I knew he was up to something." He said, looking up at Adam. "Do you think he had something to do with his mother's death as well?"

"I wouldn't put it past him."

"But how did you find out about him being responsible for his father's death?"

"One of my men heard word about de Mowbray. It seems my man's wife is related to one of the thieves that de Mowbray paid to rob and kill his father. The thief also happens to have a loose tongue after a few tankards of ale, and he was more than happy to recount the whole story to my man."

Simon nodded. "I'll leave it with you to resolve. As it is, I have another day of assize court hearings with Sir Robert now, and I need to prepare."

Adam nodded in agreement and left the room. He smiled; it would give him great pleasure to arrest Roger de Mowbray and question him over the death of his father. The man was so obviously guilty and now, he had the information which proved it.

It was only early morning, but Simon already felt exhausted and slumped back in his chair. From what Adam had told him, it would seem that Roger de Mowbray had killed both his parents; and for what? Just so he could inherit their estate and wealth. Simon sighed heavily. The last few days had not been what he was expecting. It had surprised, and shocked him, that Lord Fitzwarren was the killer of Brother Clement, and he wondered how he could ever have allowed his beloved Katherine to be betrothed to such a man? He shook his head. He suddenly felt very old and drained and wondered if he was losing his perceptiveness and understanding of people. But more than that, he felt anger at Lord Fitzwarren for his deception. At least Katherine would not have to marry him now. The betrothal was non-binding since the intended bridegroom was due to be hanged for murder. Simon thought back to how Katherine had pleaded with him to be freed from the betrothal so that she could marry Alexander de Ros; had she known something that he hadn't? Had she seen something in Lord Fitzwarren that

Simon had missed? He doubted it. At least now, he wouldn't have to fight his daughter over her marriage, which was an outcome he had not imagined would happen, but one that made him feel quite happy. He had already decided that he would give his blessing to her choice of husband. Alexander de Ros was a good man and now there was nothing to stop them being married. He doubted that the King would be concerned with the choice, but he would write to the young monarch explaining what had happened.

Simon sat up and rubbed his eyes again. He needed to focus his mind on the work in front of him. There wasn't long before the court would convene again for the final day, and he needed to ensure that all the documents were prepared ready for signing by Sir Robert de Lexington, before he left York the following day. Simon didn't want anything left to chance. He also knew that he needed to visit Abbot Robert at St Mary's Abbey, to tell him first-hand what had transpired the previous evening; though he expected that the Abbot would be already aware of it; such would have been the gossip in the city about the previous evening's banquet. Then there was Katherine. Simon knew he needed to speak with her as well, but that would wait until this evening.

Abbot Robert was expecting Simon, when Brother Michael knocked at his door and showed the Sheriff into his room later that afternoon. He had already heard a rumour about what had happened the previous evening. He got up from his desk to greet Simon warmly.

"Simon. May God bless you. It is good to see you again, my friend. I thought you might pay me a visit today."

Simon allowed himself a small smile. He had managed to slip away after the court hearings had finally concluded, knowing that he wanted to break the news to Abbot Robert in person. But, as he had suspected, it seemed the gossip had already made it to the Abbey.

"My apologies for leaving it so late in the day. I have

been occupied with the assize court. But I take it, that you've already heard the news?" He replied, as he went to sit in the chair indicated by Abbot Robert.

"I have indeed." The Abbot sat back down at his desk. "I was told that it was Lord Fitzwarren who so brutally murdered Brother Clement, which was a surprise on several levels. But why don't you tell me the full story." He suggested.

Simon nodded and proceeded to relate the whole story of Hugh de Glanville and Isabel Fitzwarren, and how Lord Fitzwarren had blamed Hugh de Glanville for his sister's death. It seemed that seeing Brother Clement that evening had given him the opportunity to take revenge for the death of his sister.

"The poor man, to carry such grief in his heart for so very long. It must have eaten away at his very soul." The Abbot shook his head thoughtfully. "I will pray for him; and, if I may, I will visit him. I will encourage him to make his peace with God and to ask for forgiveness for what he has done."

"Are you sure?" Simon was a little surprised.

"Yes, I am sure. The Lord teaches us that no-one is beyond redemption, Simon; even the man who has so cruelly taken the life of one of my brothers." Abbot Robert paused. "I want to show that there can be forgiveness in this world. I do realise that he will have access to the chaplain within the castle, but I feel that I am called personally to visit him. As Brother Clement was one of my brethren here, I need to offer Lord Fitzwarren a chance to confess his sins to me and seek absolution, before he meets his maker."

"Of course, Abbot. You may visit him whenever you want."

"Thank you, Simon." The Abbot pondered thoughtfully for a moment. "Of course, there is one other matter of which you haven't spoken."

For a brief while, Simon was perplexed at what the Abbot meant, and then he understood.

"My daughter Katherines' wedding," he acknowledged.

The Abbot nodded. "How has she taken the news?"

Simon thought back to how his daughter had supported him over the past few days. In the end, it had seemed to him that she had resigned herself to marrying Lord Fitzwarren, even though he had known her heart lay elsewhere. And then, she had not shirked from helping him find out the truth.

"Better than could be expected."

The Abbott appeared to sense there was more to the statement than the words which had been spoken and waited for Simon to continue.

"I was already aware that my daughter was not exactly happy with the betrothal I had arranged. It seems that, unbeknownst to me, her heart lay with another, and marriage to Lord Fitzwarren was not what she wanted. But I believe she would have done my bidding and been a dutiful daughter in this matter."

Abbot Robert now understood. "So, it seems the arrest of Lord Fitzwarren has been to her benefit as well."

"Indeed."

"And what now? Will you give her your blessing to marry the man she is in love with?"

"I think that I must do," Simon admitted. "She'd previously come to me to ask for my permission to marry him, but I denied her request as I had already promised her in marriage to Lord Fitzwarren. However now, I believe I should honour her wishes."

Abbot Robert nodded in agreement. "Indeed. I believe that the Lord has found a way to make good of such a terrible event."

It was a long while since Katherine had woken up and hadn't felt the weight of expectation or worry on her shoulders. This morning, she found herself looking forward to the day ahead and was eager to get up and dressed. She was singing lightly to herself when Jennet came in.

"My, you are in a good mood today."

"Yes." She paused, realising that Jennet didn't know the full story as yet. "I know I should be sad at the arrest of Lord Fitzwarren, but you know that I didn't really want to marry him, Jennet."

She watched as the truth filtered through to her maid.

"But I thought you had accepted the betrothal." Jennet protested.

"I know. I had to make everyone believe that, Jennet. But the marriage was never going to happen." She paused and saw the look of surprise on Jennet's face. "Alexander and I were planning to run away today and leave for his father's manor in Northumberland. What makes me happy now, is that I don't have to break with my family in order to be with the man I love."

The look of surprise on Jennets' face was testimony to just how well Katherine had kept her secret.

"You were going to run away? Was it me that put the idea into your head? But what would your father have said? He would have been dishonoured in the eyes of the King. You would have been cutting yourself off from him and the rest of your family!"

"I know, but I would gladly have done that in order to be with Alexander. Besides, I'm sure that, given time, father would have come round."

Jennet was still processing the information. "Did your sister know about this?"

"No, but she does now. I told her last night; but she didn't know about it before then. No-one knew except for Alexander and me."

Jennet sat down heavily in the chair, a look of shock still present on her face. "I can't believe that you would have done such a thing."

"Believe me, I didn't want to, but you know how I feel about Alexander and how distraught I was at having to marry Lord Fitzwarren. I just couldn't face going through with it."

Katherine knelt at the side of her maid, as Jennet

considered what had been said.

"And now you won't have to marry him."

"No, I won't. But it wasn't at all what I expected to happen, I can assure you. I still can't believe that the man I was betrothed to, was responsible for the death of that poor monk." She shook her head. "It was such a terrible thing to do; and all because the man had taken Holy Orders and broken the heart of Fitzwarren's sister."

"Grief can do peculiar things to a man." Jennet observed. "They hold it inside, so that it eats away at them, and the anger festers and grows until eventually it becomes such a burden that it has to be released." She paused. "He must have really loved his sister for it to have haunted him like that; for him to have been so weighed down with grief over her death must have been intolerable."

"But it doesn't excuse what he did."

"Oh no. It certainly doesn't, and he will be hanged for it," Jennet said thoughtfully. Then added, changing the subject. "So have you decided what you are going to do with Lord Fitzwarren's stable boy, young Edward?"

"Well, he can't go back to the manor, can he? And I do sort of feel responsible for him now. I mean, without his telling me what he'd seen, father would never have been able to arrest Lord Fitzwarren."

"He's been no bother," Jennet said. "He's quite a likeable soul really. And he's cleaned up a treat."

"I know, I hardly recognise him; thank you for doing that Jennet." Katherine smiled. "I suppose I should really ask him what he wants to do. He's certainly got a way with horses, so perhaps I can find him a position here."

"Shall I fetch him to you and then you can ask him?"

Katherine nodded and got to her feet as Jennet rose from the chair.

"Yes," she nodded, "I'll speak to him and see what he wants to do."

Katherine couldn't help but feel a huge debt to Edward and that she needed to repay the great favour he had done her. She thought about how he had previously been living and that she was in a position to offer him a life that previously he could only have dreamed of.

Jennet wasn't gone long before she returned with Edward. The boy had lost that fearful look in his eyes that Katherine had noticed in the previous few days. He was laughing with Jennet when he came into the room and his face beamed with happiness when Grenulf came straight up to him to be petted.

"Edward," Katherine greeted him, "come here and sit with me."

The boy obediently complied and Grenulf lolloped after his new friend to sit at his side. Edward stroked the dog and smiled at Katherine as he looked at her.

"You know how grateful my father and I am to you. What you did yesterday took a lot of courage. You were very brave and honest; and now it's time for me to give you something in return for everything you've done." She looked at him to make sure that he was listening, and she had his full attention. "You won't be going back to Lord Fitzwarren's manor, so I'd like to ask what you want to do. Would you like a job working in the stables here?"

The boy's face lit up. "Yes mistress, I would. Thank you."

Katherine smiled at the look of sheer joy in the boy's face.

"I'd like you to look after Lily for me and I'd also like it if you would look after Grenulf too. He needs regular exercise and I'm not always able to do it."

Edward smiled happily as he continued stroking the dogs' head. "Thank you, I'd like that very much."

"There is something else I'd like to do for you. And that is to teach you to read and write as well." Katherine hadn't given it much thought, but now that she'd said it; it all seemed to make sense. "Once you can read and write then you would have so many more opportunities." She told him.

"Really?" The boy looked unsure. "I don't know what I'd do with it."

Katherine smiled at his innocence.

"If you can read and write then one day you could become a steward in a household or a scribe. It will give you a lot more opportunities."

Edward thought about it for a little while, then nodded. "Yes, I'd like that. Will you teach me to write my own name?"

"Of course I will!" Katherine laughed. "Now, I'm going to spend some time with my sister and after that my father wants to see me; so, could you take Grenulf out for a long walk for me; down by the river perhaps? He likes it down there."

"Yes, of course mistress." Edward leapt to his feet and Grenulf happily followed him out of the room.

"You've really taken a shine to that young boy." Jennet observed as she watched Edward leave.

"Yes, I think I have." Katherine smiled. "I feel that I owe him so much, and taking care of him and giving him a future is the very least I can do."

Katherine spent the rest of the morning with her sister, making sure that everyone was aware there would no longer be a wedding at the minster tomorrow. Jennet had already sent a servant to the minster to make sure they were aware of the change in plans. However, it seemed that most of the city was already abuzz with the news of Lord Fitzwarren, and the clergy at the minster were not surprised by what the servant told them. Angharad had then taken charge of ensuring that everything for the planned wedding feast at the castle was also put aside.

"I think that is everything." She said sitting down and giving a large sigh.

"I'm sorry," Katherine apologised, and her sister looked at her with surprise. "I'm sorry because you had to come all the way here for nothing."

"It's not been for nothing," Angharad corrected her. "I've been able to see both you and father again and spend time with you. To be honest, I think we've got on better now than we have ever done before."

Katherine smiled at her sister, knowing that she was right. The bond between them had strengthened over the last few days, and all the previous years of petty squabbles seemed to have been forgotten.

"Perhaps it's because we don't live together anymore," Katherine joked.

"Probably; or maybe it's that we've both grown up and understand more about what is really important."

Their conversation was interrupted by a knock on the door and one of the castle servants entered.

"My lady." He said addressing Katherine. "Your father has asked if you could join him and Sir Robert in his office."

Katherine looked at her sister. "I wonder what he wants now?"

Her mind was starting to race, trying to think of the reason why both her father and Sir Robert would request her attendance. She imagined that they were putting together the documents on Lord Fitzwarren's arrest and perhaps needed to ask her something.

"Don't worry, father probably just wants to speak with you about last night, before Sir Robert signs the documents." Angharad offered.

"Perhaps, but I would think that he had enough evidence already." Katherine sighed, getting up from her chair and straightening her gown. "I mean, what else is there to ask?" She shrugged at her sister and then went to leave the room with the steward.

Her father was waiting for her when she knocked on the door. He was seated at his desk and opposite him was Sir Robert de Lexington. Sir Robert stood up and smiled at her as she entered the room, and she curtsied graciously to him. Katherine liked him greatly, even more so since the last few days and his support for her.

"Come in Katherine, I'm glad you could join us?" Her father said smiling, and indicating for her to take a seat in front of his desk.

"Katherine, it is good to see you again," Sir Robert said. "I hope that the events of last night were not too upsetting for you?"

Katherine shook her head. "No, not too much," she admitted. "I realised what Lord Fitzwarren must have done the previous day, after I'd spoken with the stable boy, Edward. So I was prepared for the events of last night."

Sir Robert nodded understandingly. "He was a brave lad, that boy Edward, to speak out against his master like that. I understand he is now under your charge."

Katherine nodded and looked across at her father. She knew she should have spoken to him about it, before taking Edward on, but she was certain he would understand, given what had happened. "Yes, he is. I want to give him a chance at a better life, as payment for his bravery."

Sir Robert nodded in agreement. "I think that is a very kind and noble thing to do."

Katherine looked across at her father. "I hope you don't mind."

Simon shook his head. He was just pleased that he and Katherine were no longer fighting over his choice of husband anymore.

"And what of the wedding arrangements?" Sir Robert asked.

"My maid, Jennet, and my sister, Angharad, have sorted that out; so, all the wedding preparations have been cancelled, and everyone is aware that it will not now be taking place."

"I'm very sorry Katherine." Sir Robert added, giving her a knowing smile. "But it was probably a good thing that you found out now what your intended husband was like, before you married him. I have told your father this morning, that I have written to the King to explain what has transpired and that you will not be married to Lord Fitzwarren as expected." Robert watched Katherine closely. She seemed remarkably composed, given what had happened the previous evening and finding herself the centre of attention and subsequent gossip. He found himself admiring her strength of character and almost wished that she was one of his own daughters.

"Thank you for that." Katherine replied.

"I also understand that Lord Fitzwarren would not have been your choice of husband; and that it was only because your father had already informed the King of the betrothal, that you were agreeing to marry him." He did not let slip that it was Katherine who had told him this.

Katherine nodded, she was aware that Sir Robert already knew the truth, but imagined that he didn't want to give away the fact to her father. "Yes, that is true."

"Your father has also told me that you were a dutiful daughter and prepared to go through with the marriage, even though you were in love with another man. That tells me a lot about your character and sense of honour." Sir Robert smiled at her.

Katherine lowered her eyes and wondered what Sir Robert would say if he knew that she had been planning to run away with Alexander and not go through with the wedding. But it served no purpose to tell either him, or her father, that there never would have been a wedding. Both men believed her to have been obedient in her intention to marry Lord Fitzwarren and even though her father might have been suspicious, he had never questioned her about it. However, she found that she could not look either of them in the eye now, in case they saw the truth in her face. It seemed that Sir Robert saw it as a reticence on her part.

"Katherine, there is no way that you could have known what Lord Fitzwarren had done. It is a credit to both you and your father that you managed to find out the truth of this matter and expose him as the killer."

"And it was, in no small part, due to your help Katherine." Her father finally spoke, and she looked up at him and saw him smile at her. "Without you finding the dagger and Edward's testimony, I would not have had any proof. I had my suspicions from the story I'd been told of

Brother Clement, or should I call him Hugh de Glanville, by his friend Peter Beaumont. But I could not have proved it without your help."

Katherine felt faintly embarrassed at the praise. Her father was not normally so complimentary about her, and never in front of anyone else; especially not when that person happened to be the Royal Justice.

"We are both thankful for your help in solving this murder, Katherine." Sir Robert told her. "And I have agreed that, because of your assistance in this, and the loss of the man you were duty bound to marry; that you should be rewarded for your actions."

Katherine was surprised, she had not expected this and wondered what her father and Sir Robert had in mind.

Sir Robert rose from his chair and went over to the door which he opened and briefly went outside. Katherine could hear voices, and she looked at her father questioningly, uncertain of what was going on, but he just smiled at her in reply. When Sir Robert came back into the room he was accompanied by another man. Katherine looked at him and gasped.

"Alexander!" She cried out, getting up from her chair and rushing towards him. "Why are you here?" She asked, as she allowed him to wrap her in his arms.

"I'm not altogether sure," he replied, letting go of her and smiling. "A message came this morning asking me to attend Sir Robert at the castle as soon as I was able."

"Please sit down." Simon told Alexander, indicating the chair that Katherine had previously been sitting in. Katherine went to stand behind him, placing a caring hand on his shoulder, smiling at him as she did so.

Sir Robert returned to his chair opposite and watched the couple carefully. "I suggested this meeting to your father first thing this morning, after we had discussed what happened last night. It seems that we are both in full agreement about the matter."

Katherine felt a little nervous, wondering what was going on and why Alexander could have been summoned by Sir Robert. She didn't dare hope, but her mind could not think of another explanation.

"Katherine." It was her father who spoke this time. "I know that Alexander was your choice of husband and that it was only because I had already arranged the betrothal to Lord Fitzwarren that you were denied your request. However, you were dutiful in *finally* agreeing to my wishes to go through with the wedding."

He gave her a small smile and Katherine briefly wondered if he knew that she had been planning to run away with Alexander and was about to expose their deception.

"But in light of what has now happened," he continued looking serious. "Both Sir Robert and I have agreed that, should you still wish to be married;" he paused, almost mocking her. "That it should be allowed."

Katherine heard the words, but felt as though she were in a dream, and it wasn't quite real. The look on her face gave away the surprise that she felt. She had considered that perhaps, after a suitable time, her father would probably agree to her marriage to Alexander, but she had not imagined that he would do so quite so quickly.

"What?" She breathed. "Are you sure?"

"Of course, Katherine, I am allowing you to marry Alexander; if that's what you still want." Her father beamed at her.

"Of course it's what I want!" She checked herself and looked at Alexander. "What we both want, isn't it?"

"Oh yes, my darling." Alexander got up from the chair and took her in his arms for a brief moment, before releasing her and turning to face her father, Simon.

"Thank you, sir, for allowing this. It is more than we could have hoped for."

"When your father told me of what had happened previously, then I suggested that it would be fitting for you to be allowed to marry now." Sir Robert smiled at them. "I take it your father will have no objection to the union?" He asked Alexander.

Alexander smiled as he held Katherine's hand tightly. He had certainly not expected this when he had been summoned to attend the Royal Justice this morning.

"I am sure not. He was aware that I desired to marry Katherine, so I believe that he will agree to our marriage." He looked at Katherine and she smiled at him.

"And I am sure that Simon can agree a dowry with your father that will be acceptable." Sir Robert suggested and saw Simon nod in agreement.

"Thank you, sir, I am certain an agreement can be reached." Alexander assured him. He wanted to say that he didn't care about a dowry, and that all he wanted was to be with Katherine, but he realised that it wouldn't be appropriate.

Sir Robert nodded. "Very well. So, it would seem there is to be a marriage after all."

"You mean tomorrow?" Katherine gasped.

"No, the bans will need to be read for the next three days, so I would suggest Monday. Would that suit you both?" Her father asked. "After all, there is no point in waiting any longer; and people are expecting a wedding, it will just be a couple of days late."

Katherine felt stunned by the news. She hadn't expected this to happen so quickly.

"But Jennet and Angharad have told everyone...." She saw her father shake his head. "You mean they already knew and didn't let on!" She exclaimed.

"I had mentioned something to them about it earlier today." Simon admitted, smiling. He was pleased to see his daughter so happy.

"But a wedding at the Minster?" She asked; it wasn't her choice. "It's not what I wanted."

"That was always Lord Fitzwarren's decision," Simon added. "And neither did I think it would have been your choice."

She had to admit that her father knew her better than she thought.

"I always thought it was a little grandiose," she

admitted. "I would have much preferred it to be in the private chapel here."

"I would like that too." Alexander told her. "Though I have to admit, I don't really care where we get married."

"Well, I think all these arrangements can be agreed. If there is nothing more, then our business here is concluded." Sir Robert added smiling.

Alexander realised that they were being dismissed. "Thank you, Sir Robert," he said giving a small bow. "I promise that I will take care of your daughter." He said turning to address Simon.

"There is just one thing." Simon added seriously.

"What?" Katherine was suddenly fearful, wondering if the dream she was now in, might suddenly be snatched away from her.

"I know you would prefer for the wedding to be held at the chapel here in the castle; however, the Abbott of St Mary's has asked if he could preside over your union. He requested this as a way of expressing his gratitude to you Katherine, for helping to find the murderer of Brother Clement. He told me that it would give him great pleasure if you would agree to hold your wedding at the Abbey of St Mary's; would you both be happy with this?"

Katherine looked at Alexander. She was just delighted that they were finally going to be married and, if it would please the Abbot to hold their wedding service at the abbey, then she was happy to agree. "Yes, of course. That is very gracious of him."

"Very well." Simon smiled, enjoying seeing his daughter so happy. "It has been agreed for the ceremony to take place at noon on Monday. I have already taken the liberty of asking for the bans to be read today, so that everything will be in place for the ceremony on Monday." He turned to Alexander. "I take it that this will be acceptable to your family as well?"

"I am sure it will be." Alexander smiled. "I will return home and tell my family at once."

Katherine put her arm around Alexander and looked at

him with such devotion that her father knew he had made the right decision in allowing them to finally marry. As they went to take their leave, Sir Robert addressed them.

"I hope that you will both permit me to be present at your wedding." He asked, smiling at the couple. "I have agreed with your father that I will delay my departure for a few days, so that I might be there."

"Of course, Sir Robert, it would be an honour." Katherine smiled and gave him a small curtsy.

EPILOGUE

Adam stood to one side, as he watched his men arrest Roger de Mowbray. He was certain now, that the young man had arranged for his father to be killed, and he had paid men handsomely for doing it. He watched as his men restrained Roger and tied him up, so that he would have to walk behind their horses as he was taken from the manor to the prison cells within the castle. All the time they were doing this, Roger was shouting and protesting his innocence and telling of how he would have Adam flogged for arresting him. Adam took no notice; his source had already confirmed the payment made to the thugs who had attacked Lord de Mowbray on his return from Durham, and there was nothing that Roger could say which would change these facts.

Adam already suspected that Roger de Mowbray had also conspired in his mother's death as well, but he couldn't prove that. However, he was content that the man should be convicted of his fathers' death at least. He suspected that none of this was now happening quite as the young man had planned. Roger de Mowbray was an ambitious man, and his desire for money and status had pushed him to commit murder. Adam was pleased that he had been able to arrest him for it, even if it wasn't the murder he had initially suspected him of.

Katherine watched the sunrise on the late July morning that was to be her wedding day. Sleep had been hard to come by that night; such was her excitement. Sitting in the window embrasure she watched the night sky lighten and be tinged with pale golds and oranges as the sun rose over the horizon.

Outside all was quiet, the servants had yet to awake and start their duties for the day and Katherine found herself delighting in the calm peacefulness. She wanted to remember every minute of this day and all that was special about it.

It was late morning when Jennet came to dress her in the wedding gown she had prepared. The gown was the one Katherine had seen her working on for her wedding to Lord Fitzwarren; it was of pale blue and richly embroidered with silver and gold. The pale colour highlighted her auburn hair which was left loose down her back. The gossamer fine wimple was pinned in place on her hair and on top of it, she wore a band of fresh picked flowers with daisies, cornflowers and white roses.

Just before noon, her father came to collect her from her room and led her down the staircase and across the bailey to the carriage which was waiting to take her to the Abbey. Outside the servants had lined a processional walkway and strewn it with flowers and herbs. The sun was blazing down and there was not a cloud in the sky, and walking over the herbs released the most beautiful aroma into the air.

Abbot Robert and Alexander were waiting for her at the top of the steps outside the main door into the abbey. Alexander had his two brothers with him and his mother and father stood to one side. At the other side, her sister Angharad and her husband waited on the steps of the abbey. As they reached the top of the steps, her father gave her hand to Alexander. As he did so, she looked at him and smiled with gratitude, knowing that this was all she had wanted. It was so difficult to believe that just a few days ago, she had been planning to run away with Alexander and none of today's celebrations would ever have happened. Instead, they would have been married in secret as they made their way north to the manor house in Wark.

Abbot Robert in front of them smiled and then gestured to the assembled crowd to be silent before he started. "May God's blessing be on all of you." He said. "I am here to marry Alexander, son of Robert de Ros, Baron of Helmsley, and Katherine, daughter of Simon de Hale, Sheriff of the County. I must first ask if anyone here knows of any reason why this couple should not be married?"

Katherine could feel her heart pounding within her as she almost expected Lord Fitzwarren to suddenly appear and object to the union. But there was silence, and she allowed herself a sigh of relief and looked up at Alexander, who smiled lovingly at her.

Abbot Robert then turned his attention to both Katherine and Alexander. "Now I have to ask both of you, that you should confess of any reason that you know of, for why either of you should not be allowed to marry. Do either of you know of any such reason?"

Both Alexander and Katherine shook their heads. "No," they said together.

Alexander and Katherine then gave their wedding oaths to each other promising to stay true to each other forever. Rings were exchanged before the Abbot formally announced that they were man and wife. A cheer rang out amongst the gathered crowd and Katherine looked around, first catching her fathers' eye and then smiling at her sister, standing to his side.

They were now officially husband and wife. Following the marriage Alexander then led his new bride into the abbey, where the monks sang as they walked along the nave towards the chancel and the high altar for the mass. As she knelt on the richly embroidered footstool, she looked across at Alexander and smiled. This had to be the most perfect day of her life.

Acknowledgements

I would like to thank the staff of the Yorkshire Archaeological Society in Leeds who, during the late 1980's, when I was originally doing research for this novel, helped me find documents and court rolls, to help with the history of York in the early 13th century. The society had a late-night opening on a Thursday evening until 9pm, and the staff would regularly have to come and find me, to inform me that they were closing, as I had invariably lost track of time.

I would also like to acknowledge several reference books which have helped with research in confirming some of the background for this novel -

- York – the Making of a City 1068 - 1350 by Sarah Rees Jones
- The Founding of St Mary's Abbey and St Leonards Hospital, York by James Raine
- England in the 13th Century by Alan Harding
- The English Medieval House by Margaret Wood
- The Art and Architecture of English Benedictine Monasteries by Julian M. Luxford

The timber castle at York is recorded as being destroyed in 1190 by fire during the riots. It is noted as possibly being rebuilt in timber and not reconstructed in stone until 1243. However, using writers' licence, I have noted that the castle keep was newly built at the time in which this novel is set.

The first draft of this novel was written in 1989-1990 - in a time before home computers and the internet. It was initially hand-written and then typed up on a manual typewriter. After that, it was put in a box and almost forgotten about; until last year, when I attended an event at the Guernsey Literary Festival in which the wonderful Anna Mazzola was holding a workshop on 'Writing Historical Fiction'. Following this, I went home and dug out the old manuscript and started to re-write the story. The arrival of the computer, the internet and email since the 1980's, has made writing this new draft of the novel so much easier to complete. I would like to thank Anna Mazzola for all her encouragement and help over the last year - quite simply, this novel would not be published without her advice.

Authors Note

This novel is entirely a work of fiction, although certain characters are known to have existed.

Simon de Hale was Sheriff of Yorkshire from 1223 until April 1225. There is no record of him having a family (except a nephew, Roger de Hale) so I have invented a family for him in his daughters, Katherine and Angharad and his deceased wife Ellen.

Abbot Robert de Longo Campo, was the Abbot of St Mary's from 1197 until his death in 1239.

Robert de Lexington (the spelling of the surname varies between Lessington, Lexinton and Lexington) was one of the Royal Justices and held the assize court in York in July 1224.

Alexander de Ros was the third son of Baron Robert de Ros of Helmsley castle north of York and although there is no record of the name of his wife, he is known to have a son who was named William.

All other characters, such as Lord William Fitzwarren, Hugh de Glanville and his parents, Adam de Burgh, Roger de Mowbray and Peter Beaumont etc., are all fictional.

Printed in Dunstable, United Kingdom